Leonid Tishkov

CREATURES

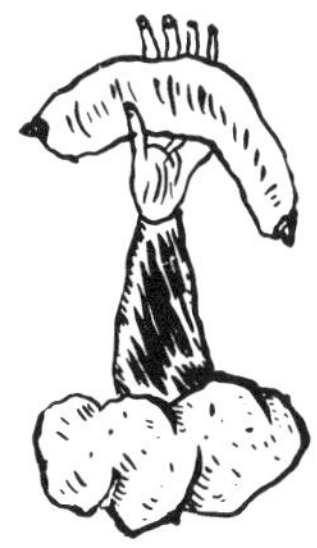

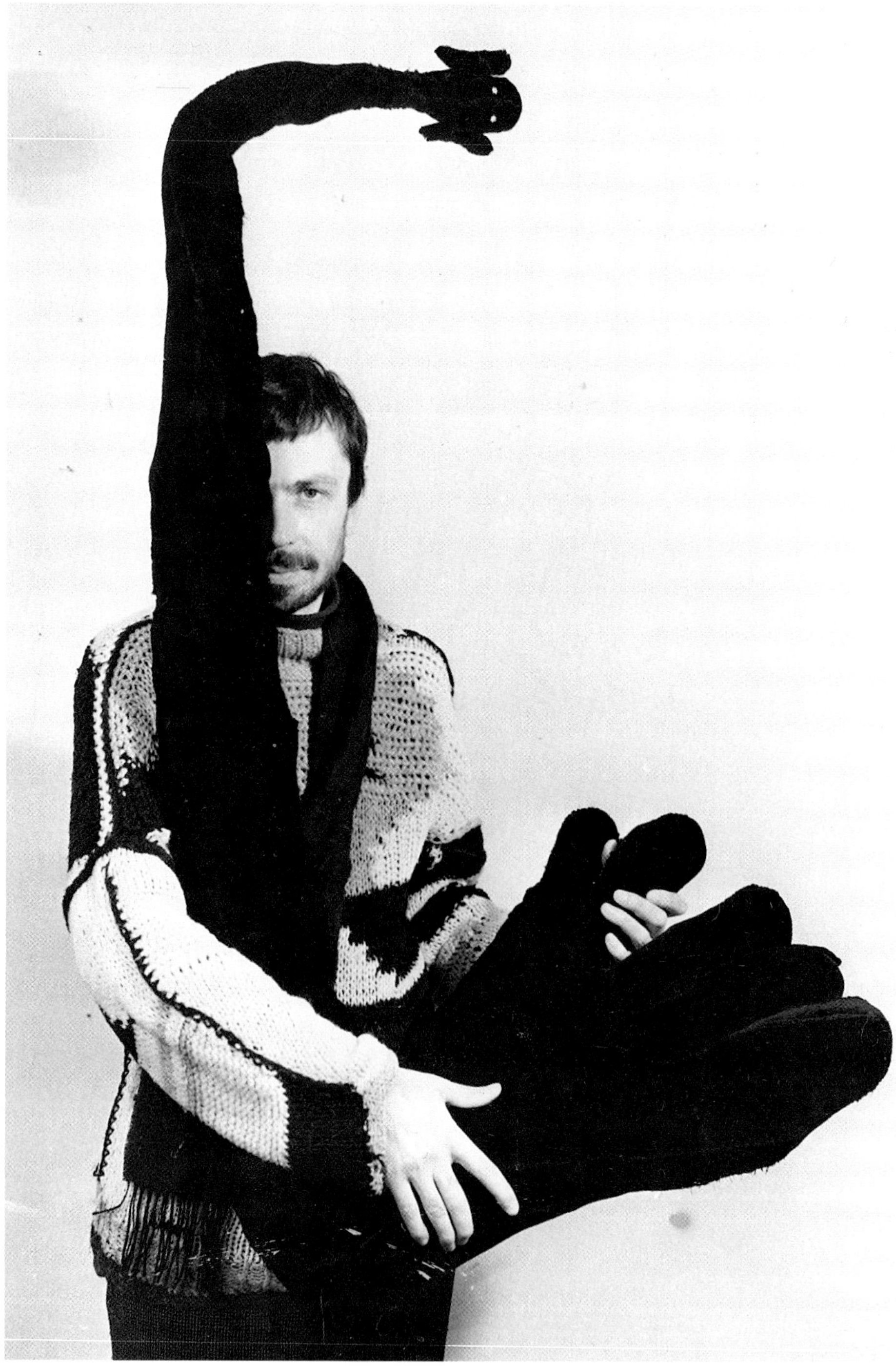

Leonid Tishkov

CREATURES

Foreword by **Michael P. Mezzatesta**

Essays by

Ludmila Lunina

Liliana Grubisic

Michael P. Mezzatesta

Ganymed
Moscow
Duke University Museum of Art
Durham
DABLUS Press
Moscow

1993

This book has been produced on the occasion of an exhibition seen at Duke University Museum of Art, November 5, 1993 - January 2, 1994.

The publication of Leonid Tishkov Creatures has been made possible by grants from the following organizations:

The Mary Duke Biddle Foundation
The Friends of the Art Museum
The Elizabeth Beswick Fund

Design - Leonid Tishkov
with assistance Sergey Stulov
and Yuri Gordon
Printed in Roma Print, Gdansk, Poland

ISBN (paperback): 0-938989-11-1
Library of Congress Catalogue Number:
93-72536

Front cover - DABLOID, 1990, oil on canvas, 200x200 cm.

Back cover - Ural's DABLOID, 1992, soft sculpture, 120x30x40 cm.

Frontispiece: Leonid Tishkov with the Dabloid
Foto S. Gurariy

TABLE OF CONTENTS

FOREWORD

Leonid Tishkov is an anomaly - a Renaissance man in a post-industrial society. Born in a small town in the Ural Mountains in 1953, he began his professional career by graduating from medical school in 1978 and practicing as a doctor. Yet, even as he was dissecting cadavers, Tishkov was drawing, not diagrams of internal organs, but caricatures. After winning a number of international awards in the late 1970s, Tishkov emerged as a full fledged artist, active on the Moscow scene in the 1980s. Drawings, prints, book illustrations, paintings, sculpture, and installations are all an integral part of Tishkov's oeuvre. In addition, he is also a publisher and founder of DABLUS PRESS, a composer, poet, and playwright. His creativity in such widely diverse media is as astounding as the richness of his work

LEONID TISHKOV - CREATURES represents the artist's first American exhibition. Featuring some 80 works - drawings, paintings, soft-sculpture, video, books and prints - the show offers a close-up of Tishkov's surreal universe. The exhibition is centered on the **Dabloids** - foot-shaped creatures of all sizes and colors who emerge magically from the Dablus, a sausage-like object that appeared one misty morning in the fields of a collective farm. Tishkov's drawings recount the history of the Dablus and the **Dabloids**. These mystical creature are at once pets and gods, beings immensely wise and yet foolish. They become guardian angels, friends, confidants - a balm for the loneliness that sometimes overwhelms us. They are surreal manifestations of the artistic consciousness even as they are symbols of our isolation. In this sense, Tishkov's roots in surrealism are charged with humorous social commentary often reminiscent of Hogarth, Red Grooms, and Robert Crumb. Tishkov draws us into his Dabloid universe because it seems natural for us to be there. If there should be, «a chicken in every pot», why shouldn't there be, «a Dabloid in every home?»

Tishkov's existential angst is seen in yet another manifestation - a suite of 26 elephant drawings. Here people live within an elephant's trunk. Tishkov has noted, «In the trunk it's warm and damp. You lie there naked, but it's safe. It's a haven, the mother's womb in which the infant hid. Be happy as a trunk: two tusks protect you, two tiny eyes always follow you.» Like Saint-Exupery's *Little Prince*, the person and elephant cannot live without each other

Of course, in Tishkov's world not everyone lives inside an elephant's nose. Some people live within a full diving suit with its round metal helmet; the air hose disappearing upward beyond the margin of the drawing. Tishkov's creatures poignantly illuminate aspects of our often lonely existence. His images, text and verse offer a poetic commentary on the human condition.

This exhibition grew out of a visit to the artist's studio in April of 1992. The warmth of Tishkov's small, cluttered space in Furmanny Lane provided a refuge from the cold Moscow weather — a haven as cozy as an elephant's trunk. It also provided a magical experience as drawings, books, watercolors, paintings, and prints appeared from the chaos in a continuous stream. At the end of several hours, and after countless glasses of tea, I had an exhibition and my own Dabloid!

Working with Leonid has been a very special experience if only because the joy he radiates when showing his work is so contagious. Even without Leonid, it is difficult to be cranky when **dabloids** are in the area. I am very grateful to him for sharing his work with an American audience and for the countless ways that he has supported this effort. I am especially indebted to him for supervising the creation of this book. With skill and sangfroid, Leonid organized the production of the catalogue in Moscow — a considerable accomplishment in light of the obstacles facing even normal daily activities.

The catalogue has been a joint-venture between Duke University Museum of Art and Dablus Press. It represents DUMA's first international collaboration. The essays also represent a collaborative effort between Russian and American scholars. Moscow critic and art historian, Ludmilia Lunina has provided a wonderful introductory essay on the artist and his work. I am very grateful to her for the marvelous job she has done. Ljiljana Grubisic, J. Paul Getty Study Center, Malibu, has contributed an essay with a particular focus on the background of Tishkov's extraordinary books. It has been a pleasure working with her. Hopefully, my essay on **Dabloids** will provide some additional insights into Tishkov's roots in Russian folk culture.

Translation is an art, not a science, and in this regard we have been favored by two extraordinarily artistic individuals. Dominique Gore, a University of North Carolina graduate student in Russian literature, translated Ludmilia Lunina's essay and all the texts which appear in Tishkov's drawings. She did an outstanding job under great time pressure. This is not surprising, for someone who can survive winter in Moscow, can do anything. Dr. Mikhail Novikov from Moscow, completing his second doctorate at the University of North Carolina, not only translated the play, **Dabloids**, but also spontaneously provided the explanatory notes that accompany it! His dedication to this effort and good humor in the face of all the other demands on his time were truly remarkable. I am deeply grateful to him and Dominique. They are remarkable people. Ljiljana Grubisic also kindly reviewed the translations for which I am most appreciative.

Special thanks must be extended to a number of other wonderful individuals, and their **Dabloids**, who helped to organize this show. Yuri Nikich and Ilya Sentsiper — two of the principals of ART MIF — were my Virgils during Moscow visits. Their appreciation of Leonid's work got the ball rolling. The staff of ART MIF ably arranged for the transport of Tishkov's work to Durham. We are most appreciative of their support. And, what can one say about Tatyana Mogilevskaya except thank you for showing me all of Moscow on the way to Tishkov's studio?

Thanks also are extended to The J. Paul Getty Study Center for agreeing to loan their collection of Leonid Tishkov's books. The Mary Duke Biddle Foundation provided a grant for the catalogue and exhibition. The Foundation has been unflagging in its support of DUMA's initiatives. Additional funding has been supplied by the Friends of the Art Museum and The Elizabeth Beswick Fund.

Finally, there is Johnny and Diane Simons. Johnny, the artistic director of Fort Worth's Hip Pocket Theatre and member of the Duke University Drama Program faculty, directed Tishkov's play, **Dabloids**. After first reading the script, he eagerly took on what I thought might be to him a strange project. But why not? As one of the leading playwrights of the southwest whose own work is deeply enmeshed in the folk culture of Texas, he felt an immediate affinity to Tishkov's universe. The spirits of Lake Worth are not so different from the spirits of the Russian forest. The appeal of **Dabloids** is universal.

Diane Simons, executive producer of The Hip Pocket Theatre, organized the production of **Dabloids** at DUMA. In addition, she created all of the costumes from designs provided by the artist. Diane is simply the most talented and wonderful theater person with whom I have had the privilege of working. To Johnny, Diane, and the entire cast and crew, we say—BRAVO—for enriching CREATURES with your art.

Michael P. Mezzatesta
Director

ACKNOWLEDGEMENTS

Radiant Dablus and I, Leonid Tishkov, express gratitude to all of our friends and loved ones who are taking part in the great project of the dabloidization of our universe: Marina Moskvina, Nina Militosyan, Rano Ismailova, Anka Odintsova, the creators of divine toys, soft sculptures and ceramic figures. Thanks to Ludmila Lunina, Ljiljana Grubisic, Dominique Gore and Mikhail Novikov who have given a voice to the Dabloids and travel with my elephants. Also, thanks to Michael P. Mezzatesta and little Marya, educator of the little Christmas Dabloid.

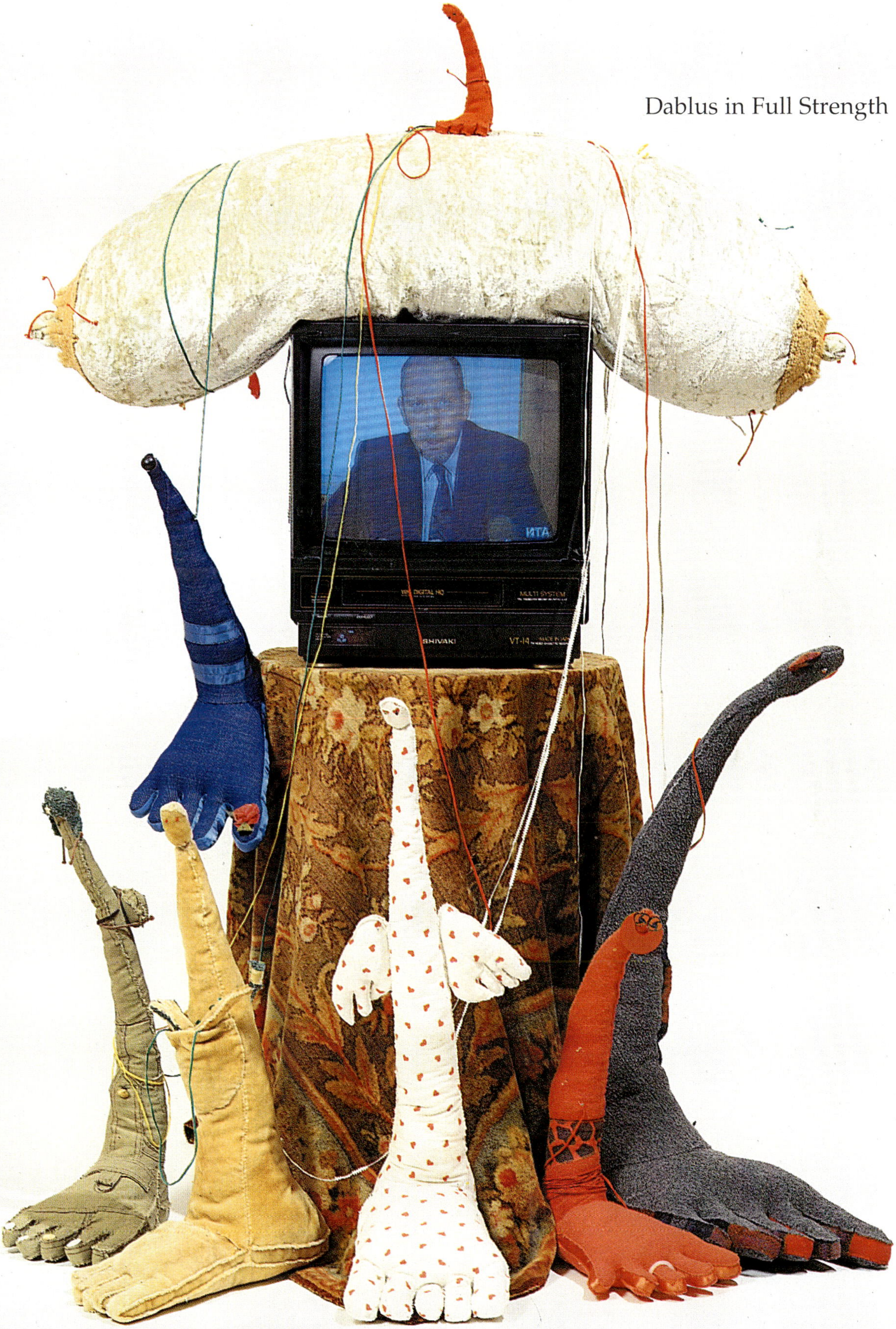

Dablus in Full Strength

Ludmila Lunina

THE MYTHOLOGY OF LEONID TISHKOV: SOURCES, HEROES, ACTIONS, TRADITIONS

Leonid Tishkov has been a part of the Moscow art scene for the last 20 years. Everything he has created in that time now appears as a most sophisticated interweaving of causes and effects, stories and images, various genres and techniques. The banyan tree could serve as a model of his art. Its shoots bend down with the branches to the ground, then the roots go into the ground and become mighty trunks. One such tree is capable of growing into an enormous forest. It becomes impossible to find the seed which yielded such an extensive crown.

One characteristic of the Tishkov epos is to combine the fantastic and the banal into a thick and inseparable mixture. He treats the *a priori* absurdity literally and firmly shuns logic. War is declared against logic; it is ignored; he allows the imagination to work as it will, as God commands the soul — with happenstance, as if in dreams, delicately noting fragments of a somnambulant frenzy. The world to which his fantasies have given birth is populated by various heroes: Dabloids, Stomachs, Blockheads, Divers. A strange life stirs in this world: a little girl saves the hero-Blockhead and a hedgehog is born of their love; the lonely Stomach walks along a cold city street. This art is calculated for our emotional receptors, for a perception equally direct as the act of creation. Children respond readily to his art. They do not need to be prepared for it; a sincere co-experiencing and co-creation are enough.

Tishkov is poet, playwright, painter, caricaturist, famous illustrator, refined professional and self-taught dilettante simultaneously. His unique style makes his work easily recognizable in every medium. This style, like Kafka's prose and Magritte's images, can be recognized from the first lines, from the fragment of a painting. His imagination, full of vital energy, yields crops on any soil and is nourished by the most unpredictable sources.

His is one of those introverted natures which draw the impulse for their work from the events of their own lives. The facts of his biography are extremely important as a key to a proper understanding of his mythology.

1. Childhood: *«I was completely excluded from the flow of life.»*

Leonid Tishkov was born in 1953 in the Urals, in the tiny provincial town of Nizhnie

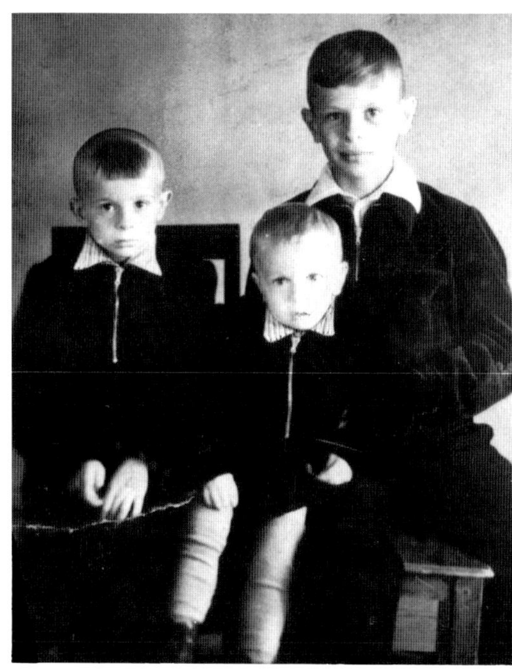

The Tishkov brothers (1-r): Evgeny, Leonid, Valery. 1956, Ural.

«In childhood I was entirely excluded from the general flow; I had practically no friends. My brothers were older than I by six and twelve years: too great a difference to become friends. I immediately refused to go to kindergarten. At one time I was a lunatic; my parents observed that I got up and wandered around the apartment at night. My strangeness was readily apparent. I walked about with my eyes cast down, and to an observer it would seem that I was examining insects and grubs on the ground. Truly, the small world of insects and plants was so attractive that I could watch the events in the grass for hours. My favorite children's book was Bragin's, In the Land of Dense Grasses.»

Sergi. His parents were schoolteachers: his father taught geography, and his mother taught elementary school. He was the third and youngest son in the family, and was always considered strange, unsociable and less capable than his two older brothers. (One of them is now a Ph.D. and director of an academic institute. The other is an anesthesiologist.)

If one recalls ancient tribes, there were always one or two individuals, shamans for example, who were considered mediators of higher powers. Such strange, blessed people still exist in any community, be it a village, a street, or a school classroom. From childhood they are already different from everyone else, «not of this world;» they fantasize and mumble weird sounds to themselves and, it seems, communicate with another world.

From childhood, he studiously avoided any collective in which it would have been necessary to obey the established rules and willy-nilly to establish ties with his peers. As a four-year-old child he gave his parents an ultimatum: he would never go to kindergarten. He had to be left home alone. He avoided noisy games in school. Two of his best friends, as great introverts as himself, later went out of their minds. Perhaps because of his refusal to accept the common norms of social behavior, Tishkov found a solace in art, a fact which may have saved him from the sad fate of his closest companions.

He never speaks of his childhood solitude with regret. He compensated for the lack of friendships with the observation of nature and by reading books (he gulped down books of fantasy). A picturesque locality in a valley surrounded by mountains and woods on the shore of a lake, Nizhnie Sergi provided far more opportunities for observing nature than a city would have. An important and, according to Tishkov, a determining fact, is that he was born on the border between two parts of the world. The symbolic border between Europe and Asia is right next to Nizhnie Sergi. He does not identify exclusively with the European cultural tradition; his contemplative perception of life is akin to a Buddhist understanding of life.

In the Urals, the centuries-old traditions of folk art are still strong. In the 1920s and 1930s the writer Pavel Bazhov gathered

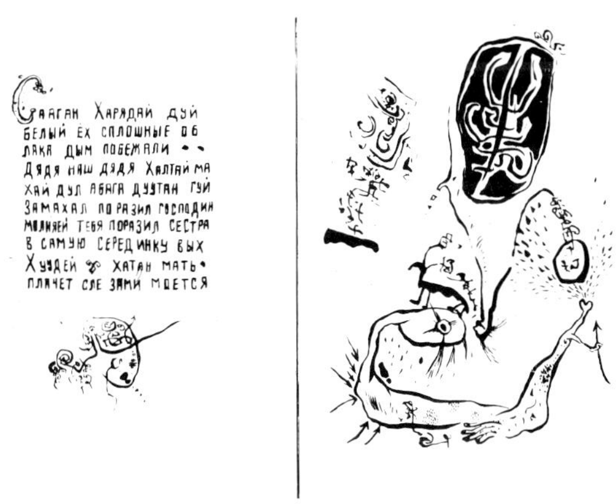

New Songs. Two pages from book, 1991

unique folklore materials here for his famous book of folktales, *Malachite Box*, which has become a classic. Therefore, there is nothing surprising in the fact that Tishkov's poetry is closely tied to folklore. His poems are similar to traditional Russian wandering minstrel (*skomorokhi*) songs, sharing the same rhythm and the same love for a taboo lexicon.

Nizhnie Sergi played a role in Tishkov's biography similar to that played by Vitebsk in Chagall's life. His art, except for clearly fantastical personages, is a constant recollec-

«They always said: «he's like Grandfather.» And grandfather was also a bit strange. Illiterate, he worked as a foreman at the Demidov factory and thought up his own alphabet. In a special booklet he wrote some sort of signs and knew how to read them. In hindsight, I can say that of all my relatives, only my grandmother was an artist. She copied flower bouquets from postcards into an album.»

«Of course, the Urals for me are a land comparable with nothing else. I now collect books with the epics of the Siberian peoples and find there what I have long known: cliff drawings on the Chusovaya *river, the* Katnikov *cavern,* Bazhukovo, Ledyanaya *cavern,* Kungurova. *These are all ancient paleontological sites. Tartar villages surrounded our town. Tartars have lived in the Urals for a very long time. «Sergi» means «rings» in Tartar. In our locale there was a unique microclimate created by the mountains:* Kukan, Sholom *and* Kabatskaya.
We buy cherries in sacks made of newspaper from the Tartars. I eat all the cherries, turn the sack, all covered in lilac spots, inside out, and a strange translogical text is written in Russian letters on the newspaper page. Although the Tartars wrote in the Cyrillic alphabet, it read as complete abracadabra, sprinkled with chance familiar words. Tartar writing was one of the strongest emotional shocks of my childhood. The book New Songs *is about this.»*

«Three generations of my family lived in the Urals. My father is from the village Korkino, in the Tuvinsky district. This is also the Central Urals, but is different from Nizhnie Sergi. The regions of the Urals differ strongly from one another: there are the Upper Urals, Tagil, Chelyabinsk. In Nizhnie Sergi «gamayuns» (mythical birds) live: they don't talk, they sing. After perestroika, *I even suggested that the newspaper* Lenin Banner, *change its name to* Gamayun, *but they didn't listen to me. All of my relatives, grandmothers and aunts, sang wonderful folk songs. Whenever there was a wedding, everyone would gather on the large lawn, and compose and sing songs. There was no particular perception of this as art; it was simply how they lived. Women would go around, wretched and crazy.* Katya Selyabina, *and another one all in medals whose name I don't recall, told folktales as in Bazhov's time.»*

«I came to Moscow to enroll in the Biology Department at Moscow State University, but failed. I got an F in Math. My older brother said: «Go to the Medical Institute; they teach biology there too.» This was the right decision. They write about the «Russian path:» the search is more important than the goal. My biography is a direct illustration of that: my roundabout path to the goal proved to be the shortest.»

tion of his native town. Thus, one of the central parables about the origin of the Dablus and the birth of Dabloids is called «My Village Folk.» He describes the most commonplace events, events which he observed often in his childhood: a call-up to the army, a wedding, drinking bouts, a scuffle, washing in the baths, feeding children, digging a garden. All of Tishkov's characters, regardless of how whimsical they may seem, are inhabitants of the provinces, «natural» people, connected to the earth by an uncut umbilical cord. He has one enormous red canvas that literally affirms this idea: a person wrapped in a spiral umbilical cord. Provincialism, a universal characteristic of Russian art — Petersburg compared to Moscow, and Moscow compared to Europe — is strongly accented in Tishkov's work. He has smelted the «complex» of provincialism into a unique artistic image.

Tishkov's childhood interests became the foundation of those scenarios that he would draw upon in his future life.

When he was six he almost drowned in an icehole. Since then he has always feared water and he never learned to swim. In his drawings, the natural force of water always signifies the plane of non-Being, whether it appears as a symbol of the subconscious depths, as a metaphor for sleep or depicts an immanent underwater kingdom in which divers live.

As a schoolboy he loved to spoil textbooks, to mark up the pages with drawings and patterns, a trait later seen in the hypertrophied decorativism of his illustrations.

The years produced few changes in his character. In his current artistic activities he remains an extreme individualist. He never joined any of the Moscow artistic groups: his egocentric philosophy would have difficulty fitting within the limits of collective actions. He has many imitators, but no students and, likewise no teachers. His only advisors are experience and books. The man who has thought up the character Dabloid, a foot with splayed toes, would naturally be intrigued by the strange form of his own extremities. Such a person can easily disengage himself from the noise of the surrounding world: he is completely focused on himself.

2. Medical School: *«My roundabout path to the goal proved to be the shortest.»*

When he graduated from high school Tishkov came to study in Moscow. There was not the slightest hint that he would become an artist. He dreamed of devoting himself to biology; fauna and flora seemed to him much more worthy of attention than the world of humans. But as it turned out, he enrolled in the First Moscow Medical Institute. It seemed that all future events were already predetermined. A career as a doctor awaited him: not the worst occupation in any country.

Time made its own corrections in his life. Tishkov arrived in Moscow at the beginning of the 1970s. It was the Brezhnev era, the height of the Cold War; the country lived behind the Iron Curtain. The atmosphere of stagnation penetrated into all areas of life, even those most removed from ideology. These times left individuals very little space for self-realization. Therefore, art was an existential occupation: it offered the possibility to be relatively free in an unfree country. The 1970s was an introverted era. The civic-minded dedication and social ferment of the 1960s was cut short. Under the conditions of censorship, art was allowed to pose ethical, but not ideological, questions. Subjective experience and personal moral issues acquired an immense significance. Art was occupied with the private and particular: Chekhov was the most popular playwright and «the little man» the most popular hero. Tishkov's self-absorption, his «digging into himself,» were in unison with the mood of the times. Perhaps because of this he was very easily absorbed into artistic life.

His work in medicine foreordained much in his future art. He studied anatomy from corpses floating in a solution of formaldehyde. Therefore he perceives the metaphysics of life and death surprisingly simply. This explains a peculiar physiological aspect of his works. Shame is unknown to Tishkov's art. There are no taboo themes: he draws the sexual act, feces, and suicide without emotion or passion, as if he were composing a list of symptoms of an illness. His books even remind one of a detailed case history. Pictures from anatomy and biology textbooks became a part of his memory and an analogue to intuition. Following the Surrealists, Tishkov propagates the cult of automatic writing. When he relaxes, «turns off» the rational, and frees the subconscious, he produces not geometric patterns on a piece of paper, but throbbing simple organisms. Even in the most fantastic of his abstractions, the contours of living bodies can be discerned. The action of his myth is based on perpetual biological motion, as it is in life. This world is constantly occupied with the reproduction of itself. The act of birth is one of the central events in the Tishkov mythology.

At the Medical Institute he began to write: poems, stories, and plays. In the library he found the literature which corresponds to his personal understanding of the world: Khlebnikov, Beckett, Ionesco, Kharms. His preferences were clear: Symbolism, Surrealism, the Absurd. In a year it became clear that medicine didn't interest him at all. Nonetheless, the Institute was the only way to avoid military service. The tragic lack of correspondence between his activities and interests over the course of two years led to a nervous breakdown. Art saved him. He began to work seriously in caricature.

In the first humorous drawings he took to the magazine the complexes of the future doctor were sublimated: their black humor constantly revolved around the anatomical theater and the morgue. It came out surprisingly fresh. His work was printed in newspapers and magazines and within a year he was one of the top five caricaturists in the country. All that he had done up to then, his exercises in black humor, his artistic thinking, was realized through a poetic or visual paradox.

His career as an artist became simply a matter of time. In 1983, the publishing house Kniga offered him the opportunity to illus-

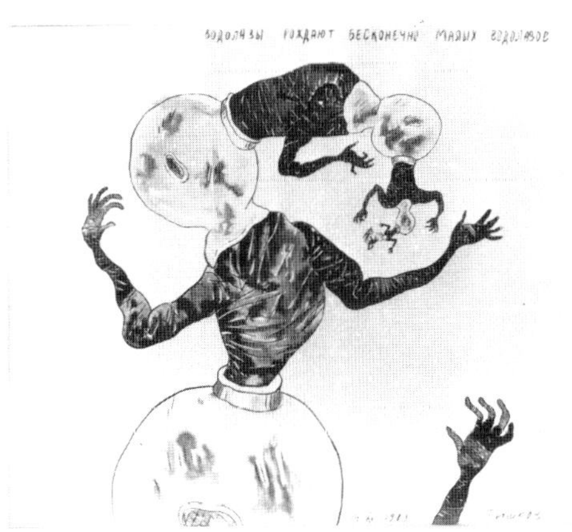

The Divers. Page from album, 1990

«Medicine also oppressed me a great deal, it was simply horrible. Even now in front of my eyes is a morgue, forensic medicine, opened-up dead people. I just couldn't learn anatomy. And in the skull, by the way, are more than sixty bones, all of which have to be learned in Latin. What's more, in this system everything was calculated in class hours: if you missed an hour you had to make it up in the evening. I remember how I would come to the anatomical theater on Mokhovaya *Street and grab some hand or foot from the formaldehyde (the smell of formaldehyde follows me to this day). And I had to learn all of this. Afterwards I went to the Nekrasov Library and found* The Unpublished Khlebnikov *there! Almost no one knew about Khlebnikov then. Morgues, dead bodies, poetry, plus an introverted nature and a wild fantasy. I did one thing, thought about another and, naturally, this led to a stressful situation. I got sick. I had vegeto-vascular asthenia, arterial hypertrophy, and the beginnings of jaundice. They decided that it was Botkin's disease and put me in the hospital. I lay among yellow people, although I didn't have jaundice at all. They gave me clothes in the hospital: huge canvas pants and a huge jacket. I put them on and asked if it was possible to change them. They answered: «You need to drink less.» Then they added: «Tie them up with a string.» And I tied them up with a string.»*

«At precisely that time I suddenly came upon a book of French caricatures titled French humor. *I found there great examples of black humor -- the drawings of Maurice Sinet. By the way, caricaturists often have psychological problems. Chas Adams was periodically hospitalized in a psychiatric institution. Sinet, Bosque, Roland Topor. . . My art is similar to Topor's and the group «Panic» -- Arrabal, Topor, and Olivier O. Olivier. And when I saw this, naturally I began to draw strange and absurd series about funerals and suicides. I did a whole pile of these drawings and went to the journal* Smena. *There I met Oleg Tesler and he liked them very much. Suddenly* Smena *published my drawings.*
Oleg Tesler told me: «We can't publish everything, but you draw. Don't pay attention to anyone else.» And I drew. It was constant mental activity: I would even wake up at night. There were hundreds, thousands of drawings, a stream: one drawing would come up on paper, I'd already thought up another, and a third would begin to gnaw at me. Caricature pushed aside my poetry for a while.
I drew amateurishly, but caricaturists are rarely good artists, just as professional artists rarely become caricaturists — they're weak on ideas. Caricature is a philosophy, and the people who do it think amazingly strangely. Skill in drawing comes second. For me, a caricature is more than just a humorous drawing. A paradoxical image is always retained in my work. Marcel Duchamp was also a caricaturist. Philip Guston was an abstractionist at the beginning, and then he began to draw caricatures.

trate Karel Chapek's novel, *War With the Newts*. He received several prestigious awards for this work, he began to be imitated, and the drawings themselves were bought by the Tretyakov Gallery. An artist who was practically unknown now outshone the leading lights of contemporary Moscow illustration.
He came to illustration at a time when there was already an established, standard style of «metaphysical graphics.» The stamp of this style was a minimal set of visual images, based on the metaphors of surrealism. Tishkov worked in an entirely different manner: parallel to Chapek's text he drew his own remarkably original and funny stories about newts. He did not cultivate a strictly planned composition, but filled the page completely chaotically and extremely densely with personages and subjects. This baroque (or eclectic, or post-modern, which are all one and the same) excess, this supersaturated visual solution, this extravagant narrative became the foundation of his visual vocabulary and his aesthetics.
His is one of those types of universal artistic natures for whom the boundaries of genres are transparent. In 1986 he tested himself in painting for the first time, and very successfully. His large paintings were shown at the Moscow Art Fair, ART-MIF 90. A bit earlier he began to produce artist's books, uniting word and image in an integral visual-poetic text. These books conclusively shaped his mythological legends. In order to renew the tradition of limited editions of the Russian Futurists, Tishkov founded the publishing house Dablus. He views it as part of a single project, one which includes the work of other artists within the orbit of his own myth. For his one-man show in Moscow, he prepared an installation of stuffed toys. He composed and recorded music on the harmonium which was then played at the exhibition. In 1992, the play *Dabloids* was first published in the literary journal *Mesto pechati*. To all appearances, we should await the opening of a massive monument to Dabloid and the founding of the amusement park «Dabl-land.» Tishkov's plans include the Dabloidization of the entire world!
Tishkov's favorite poetic imagery is that of the full-watered Nile. In this sense, his artistic activity is similar to that great river. Regardless of how diverse his interests or how varied the media in which he works, the flow of his creative will, like the waters of the Nile, is the same at any given point. Whether illustrating Lewis Carroll, composing and drawing his many books, or working on a monumental canvas, he is occupied with one and the same thing: he reproduces now and forever his mythopoetic world.

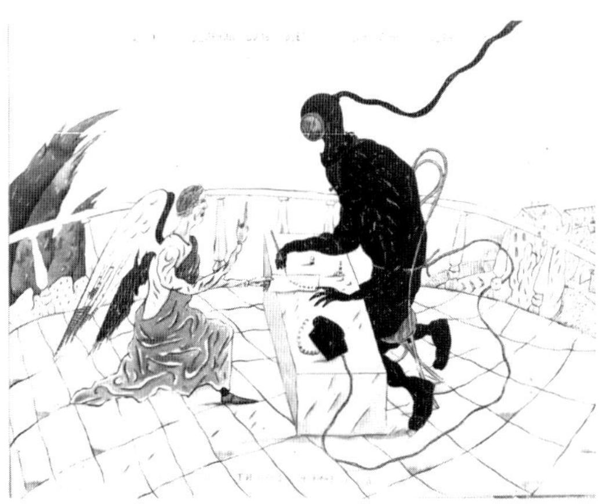

Angel and The Diver, 1989.Drawing .

3.The Mythology of Leonid Tishkov: Heroes

Dabloids, Stomachs, Blockheads, Divers, and Living In a Trunk are characters with whom the artist has lived for a decade. They are indivisible atoms of his invented world, a mythological constant.

Dablus is the most important hero. Dablus looks incredibly simple: a divan bolster with a nipple on each end. It appears that two female breasts have grown together, but in the shape of a phallus. The myth of Dablus can be traced back to the theme of the cosmic egg in Hinduism. Dablus is the same thing as Hiranyagarbha in ancient Indian mythology — the egg-like Golden Embryo of Brahman, which began the universe. Dablus gives birth to Dabloids and thus leads Tishkov's cosmos into movement.

Yet another meaning of the Dablus is parodic. By illustrating the unity of the masculine and feminine principles too literally, Tishkov parodies the idea of the androgyne, so popular in Russian philosophy at the turn of the century. Vladimir Solovyov, and after him Vyacheslav Ivanov, saw the possibility of resolving the contradictions inherent in man (the division into two sexes) and in the world's structure (oppositions such as darkness and light, man and nature, cosmos and chaos) through love and the flowing together of souls. The androgyne was a sort of hypothetical creature who had achieved perfection. In Tishkov's mythology, the androgyne is cast down from the metaphysical heights into daily life, moved into the Russian countryside. The villagers find Dablus in a field, place it in a shed, take it to the baths. This recontextualization unavoidably changes the image; it becomes a caricature of itself.

The next image in the hierarchy is Dabloid, a foot with splayed toes, crowned with a tiny head. The etymology of the word is traced to the word «dual.» The image is constructed on the opposition of the concepts «upper-lower,» and «reason-action.» Analogies for these oppositions are found in Russian folklore, in proverbs: «Because of a stupid head, the feet get no peace.» The Dabloid is a sort of universal sign. It is a word which means everything at once: metaphysical concepts and daily objects, homeland and tap water. It is a sign of human destiny, a predestined life path. It is an emblem of the Chinese hieroglyph Tao, which is made up of two parts: head and to walk. At one of his exhibitions, Tishkov prepared the action called «To Each His Dabloid,» in which visitors were invited to choose their favorite portrait of the Dabloid, that is, to choose a portrait of their destiny.

The dual nature of the Dabloid lies in the fact that, as the central personage of the Tishkov epic, he is a hero without deeds, a foot that can't move, and a head that doesn't think. Dabloid reveals itself only through other peoples' actions. Taken in its pure essence, Dabloid loses all meaning, becomes transparent, and disappears.

The Stomach is a hallucination, born of vigils over medical texts. The Stomach is the

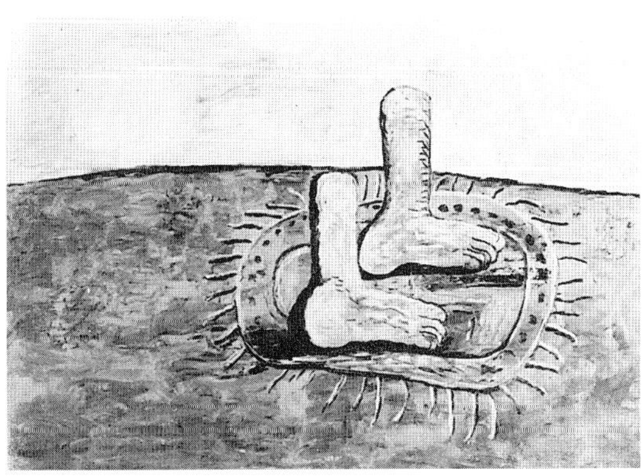

Philip Guston, Feet on Rug, 1978. Oil on canvas.

«My brother was very interested in Western art, painting and jazz. The beginning of the 1960s was a time of general interest in America: rock, Elvis Presley, etc. Somehow a copy of the journal America made its way to Nizhnie Sergi. To this day I can see before me cut-out illustrations of Rothko, a «Golden 5» — I don't remember the artist. I saw these things by chance in my childhood, but as I now realize, memorized them very well. I was seven years old. I didn't know Russian art and knew nothing about the history of art, but I looked through these American journals and liked everything I saw there: Arshile Gorky, Boogie Woogie on Broadway. Piet Mondrian, Mark Tobey, Abstract Expressionism, Jackson Pollock. That was the most tremendous impression: Jackson Pollock in large format in the journal America.

Music was always playing in the house. My oldest brother studied then in Moscow and sent presents, records: Benny Goodman, Frank Sinatra, Harry Belafonte. I remember, they would put on a record and my brother and his friends would gather together to play cards. Sometimes they would be a person short and call me. Although I was small, I knew all the card games. My childhood was truly happy. I didn't go anywhere — I just sat at home, read books, listened to jazz and played cards.»

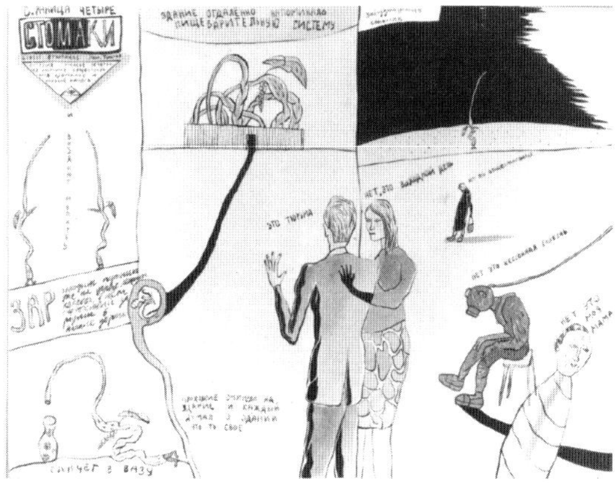

Stomachs. Page from album, 1990.

human insides, the quintessence of his physical and physiological hypostasis, and the mirror image of the metaphysical hypostasis — the soul. The Stomach is a caricature of the soul, the soul inside out. When a person sleeps and the fetters of reason don't reign over his soul, the delicate shoots of the Stomach grow out of his body as from the earth.

Within the Stomach, in the place which corresponds to the rectum in the human organism, a person is hidden. With the person's help, that is, by means of his feet, Stomachs can move about the earth. This strange visual image comes from the Russian saying, «to sit in the butt,» that is, to be in an incredibly awkward position. Practically all of Tishkov's stories, or their fragments, are built upon the provocative use of such strange situations — elements of his larger myth.

«I was interested in dreams, I copied them down and constantly depicted sleeping people in my drawings. My work can be divided into two parts: spontaneous-automatic writing which includes latent Surrealistic images, and analysis. «Living In a Trunk» is the result of vision. «New About Dabloids» is pure analysis.»

The active hero Blockhead is counterpoised to the shy and subtle Stomach. The Russian word for Blockhead is «*Churka*.» «*Churka*» means both a roughly hewn beam and, in the figurative sense, an illbred person, a bumpkin. The Divers are sublimated memories of childhood, strange people seeking a dead person in a lake. The history of the Divers is a separate myth. Its essence lies in the contemplation of freedom and/or the lack of freedom. Divers are the incarnation of fatal dependence: their life is cut short the moment someone steps on the hoses that carry oxygen from an unknown source. Divers aren't even heroes, they are simply protective membranes. The actual beings hide within the suits.

The Living In a Trunk series, LIT, (in Russian *ZhVKh*), is semantically similar to the stories of the Divers. The LIT folio is perhaps the most epic of Tishkov's creations. It is done in the spirit of Chinese drawings with India ink, and is accompanied by aphoristic titles in the style of haiku. Living In a Trunk is an indivisible creature, both person and elephant simultaneously. The naked person is hidden in the trunk of an enormous elephant who is at once the tenderest nanny and a merciless jailer. LIT can be viewed as a grandiose metaphor, an epic unfolding of one of the central issues of existentialism: the problem of freedom and limitation of choice. An African folktale tells how one day a person came from the desert and he was lonely and sad. An elephant, who met him along the path, took him on his back and carried him everywhere for many years. He showed him the forests and savannahs, and all the beasts who lived there. The person lived on wild honey and the fruits of the forest, which the elephant got for him. The elephant initiated the person into the secrets of hunting and made him into a great hunter. Now the ungrateful human kills the elephant for the beauty of his tusks. But that is already contemporary history.

Symbolic parallels to of this parable can be found in Eastern myths. The image of the elephant-universe is seen in ancient Indian mythology: eight elephants that appeared from the cosmic egg of Brahman became guardians of the eight parts of the world. In Vedic mythology there is the solar deity Vivaswat, «the Radiant One» — a naked person, born deformed. Later he is compared to the gods, and an elephant arises from the parts of his body. The parable of Living In a Trunk resonates with the most ancient cosmogonies.

4. Actions of the Myth

Tishkov's myth is concerned less with actions than with the description of situations. There are several such moments that define the boundaries of this myth.

The first of these moments is the act of birth. Tishkov's world constantly thirsts for renewal. By means of germination, division, copulation, and birth it tries to jump out of its own membrane: Dablus generates Dabloids, Divers give birth to more Divers. On the one hand, birth reaffirms the ontological continuity; on the other hand, it supports the intention of the poetic language itself to go beyond its limitations and become a metalanguage. Tishkov's texts are simultaneously stream-of-consciousness and commentary on it. This pulsating and twinkling is one of the most characteristic features of his work. This is why he is so fond of giving interviews: explaining absolutely nothing, he strengthens the body of his own myth.

The idea of refuge is in opposition to the idea of birth. The newly arrived hero is in need of protective cocoons and membranes — the trunk of an enormous elephant or the suit of a diver. The idea of refuge also finds its expression in repetition, in a constant return to one or another image. The crying or sleeping person, a flying bird, washing in the baths, the heart going away down a freshly plowed field are all images that present a closed circle, the unique repeating cycle of the life of Tishkov's heroes.

The twinkling or pulsation of the Tishkov text is expressed in the opposition of artistic devices, from which his creative gesture is composed: intuitive writing, the fixing of the flow of consciousness in images and text and, a function of opposites, the strengthening of these intuitive insights with the mixture of memory. In this, he strongly echoes the manifestos of «Panic» art, whose ideologue, Fernando Arrabal, divided the mechanism of creative inspiration into three fundamental moments: chance, memory (appearing through the repetition of chance) and confusion (violation of the logic of chance).

Tishkov's work is a form of palimpsest. One level constantly shines through another: through abstract patterns figurative painting

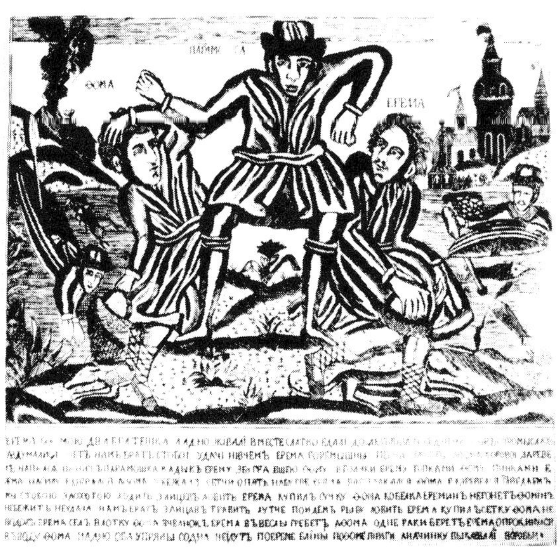

Russian folk picture.

is seen; through the arabesques of the handwriting the sense of the text appears; through entirely fantastic subjects thoroughly realistic situations develop. The sharpness fluctuates: the image at one moment is unclear, then is brought sharply into focus. It twinkles, is not entirely comprehensible, and therefore complicates perception of the text and provokes constantly increased attention.

5. The Morphology of the Poetic Language

It is impossible to define what Tishkov is first — artist or poet. He is both simultaneously. The word and the visual image exist on an equal basis in his art: they are interchangeable. For example, it is possible, not knowing a word of Russian, simply to look at the pictures; their grotesque expressiveness retains a clear message. Similarly, it is possible to read the play without seeing the drawings and thus create an integral concept of Tishkov's world. His art is essentially tautological: the principle of doubling lies at its base. The word and the text are superimposed upon each other. By various means he repeats himself and cites what he has just said. The question of citations, so essential for contemporary post-modern practice, acquires a completely different meaning when applied to Tishkov. He quotes willingly and often, without any consistency or logic. The citations cease to be a retelling of someone else's thought; he «dequotifies» them and turns them into direct speech. For Tishkov, polemic with other authors does not exist for there are no authors besides himself. His art is akin to the most delicate membrane tightly pressed to the world, lacking the springs of culture. This membrane shakes with the tiniest breath of air. His drawings contain responses to everything he has experienced, read in the newspaper or heard on the street. The sheet, «His elephant died of radiation...,» appeared after the Chernobyl catastrophe, and the mention of «Committee Women» has its source in the name of the official organization the «Committee of Soviet Women.» There are hundreds of such splinters of citations.

«There is a remarkable story about a turnip in the collection of Russian folktales gathered by the famous 19th century folklorist Aleksandr Afanasyev. A grandfather, grandmother, granddaughter, dog and cat were pulling an immense turnip from the ground (doesn't it look like Dablus?). And when they were completely worn out, they called Foot, and then another, and another, and all together they coped with the turnip. The Personage-Foot is found not only in Russian, but also in Georgian folklore.»

6. The Question of Traditions

Morphologically, Tishkov's world is alogical and absurd. This type of storytelling is called mythological. The cause-and-effect ties lead to links between events and have no other motivation, either psychological or historical. In Russian culture, the tradition of such art originates in folk culture, in the grotesque assumptions of Nikolai Gogol, Saltykov-Shchedrin, and Fyodor Sologub. In some sense, Gogol's «The Nose» can be seen as a prototype of Dabloid.

True forerunners of Tishkov's style, examples which he consciously imitates, are the artistic experiments of this century, specifically, language practices that can be considered «antiphilological linguistic utopias» (as contemporary Russian philosopher Valery Podorogy has expressed it). This includes the automatic writing of Andre Breton and the first Surrealists, the brutal absurd of Franz Kafka, the global mythopoetic experiment undertaken by Velimir Khlebnikov and later continued by the OBERIU group (Kharms, Oleinikov, Vvedensky), and the work of adherents of the theater of the absurd such as Beckett and Ionesco. Tishkov's ideas can most fittingly be compared (although due to different life experiences, are not at all similar) to the work of the group «Panic»: Fernando Arrabal, Topor, Olivier O. Olivier. He is close to «panic art» in his interest in the deliberately degraded sphere of human existence, and in the mix of profane and sacred, high and low.

Reading such texts, we are engulfed in the flow of nonsense. These works actively push aside any scientific instrumentation; they counteract any philological analysis directed towards the dissection of their inner logic and structure. In his time Ionesco, quoting what he had learned in a teach-yourself English textbook, confused many scholars with his logical explanation of the nature of the absurd. Social criticism is not the chief raison d'être of Tishkov's art and certainly not its only justification.

The bewitching puzzle of such texts is in their primordial immanence within themselves. Symbolic subtexts are absent; their narratives give birth anew to fresh and unique symbols. Only thus is it possible to find parallels in ancient mythologies and in folklore, that is, in that literature which in the very beginning was narrative. Tishkov's audacity, like that of his predecessors who opened the «logic of the absurd» to the world, consists in the fearless attempt to build the world anew from nothing, to erect what Beckett called the «total object,» a «powerful impulse to the most adequate expression of natural experience.»

Tishkov's cosmos has not yet been completed: birds and fish await their history. We still don't know what death looks like in this world, or if there is a soul. Or perhaps, as is usual in nature, this world is immortal, endless in space and time, just as human fantasy is endless and just as reality created by the artist is not subject to oblivion.

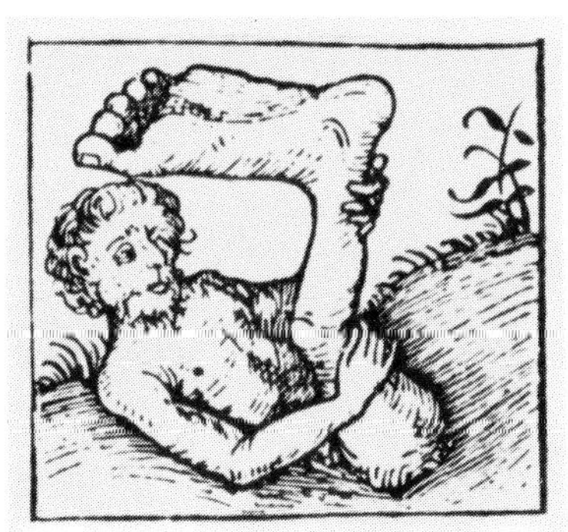

Fantastical Series.
De La Weltchronik
de Schedel

Ljiljana Grubisic

TRADITION AND INNOVATION IN THE WORKS OF LEONID TISHKOV

The work of Moscow artist Leonid Tishkov is fundamentally *uncategorizable*. To introduce Tishkov is not to place him within a contemporary artistic school or a particular style. Rather, it is to make a list. Although trained as a medical doctor, Tishkov is a successful painter, book publisher, illustrator, graphic artist, caricaturist, poet, dramatist, sculptor, composer, and exhibition organizer.

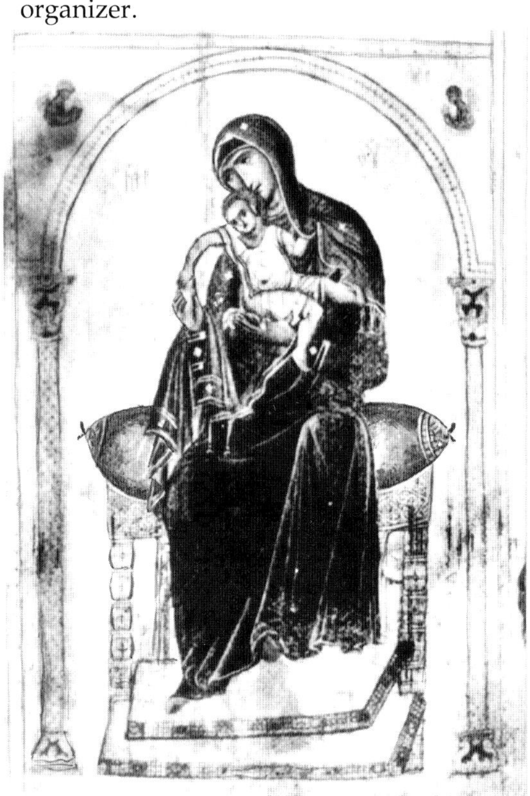

Mother of God. *Icon fragment of the Monastery of St. Ekaterina on Sinai, Byzantine, 1st half of the 12th century.*

To extract the peculiar essence from the dazzling versatility of this artist's oeuvre is possible only by calling attention to recurrent clusters of images. One of their main features is the migration from one artistic medium to another. The subjects of Tishkov's paintings are elaborated in his books and interviews, while the images in watercolors are transformed into three-dimensional sculptures. As a result, his work is highly self-referential, as ideas are related to one another in the most fundamental way. To understand Tishkov's paintings, one has to be able to read his play *Dabloidy* (Dabloids, 1991). To understand his play helps us to establish a broader frame of reference, one that defines Russian culture as a whole. It is only in this larger context that the critic can identify the underlying principle that unites all of Tishkov's work into a coherent artistic and philosophical system and can determine how this complex and seemingly eccentric system fits into the mainstream of Russian culture.

Central in Tishkov's art is the image of Dablus, the archetypal symbol of fertility and, as such, related to the myth of birth. Its oval shape reflects the androgynous nature of the creature — Dablus unites both the feminine and the masculine principle, the breast and the phallus. Because it is integral despite its duality, Dablus could be considered the contemporary variation of the quest for the lost ideal of androgynous wholeness, in which the opposites have not yet flown apart.

Furthermore, Dablus has a dual relationship to both the sacred and the profane. In regard to the former, the oval-shaped Dablus is related to the bolster on which the Virgin Mary sits, a scene familiar from Russian icons. In respect to the latter, Dablus recalls both bread and sausage, two essential components of the contemporary Russian diet and, as such, signs of the material and the mundane mode of human existence.

The red, foot-shaped offspring of Dablus are called Dabloids. This appellation is derived using the same morphology that governed the formation of the artist's own name. Tishkov explains this in his *Ne tol'ko dabloidy: Izbrannye besedy illiustrirovannye avtorom* (*Not Only Dabloids: Selected Conversations Illustrated by the Author*). There he states: «I am Leonid, the son of Leon. Dabloid is the son of Dablus.»[1]

Besides Dabloids, the other creatures that populate Tishkov's artistic world are Divers, Elephants, Stomachs and Blockheads. Dabloids are usually, but not always, the symbols of human complexes, misconceptions, ignorance, illusions, stupidity and fear. The Blockheads are closely related to Dabloids in that they symbolize human arrogance. Aggressive, they like to insult the lonely gentle and dangerously naked Stomachs. Divers are hidden behind their masks while their entire well-being depends on the network of hoses that could be cut by anybody at any time. Living In the Trunk (Elephants), the Stomachs and the Divers are all related to one another through the type of space they live in or represent — the tight and close space of our subconscious.

In a play titled *Dabloids*, Leonid Tishkov recounts the history of Dablus and explains how its offspring, Dabloids, came into being. The action of the play takes place in 1989 on the collective farm called «Garden Giant» in the village Bazhukovo. There, one foggy morning, Dablus is found in the fresh soil. Although situated in the heartland of Russia, far from Moscow, the collective farm has a broader symbolic meaning that transcends its narrow geographic and cultural boundaries.

Emerging from the soil, and having been sent down from above, Dablus is a contemporary variation of the cosmogonic myth of the original unity and subsequent separation of Mother Earth and Father Sky disseminated in various cultures.[2] A chorus, similar to those found in Greek tragedies, sings a hymn to mark this event which has truly mythic proportions. Here, characteristically called the «father and the mother,» Dablus is described as the «immortal dual-titted object,» the «simple light-carrying organism,» and the «vessel full of bliss.»[3] The villagers who find Dablus are puzzled by its shape and purpose. Determined to establish some familiar frame of reference, they compare it with human feces, breasts, sausage, bread and the bolster, that is, with the symbols of their profane and material existence. Instead of embracing this heavenly gift sent from above to bring «deliverance, eternal joy, peace and progress,»[4] the villagers view Dablus as an evil and corrupting force. Their fears and misconceptions ultimately turn the divinity into their own terror.

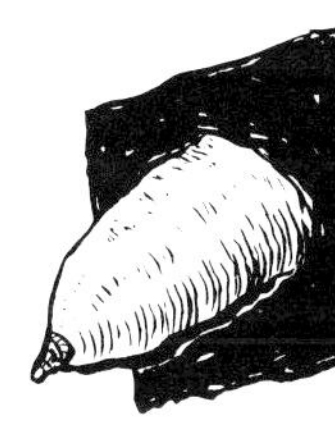

Birth of the Dablus from the Black Quadrant.

After they realize that the local girls spend nights and days in a bath-house, engaging in what appears to be sexually explicit, thus dangerously corruptive games with Dablus, the concerned fathers of the village decide to stage an all-out war against this creature. As in Greek tragedies, a blind madman, the voice of reason, appears and warns this angry mob not to bother Dablus. Tishkov's blind madman exhibits some of the traits of the traditional fool figure found in European literature. He has an ambiguous position of being both inferior and

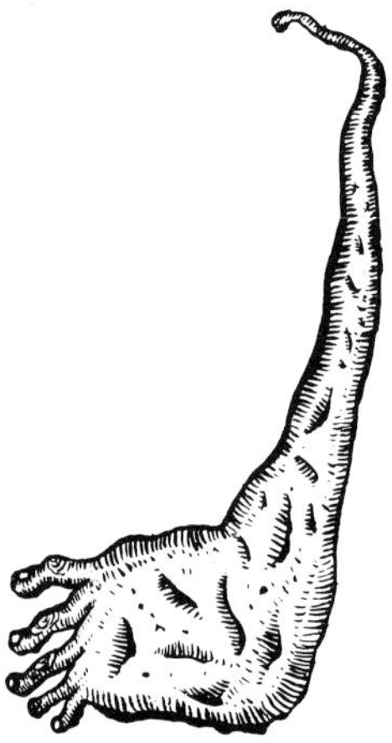

superior. His blindness and mental deficiency makes him inferior with regard to the villagers. Yet his understanding of the divine nature of Dablus distinguishes and elevates him above the banality of his fellow-villagers.

Despite the blind madman's warnings, the villagers decide to assault Dablus. Injured by the people, Dablus suddenly starts to «tremble, swelling, lights up red, and out of it come dabloids, slowly at first, then faster and faster.»[5] The villagers fight against the multiplying Dabloids, but shortly thereafter give up. In the end, everybody has his or her own Dabloid.

Tishkov's text is actively engaged in a dialogue not only with the theme of androgyny and the myth of the birth of the hero but also with the nature and moral norms of Russian society. The setting of the play, as well as the language of its protagonists, are deliberately profane. The protagonists verbally abuse each other, and obscenities and clichés are easily and frequently uttered. Yet, the semantic paradigm of insults, profanities, political clichés and the absurd are occasionally interrupted by lyrical digressions. In one a character gives an inappropriately philosophical and poetical response to the question concerning the ownership of the object found in the fresh soil. He states:

No, I did not loose anything
Everything has been already lost
I have nothing, lonely
is Petrusha in the universe.[6]

In yet another, the narrator describes the setting as a «sad landscape of Russia.»[7] Similarly, a long enumeration of characters and a list of the weapons they plan to use in the war against Dablus is suddenly interrupted by the narrator's statement that «there is no truth on earth and unhappy people live in the village.»[8]

Ancient sign of the Dabloid

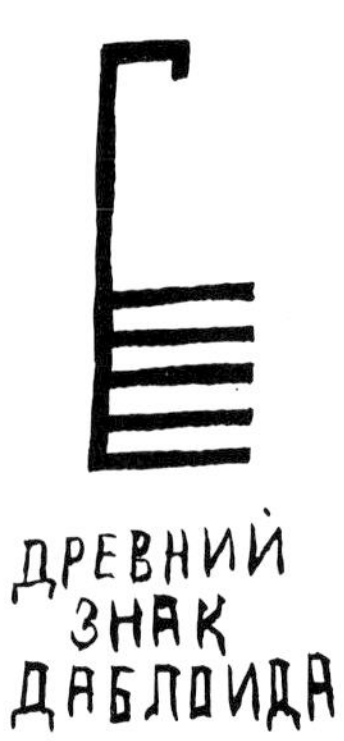

Furthermore, one of the characters thinks that time should not be wasted and that Dablus should be shot «like a Fascist.»[9] This, and the villagers' subsequent fight against the offspring of Dablus, characteristically called the Great Battle, are obvious references to the Great Patriotic War, as World War II was known during the Soviet period. The Great Patriotic War, an enormous ordeal and a triumph, which in the Russian mind happened only yesterday, has been the undiminished source of officially sponsored patriotism. The villagers' claim that the invasion of Dabloids presents danger to both the «motherland» and «the creative labor of the Soviet people»[10] is derived without any modification from the rich arsenal of clichés found in official Soviet propaganda.

The play ends with a state of tranquility returning to the village after its inhabitants simply get used to the Dabloids. Ultimately, Dabloids are found not only in the villagers' houses where children are seen playing with them but also in the «red corner» of the collective-farm clubs.

The latter image indicates that Tishkov is again targeting the socio-political clichés of Soviet culture. The «red corner» in the Russian Orthodox tradition is the place in a dwelling reserved for sacred objects — the icon, the Bible, oil lamps or candles. However, in order to eradicate religion, Soviet propaganda called for the replacement of these traditional religious objects with the portraits of Lenin and Lenin's works. They were placed in what ironically continued to be called the «red corners,» a practice especially exercised in schools, Pioneer Centers, workers' and collective-farm clubs.

A book project published by Dablus Press in 1991 in an edition of 500 copies and called *Dabloidy* (*Dabloids*) further illuminates the foot-shaped creatures. The portfolio-sized and lithographically produced pages open to a near-empty left and overloaded right side. The left side presents a single image and is accompanied by a short caption. While the first one depicts Dablus, the «beautiful androgyne,» most of the remaining thirteen images are parodic variations of the Soviet type of Dabloid. They include a Dabloid called «Makarenko» a reference to the famous Soviet authority on education, Anton Makarenko (1888-1939), who worked on transforming the delinquents (*besprizorniki*) into «new Soviet men;» an inscription «Dabloid» which replaces Lenin's name on the entrance to the Mausoleum («Let Us Pay Respect»); and the Dabloid with a Pioneer tie attached to its neck («The Pioneers Salute Him»). Others, like the one depicting a cigarette-smoking Dabloid, is an ironic play on the banality of everyday Russian clichés — »He Smokes, But Where Did He Get the Money From?» The fourteen plates on the right side of Dabloids are either purely ironic and comic or they take issue with other clichés of Soviet culture which produced a peculiar type of mentality. They are presented in a distinct cartoon-like format. While each window can exist independently on its own, it is also a necessary component of the overall structure.

In Tishkov's paintings and writings, parts of the human anatomy — the foot, the stomach, the liver, the heart, the breast, the phallus — are transformed into symbols. One of Tishkov's books of poems and drawings called *Zhizn' chelovecheka* (*Life of a Little Fellow*, 1991) carries two vivid images. The left page depicts a man embracing his own larger-than-life heart. The image is accompanied by a caption «Don't leave me, my heart,» an obvious parody of romantic clichés. Despite the man's plea, the heart is seen on the opposite page literally turning its «back» to its master. The symbolic separation that takes place between the man and his heart is captured by yet another cliché, «Where are you going, my heart?» Other exemplary illustrations supplement Tishkov's *Selected Conversations* including the one in which a boy is depicted holding a stomach in his hands («Son Found A Stomach Somewhere») and the flower-pot with a liver («Beautiful Flower Called Liver») which decorates the book's margin. Because they exist independently, these parts of human anatomy are viewed as signs of human existence. They lend themselves to various types of analysis, such as psychoanalytical or literary. Indeed, in his *Selected Conversations* Tishkov admits that his art in all its dimensions and forms is an exercise in psychoanalysis.[11] Tishkov's Dabloids can also be viewed as a sophisticated literary parody. In Russian culture, the concept of a part of the body leaving its master and assuming its own identity goes back to Nikolai Gogol's (1809-1852) «The Nose,» a short story about Major Kovalev and his anguished pursuit of his runaway proboscis. Thematically, dabloids are also related to Aleksandr Pushkin's (1799-1837) pedal digressions in

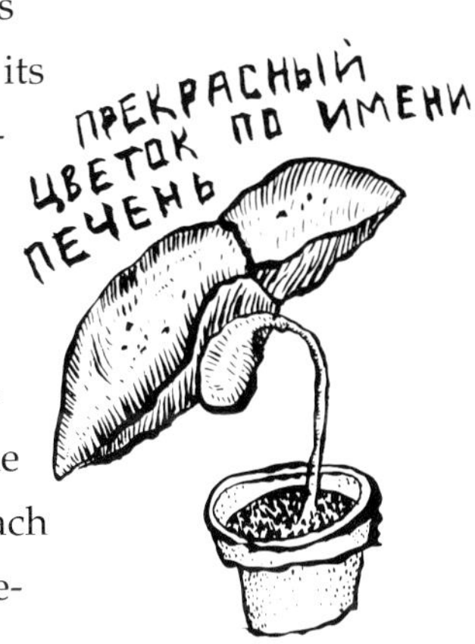

«Beautiful Flower Called Liver»

the novel *Evgenii Onegin*. However, unlike the elegance of the small and slender lady's feet in Pushkin's text, Tishkov's foot-shaped Dabloids are stodgy and fundamentally ugly. They are grotesque, horrible, comic, threatening, benevolent all at the same time.

A.S. Pushkin

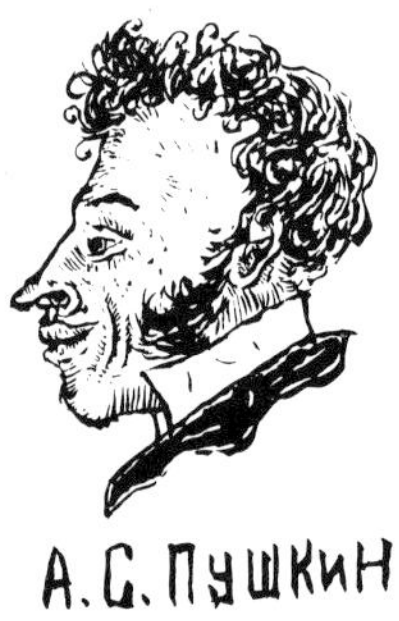

Tishkov explains the element of ugliness in Dabloids in his *Selected Conversations*. He agrees that dabloids do look strange, but the same can be said about the portrait of Lenin. Nobody asks, Tishkov continues, why Lenin has a beard or a high forehead. This is because, Tishkov concludes, «we are just used to it.[12] The artist also warns that the red in the depiction of Dabloids should not be associated with the Soviet symbolism of the color red. Dabloids are red because they are very alive. Ironically, the redder the individual's Dabloid, the less alive the real individual becomes.

One of the main features of Tishkov's artistic system is the pre-eminence of the word. He often calls his paintings «pages of a book.» Usually numbered, they often appear in a series and, as a rule, carry some type of text, description or at least a caption. Because the painting usually cannot «tell» all the «secret thoughts of the artist-graphomaniac,» Tishkov explains in a short article titled «My Books Are My Silent Feet,»[13] that he often resorts to the word, both spoken and written. Consequently, Tishkov readily gives interviews, he writes poetry and plays as well as books about Dabloids, Stomachs and other creatures. It is not coincidental, therefore, that Tishkov called one of his recent Moscow exhibitions «Graphomania.»

Related to the pre-eminence of the word in Tishkov's work is his successful activity as a book publisher. Founded in 1990, Dablus Press produces artists' books in limited editions ranging from 30 to 200 copies.[14] In addition to Tishkov's works, Dablus Press has produced a series of artists' books that include Rezo Gabriadze's *V malen'kom sadike imperii* (*In a Small Garden of the Empire*, 1990), Iuliia Kizina's *Neznachitel'nye izmeneniia* (*Insignificant Changes*, 1991), Konstantin Zvezdochetov's *Efemeridy* (*Ephemerydes*, 1991) as well as others.

Tishkov's own writing style — simple, laconic, and at times absurd — is reminiscent of the infantile speech, nonsense and parody found in the works of Daniil Kharms' (1905-1942?), a member of *Oberiu*, the last Russian avant-garde group. Tishkov's poetry evinces an indebtedness not only to Kharms' automatic writing, in which a passive hand is allowed to record the dictations of the subconscious, but also to Aleksei Kruchenykh (1886-1968) and his transrational poetry or *zaum*.[15] *Zaum* was the most radical expression of the new concept of poetry introduced by the Russian Futurists in the 1910s. According to them, the poetic word was to be treated as «self-sufficient,» that is non-referential. Primarily a language of invented words, illogical combination of sounds and raw verbal material, *zaum* was best represented by Kruchenykh's poem which started with a famous line «dyr bul shchil,» published in 1913 in a booklet titled *Pomada* (*Pomade*).

Most of Tishkov's books of visual poetry such as *Gazeli* (*Gazelles*, 1990), *Life of a Little Fellow* (1991) and *Novye pesni* (*New Songs*, 1992), all published by Dablus Press, further develop not only the Futurist tradition of *zaum* poetry but also the rich tradition of Futurist book-making. This is particularly true for the latter two in which the visual unity of the works is achieved by having been written and drawn by the same hand. This technique was often used by the poets Kruchenykh and Velimir Khlebnikov (1885-1922) and artists Mikhail Larionov (1881-1964) and Ol'ga Rozanova (1886-1918) to name a few. By producing esthetically shocking books such as *Vzorval'* (*Explodity*, 1913), *Mirskontsa* (*Worldbackwards*, 1912-1913) or *Igra v adu* (*A Game in Hell*, 1913, 1914), these poets and artists ultimately challenged the conventional notions that defined the relationship between text and illustration.

Tishkov's own books further develop this rich tradition. Each copy of *Gazelles*,[16] published in an edition of 200 copies, is illustrated by the author with silver paint superimposed over both the poems on the left and the black drawings on the right. Ultimately, each book can be considered a unique creation despite the fact that the poems and the drawings printed in black are the same in all 200 copies. Six visual poems published in *Gazelles* consist of unintelligible and illogical combinations of syllables that are sharply separated from the illustrations by a black border. The illustrations on the right side spill over their border into the whiteness of the margins. These illustrations consist of abstract images and blocks of «texts» written to look like letters of an unknown script. The overall effect of the two types of «texts» in Tishkov's book is the same in that they are equally unintelligible. The poem on the left represents a nontraditional combination of the existent letters of the Russian language, while the «text» on the right is merely a combination of letters of an non-existent language.

By having the text of the poems «framed» exclusively on one page, the overall structure of the book reinforces the traditional boundary between and separation of the text from illustration. Yet, this tradition is also undermined by having the silver paint, applied manually by the artist, spilling over the text of poems on the left to the margins on the right. The text and the illustrations are physically separated by the frames yet intimately linked with one another through the silver paint.

Tishkov's *Gazelles* is related to the Futurist tradition in yet another way as it seeks to synthesize various forms of art into a piece to be performed. The six poems are to be read by the author softly while, at the same time, his voice is amplified through loud speakers. His reading is also to be accompanied by Georgian folk songs. Normally performed forte by a men's chorus, these songs are here played so that the music and the poetry are of equal volume.

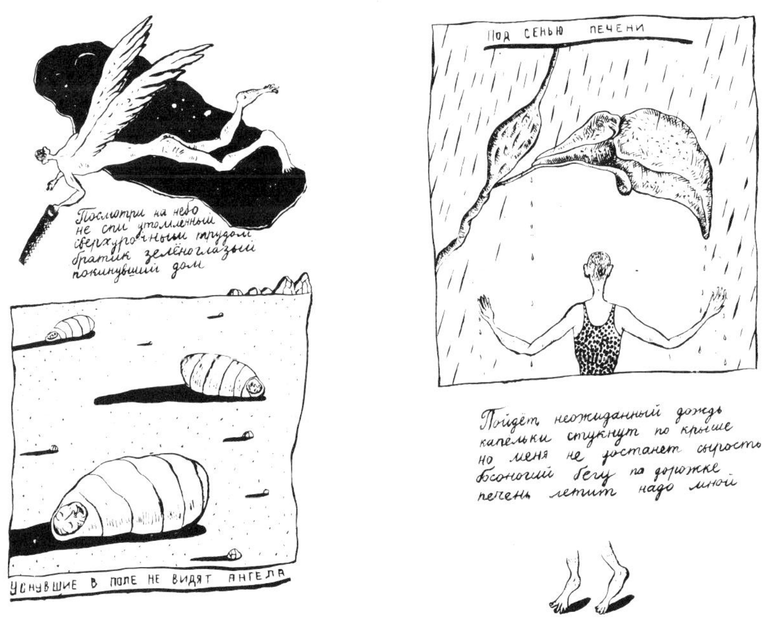

«Dream of the Fisherman», 1990
Pages from the book

Tishkov's interest in books has recently been supplemented by a turn to sculpture. His latest shows present not only two-dimensional images of Dablus and Dabloids, but also their three-dimensional manifestations. The centerpiece of his recent exhibitions are foot-shaped sculptures of Dabloids

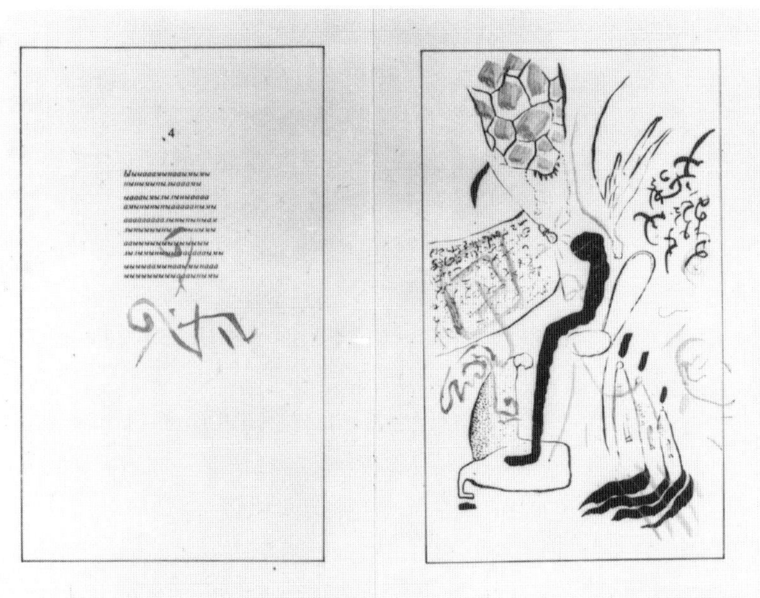

Gazelles, 1990.
Pages from the book

which are symbolically and literally connected through a network of cords to a large, double-breasted Dablus. His sculptural Dabloids come in all shapes, sizes and colors. Captions such as «Touch me, I am soft and warm,» «I am loved by children and women,» or «I love you» are attached to some of them. One of the watercolors, part of the overall installation, describes how to make your own Dabloid and which steps have to be taken to transform a sock into a foot-shaped creature. The three-dimensional Dabloids are united with Dablus until the end of the show when a ritualistic ceremony of cutting the cords takes place. The cut cords are left hanging from Dablus as a sign of their primal connection and subsequent separation.

In addition to the sculptures, these recent shows also have been accompanied by Tishkov's own music which the artist performs on an organ. To music Tishkov adds primitive verbal improvisations which consist of whispers, sighs and combinations of various phonic elements. Generated by the artist himself, the overall effect of these improvisations is almost hypnotic. They are reminiscent of Kruchenykh's fantastic philology and his concept of *zaum* as the manifestation of a spontaneous non-codified language. In that sense, Tishkov can be compared with the Russian religious sectarians who, as Kruchenykh often liked to mention, in moments of ecstasy spoke in foreign tongues or non-existent idioms. Ultimately, Tishkov's improvisations possess what James Billington calls «hieroglyphic quality,» a vocal ornamentation of the old Muscovy.[17] This «hieroglyphic quality» places Tishkov's musical and vocal experimentations firmly in the broader context of Russian culture.

In the final analysis, Tishkov stands in the same relationship to Russian cultural tradition as Dabloids stand to Dablus. Materialized either as poems, paintings, drawings, sculpture, music, book illustrations or caricatures, they are all the products of that culture. While generated by the Russian tradition and intimately linked with it, Tishkov's works are at the same time a sophisticated parody of it. As a synthetic reaffirmation and a subversive displacement of the symbols found in Russian culture, Tishkov's works lend themselves to a dual interpretation. His illustrations may appear as both foolish and wise, his writings as vulgar and lyrical, his world-view as childish and serious, and his paintings as both ugly and refined. If his painting does appear «ugly,» it is because Tishkov is not concerned with the traditional questions of style or beauty. In that sense, he is deeply rooted in the Russian tradition. For unlike Westerners, Russians remained consistently, as James Billington points out, «more interested in the ideal represented by a painting than in its artistic texture.»[18] Consequently, it is important for Tishkov not how the painting conveys the message, but *what is said* in it.

NOTES

1. Leonid Tishkov, Ne tol'ko dabloidy. Izbrannye besedy, illiustrirovannyc avtorom. Moscow: IMA-Press, 1992.
2. See, for exaple, Mircea Eliade, *The Sacred and the Profane. The Nature of Religion.* (New York: Harcourt,, Brace & World, Inc., 1959), 145-146; Joseph Campbell, *The Hero With a Thousand Faces* (Princeton: Princeton University Press, 1973), 283. The separation of the Mother Earth (Gaea) and the Father Sky (Uranus) was rendered in great detail by Hesiod in his *Theogony*.
3. *Dabloidy,* Prologue.
4. Ibid., Part One, Episode Two, Scene One.
5. Ibid., Part Two, Episode One, Scene One.
6. Ibid., Part One, Episode One, Scene Two.
7. Ibid., Part One, Episode Two, Scene One.
8. Ibid., Part One, Episode Four, Scene Three.
9. Ibid., Part One, Episode Four, Scene Two.
10. Ibid., Part One, Episode Two, Scene One.
11. *Ne tol'ko dabloidy*, 11.
12. Ibid, 6.
13. Leonid Tishkov, «Knigi - moi molchalivye nogi,» *Dekorativnoe iskusstvo*, 1991, no. 9/10.
14. For Tishkov, books published by Dablus Press are also dabloids. The ultimate goal of these books, the artists explanes, is to «dabloidize» the entire population.
15. *Zaum* literally means «beyond mind»
16. Based on Eastern poetry, *gazelle* is a type of Russian versification in wich the rhymes of the first two lines are repeatead in each even line, while the odd ones are not rhymed.
17. James H. Billington, *The Icon and The Axe. An Interpretive History of Russian Culture.* (New York: Alfred A. Knopf, 1967,) 38.
18. Ibid, 36.

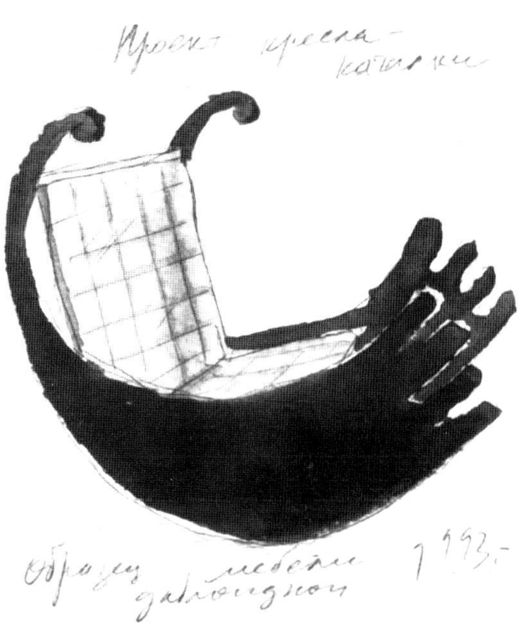

Design of a rocking chair «Dabloids»

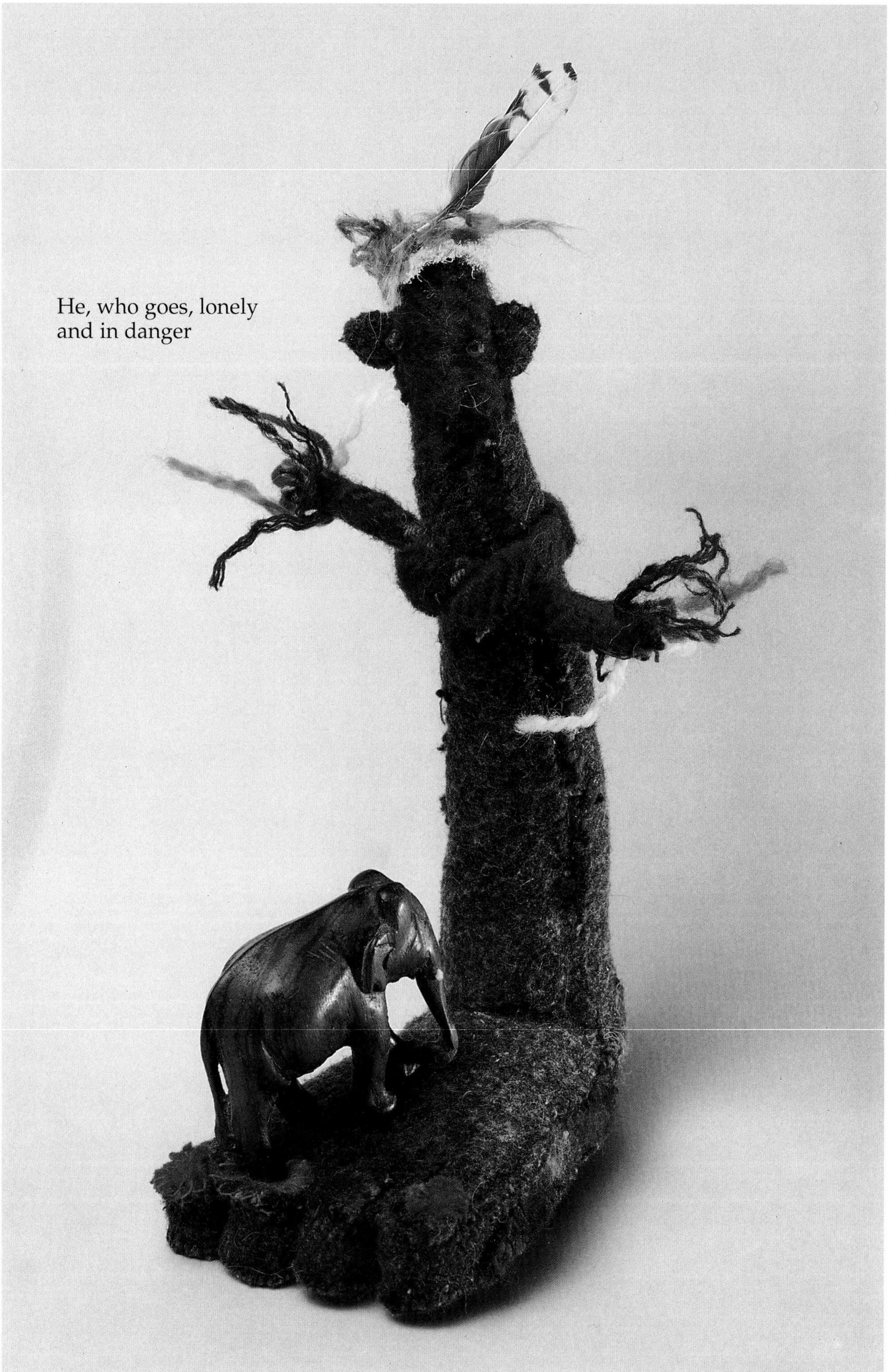

He, who goes, lonely
and in danger

LIVING IN A TRUNK

«Living In a Trunk» is almost a Chinese story, drawn in India ink. It tells about a frightened rabbit, about how standing next to a person there is always something Huge. Maybe it's God, the subconscious, eternity or the state. Sometimes you think something is following you in your sleep — don't be afraid: it's only an elephant and you — his trunk. This is your world, from which you can't leave. You don't even want to give up this world. In the trunk it's warm and damp. You lie there naked, but it's safe. It's a haven, the mother's womb in which the infant hid. Be happy as a trunk: two tusks protect you, two tiny eyes always follow you. Tomorrow the elephant will show us a valley of violets and how to pick bananas. «Living In a Trunk» is the little prince of Saint-Exupéry, in which the person and elephant can't live without each other, and each dreams about freedom, forgetting about the rose of love.

On a mountain called Sholom a herd of elephants lives like clouds, and slow time passes them by. Below this mountain stands my paper hut. My parents left. I'm alone again and fear the arrival of the Divers. Oh, Dablus, great and powerful, give me the strength to smile at eternity. Where have my golden days gone to? The autumn leaves have flown by; the owls have jumped from the fence; lovely toads sleep neatly on soft little beds. I read magazines and books; the stars shine over my head.

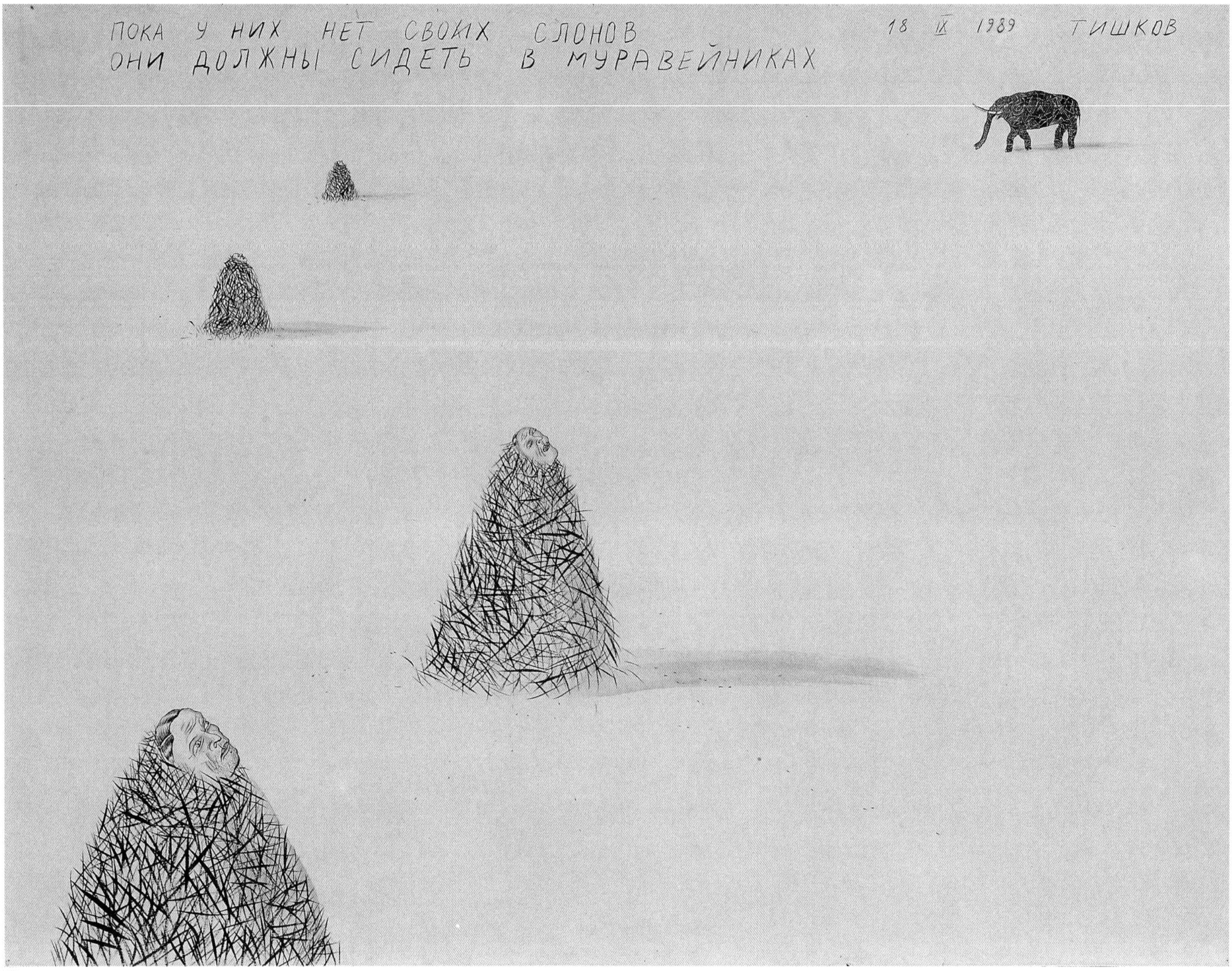

India ink on paper,
75x100 cm.

While they haven't their own elephants
they must sit in anthills, 09.18.1989

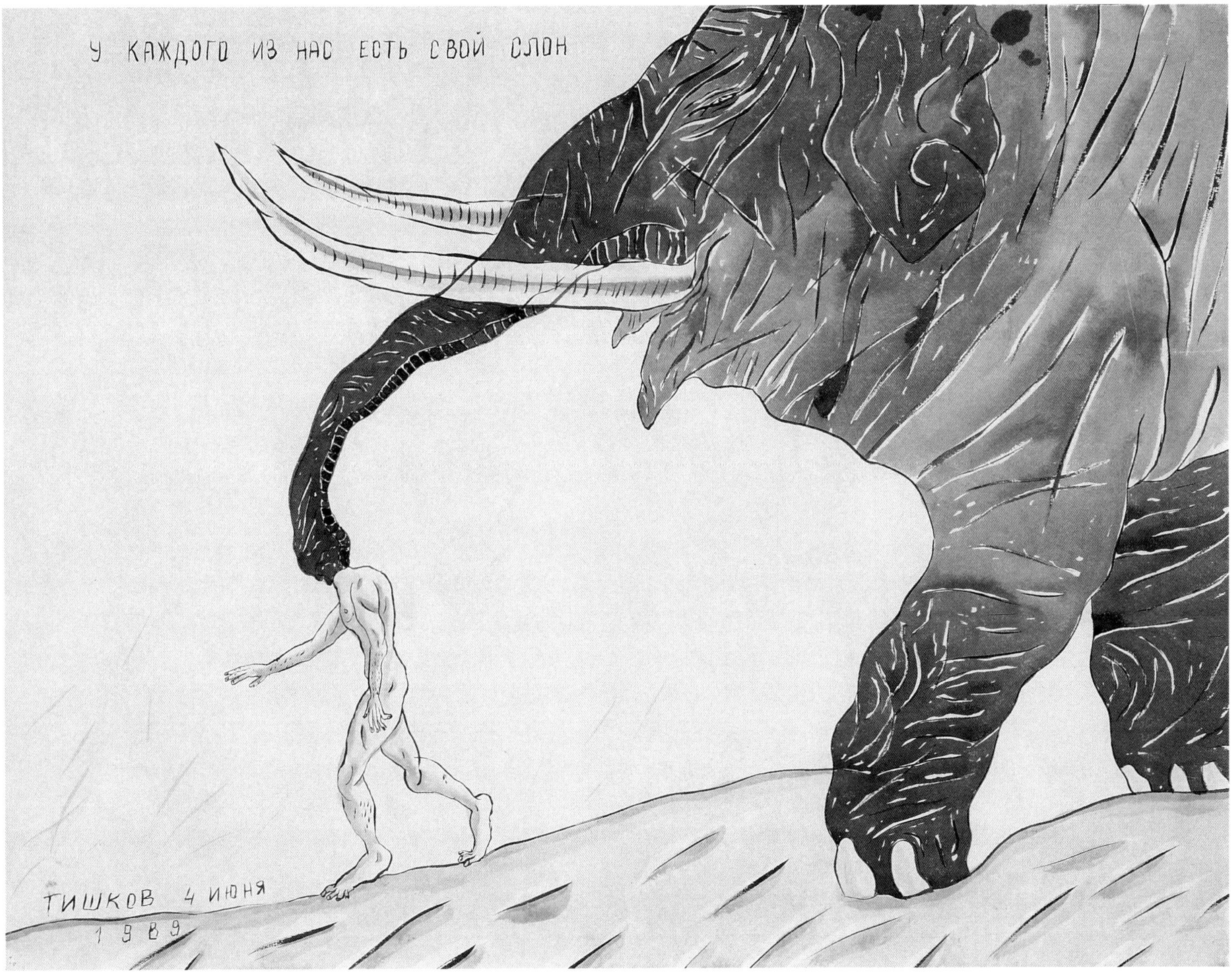

India ink on paper,
75x100 cm.

Each of us has his own elephant,
06.04.1989

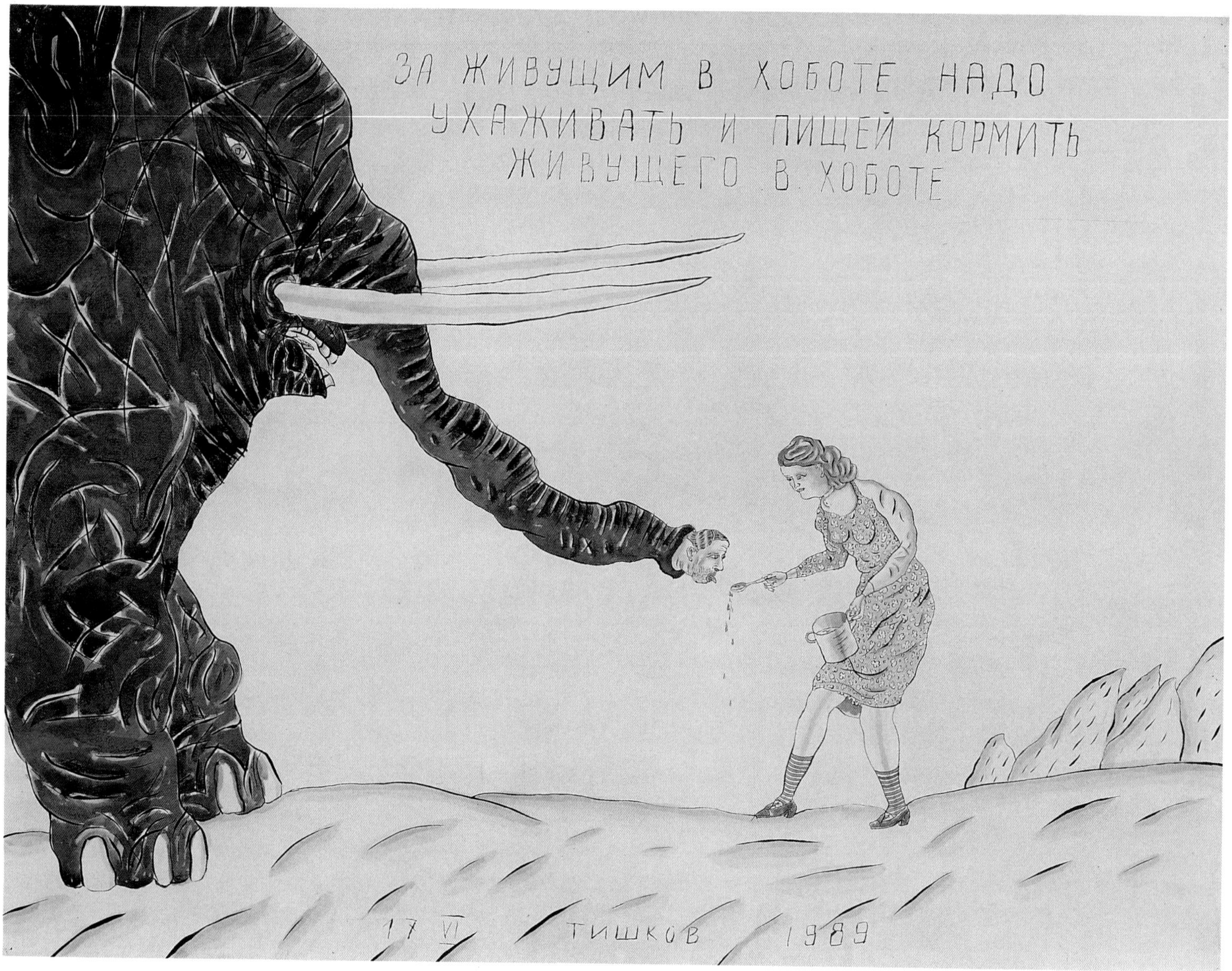

India ink on paper,
75x100 cm.

One must look after Living In a Trunk and with food nourish living in a trunk, 06.17.1989

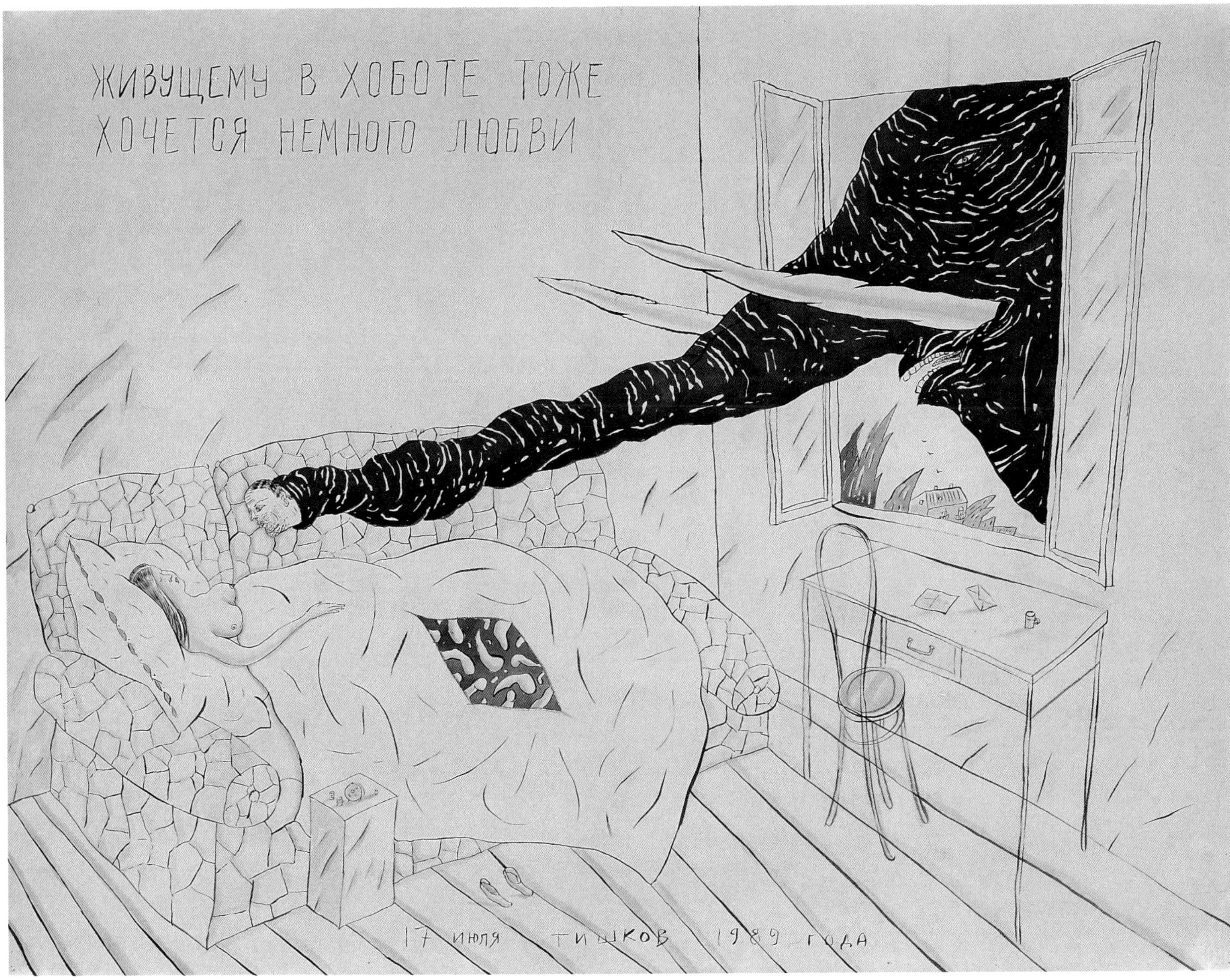

*India ink on paper,
75x100 cm.*

Living In a Trunk also wants a little
love, 06.17.1989

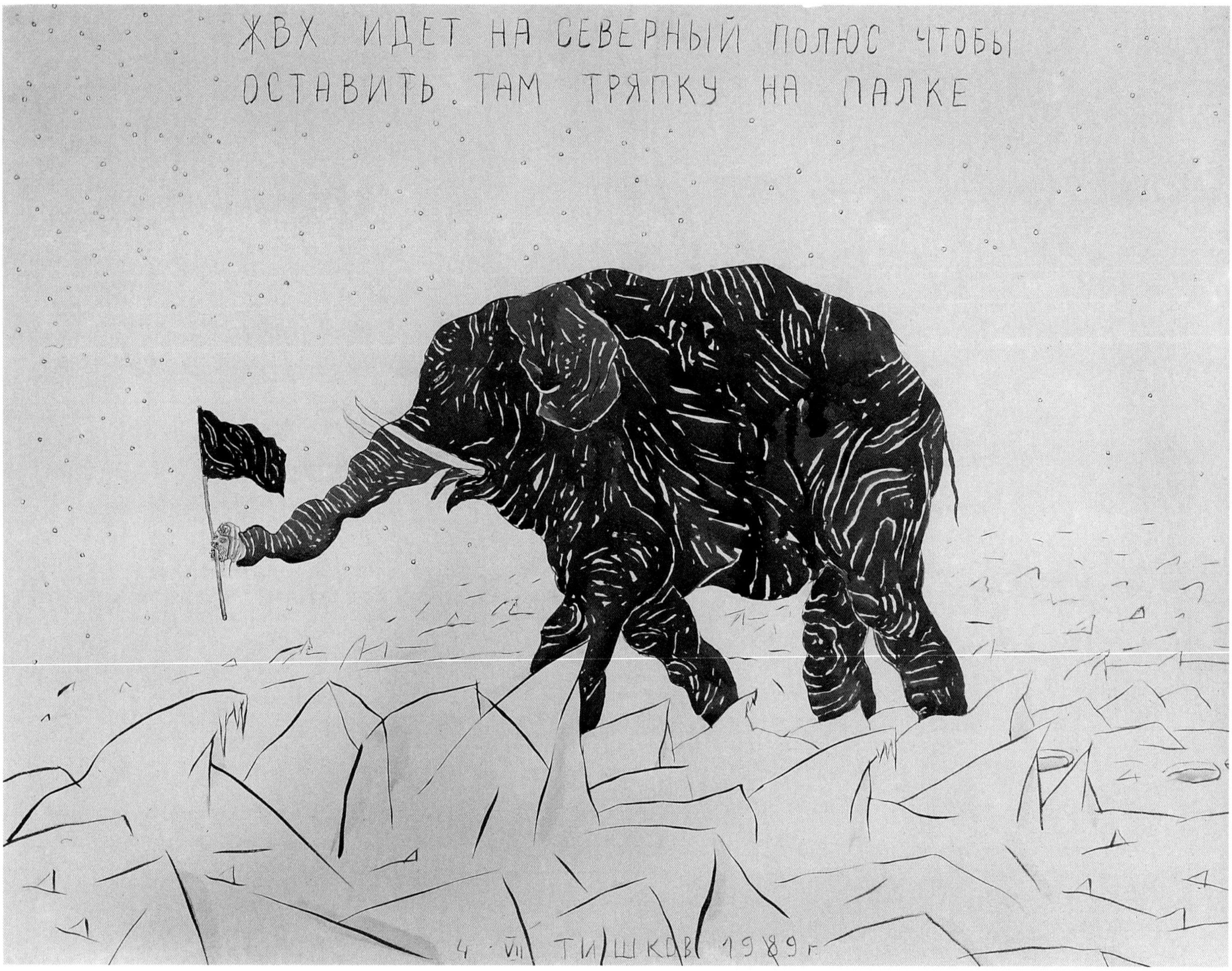

India ink on paper,
75x100 cm.

L.I.T. goes to the North Pole to leave
a rag on a stick there, 07.04.1989

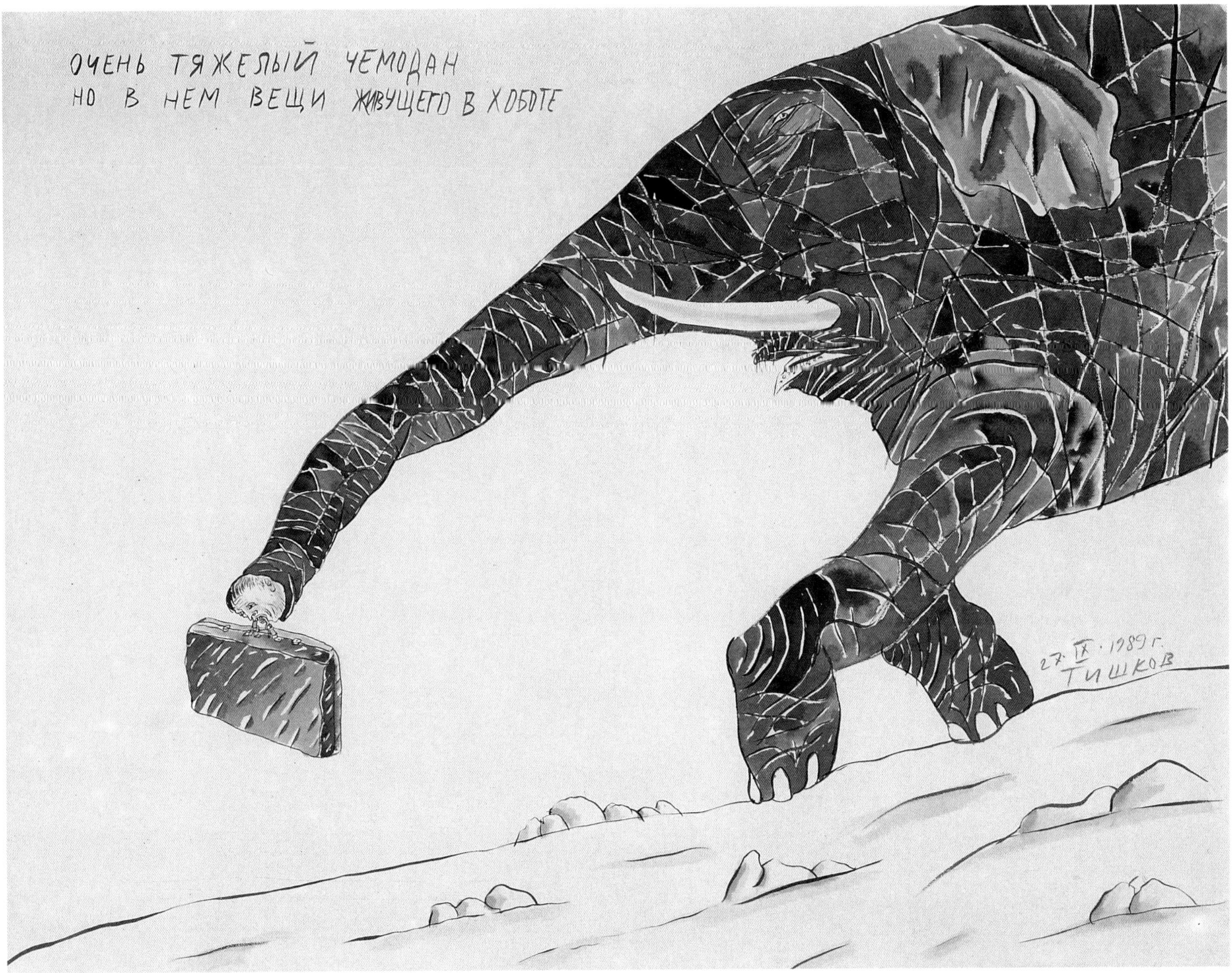

India ink on paper, 75x100 cm.

A very heavy suitcase but in it are
Living In a Trunk's things, 09.27.1989

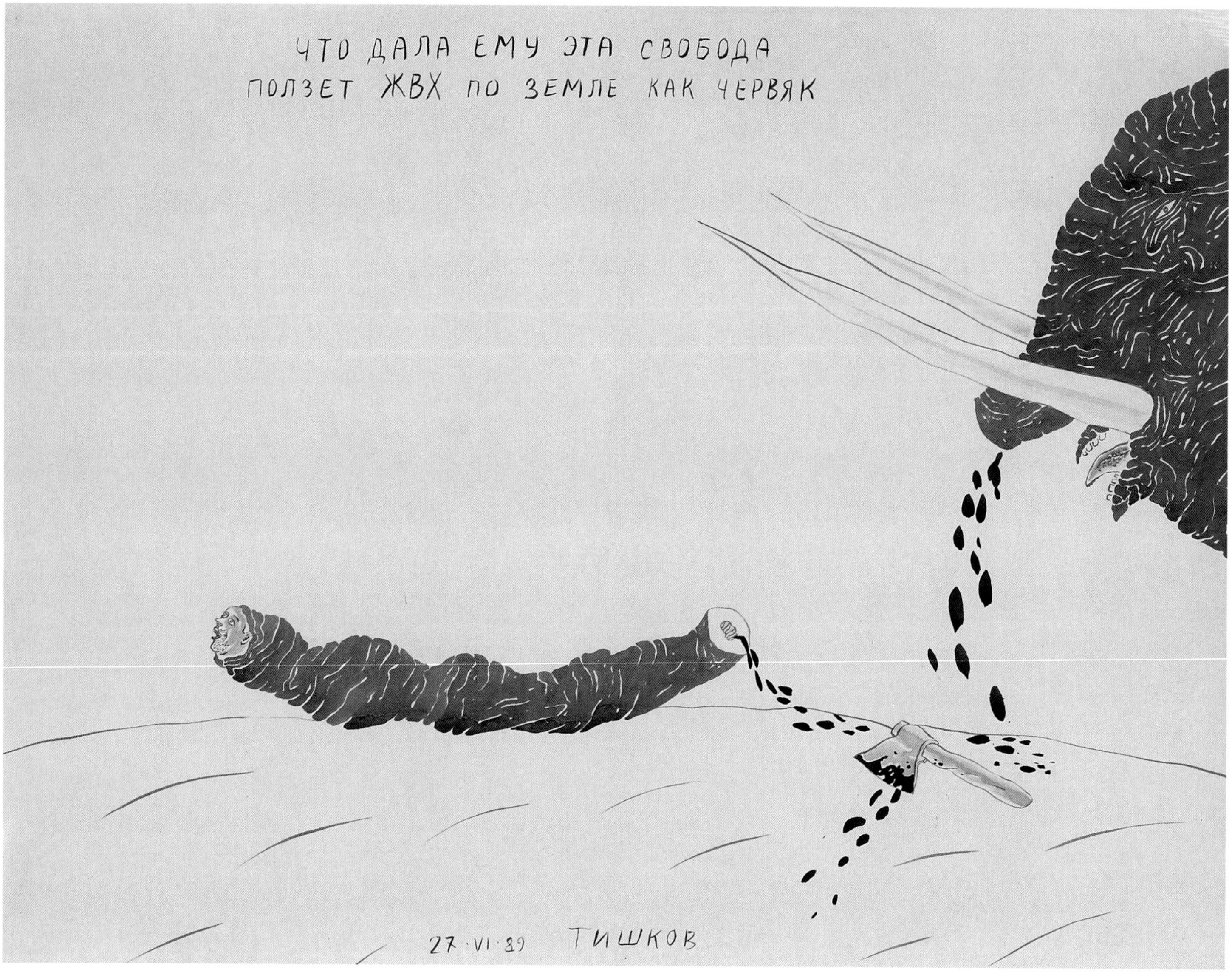

India ink on paper,
75x100 cm.

What has this freedom given him
L.I.T. crawls along the ground like a
worm, 06.27.1989

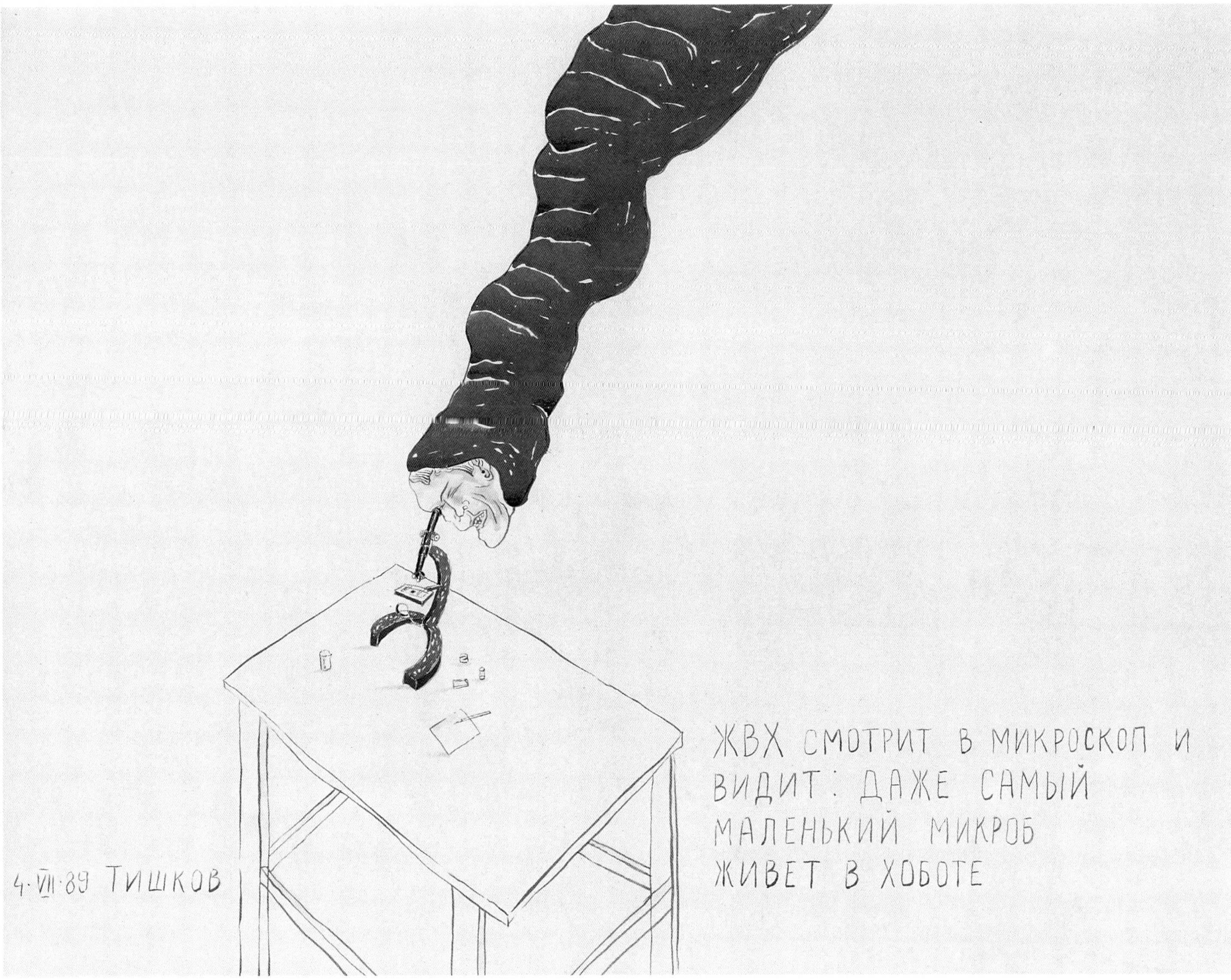

India ink on paper, 75x100 cm.

L.I.T. looks in a microscope and sees: even the smallest microbe lives in a trunk, 07.04.1989

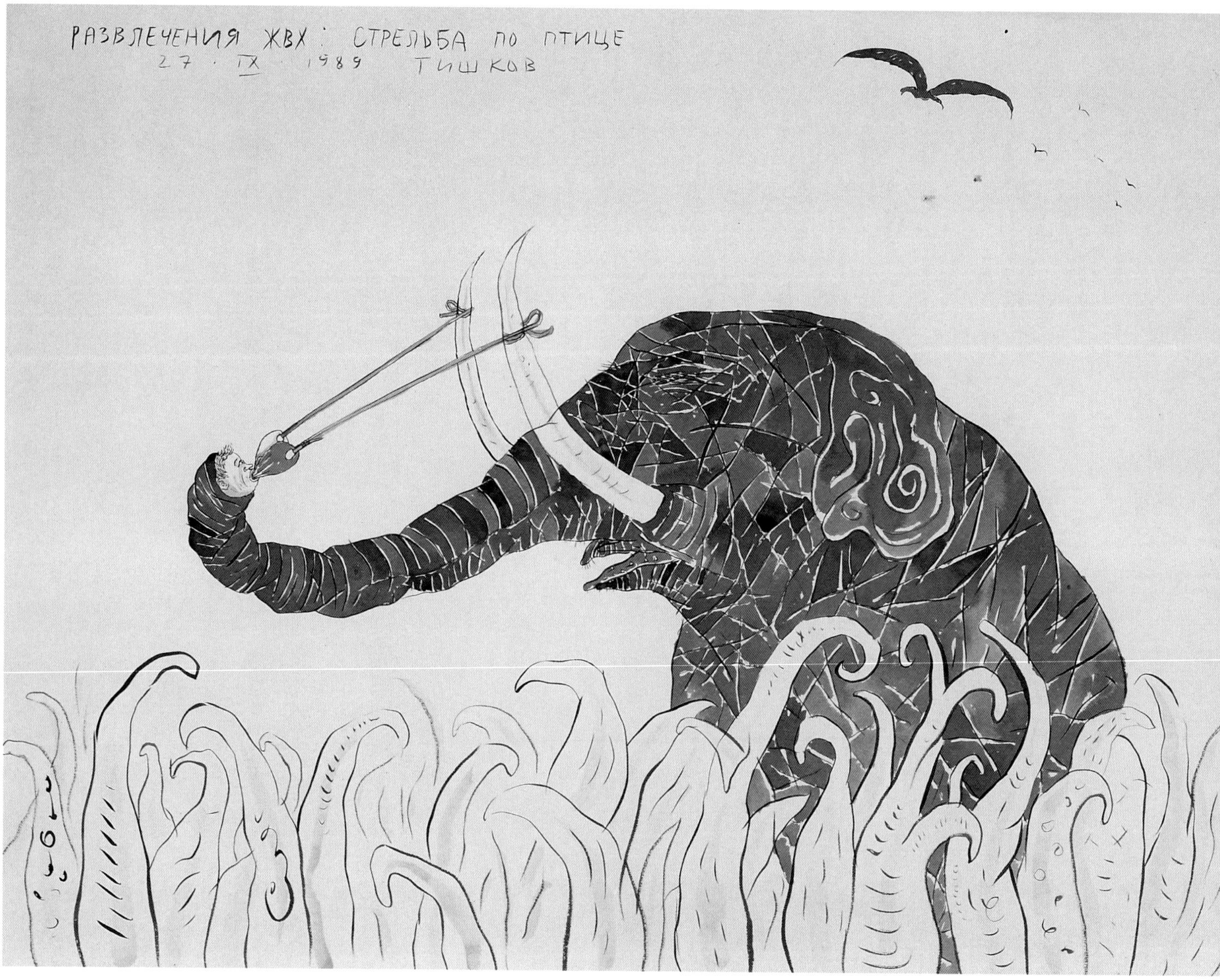

India ink on paper,
75x100 cm.

Entertainment for L.I.T.: bird-shooting, 09.27.1989

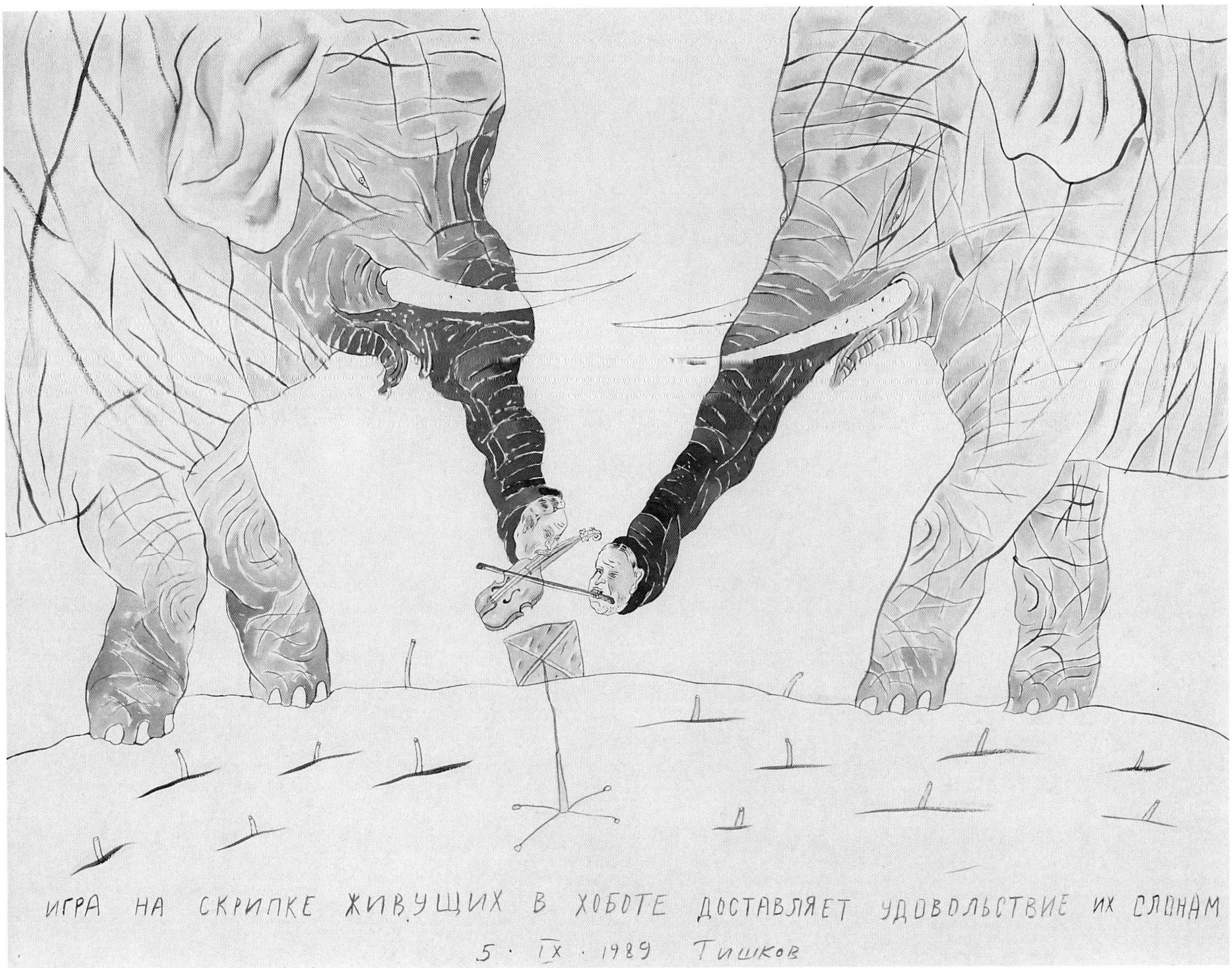

India ink on paper,
75x100 cm.

Living in trunks' play on the violin
pleases their clephants, 09.05.1989

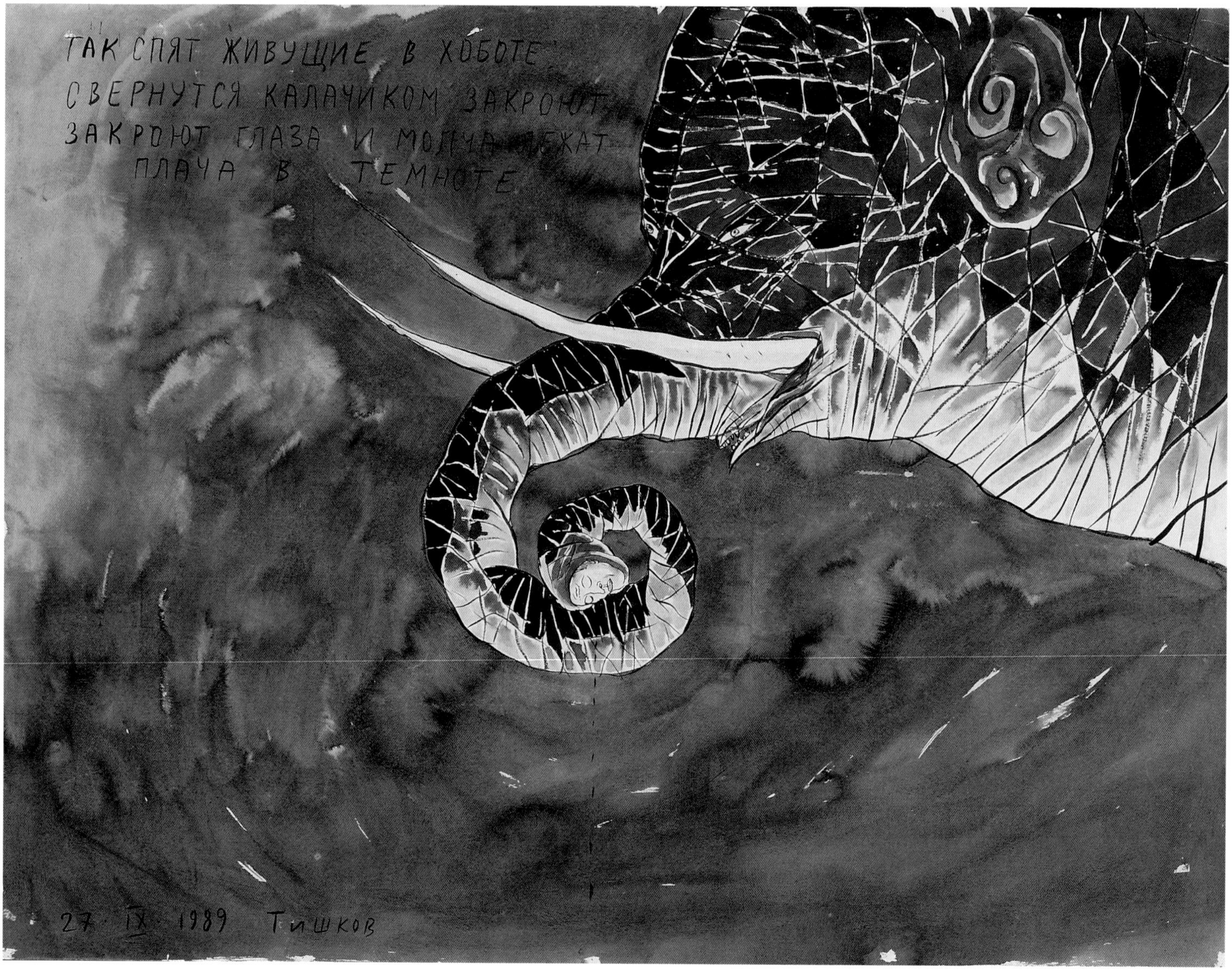

India ink on paper,
75x100 cm.

Thus sleep living in trunks roll up in
balls close their eyes and silently lie
crying in the dark, 09.27.1989

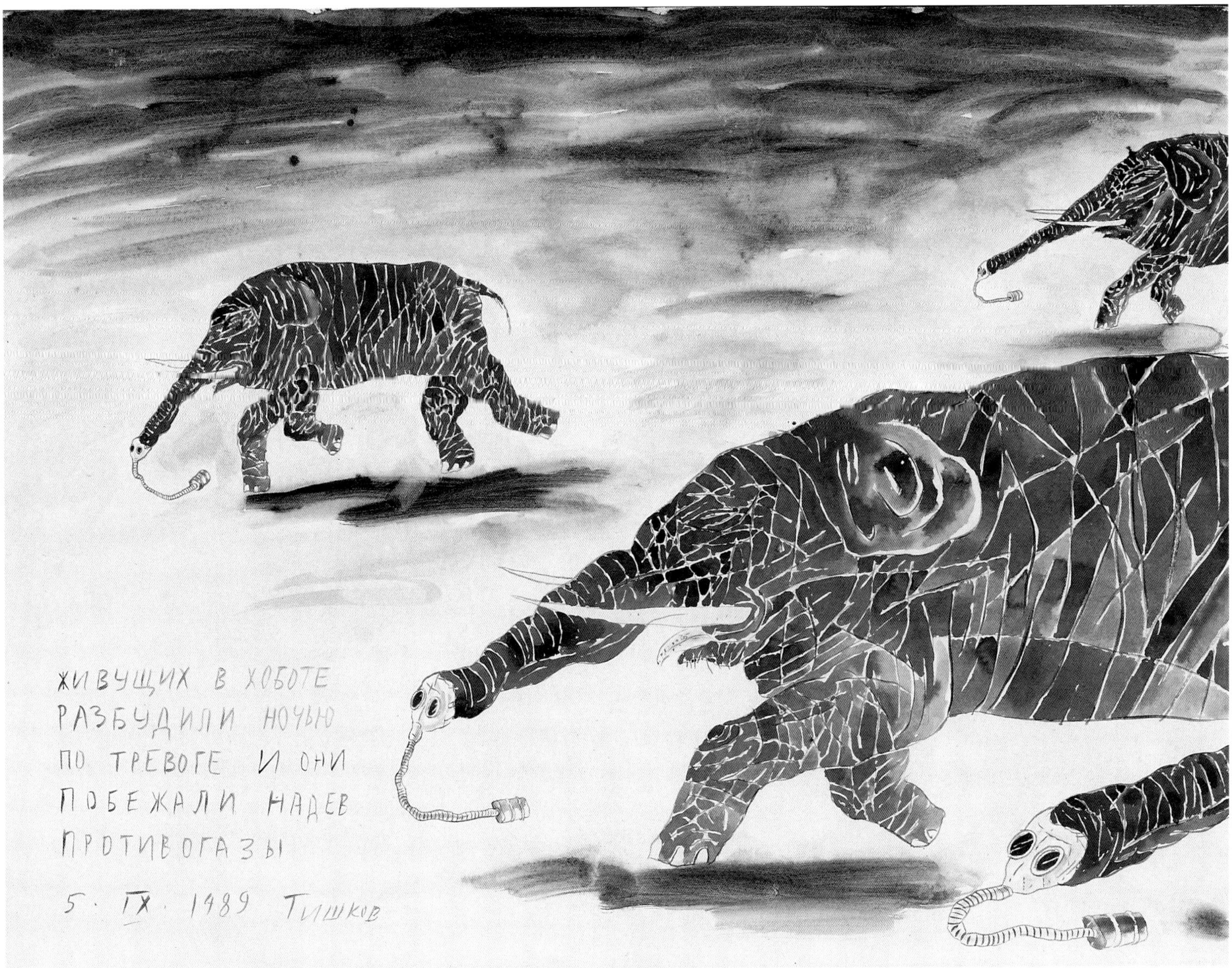

India ink on paper,
75x100 cm.

At night they awakened Living In Trunks in alarm and they ran with gasmasks on, 09.05.1989

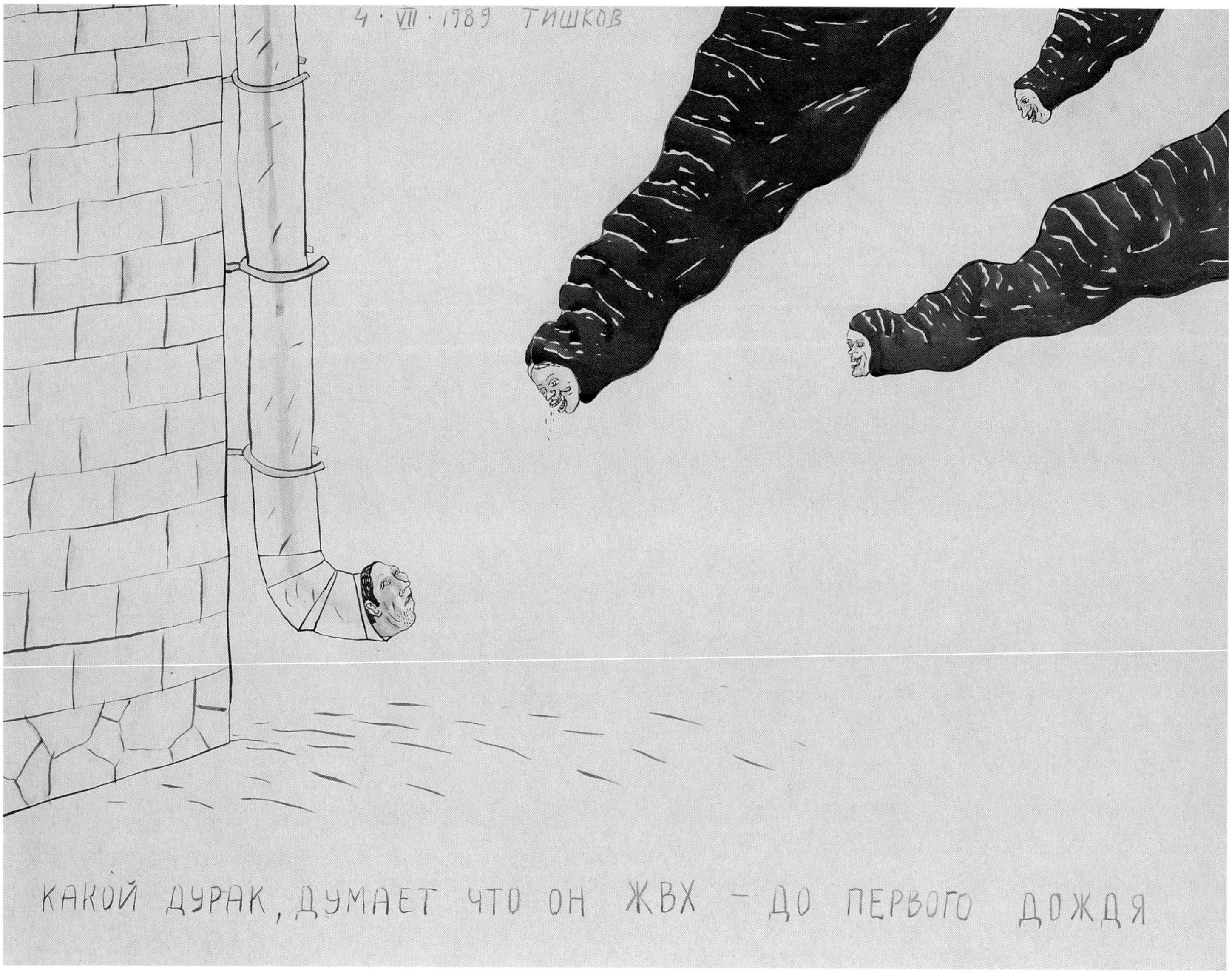

India ink on paper,
75x100 cm.

What a fool, thinks he's L.I.T. — until the first rain, 07.04.1989

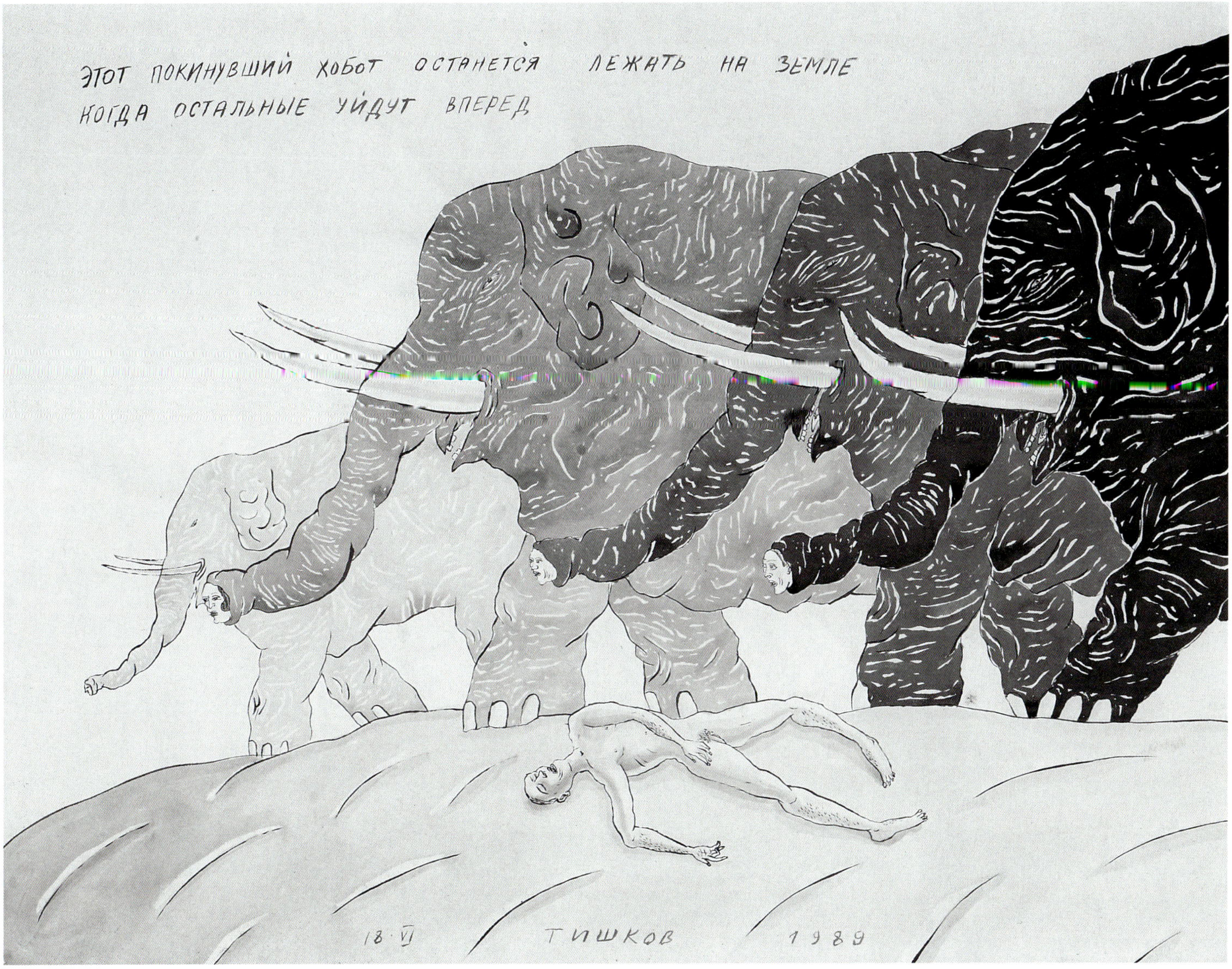

India ink on paper, 75x100 cm.

This onc that's left his trunk will still be lying on the ground when the others move ahead, 06.18.1989

India ink on paper, 75x100 cm.

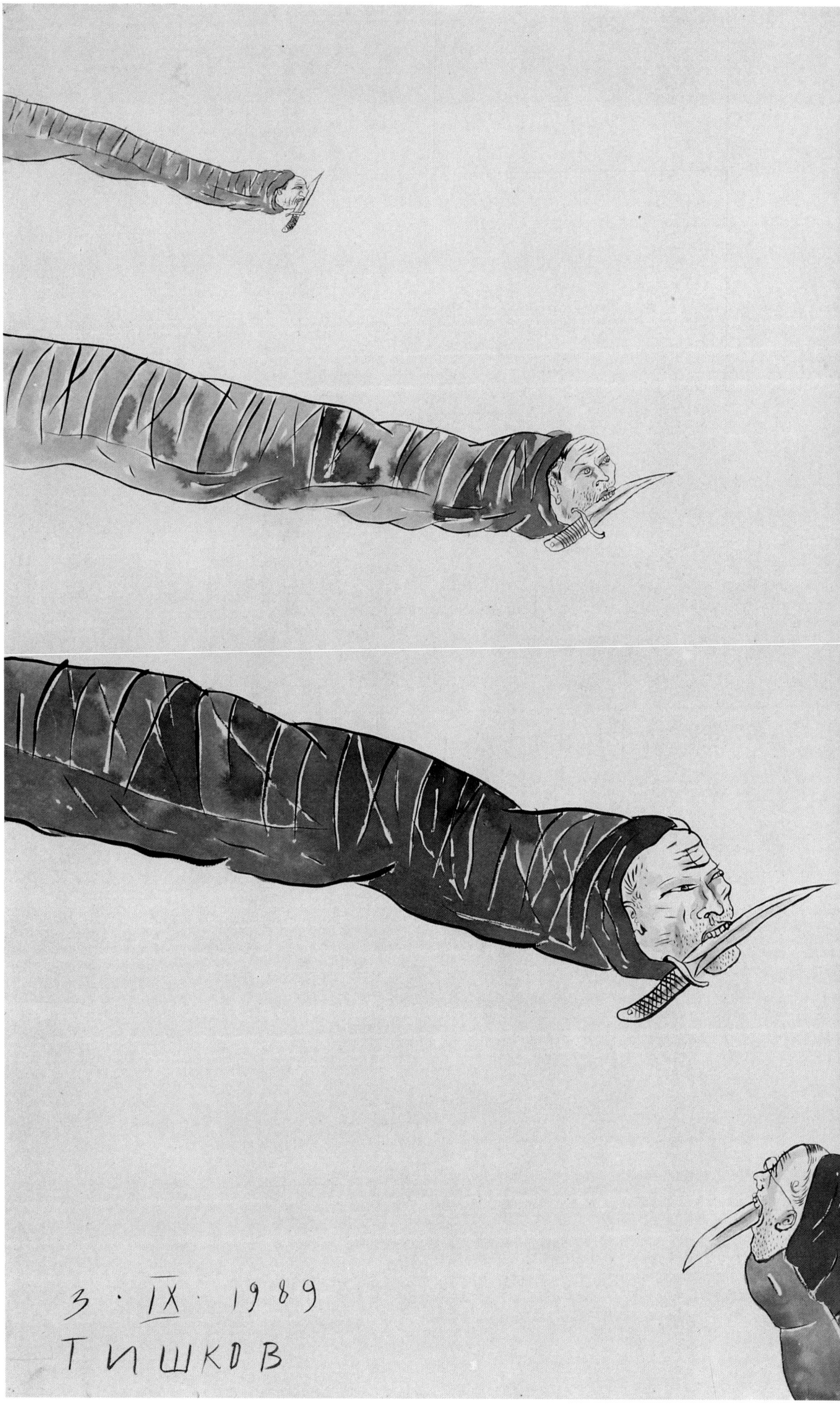

Living In Trunks are armed to the teeth both these and those, 09.03.1989

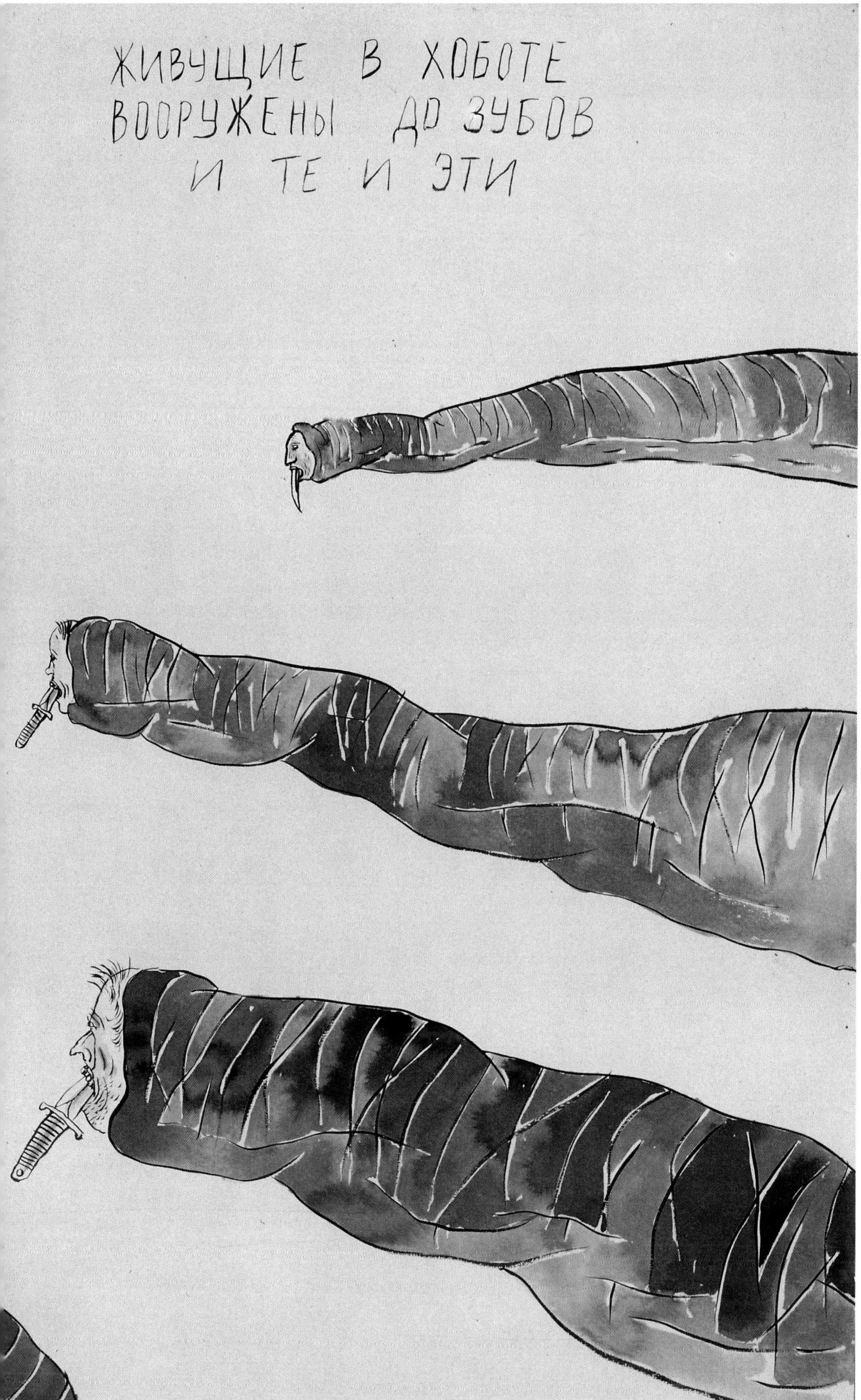
ЖИВУЩИЕ В ХОБОТЕ
ВООРУЖЕНЫ ДО ЗУБОВ
И ТЕ И ЭТИ

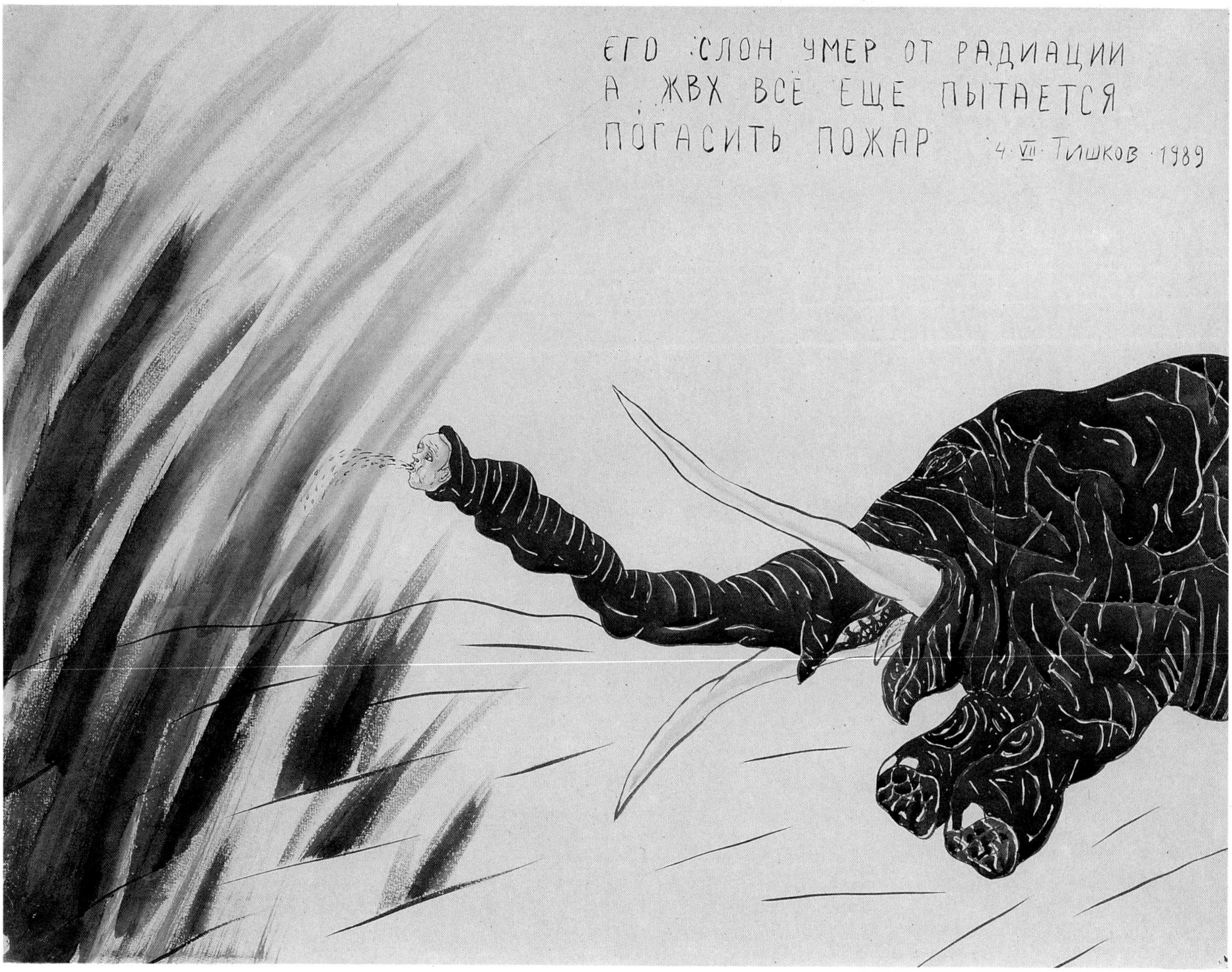

India ink on paper,
75x100 cm.

His elephant died of radiation and
L.I.T. is still trying to put out the fire,
07.04.1989

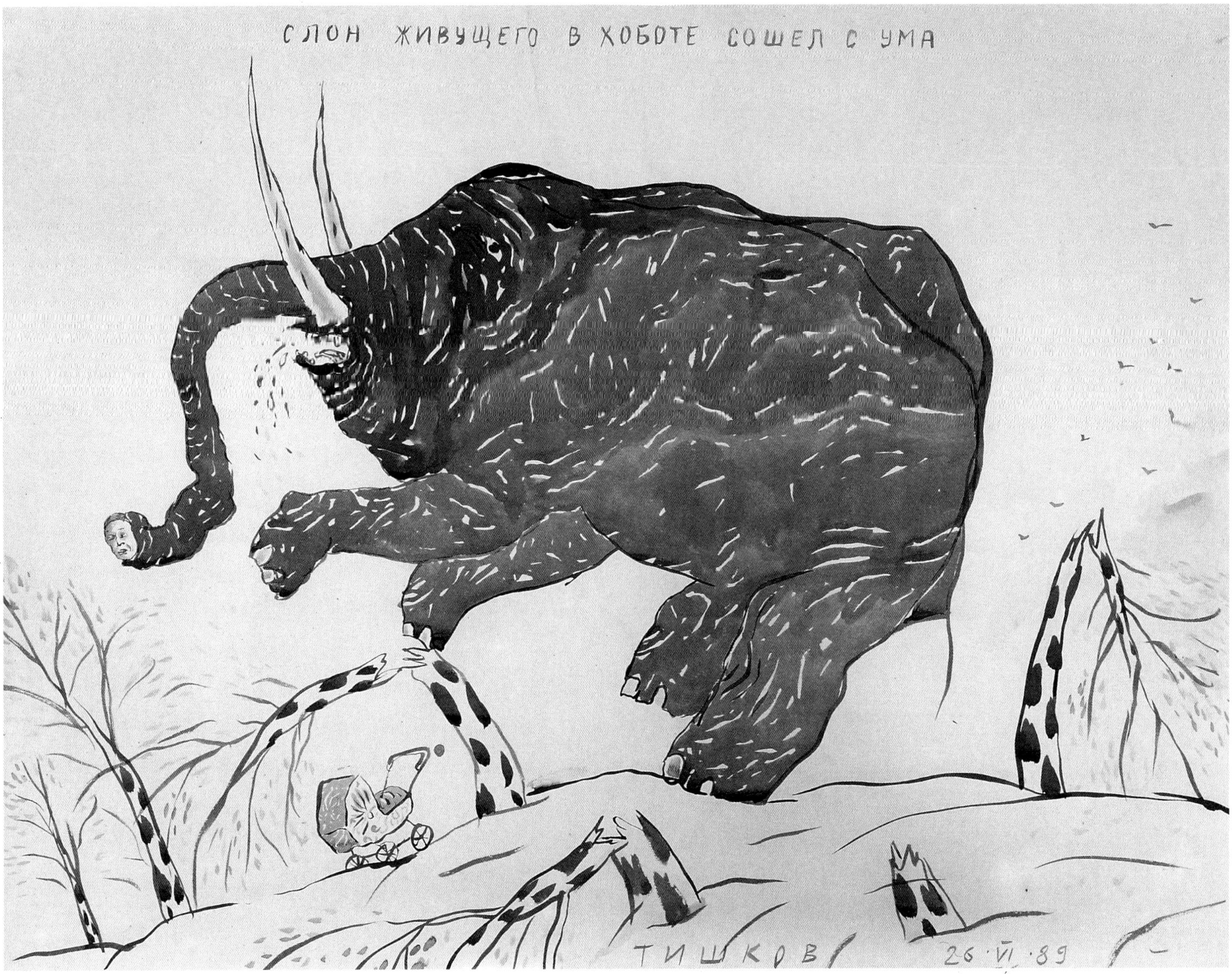

India ink on paper,
75x100 cm.

Living In a Trunk's elephant went
out of his mind, 06.26.1989

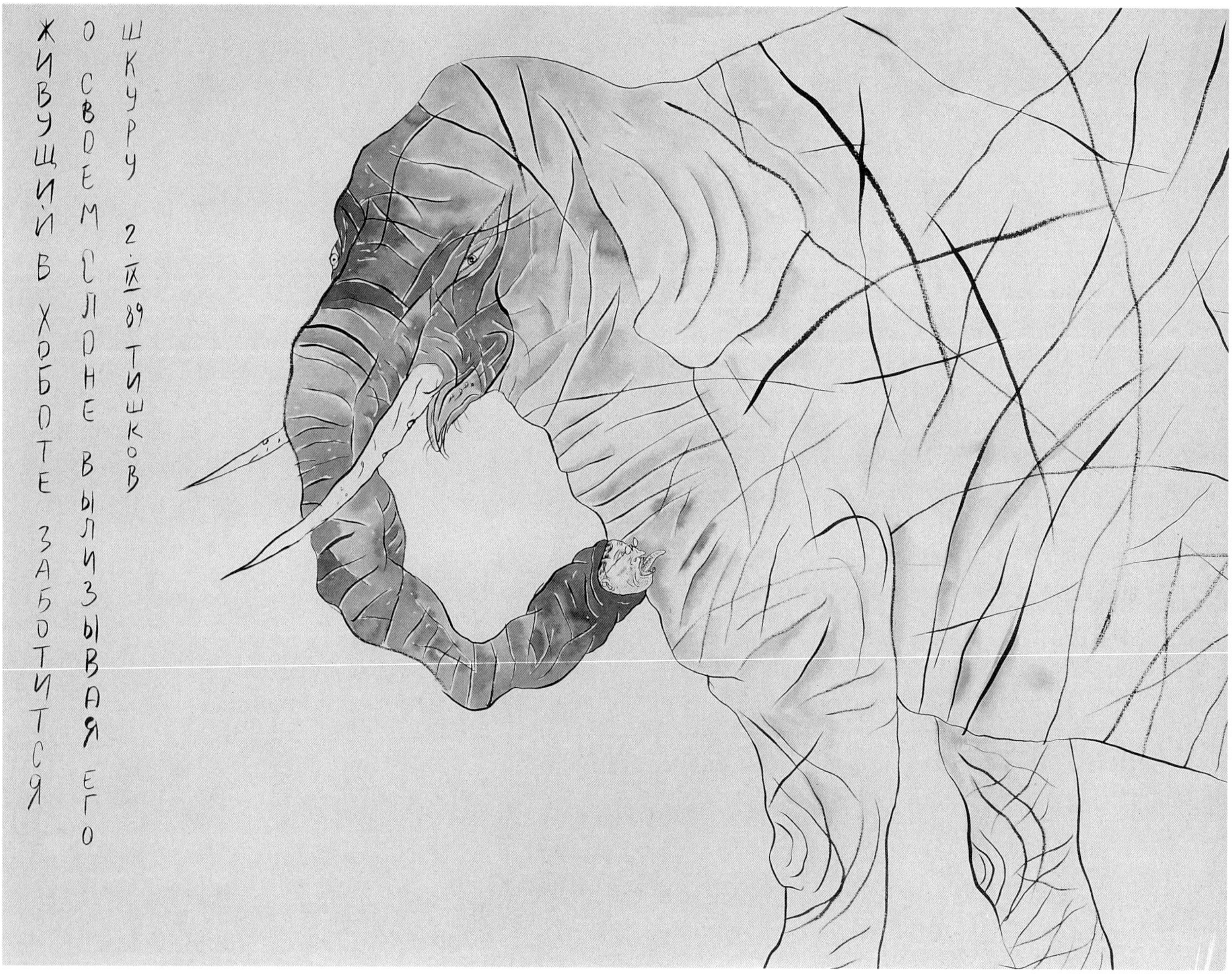

India ink on paper,
75x100 cm.

L.I.T. takes care of his elephant licking his hide, 09.02.1989

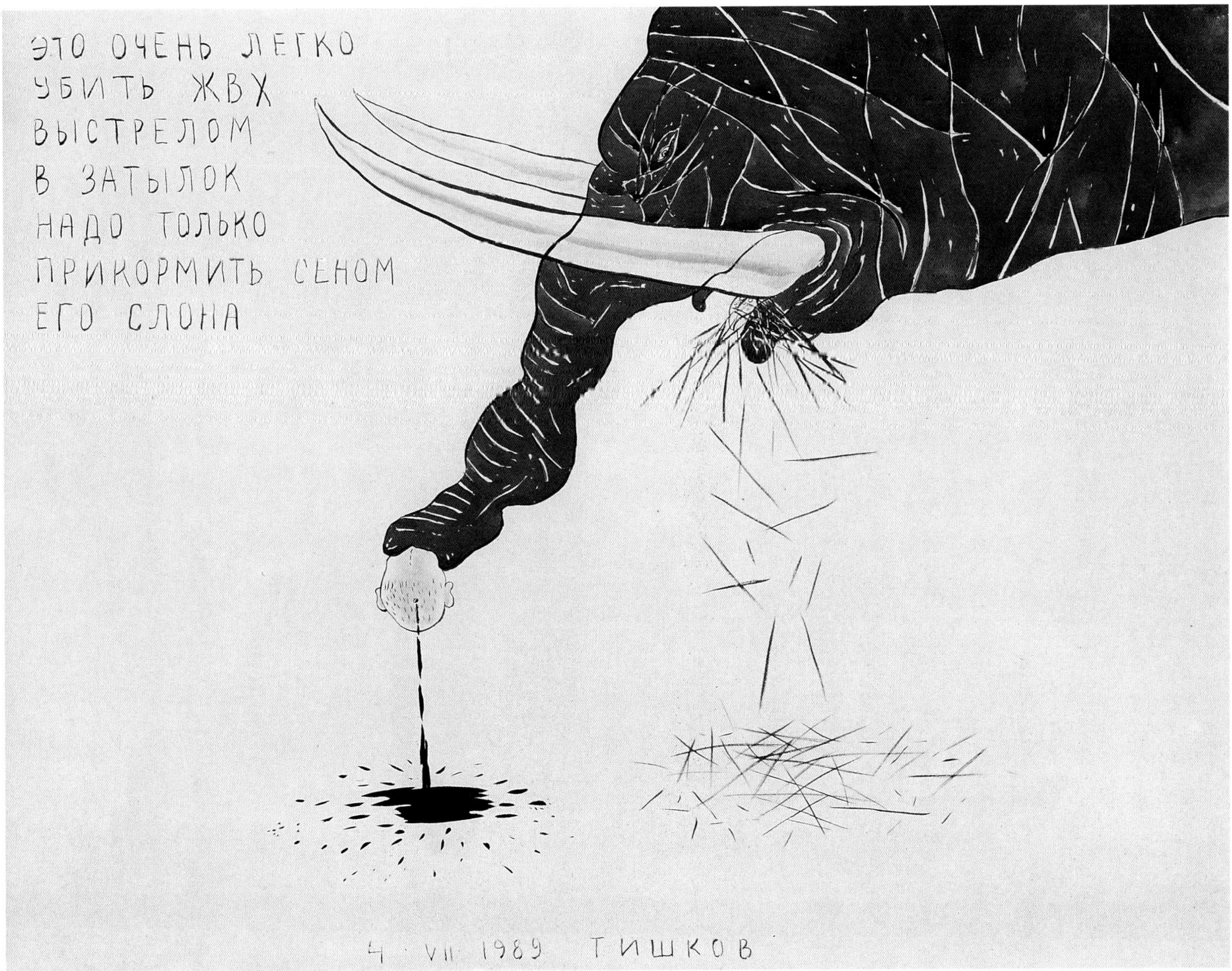

India ink on paper, 75x100 cm.

It's very easy to kill L.I.T. with a shot to the back of the head just feed his elephant hay, 07.04.1989

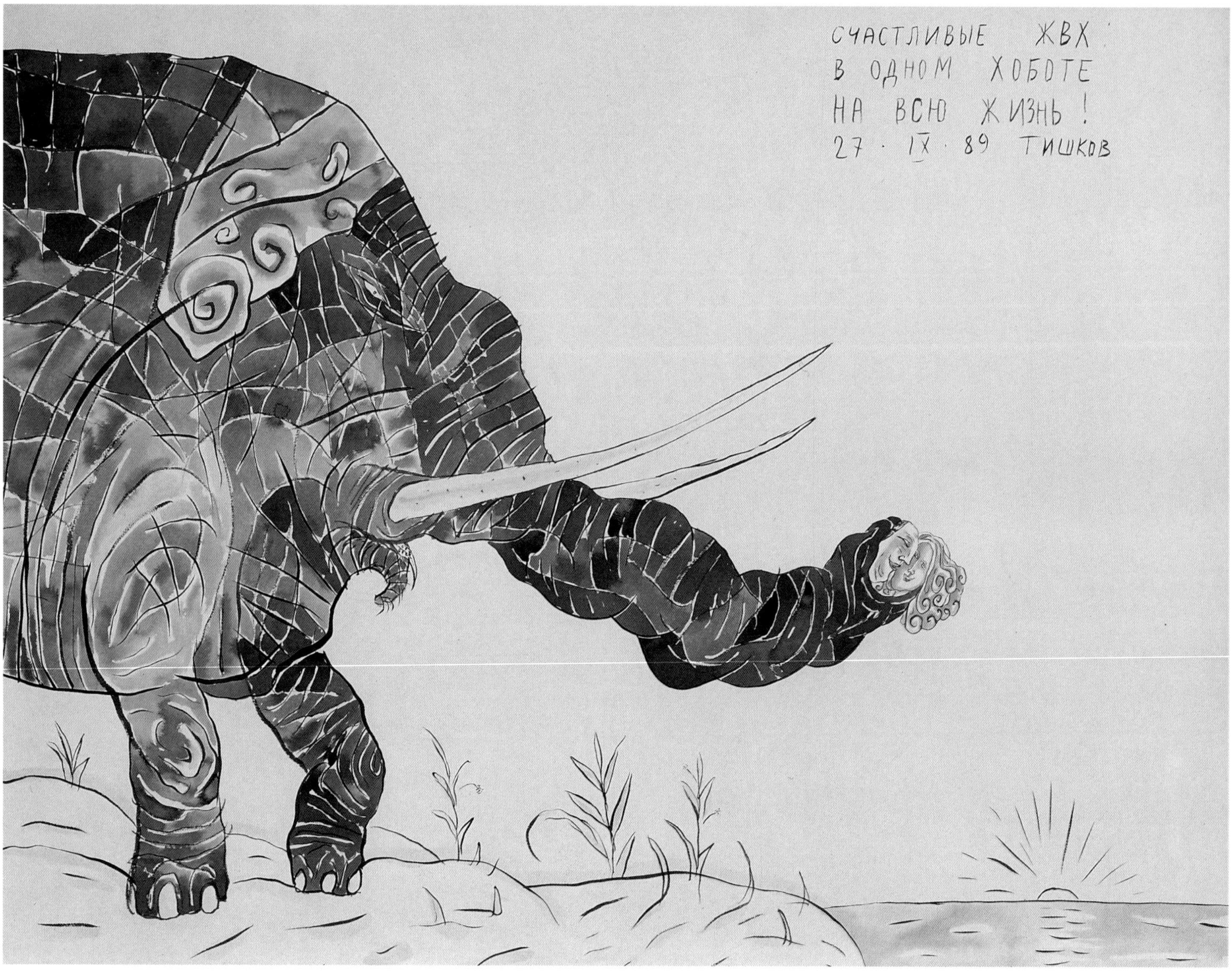

India ink on paper,
75x100 cm.

Happy L.I.T.s: in one trunk for life!,
09.27.1989

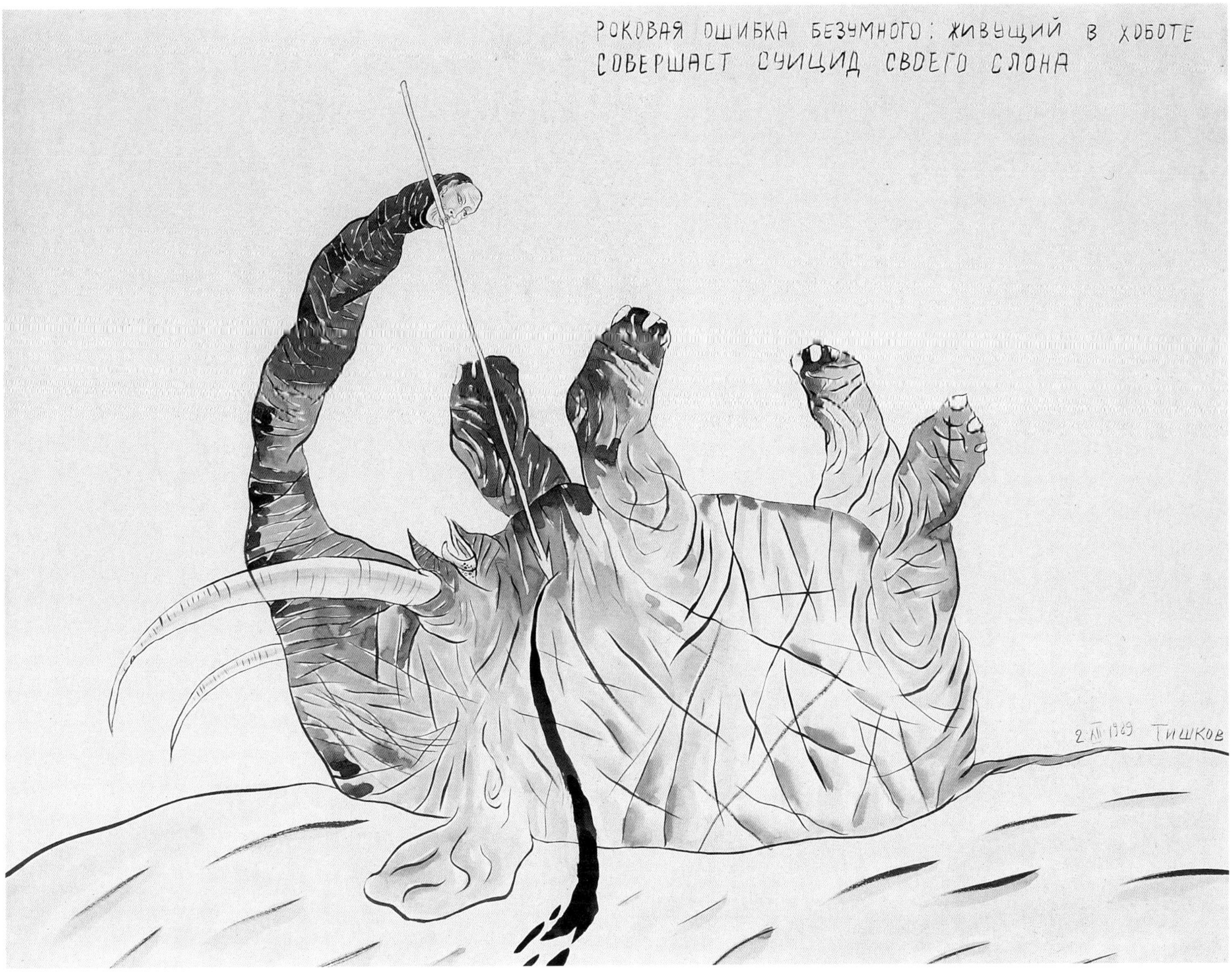

India ink on paper, 75x100 cm.

Fatal mistake of a lunatic: Living In a Trunk commits the suicide of his elephant, 12.02.1989

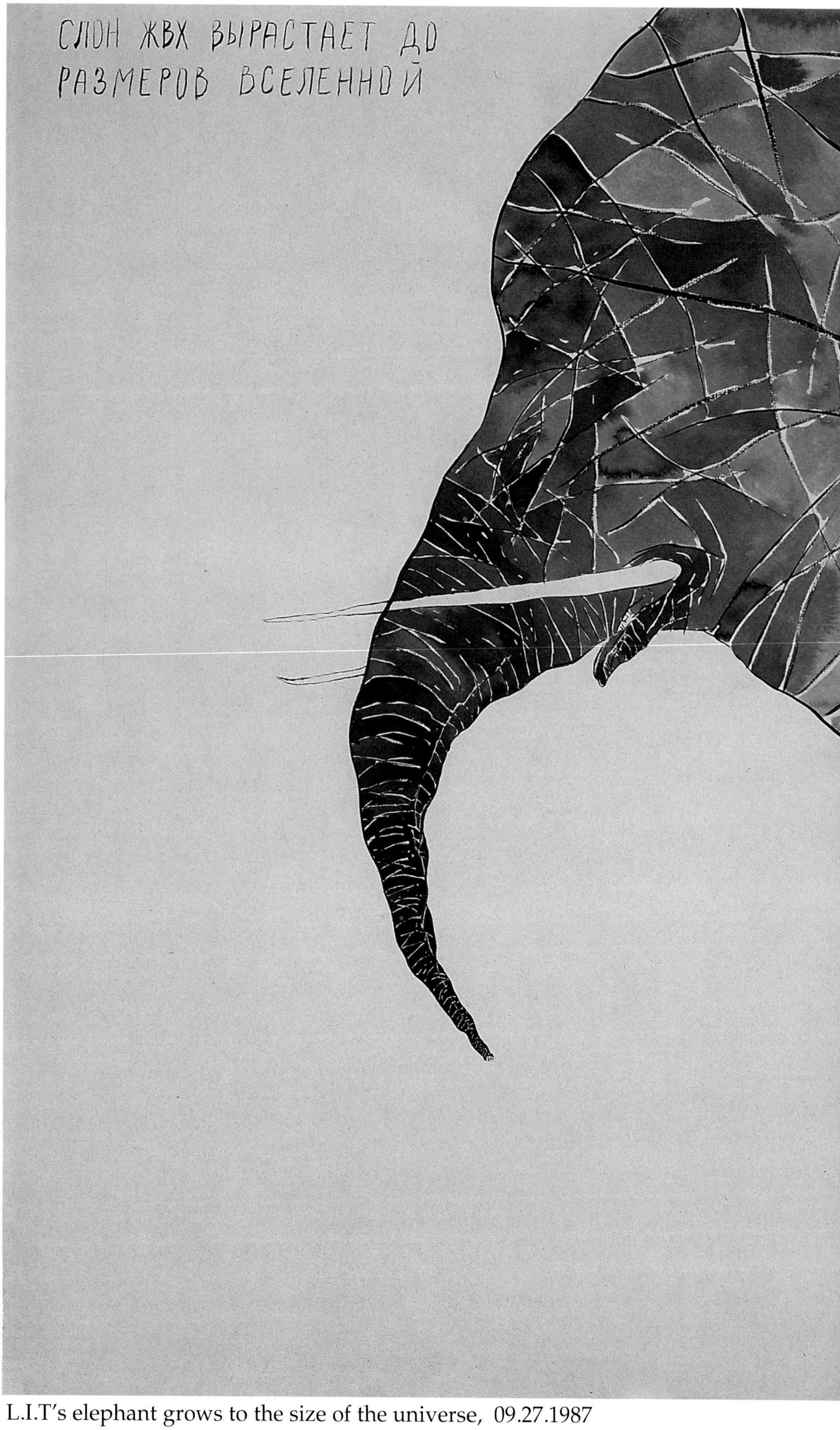

India ink on paper, 75x100 cm.

L.I.T's elephant grows to the size of the universe, 09.27.1987

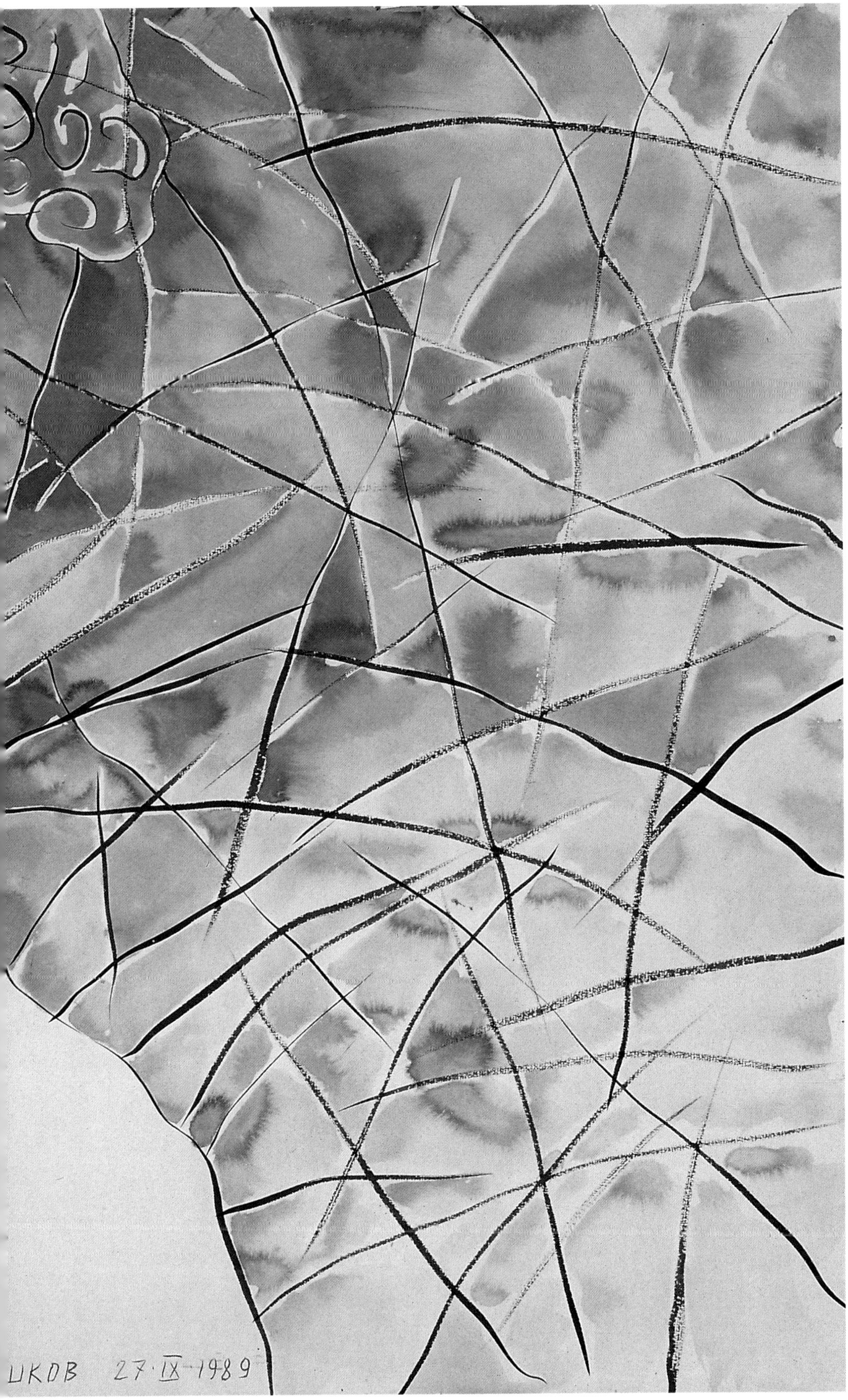
UKDB 27·IX·1989

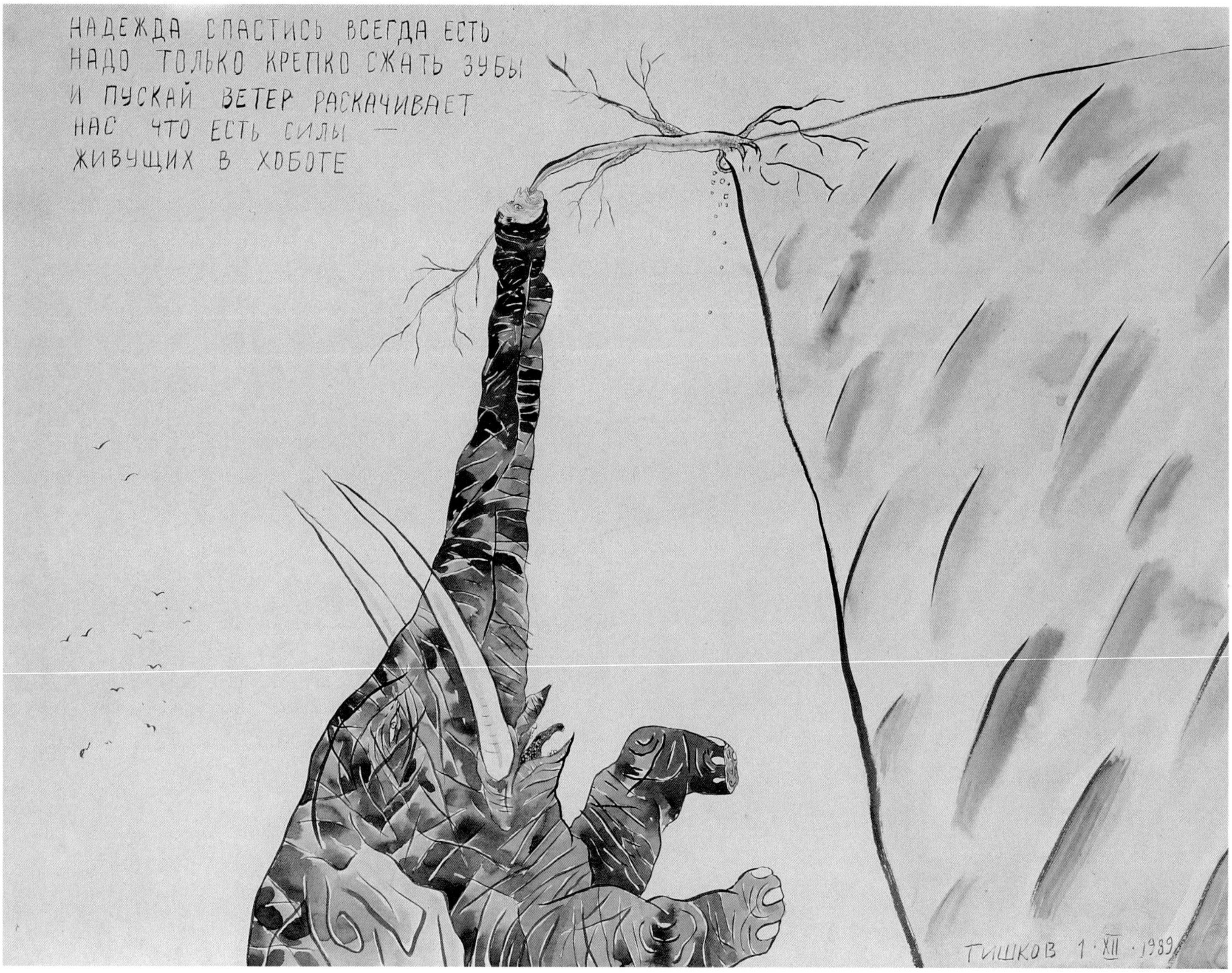

India ink on paper,
75x100 cm.

There is always hope to save yourself
just firmly clench your teeth and let
the wind rock us all it can — Living
In a Trunk, 12.01.1989

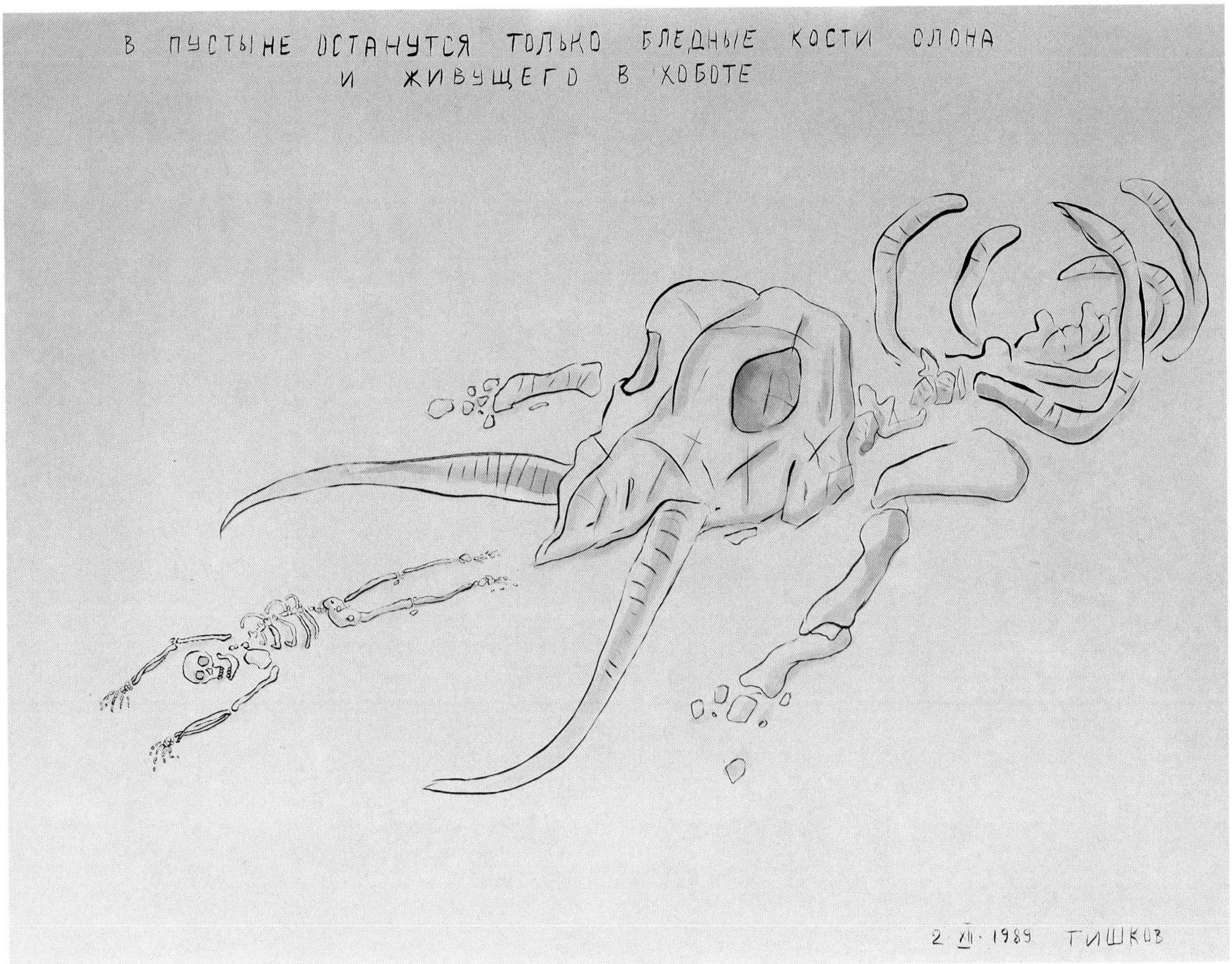

India ink on paper,
75x100 cm.

In the desert will remain only the
pale bones of the elephant
and Living In a Trunk, 12.02.1989

THE DIVER'S LIBRARY

In the foothills of the Urals, on the shores of ponds, watching the search after a wedding or army call-up, I first saw the divers. My frightened eyes were reflected in their observation windows.

As Vishna created the world in his sleep, I imagined my world of divers, creatures without faces, their hearts kept deep within diving suits, when I immersed myself in sleep, in the depths of the subconscious, where underwater fish surrounded their loneliness with Christmas trees.

All of my characters are connected by one idea, like a life line. Living in a cramped trunk, born in a heavy diving suit, the person existing in the rectum the lonely passing Stomach — these are all variations of movement within. To hide away in your own space, to build your own home. This is a symbol of the eternal loneliness of man. Beckett has something similar — life in a trash bin; in Beuys — clothes of thick felt; snail builds its own little house from silt, sand and blades of grass.

Books are drawn about divers and a play written on the motifs of the drawings. In the last three years the Great Diver's Library has appeared. «Yellow Nile,» «The Dead Perch Sutra,» «The Reed Hut,» «A Diver Abecedarian,» «Various Fish,» «The Accountant,» and «One Hundred and Thirty Six Notions About the Unrealized» are already on the shelf. A book is being written «About Bird Flight» — a very important and necessary work for the Diver-Reader.

The abstract character of the drawings is mere surface. Everything is clear to the diver. He understands the twinklings of color, the interweaving of lines of letters and spots. The irrationality and monotony, the black color of the depth, the palpable rustle of ironing out the wrinkled tracing paper, fragments of some essential phrases, an unintelligible language, all of this is the deep-watered Urals where I, a little boy, either on the very top of the mountain called Kukan, or on the bottom of a foundation pit, stand surrounded by earth like sky.

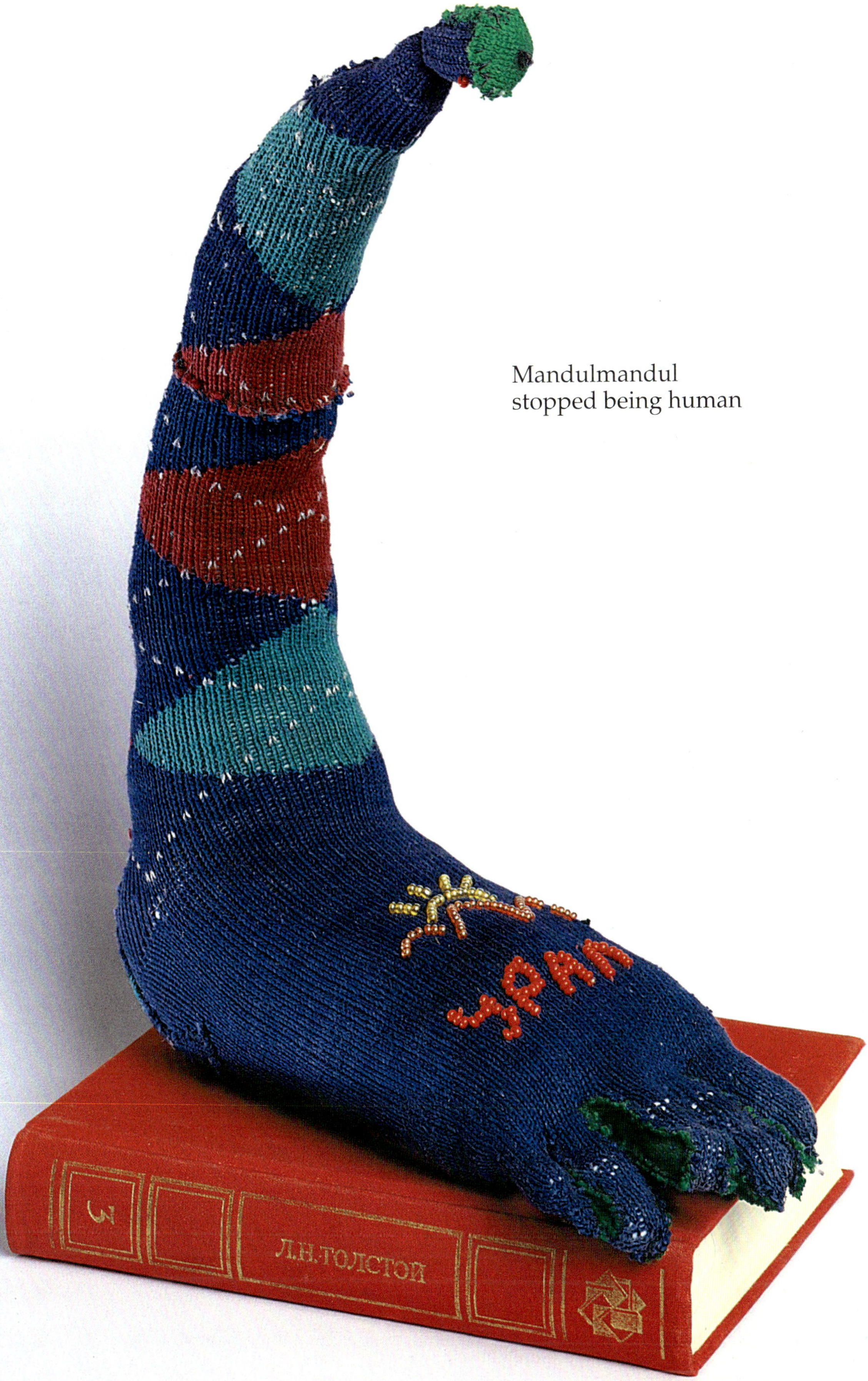

Mandulmandul
stopped being human

When all the room is in gloom, light and music come from the helmets of the divers

Diver's sculptures

Scroll «Yellow Nile»

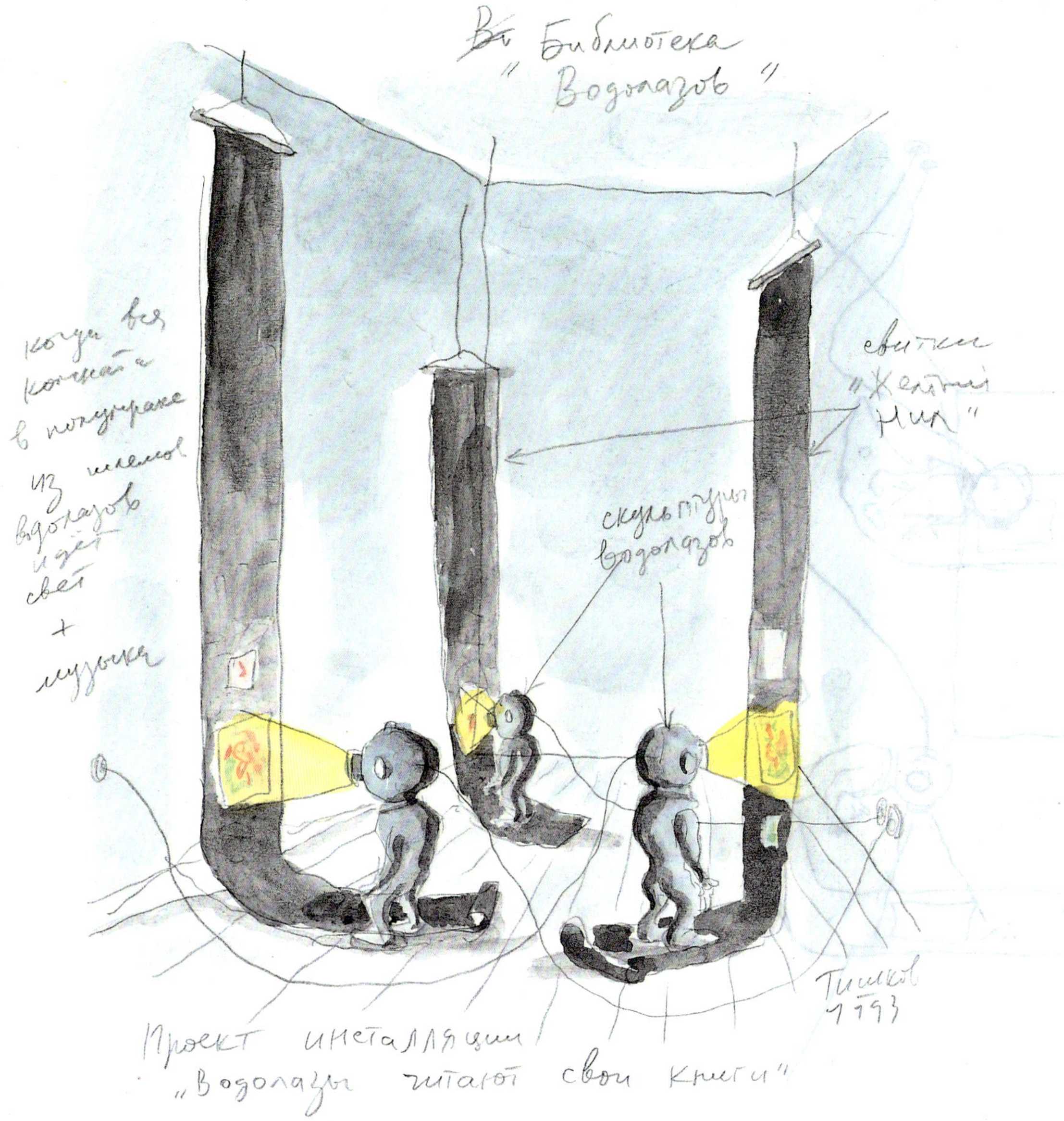

Installation project
«Diver's Read Their Books»

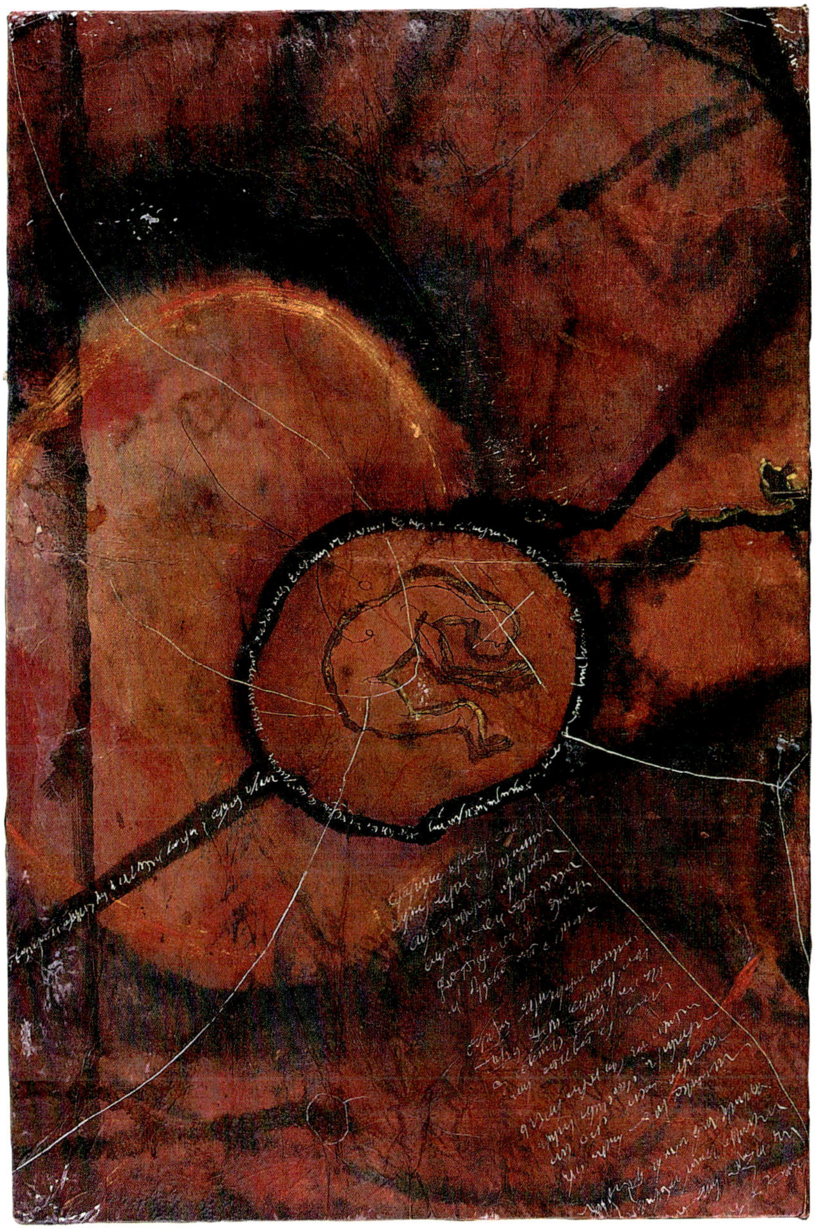

1992, watercolor, India ink, tracing paper, collage on paper, cardboard, 44x31 cm.

Reed hut, book from the Diver's Library.

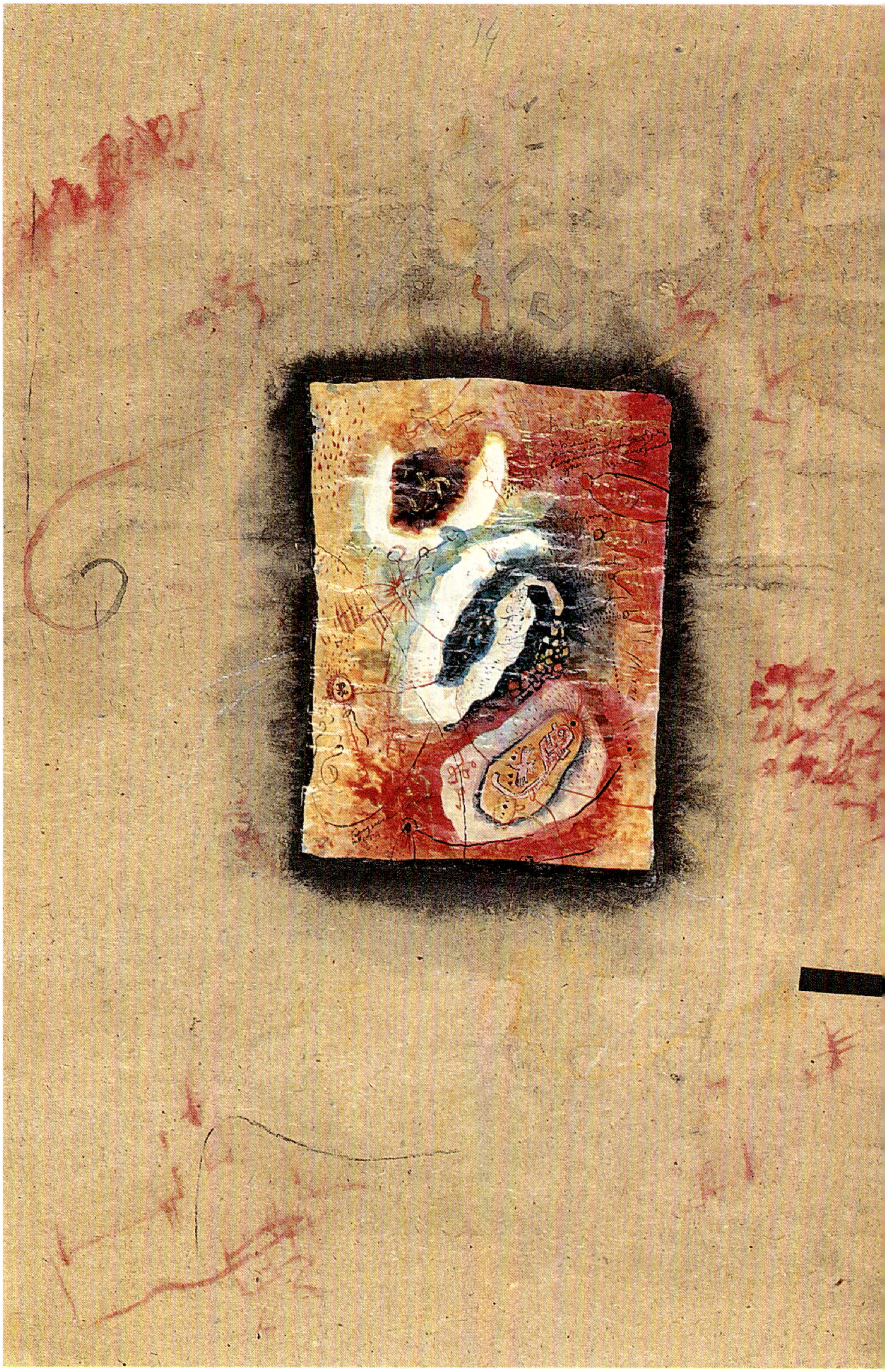

Reed hut, book from the Diver's Library, two pages.

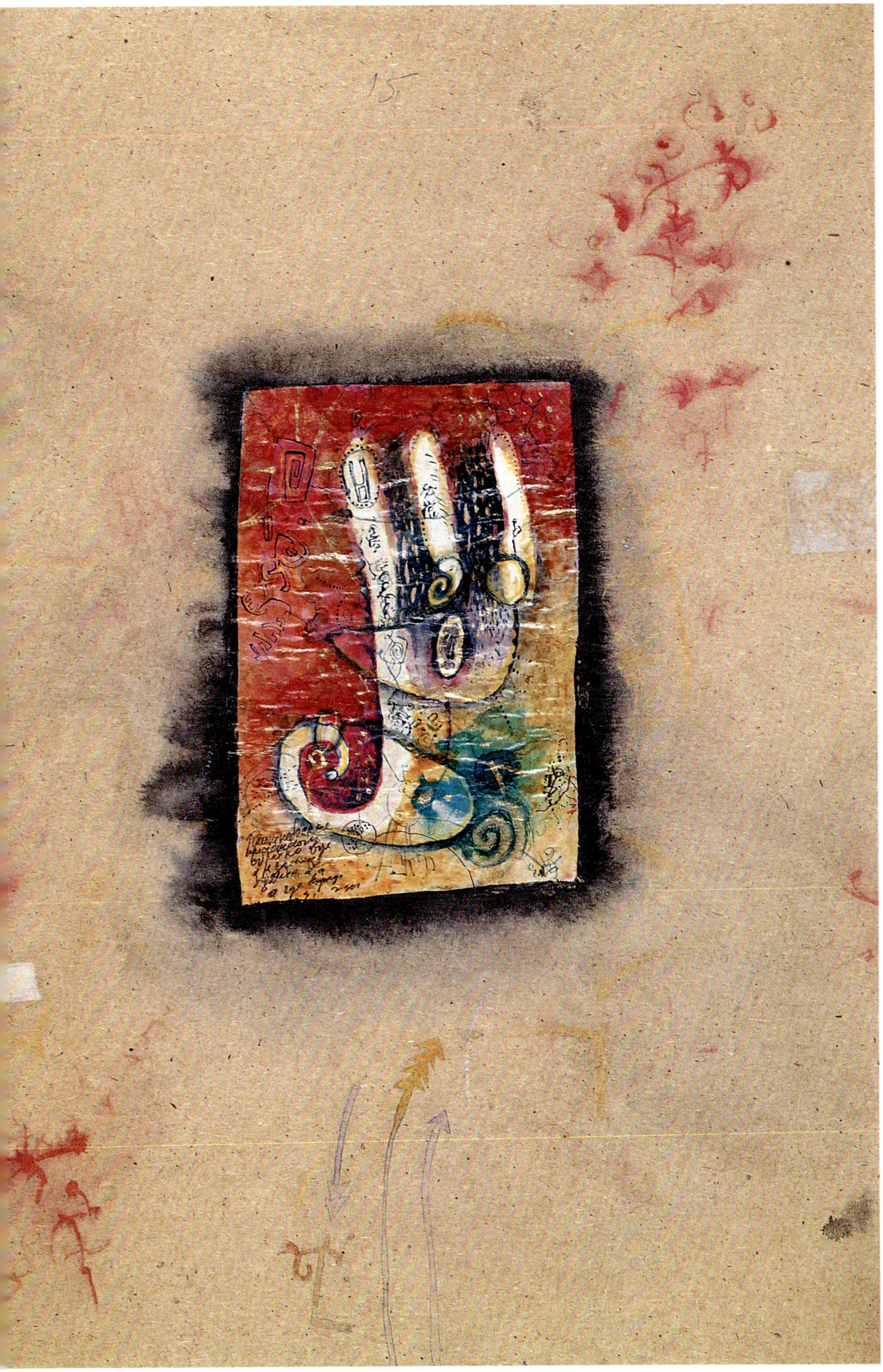

*1992,
watercolor, India ink,
tracing paper, collage on
paper,
cardboard, 44x31 cm.*

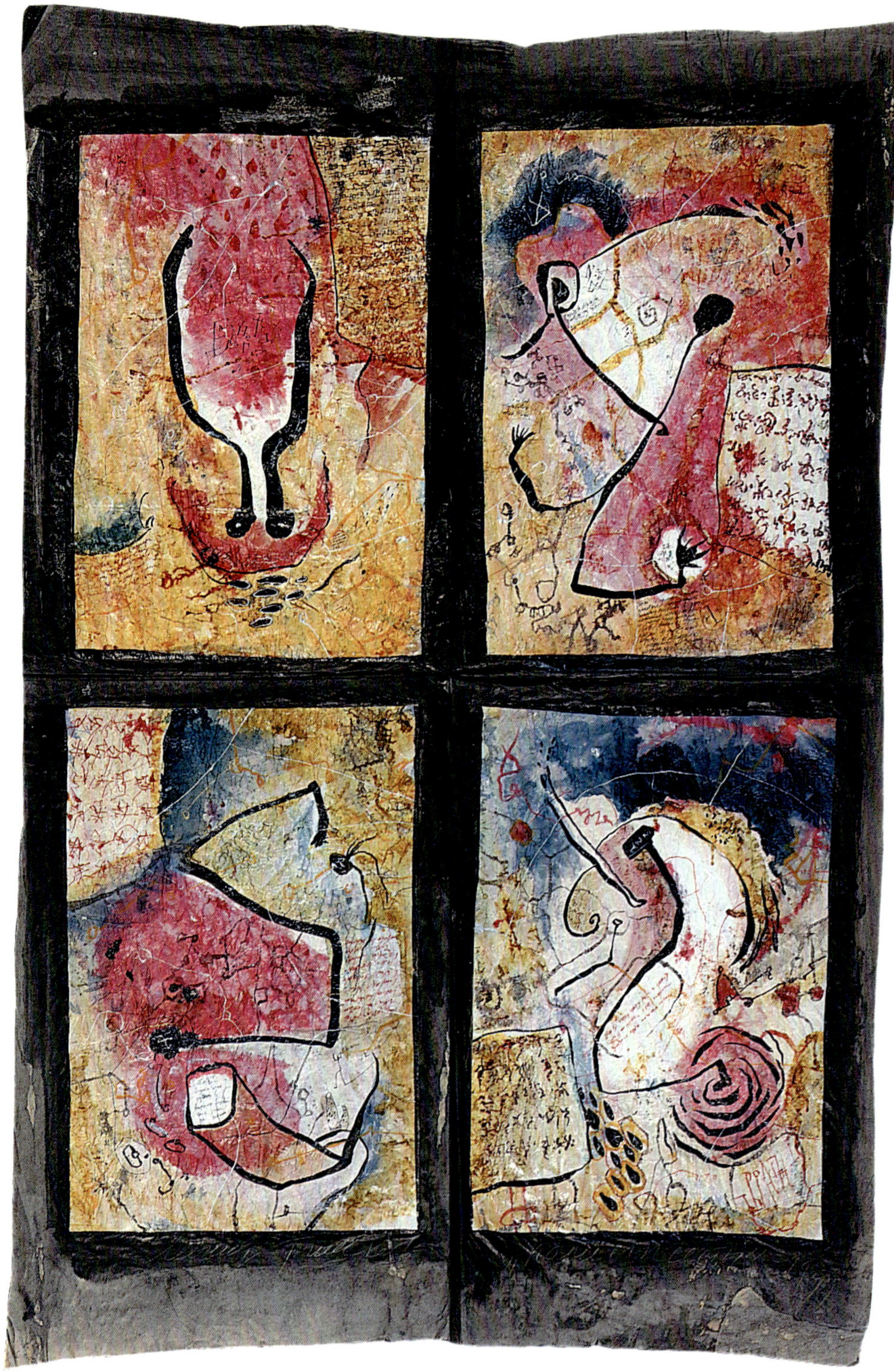

1989, paper, tracing paper, India ink, ink, glue, collage, 105x77 cm.

Windows facing within I

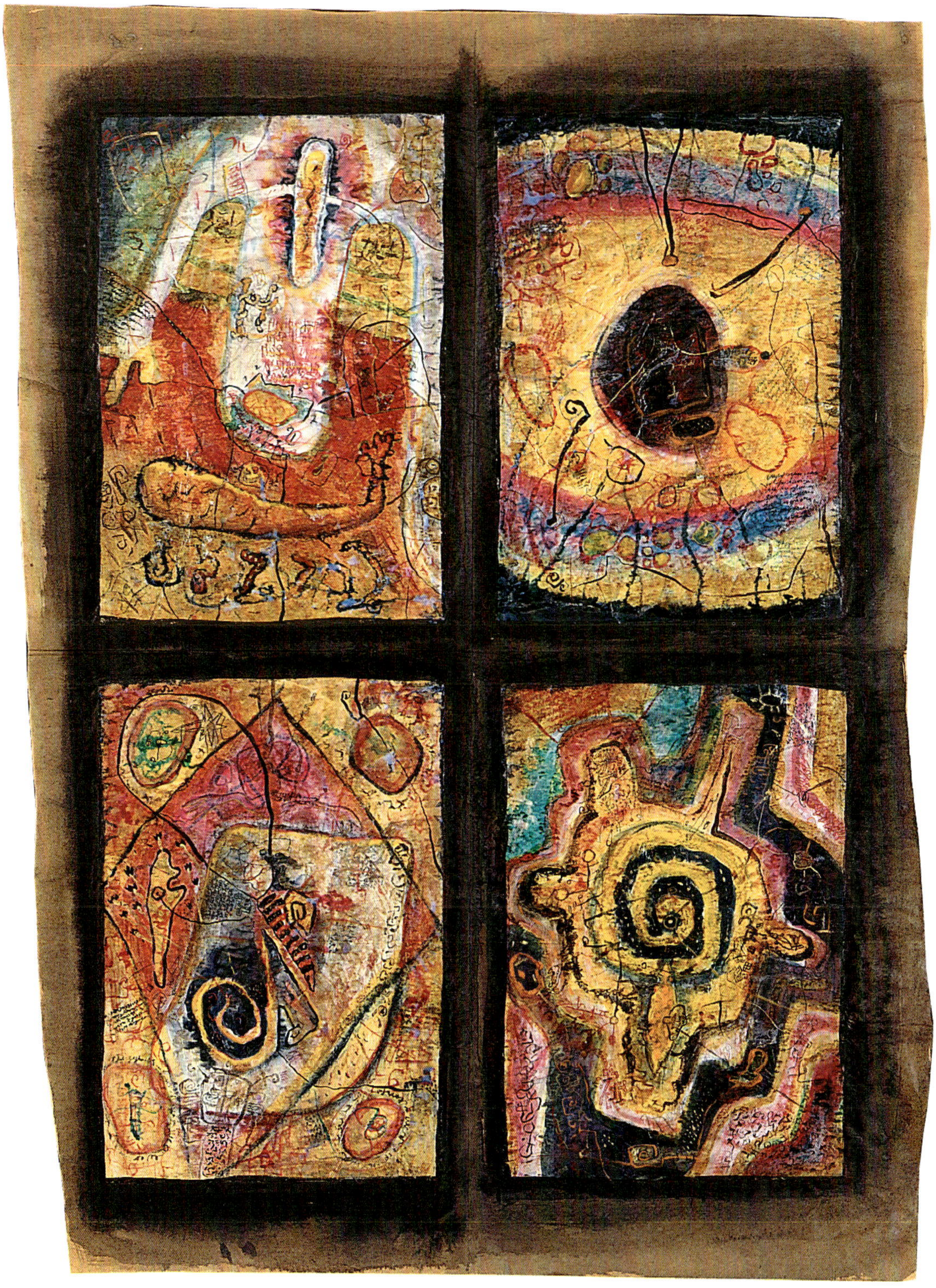

1989, paper, tracing paper, India ink, ink, glue, collage, 105x77 cm.

Windows facing within II

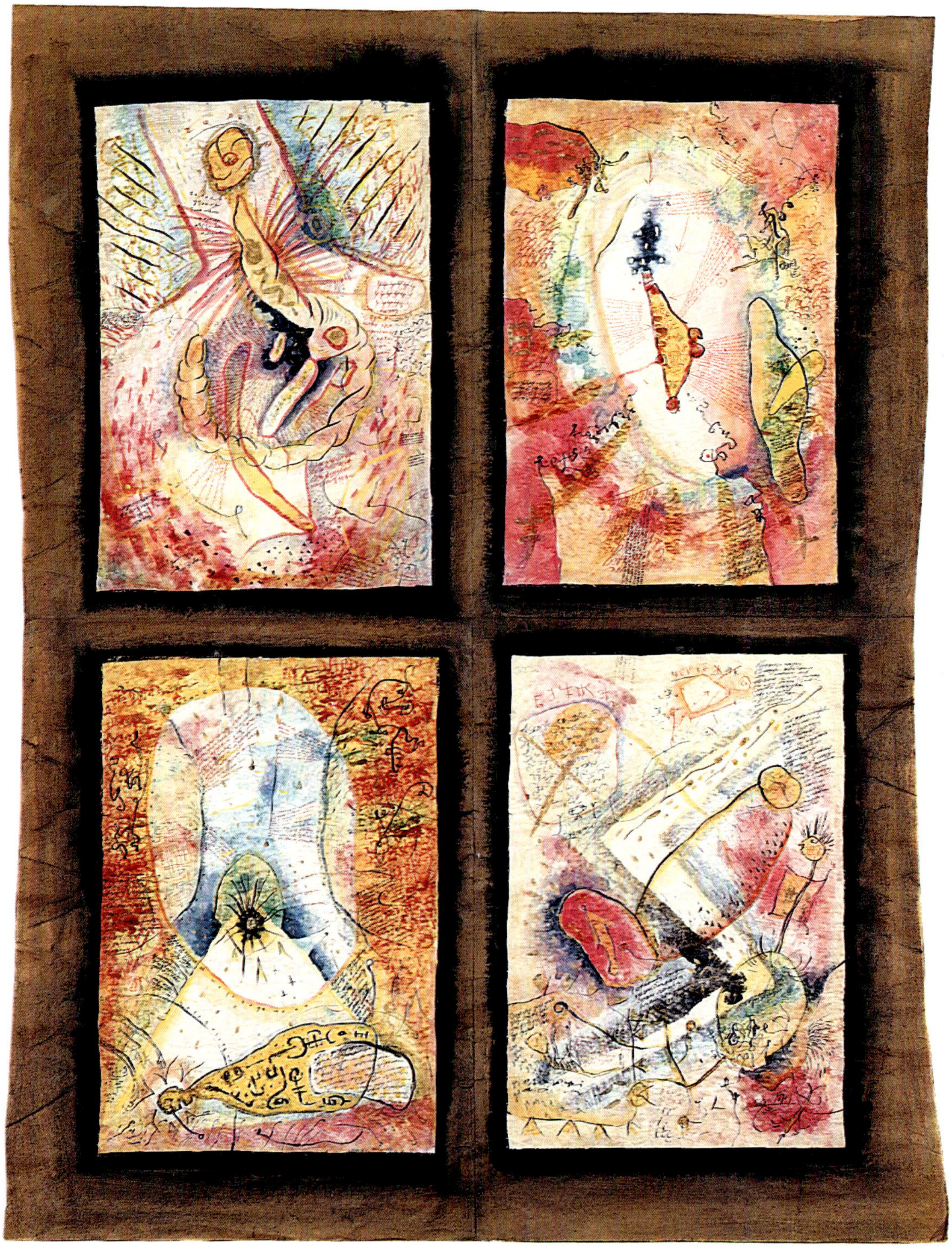

1989, paper, tracing paper, India ink, ink, glue, collage, 105x77 cm.

Windows facing within III

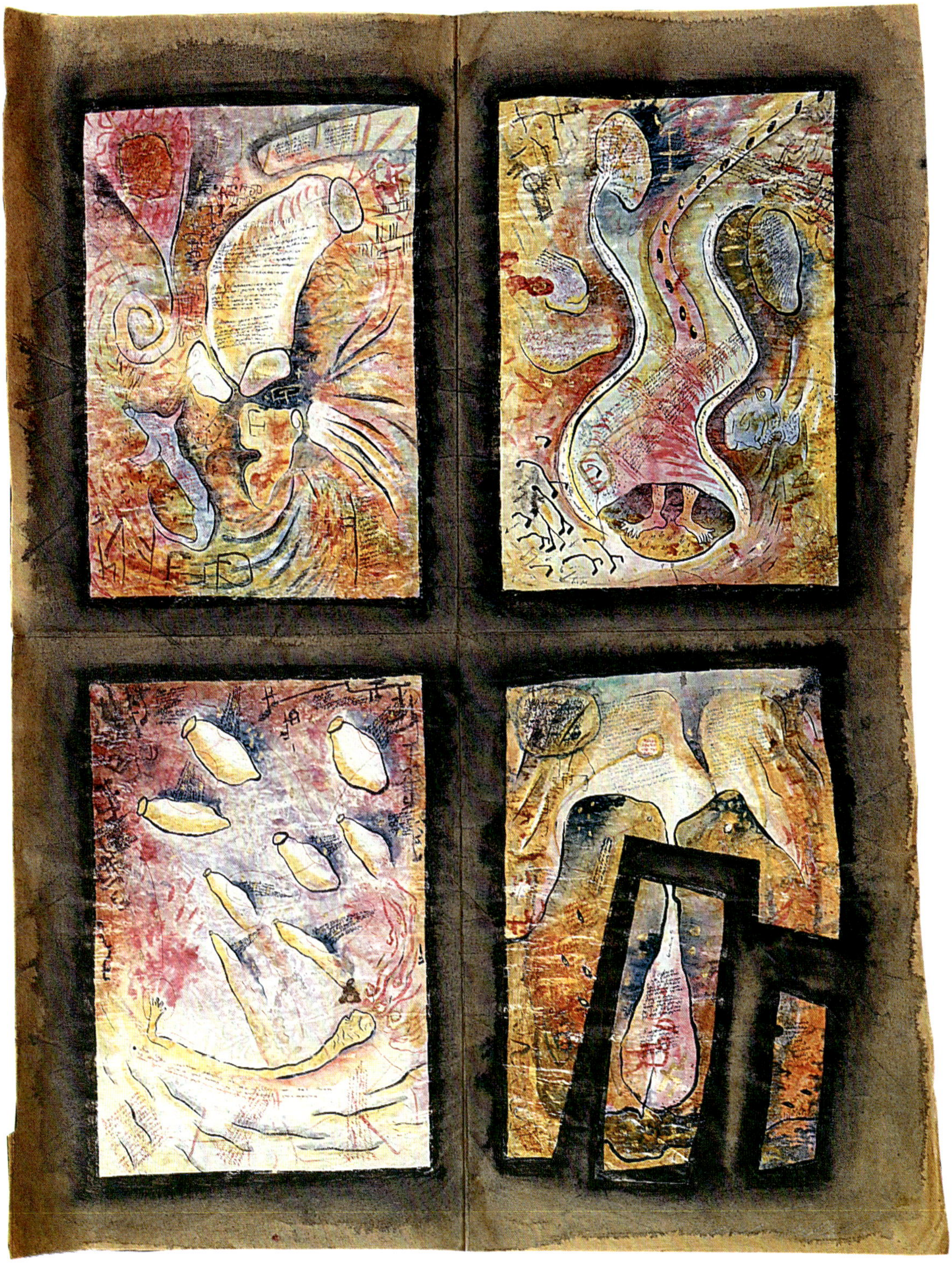

1989, paper, tracing paper, India ink, ink, glue, collage, 105x77 cm.

Windows facing within IV

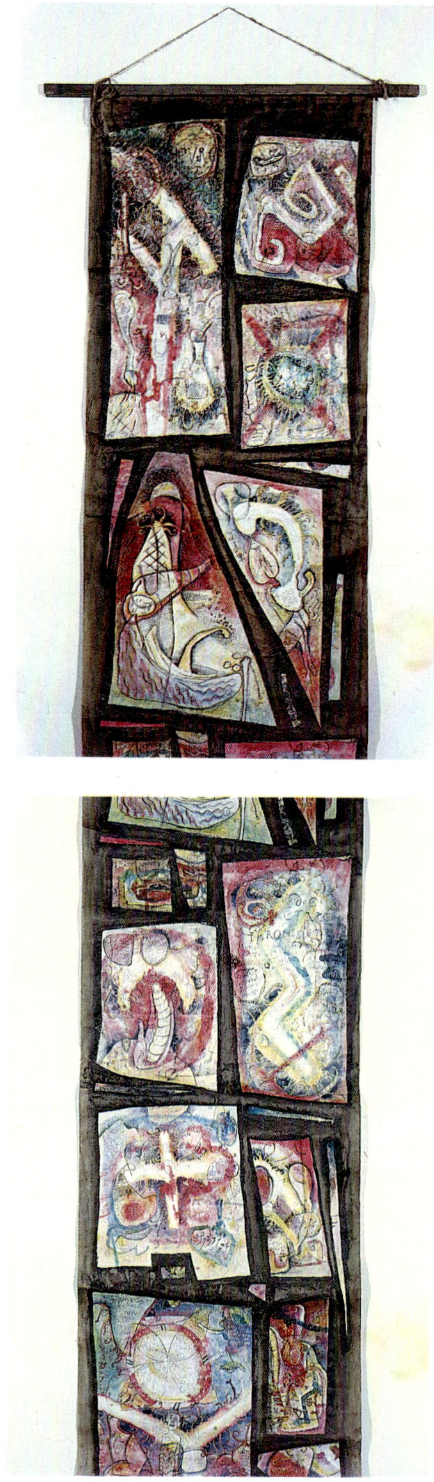

Yellow Nile I, scroll from the Diver's Library

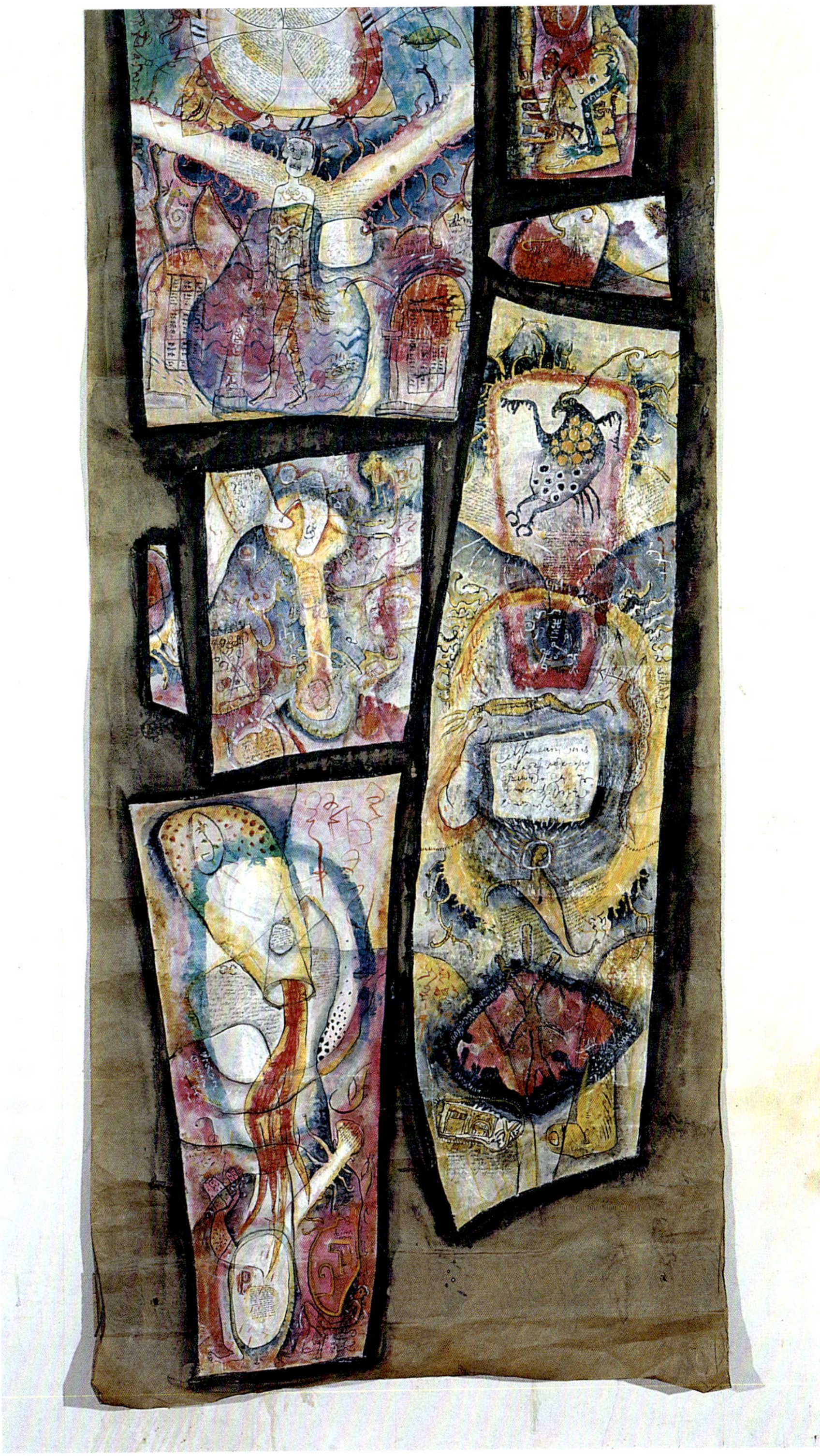

1989, paper, tracing paper, acrylic, India ink, ink, collage, glue, wood, twine, 104x650 cm.

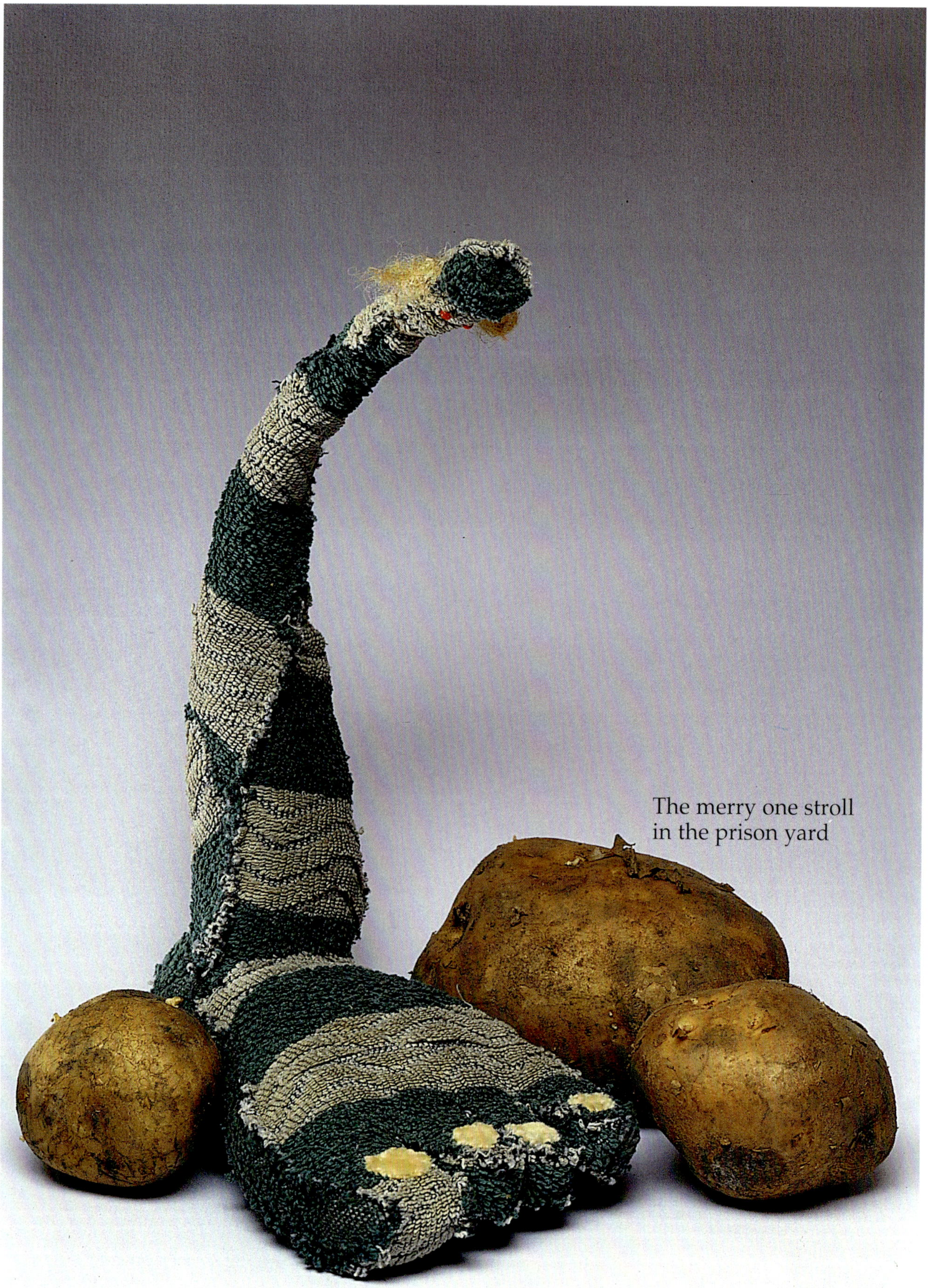

The merry one stroll
in the prison yard

STILL LIFES

After a long time depicting an imaginary world, a black diver plunging deep into myself, I finally decided to return to a real object. I recollect early childhood and see before me a stool standing on three legs like the Earth on three whales, and on that Great Stool everything imaginable. Thus it became a stage in the theater; animate objects perform on it a play called «Still Life.» Simple balls, a pyramid and a cube, a lonely bottle casting a sad shadow, three potatoes hunched together — now not even a knife is scary, green flowers and a blue fish, a violet dwarf at the edge of an abyss (reach a hand out to him, comrade!), a cheery hoe, a shadow — a living soul half rises from the stool. And there — neatly placed twiglets in place of fruit, sausage and a murdered turkey — a hungry stomach lies there. Here the «Titanic» says «Farewell,» Gorky's heart shines in the dark, a head turned yellow lies there. And certainly, Dabloid, my bosom friend. And everywhere, above everything, the absurd words «nature morte»...There is no more absurd conjunction: dead nature. Even the stool on which this takes place is more alive than you, standing alongside, young and strong.

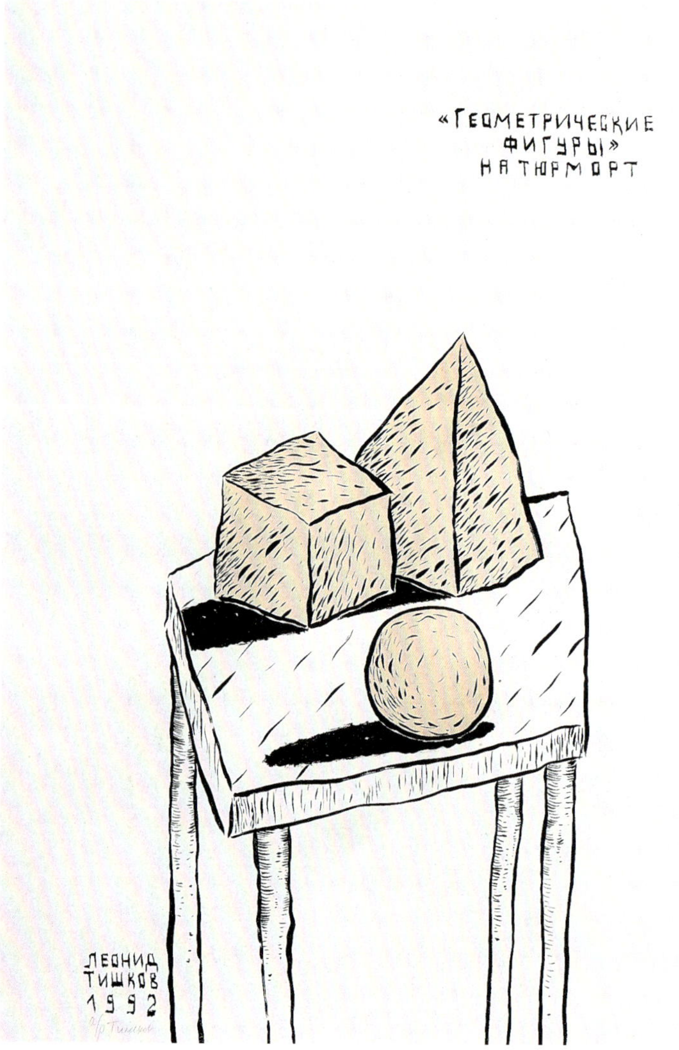

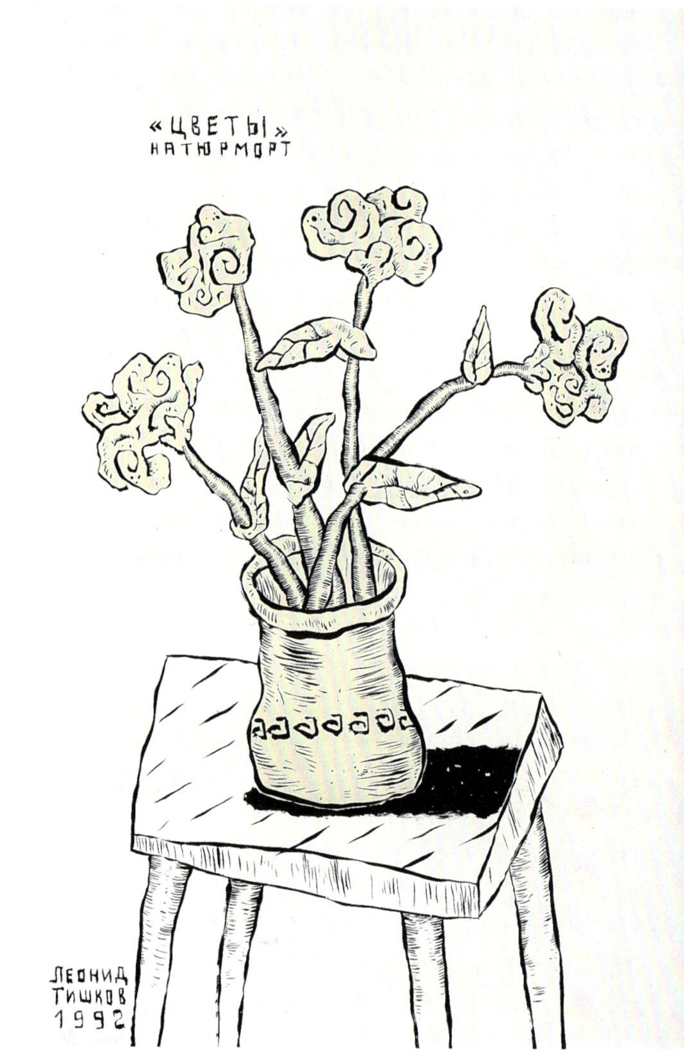

1992, Lithograph,
62x43 cm

Geometric Figures
Still Life

Flowers
Still Life

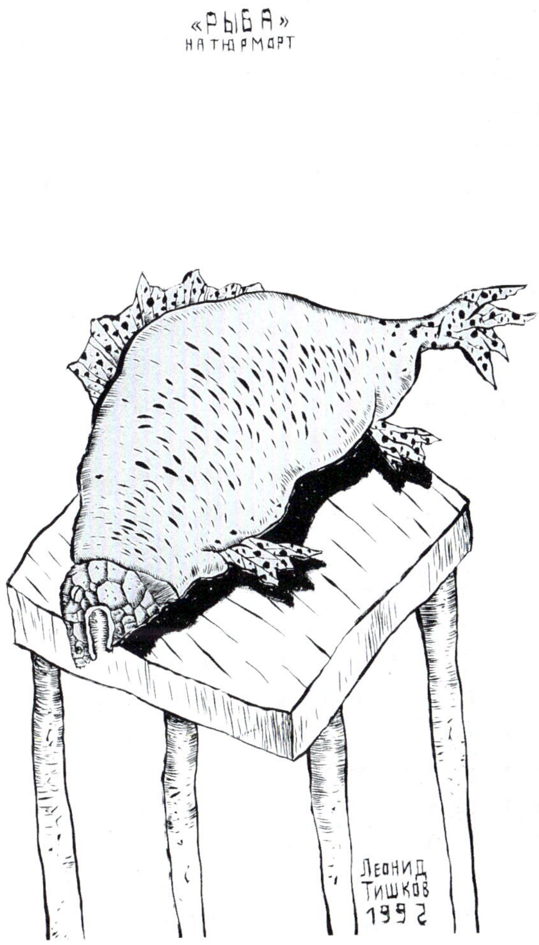

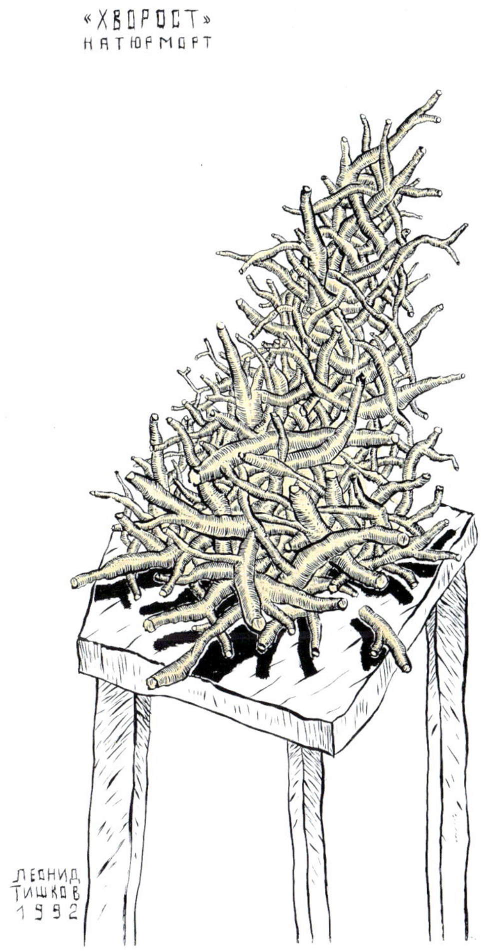

1992, Lithograph,
62x43 cm

Fish
Still Life

Twiglets
Still Life

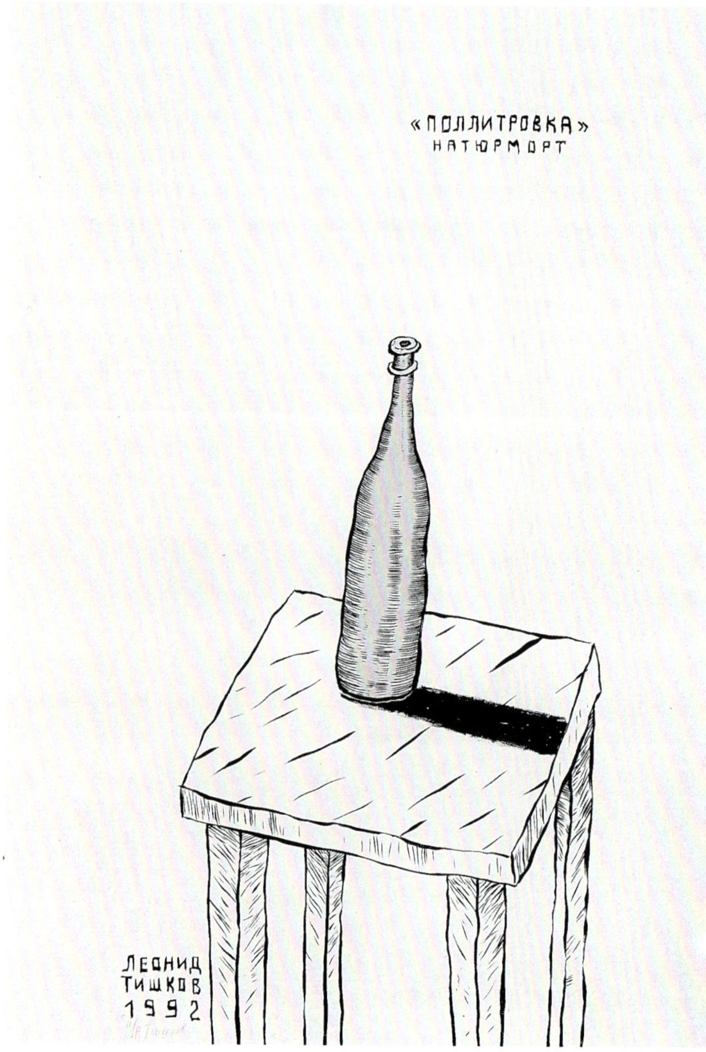

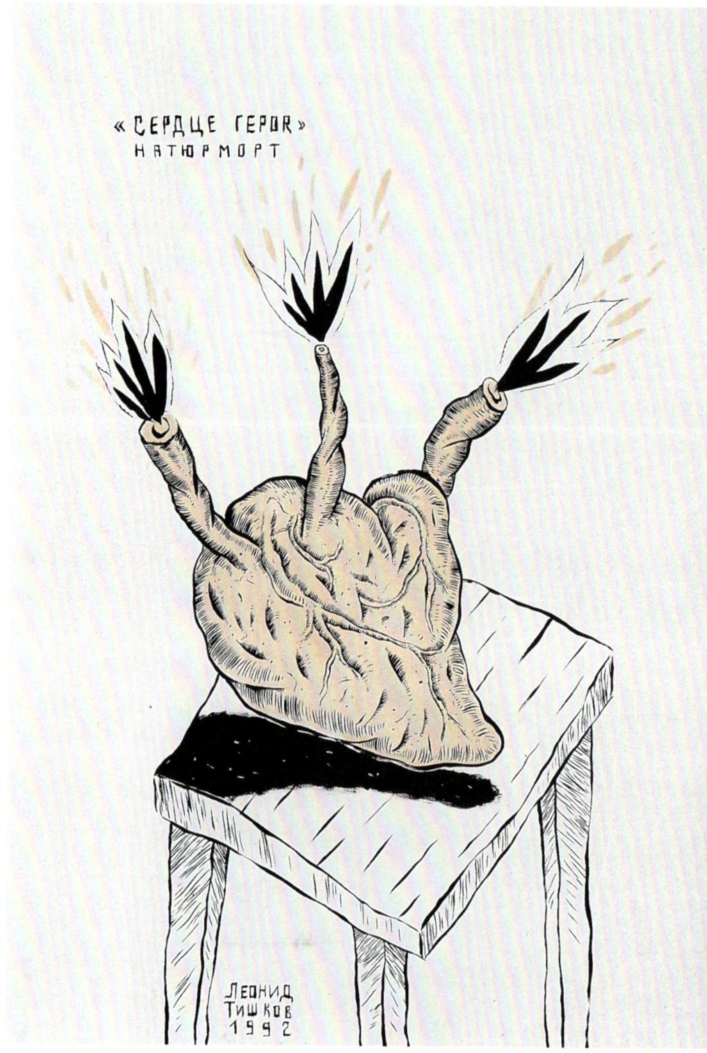

1992, Lithograph, 62x43 cm

Half-liter Bottle
Still Life

Heart of a Hero
Still Life

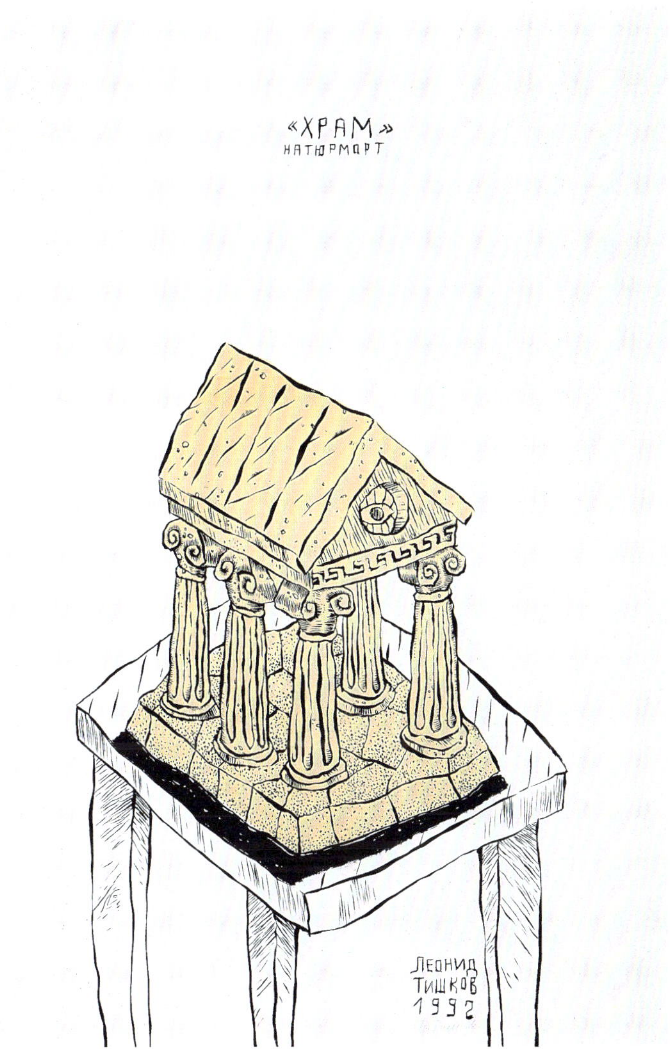

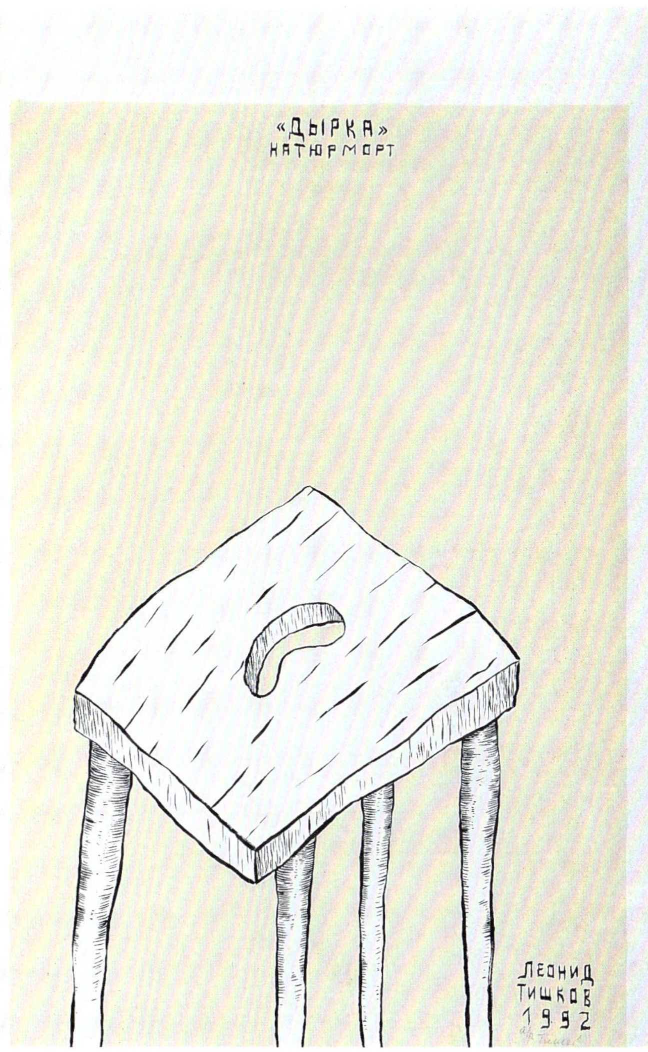

1992, Lithograph, 62x43 cm

Temple
Still Life

Hole
Still Life

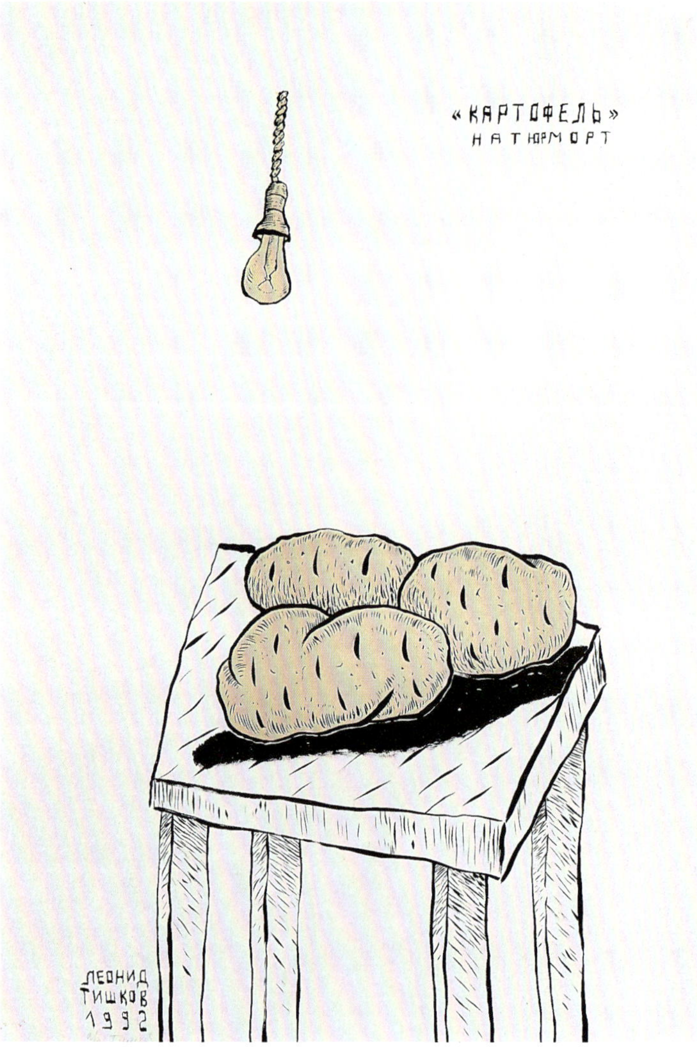

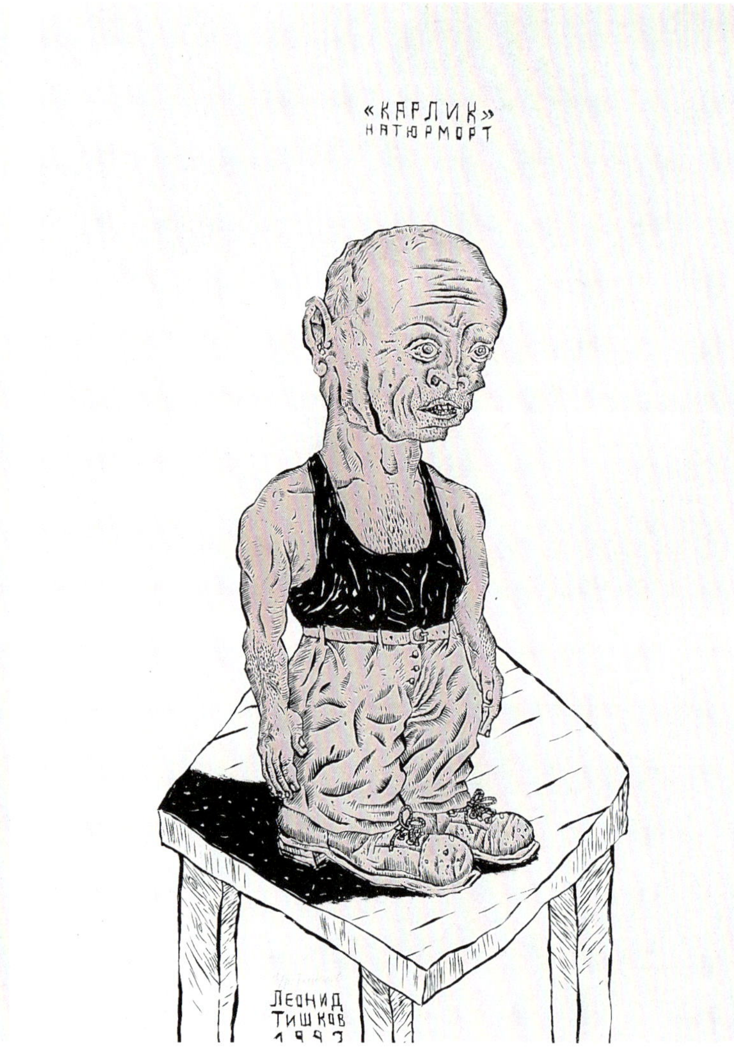

1992, Lithograph,
62x43 cm

Potato
Still Life

Pygmy
Still Life

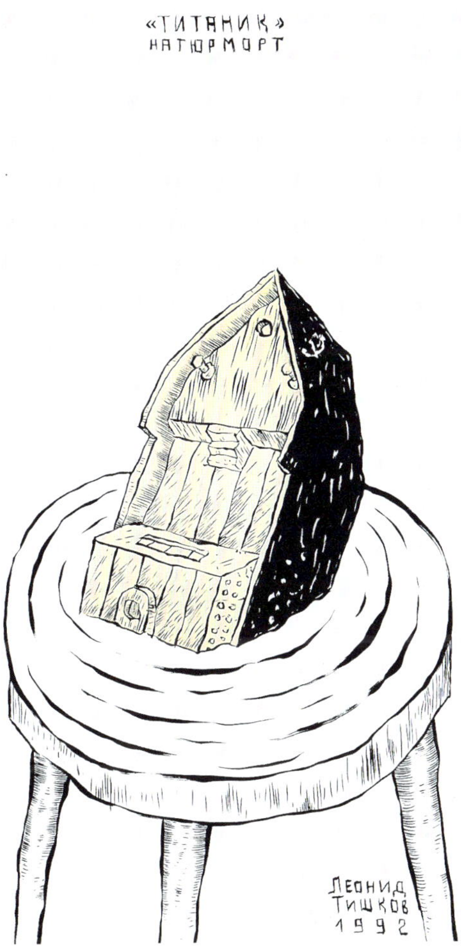

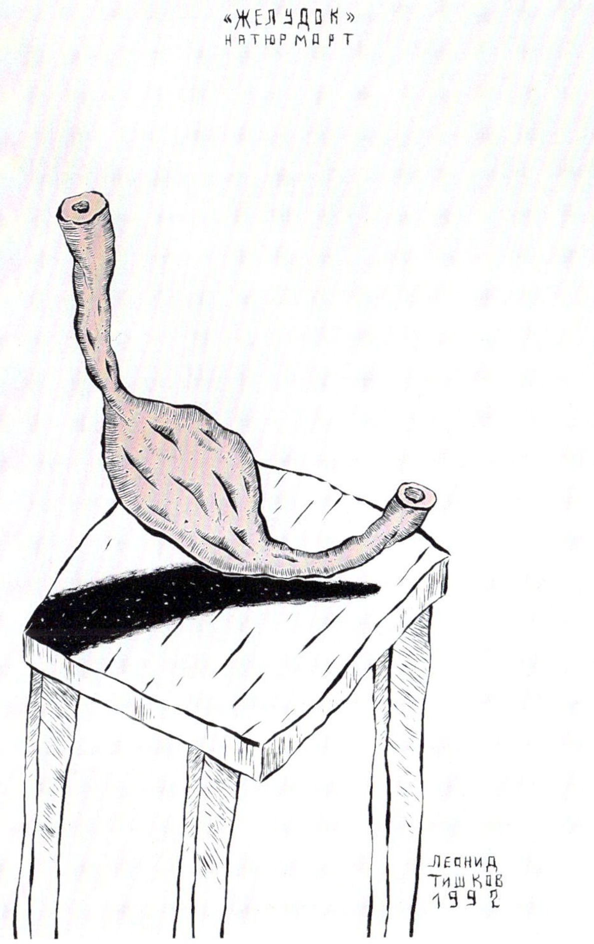

1992, Lithograph, 62x43 cm

Titanic
Still Life

Stomach
Still Life

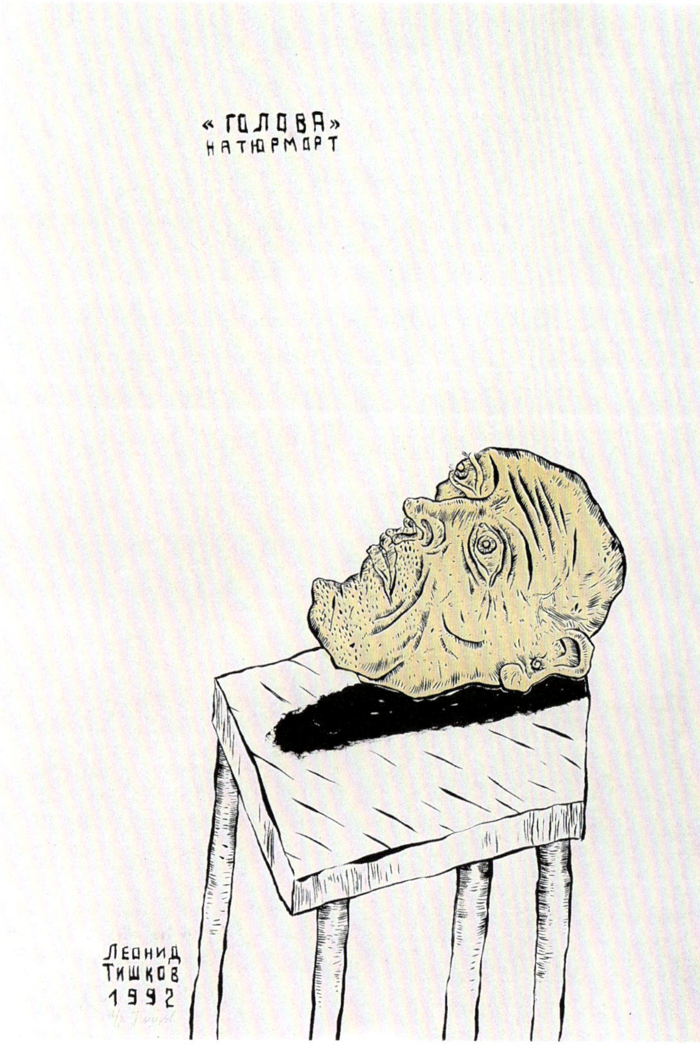

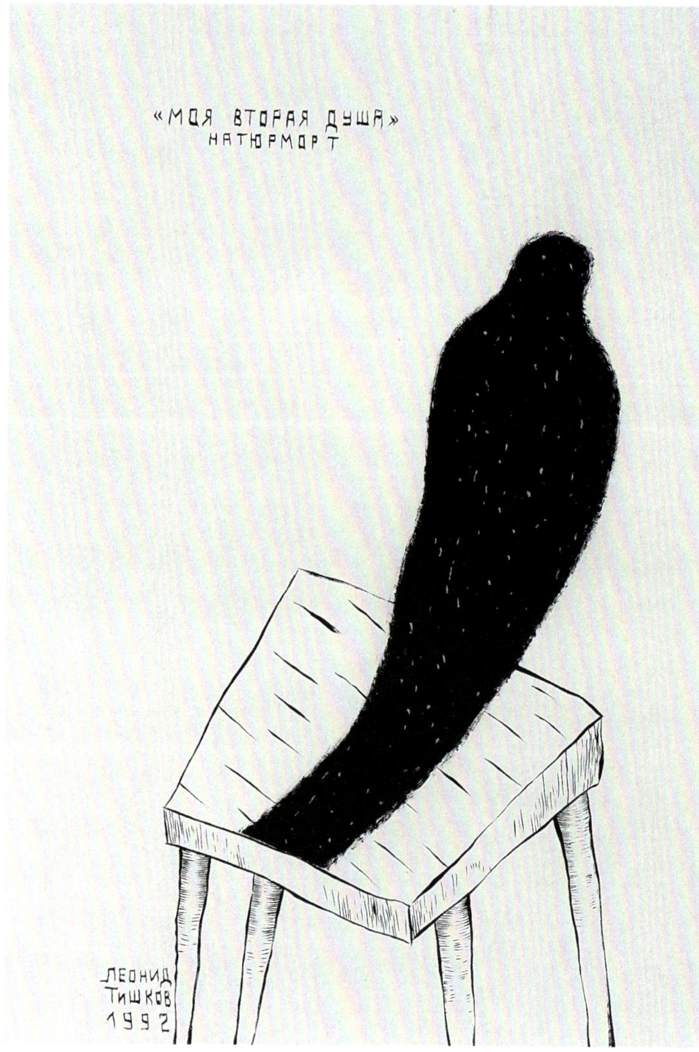

1992, Lithograph,
62x43 cm

Head
Still Life

My Second Soul
Still Life

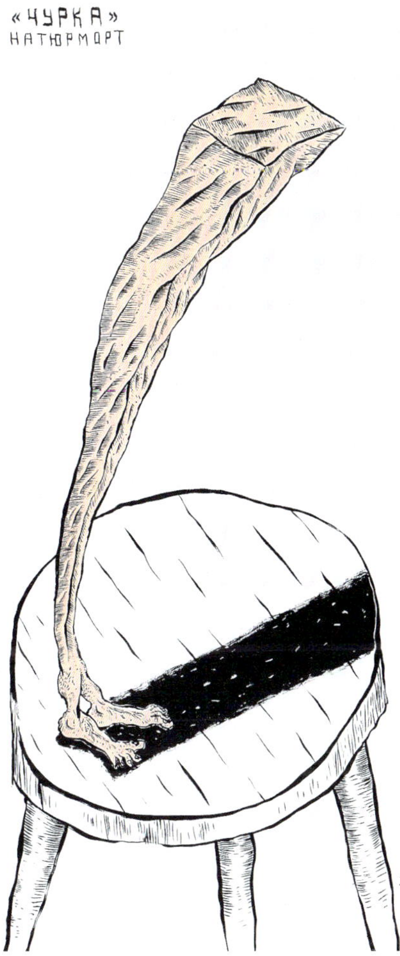

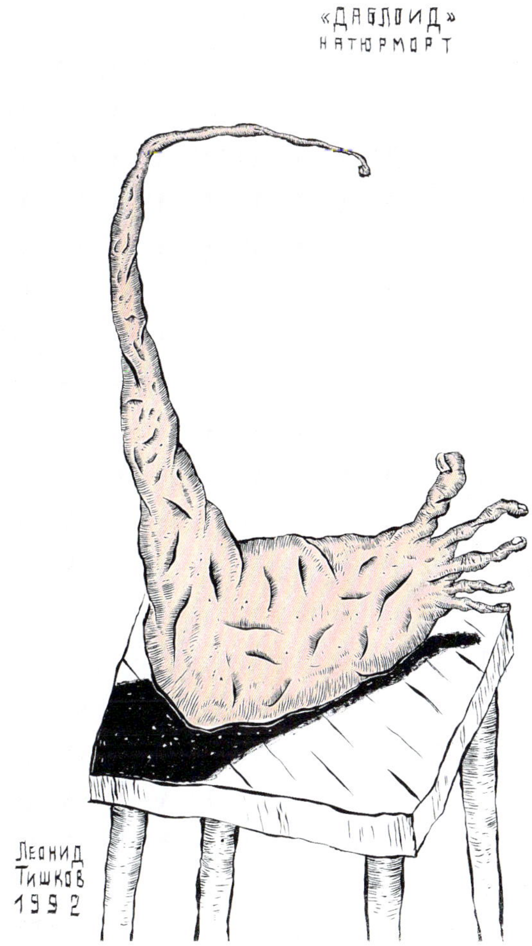

1992, Lithograph, 62x43 cm

Blockhead
Still Life

Dabloid
Still Life

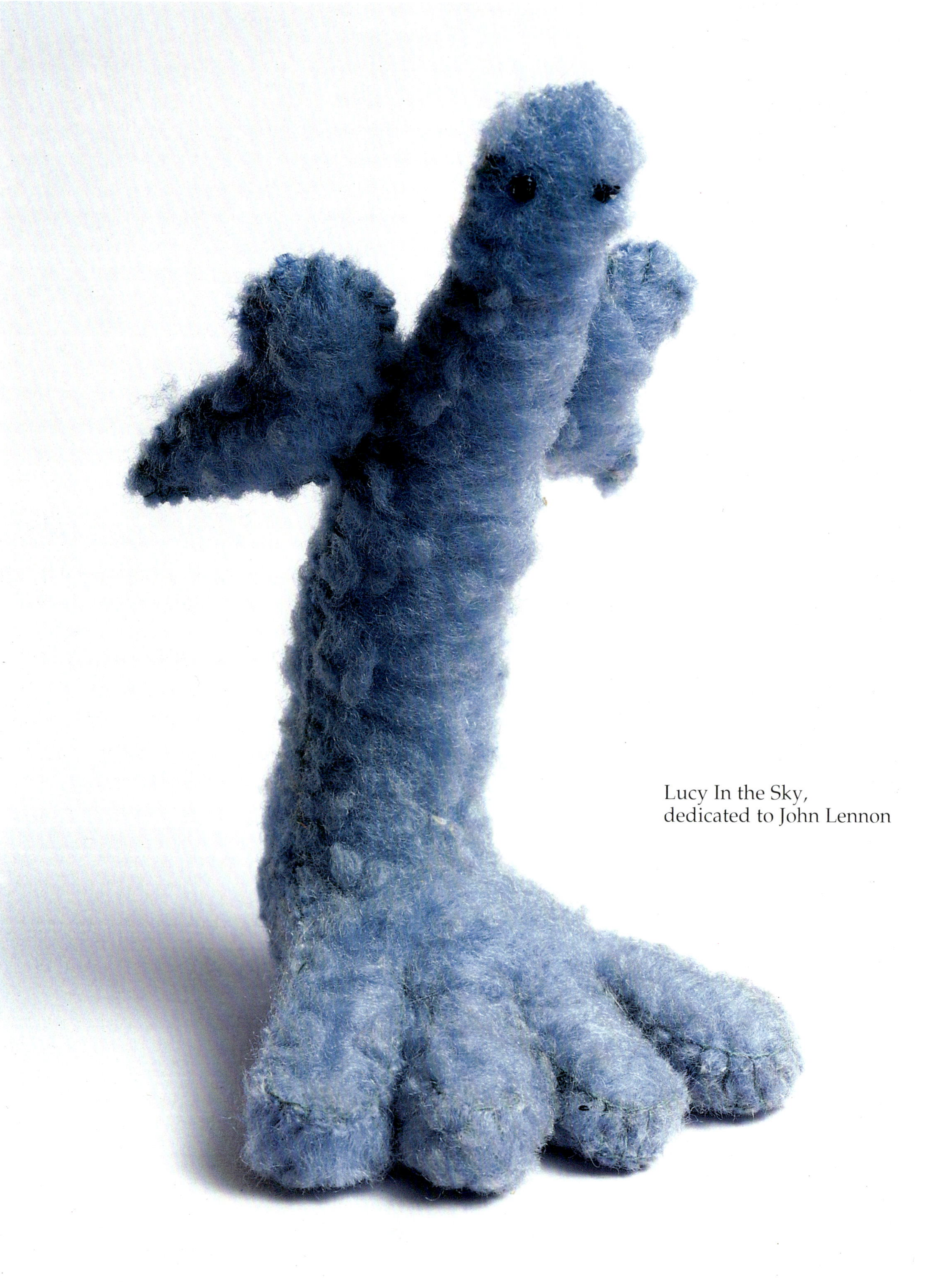

Lucy In the Sky,
dedicated to John Lennon

DABLOIDS

In a neurology text is a diagram of a person depicting with the nerve endings. This person has a small head and big feet, because the greatest num-ber of receptors is concentrated in the soles of the feet. That is science, and here is a fairy tale: Achilles'soul went into Achilles' heel, the soul went into the heels (Russian tale), and lives there all day. Wisdom, consciousness, life, low and high, movement and intellect are in the foot. Dabloid is the symbol of the path, or Tao, its hieroglyph is made up of two Chinese words: head and foot. This is the sole of Brahman, the track of God, a symbol of straight-walking man, five toes are the five parts of the world, an attractive creation, simple and furry like a teddy bear.

But the Dabloid is also that which is created by our thoughts, the totality of life conditions, the mold of complexes and confusions, a product of consciousness and instincts. A person lives — and his Dabloid lives. One must simply realize that he is, live with him, and await enlightenment. You are aggressive — and your Dabloid becomes red, gathering life forces. You are calm and happy, full of life — your Dabloid is transparent, his surface twinkling in space. Perhaps he will disappear and a blue light will pour around us?

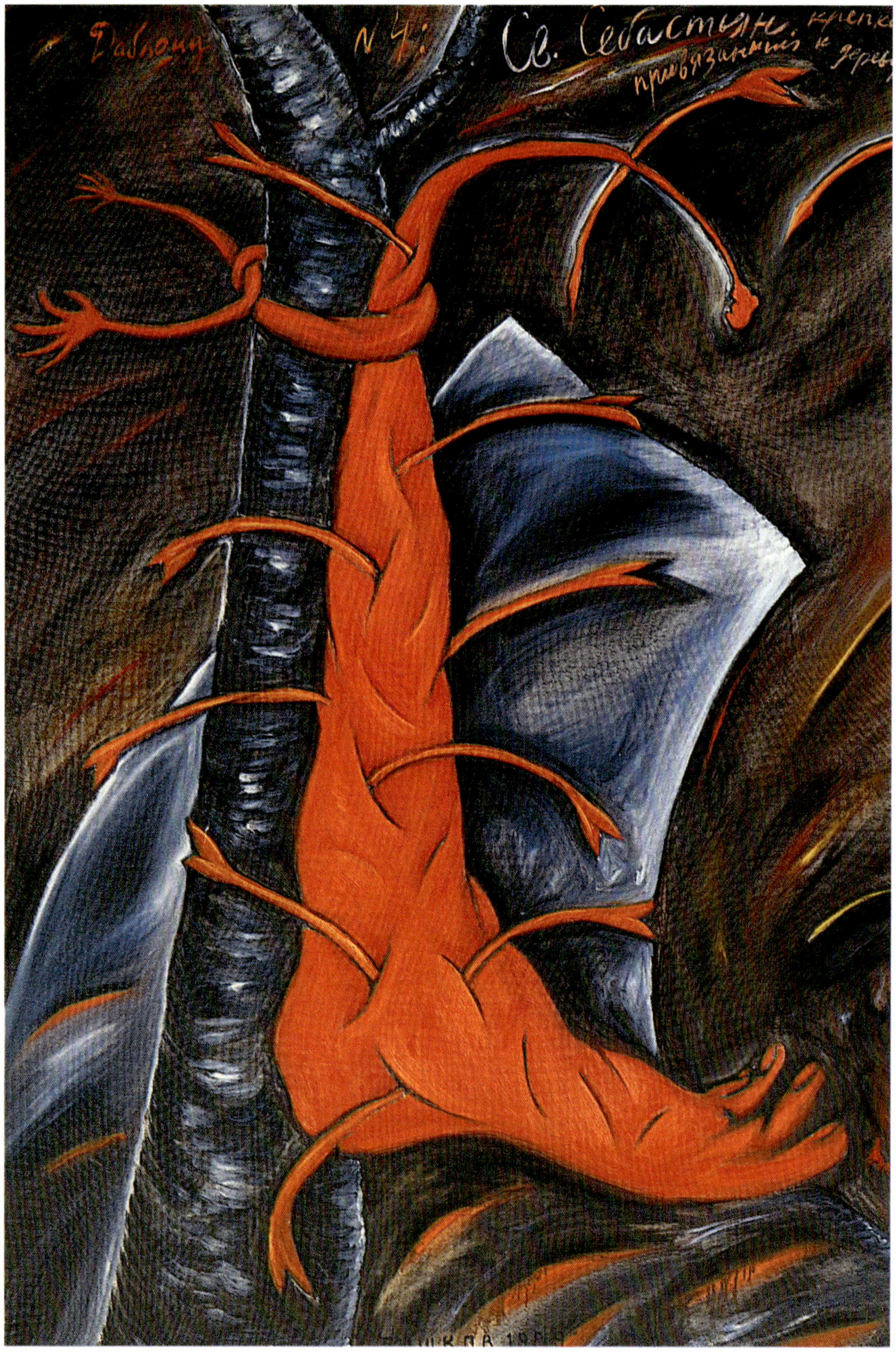

1989, oil on canvas,
200x150 cm.

Dabloid no 5;
St. Barbara extinquishes the burning tree
with her own blood flowing from her body

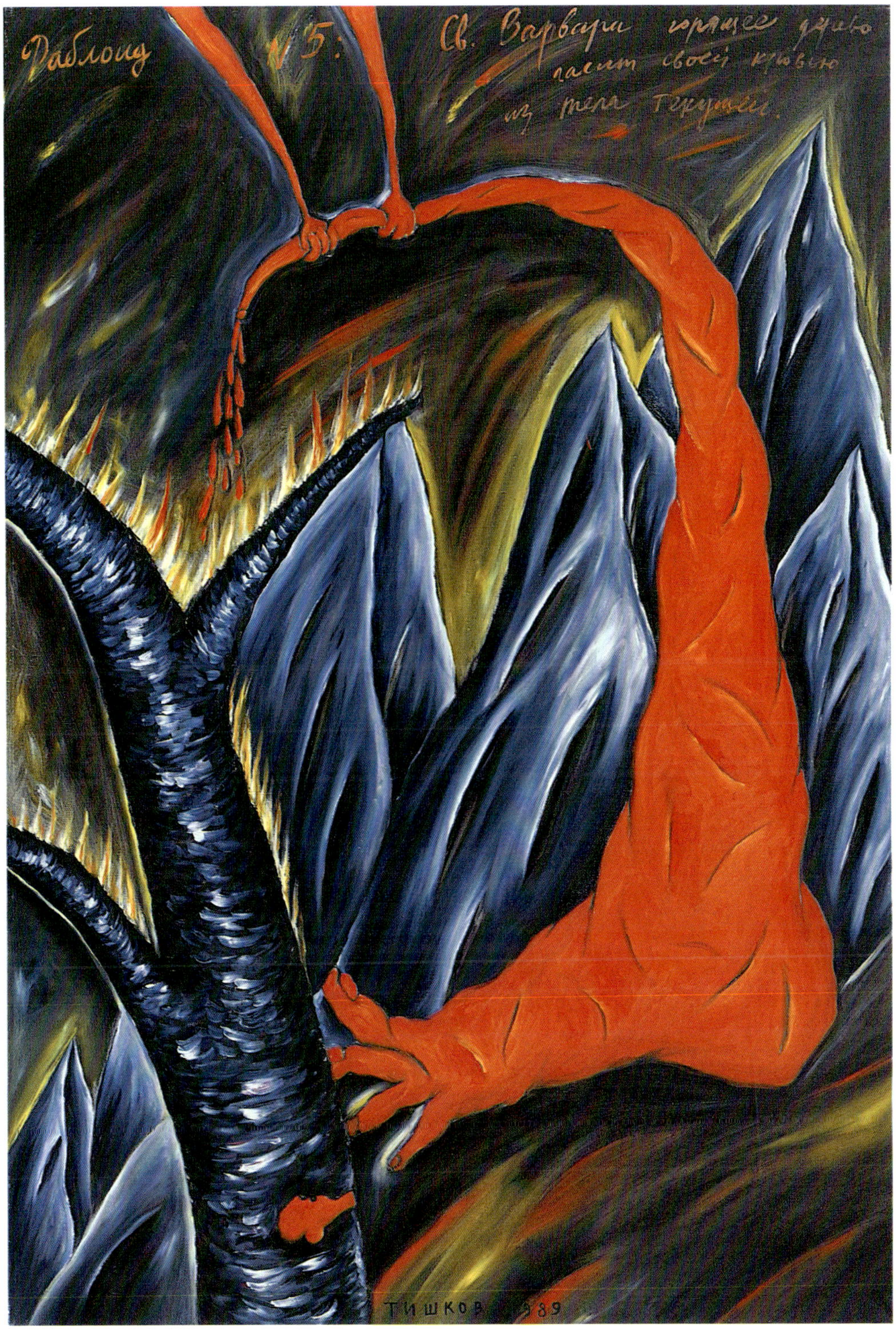

1989, oil on canvas, 200x150 cm.

Dabloid no 4;
St. Sebastian firmly tied to a tree

LEONID TISHKOV

NEW ABOUT DABLOID

Pictures
with texts

GIRLS WITH DABLOIDS

PHOTO BY V. ORLOV

DABLUS

1992

Леонид Тишков

НОВОЕ О ДАБЛОИДЕ

картинки с текстами

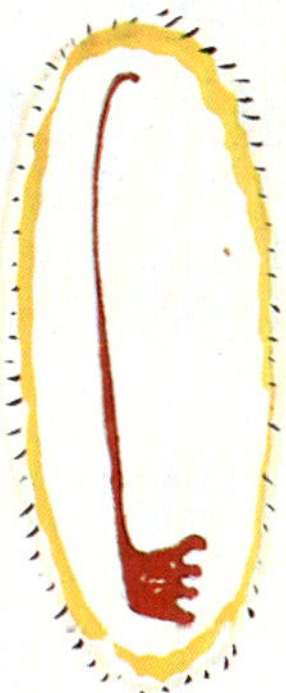

Девочки с даблоидами

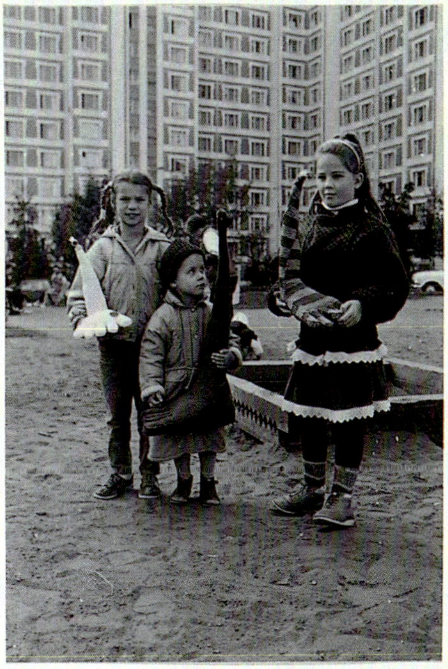

Фотография В. Орлова

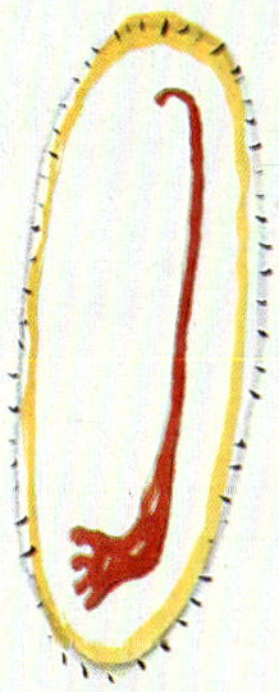

ДАБЛУС

1992

The Urals - golden land
L.A. Tishkov
in childhood
on the
mountain
Kukan

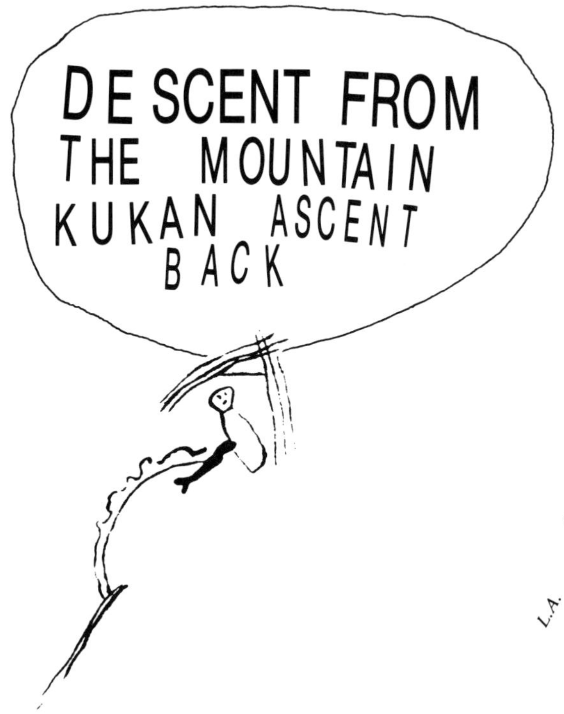

1st MMI
institute
L.A. reads the book
"Anatomy"

Moscow

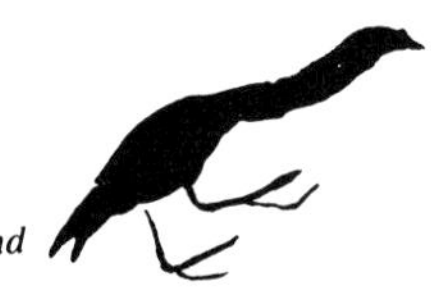

L.A. walks around
the city

Leonid Tishkov
got sick and he hallucinated
a dabloid

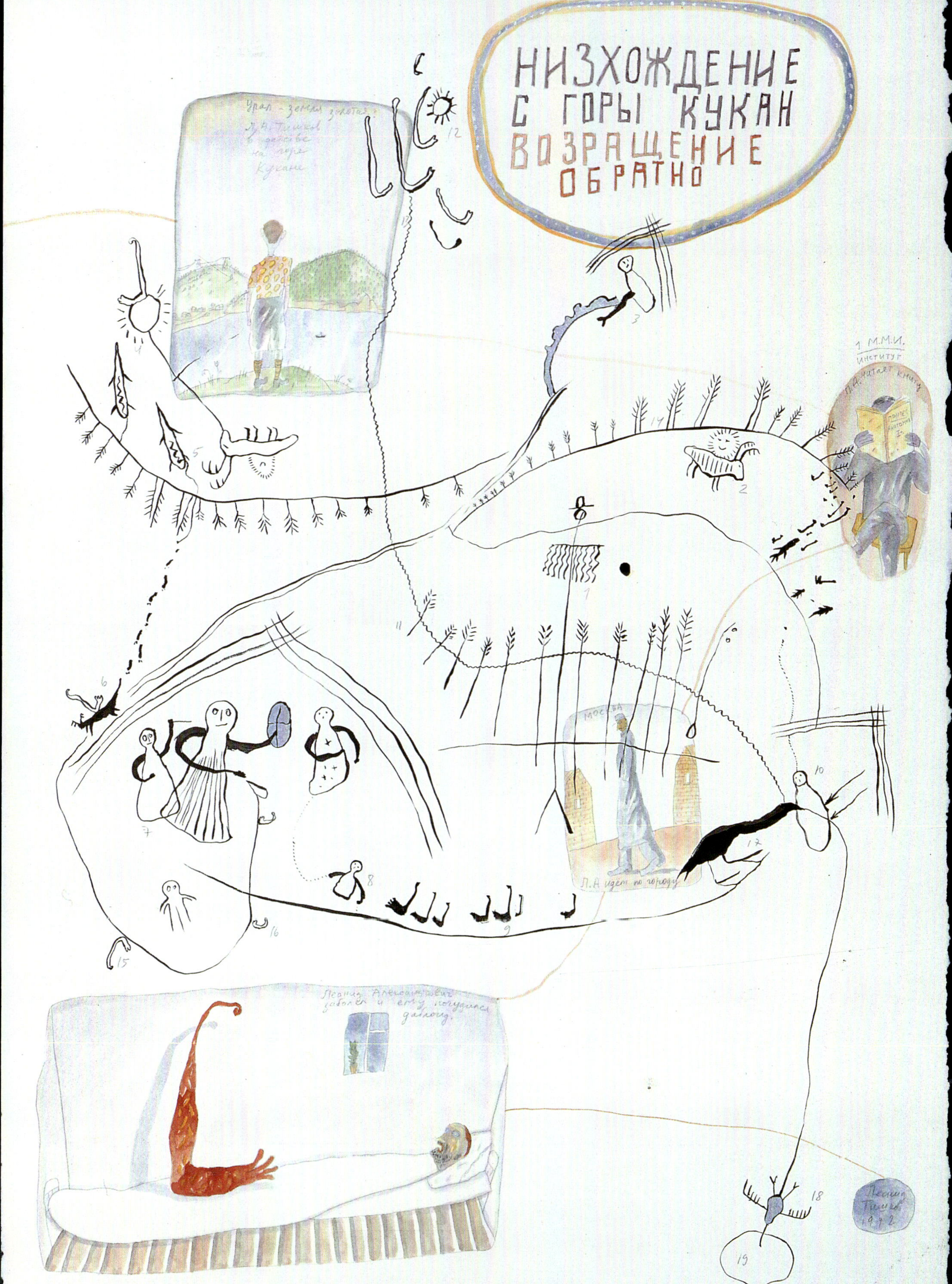

НИЗХОЖДЕНИЕ
С ГОРЫ КУКАН
ВОЗРАЩЕНИЕ
ОБРАТНО
1 М.М.И.
институт
Москва
Л.А идет по городу

WHERE DID DABLOIDS COME FROM

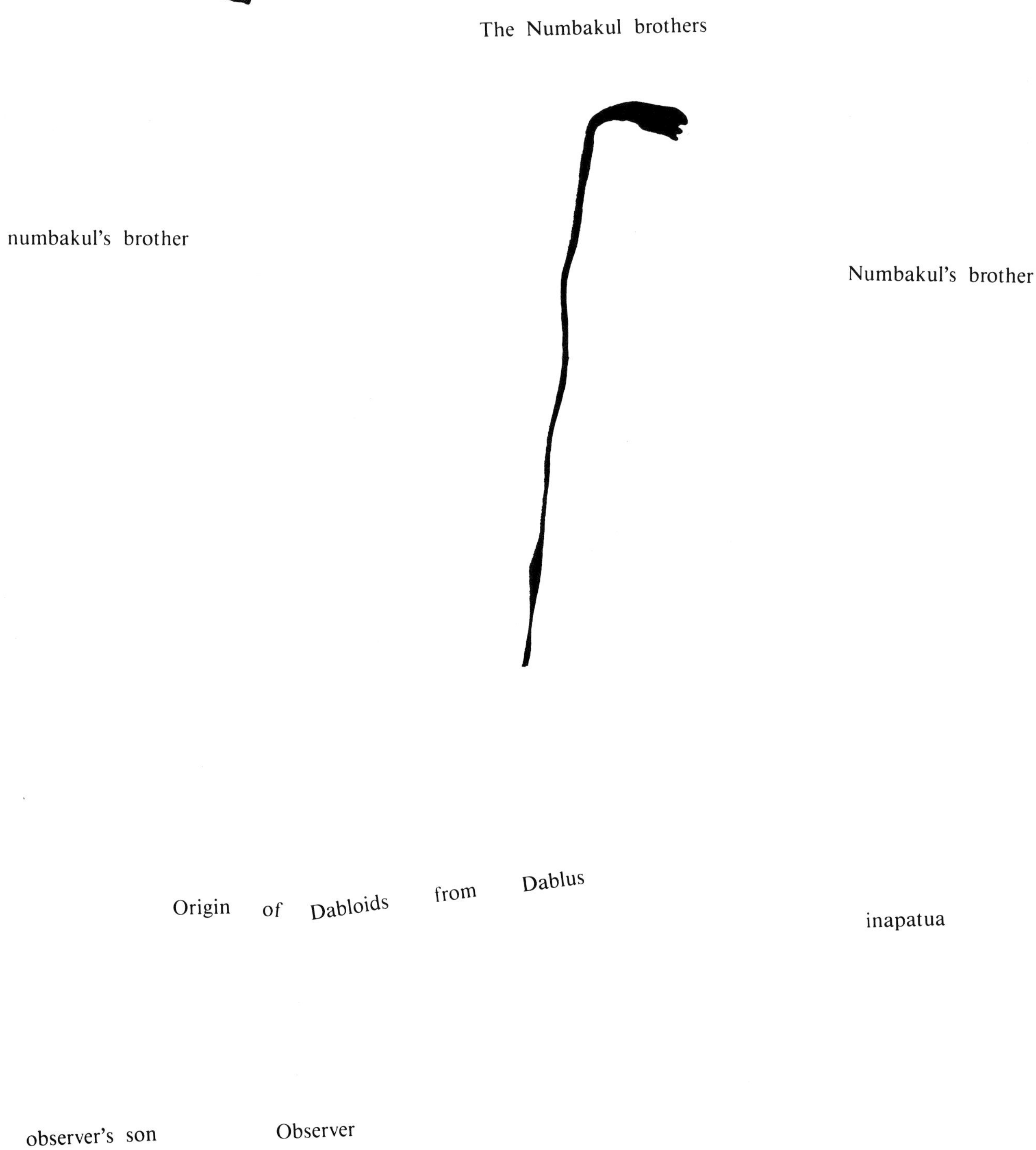

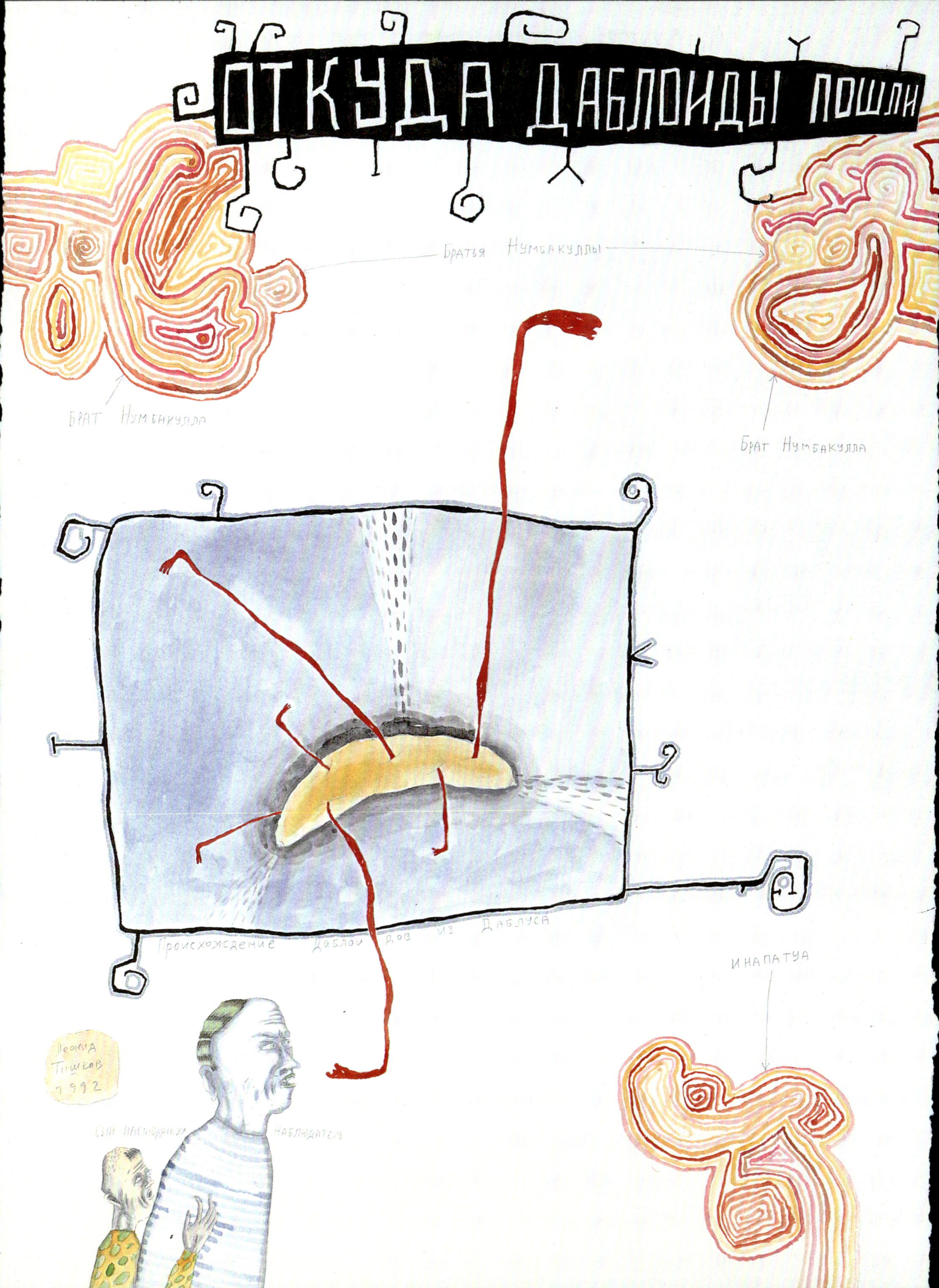

ОТКУДА ДАБЛОИДЫ ПОШЛИ
Братья Нумбакуллы
Брат Нумбакулла
Брат Нумбакулла
Происхождение Даблоидов из Даблуса
Инапатуа
Леонид Тишков 1992
НАБЛЮДАТЕЛЬ

FLAT-FOOTEDNESS GIVES US THE JOY TO FEE LIFE MORE FULLY

Fig. 4. Plan of the position of the bones of the foot within the norm (a), and with lengthwise flat-footedness (b). In cases of flat-footedness almost the entire sole of the foot is in contact with the ground. The ground,, the grass, warm sand on lonely shores of a warm sea, where joyful seagulls sign and the water invites you.

Fig. 6. Insertion of arch support in shoe.

Dabloid stands
in a meadow pressing
its entire body to the ground
sensing the growing grass the
smell of flowers the dear heart
of the black earth of the
Urals is warm.

Dabloid Track

The surface
of the Dabloids
sole leaves its
mark on my land
on sand on
ashes on white
paper

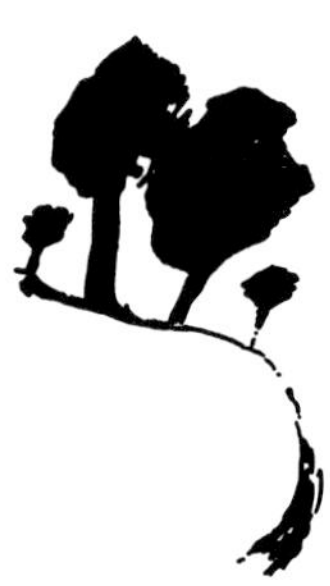

orthopaedists stand on guard

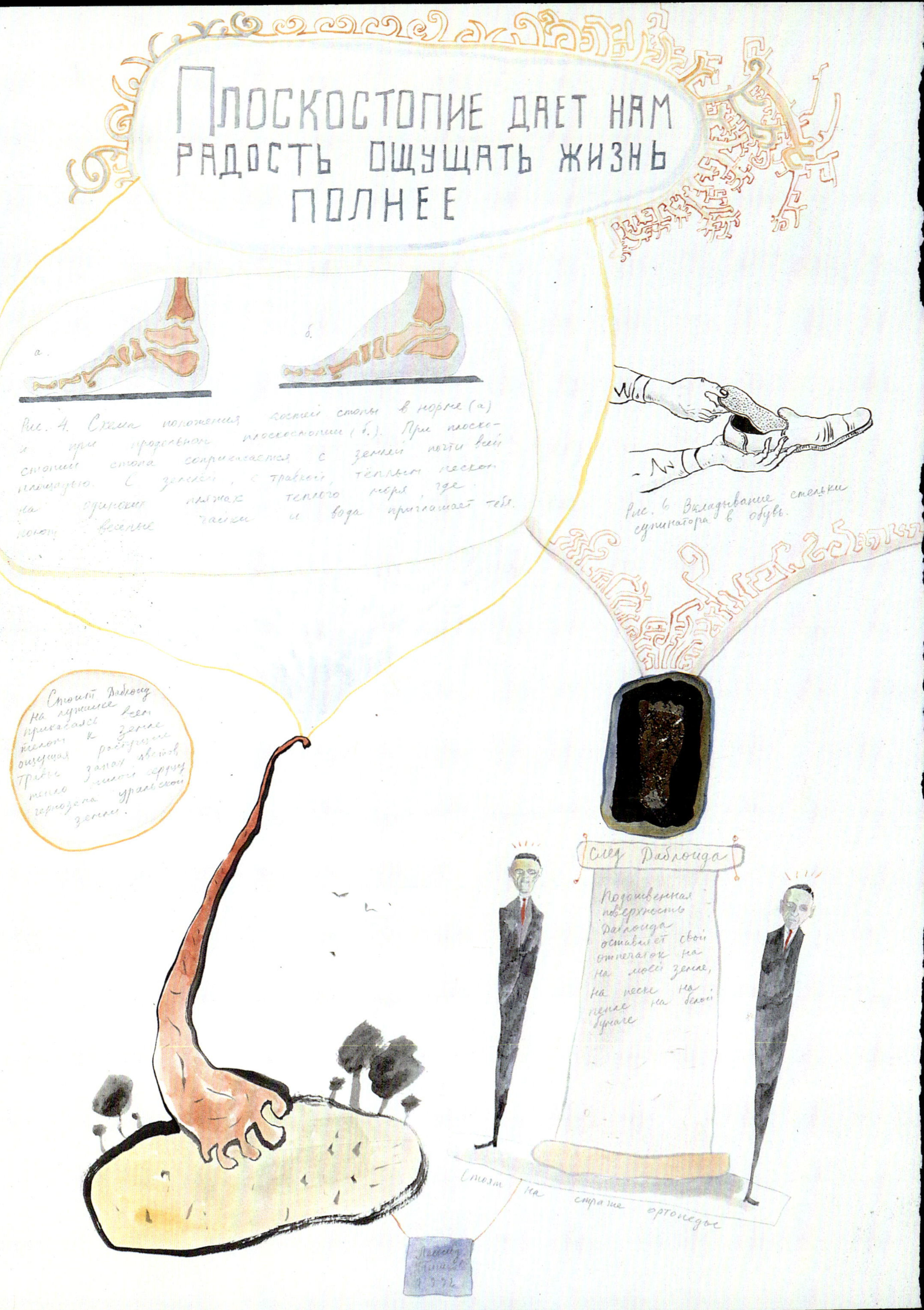
ПЛОСКОСТОПИЕ ДАЕТ НАМ РАДОСТЬ ОЩУЩАТЬ ЖИЗНЬ ПОЛНЕЕ
а.
б.
Рис. 4. Схема положения костей стопы в норме (а) и при продольном плоскостопии (б.). При плоскостопии стопа соприкасается с землей почти всей площадью. С землей, с травкой, тёплым песком на одиноких пляжах теплого моря, где поют веселые чайки и вода приглашает тебя.
Рис. 6 Вкладывание стельки супинатора в обувь.
Стоит Даблоид на лужайке всем прикасаясь телом к земле ощущая растущие травы запах цветов тепло милой сердцу чернозема уральской земли.
След Даблоида
Подошвенная поверхность Даблоида оставляет свой отпечаток на на моей земле, на песке на пемзе на белой бумаге
Стоят на страже ортопеды

TAKE US TO THE TEACHER'S HOUSE

BULL

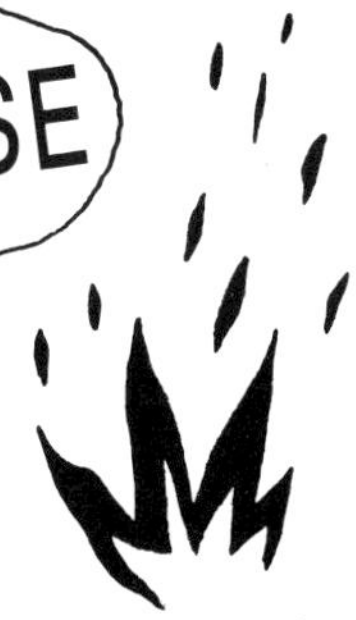

FIRE

The Eastern side is
part of his dabloid,
The Western is part,
The Southern side is part,
The Northern side is part.
Truly, dear one, this is the
four-part dabloid of Brahman,
called the SHINING *one.*

1

Earth is part of his dabloid
Air is part
The sky is part, the ocean is part,
The four-part dabloid of Brahman
called
ETERNAL

2

There he stands
beautiful and
proud from
the windward side
uniting all
parts of the world

the sun is that which
shines above the water
which flow down
the soul is that which
lives inside you

GOOSE

I will tell you
about the foot
of the true one
Fire is part of
his dabloid, the sun
is part, the moon is
part, lightning is part,
Truly, dear one, This is
the four-part dabloid called
LUMINOUS

3

And I tell you about the Dabloid

4

Breath is part
of his dabloid,
the eye is part,
the ear is part,
reason is part.
Truly, dear one,
this four-part
dabloid is called
ENDOWED WITH
THE FOUNDATION

DUCK

Dablus Radiant

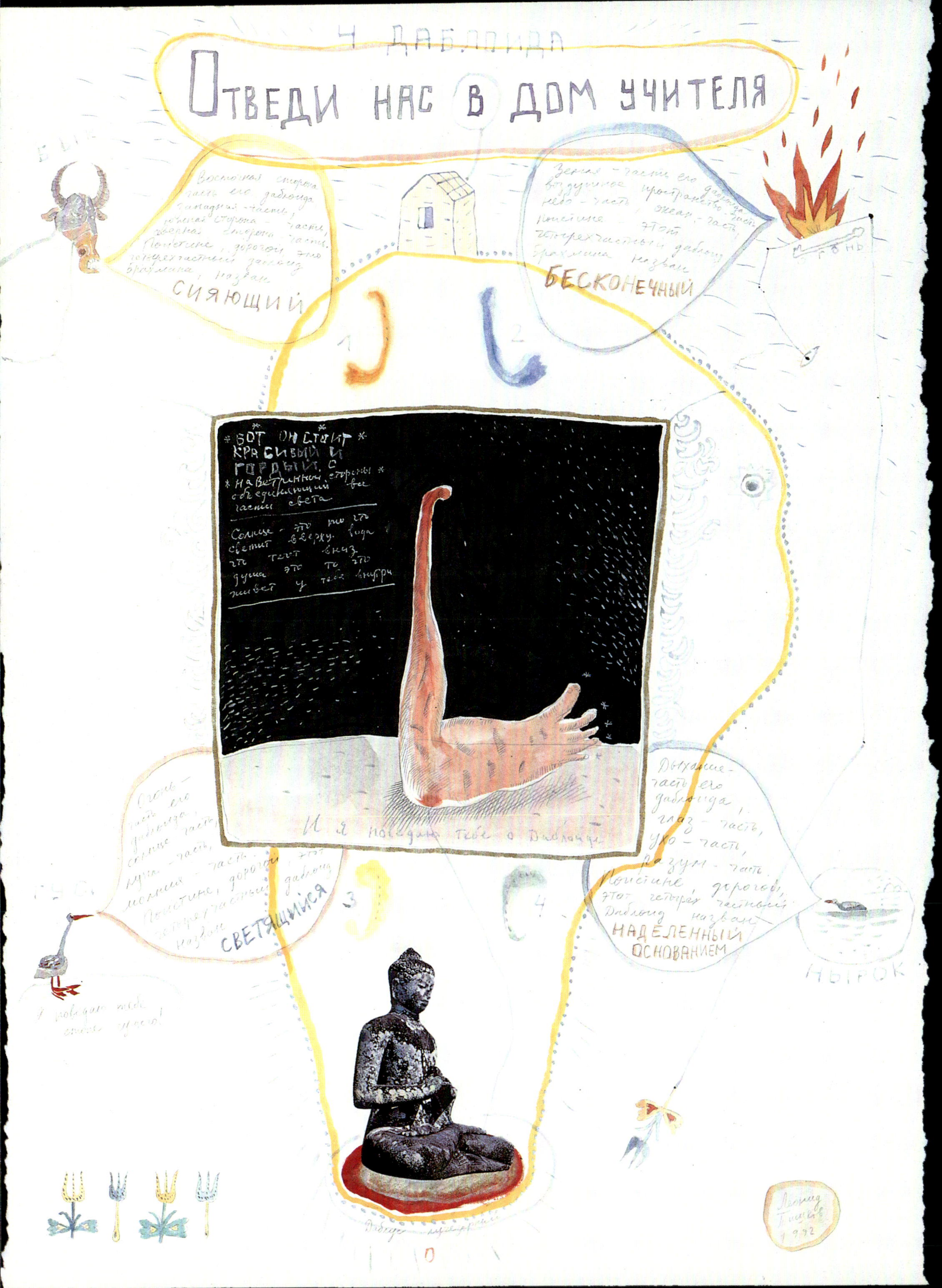

4 даблоида
Отведи нас в дом учителя
Бык
Восточная сторона часть его даблоида, западная - часть, южная сторона - часть, северная сторона - часть. Поистине, дорогой, этот четырехчастный даблоид брахмана назван
Сияющий
Земля - часть его, воздушное пространство - часть, небо - часть, океан - часть. Поистине - этот четырехчастный даблоид брахмана назван
Бесконечный
Огонь
Вот он стоит красивый и гордый. С наветренной стороны объединяющий все части света
Солнце - это то что светит вверху. вода это течет вниз. душа это то что живет у тебя внутри
И я поведаю тебе о Даблоиде
Огонь - часть его даблоида, солнце - часть, луна - часть, молния - часть. Поистине, дорогой, этот четырехчастный даблоид назван
Светящийся
Дыхание - часть его даблоида, глаз - часть, ухо - часть, разум - часть. Поистине, дорогой, этот четырёхчастный Даблоид назван
Наделенный основанием
Нырок
Леонид Тишков 1992

BRAHMAN

NEW ABOUT D.

OR .. LEONID'S DABLOID

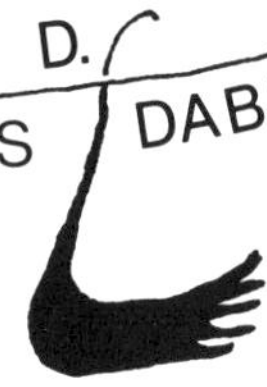

This brahman has four feet: speech is a foot,
breath is a foot, the eye is a foot,
the ear is a foot.

Now as regards the godhead:

This is as regards the body.

fire is a Dabloid, wind is a Dabloid the sun is a Dabloid,
the four corners of the world are Dabloids.

Beautiful and astonishing Dablus

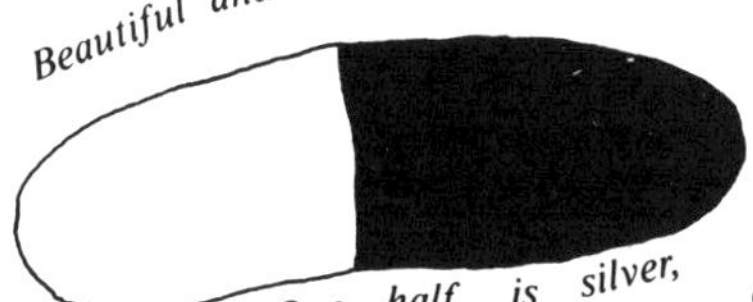

One half is silver,
The other is gold.

Once he came to exist. Began to grow. Then he lay like an egg for a year. Suddenly he broke into two halves.

And were born the sun, wind,
fire and four corners of the world.

Girl with
a bananas

4

1

2 3

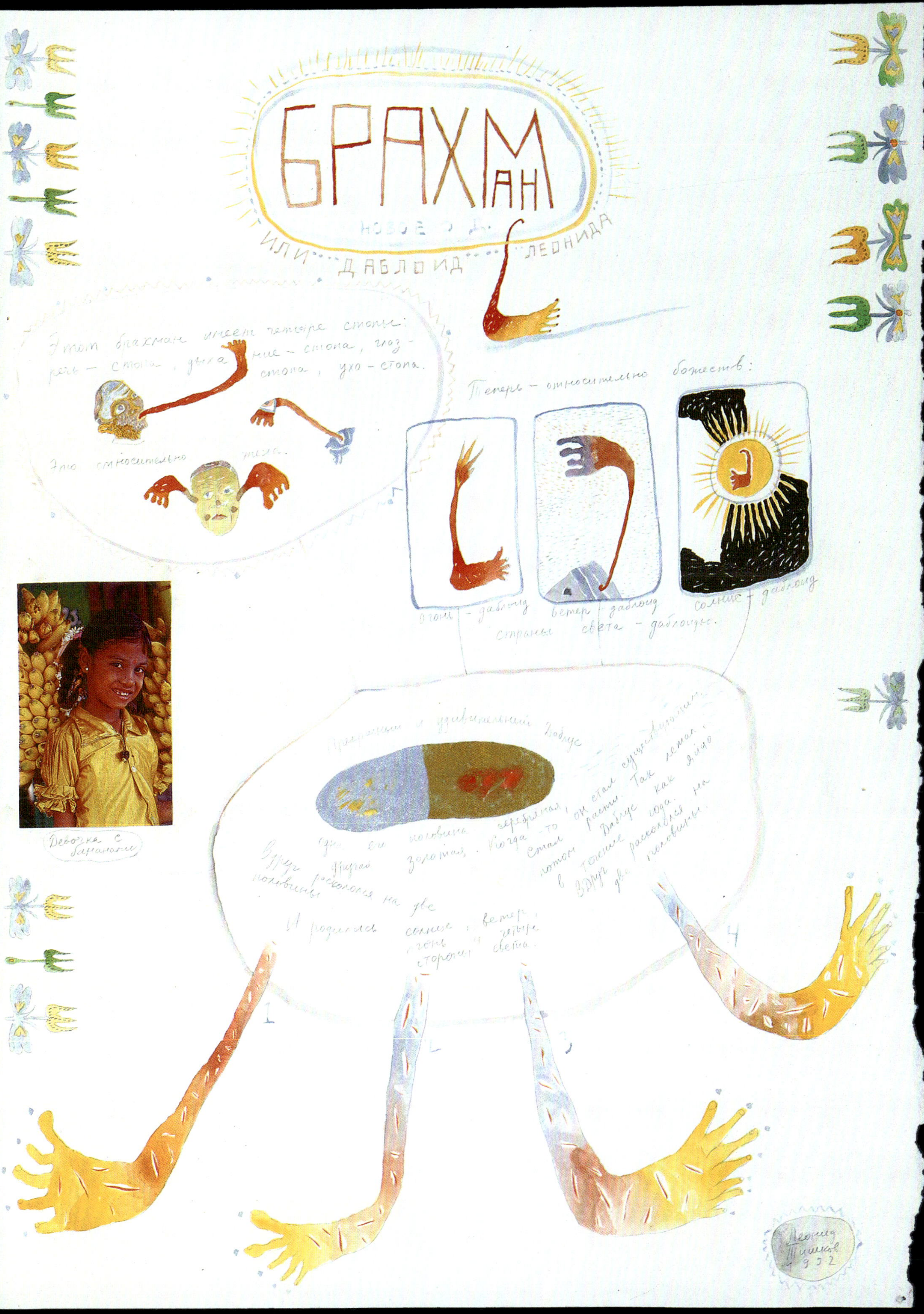
БРАХМАН
ИЛИ ДАБЛОИД ЛЕОНИДА
Этот брахман имеет четыре стопы: речь — стопа, дыхание — стопа, глаз — стопа, ухо — стопа.
Это относительно тела.
Теперь — относительно божеств:
огонь — даблоид
ветер — даблоид
солнце — даблоид
страны света — даблоиды.
Девочка с бананами
Вдруг он раскололся на две половины.
И родились солнце, ветер, огонь и четыре стороны света.
1
2
3
4
Леонид Тишков
1992

CHINESE MONEY

movement conquers cold

he
knows
how to
stand
firm

he
is full
of peace

The nameless is
the beginning of the
heaven and the earth
that which can be named —
mother of all things:
DABLUS.

he does
nothing

nothing
is necessary

I am
very weak

The head and foot is a way
way is tao
head and foot is the dabloid
dabloid is a way
The way of the dabloid

calm conquers heat

Where is the carriage rolling

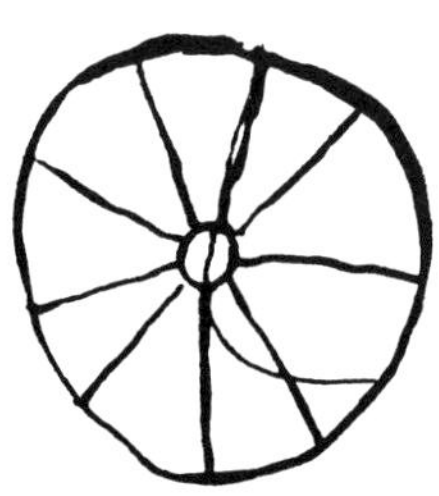

water is unconquerable

tranquillity
creates a new order in the world

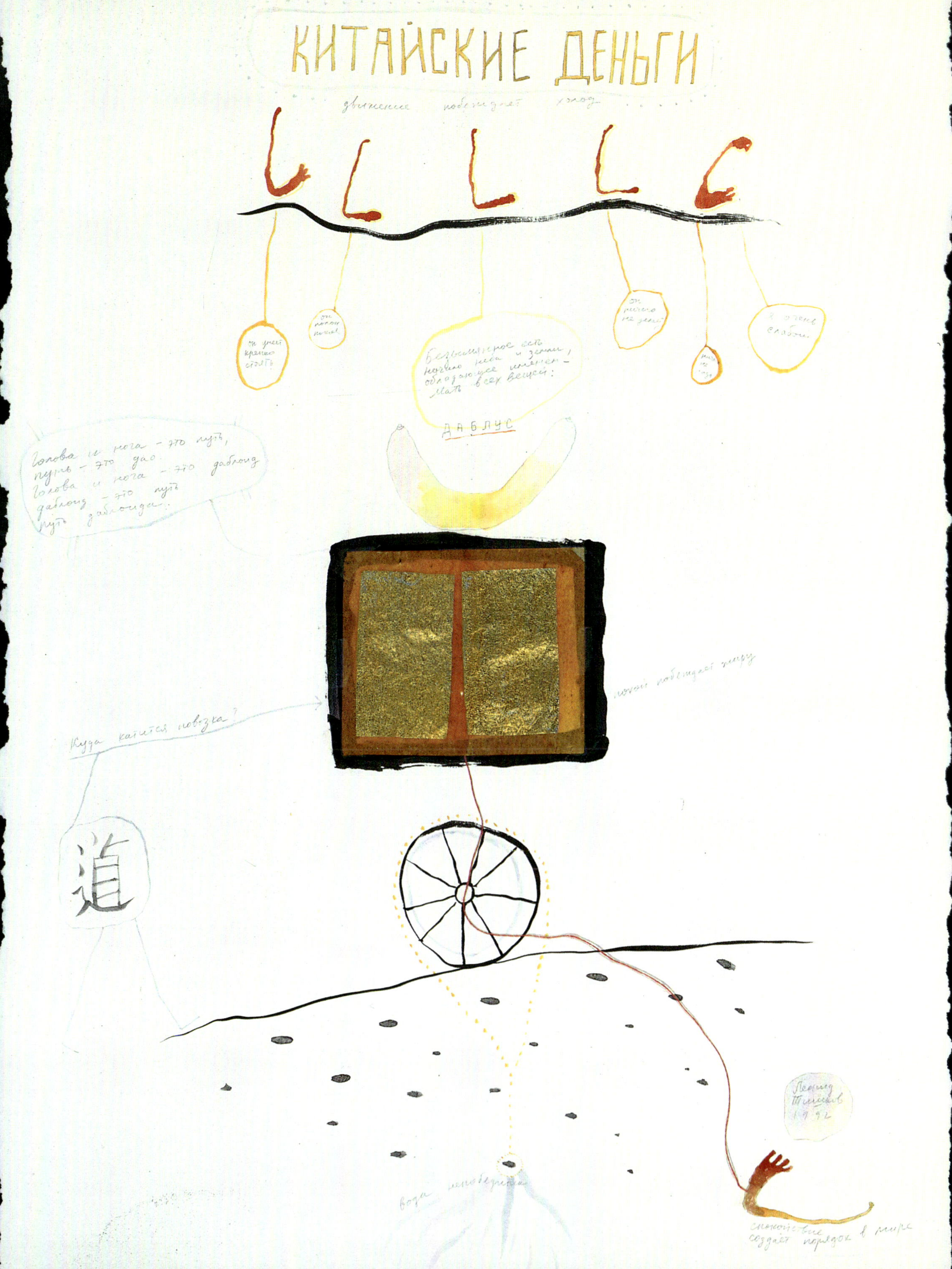
КИТАЙСКИЕ ДЕНЬГИ
движение побеждает холод
Безымянное есть начало неба и земли, обладающее именем — Мать всех вещей:
ДАБЛУС
Голова и нога — это путь, путь — это дао. Голова и нога — это даблоид даблоид — это путь путь даблоида.
покой побеждает жару
Куда катится повозка?
道
вода непобедима
Леонид Тишков 1992
спокойствие создаёт порядок в мире

DABLOID MUSIC

The northern pyramid

is the coolest

Second performance of "Composition no 4"
13 September 1992 in
the exhibition hall on Kashirka

the meditation went
something like this.
Title "At the Feet
of Brahman"

The pyramid of the east
is the sweetest

Fist performance of
"Composition no 4"

To the memory of Beuys

35th page of the book of the dead and the living

I 20 m

II 20 m

III 20 m

Symphony for organ.

1992 9 September

for voice and organ

Compotion n 4

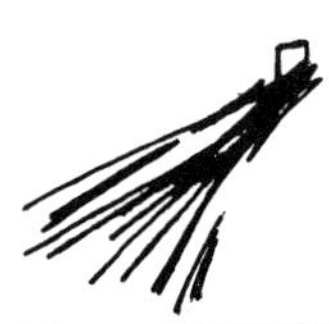

Four pyramids

The southern pyramid
is warming

The pyramid of the
west is satisfying

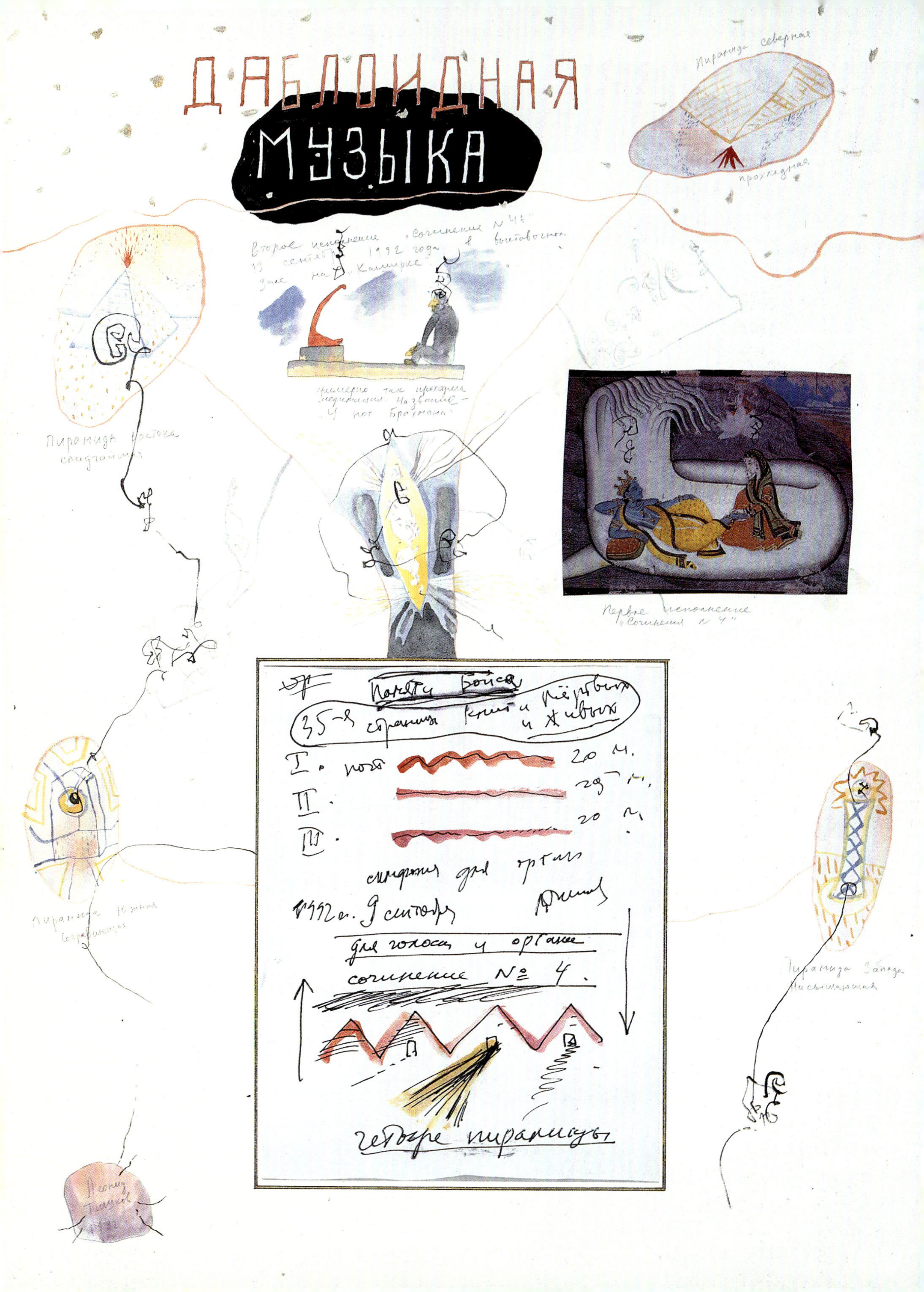

ДАБЛОИДНАЯ
МУЗЫКА
Пирамида северная
прохладная
Второе исполнение «Сочинения № 4» 13 сентября 1992 года в выставочном зале на «Каширке»
Примерно так проходила медитация. Название — «У ног Брахмана»
Первое исполнение «Сочинения № 4»
Пирамида Запада
Памяти Бойса
I. 20 м.
II.
III. 20 м.
симфония для органа
1992 г. 9 сентября
для голоса и органа
сочинение № 4.
четыре пирамиды
Леонид Тишков

HOW TO MAKE YOUR OWN DABLOID

SISTER'S THREADS

FATHER'S SOCK

MOTHER'S COTTON

GRANDMOTHER'S SCISSORS

Take your sock,
Left at some point alone,
the other was tossed out with a
hole on the heel, but THIS one
seemed a shame to throw out and you
placed it neatly and
hid it in a far corner of the drawer
of the dresser. And now, take your unpaired
sock, or your son's sock, or your brother's,
or your husband's. Father's sock. It remembers
your father's foot.

1

Cut off a little
piece of sock
for the upper part
of the dabloid.

Cut toes on the sock

2

maybe
four,
may maybe
be five

3

Sew a
ribbon on
toes are
formed

4

Stuff
it with
cotton,
oakum,
sheep's
wool.

Now - it's
ready!

A golden
portait of the
Dabloid's creator
the Russian
artist and poet
Leonid Tishkov

A DABLOID CASTING A SHADOW

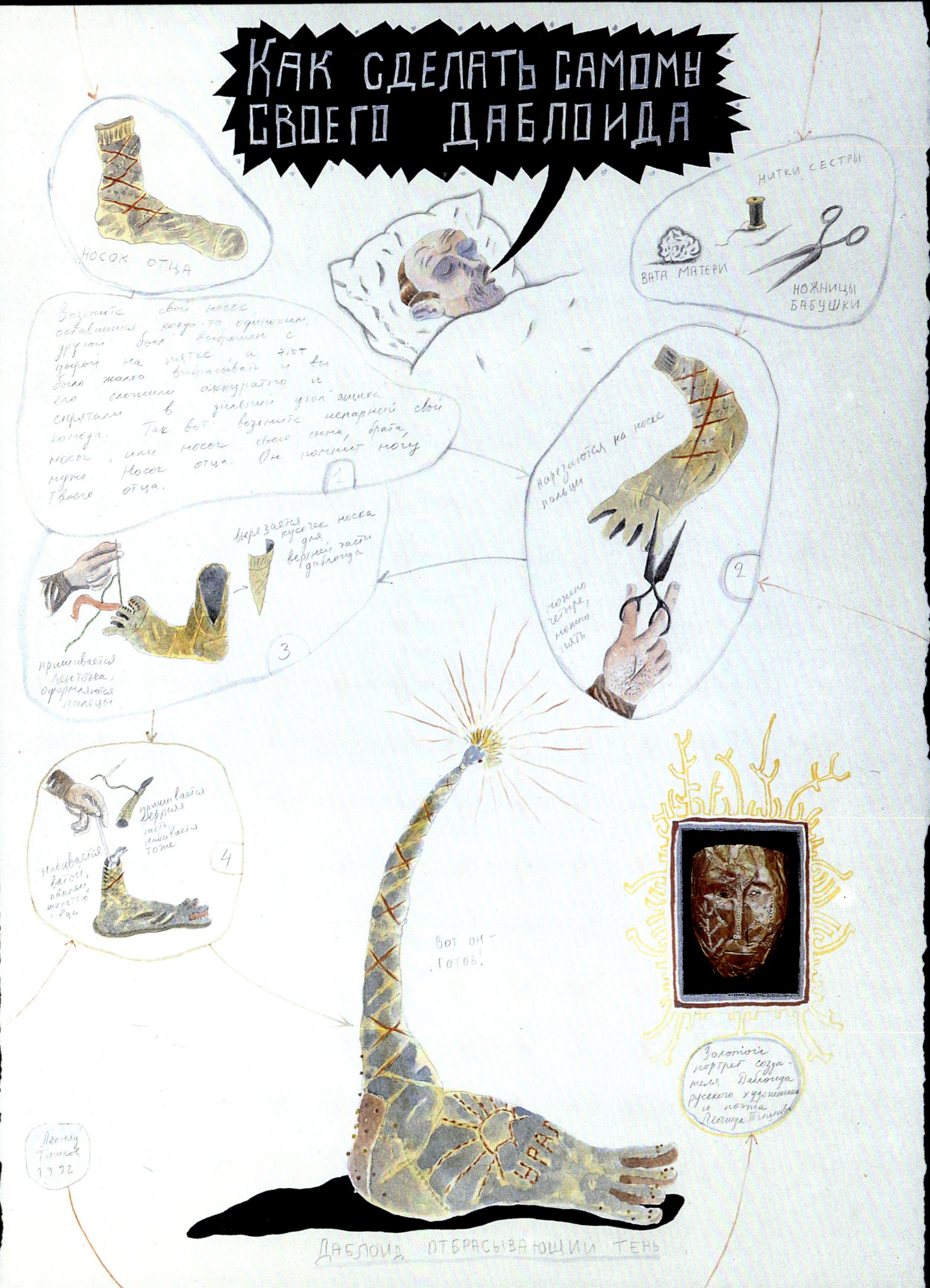
КАК СДЕЛАТЬ САМОМУ СВОЕГО ДАБЛОИДА
НОСОК ОТЦА
НИТКИ СЕСТРЫ
ВАТА МАТЕРИ
НОЖНИЦЫ БАБУШКИ
Возьмите свой носок, оставшийся когда-то одиноким, другой был выброшен с дырой на пятке, а этот вы было жалко выбрасывать и вы его сложили аккуратно и спрятали в дальний угол ящика комода. Так вот возьмите непарный свой носок, или носок своего сына, брата, мужа. Носок отца. Он помнит ногу твоего отца.
1
нарезаются на носке пальцы
можно четыре, можно пять
2
вырезается кусочек носка для верхней части даблоида
пришивается ленточка, оформляются пальцы
3
пришивается верхняя часть, набивается тоже
набивается ватой, паклей, ветошью
4
Вот он — готов!
Золотой портрет создателя Даблоида русского художника и поэта Леонида Тишкова
УРА!
ДАБЛОИД ОТБРАСЫВАЮЩИЙ ТЕНЬ

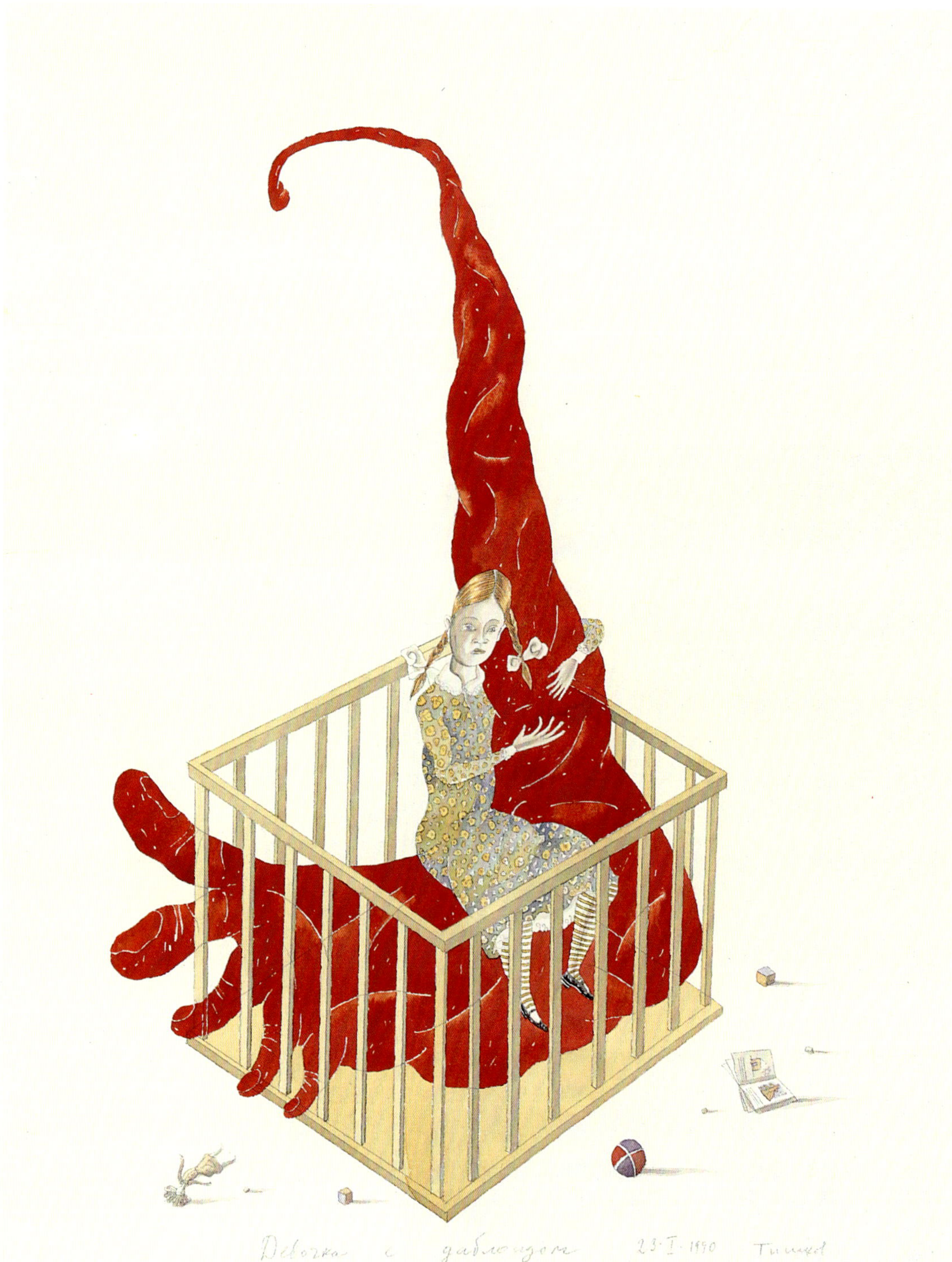

01.23.1990, pencil, watercolor on paper, 48x36 cm.

Little girl with Dabloid

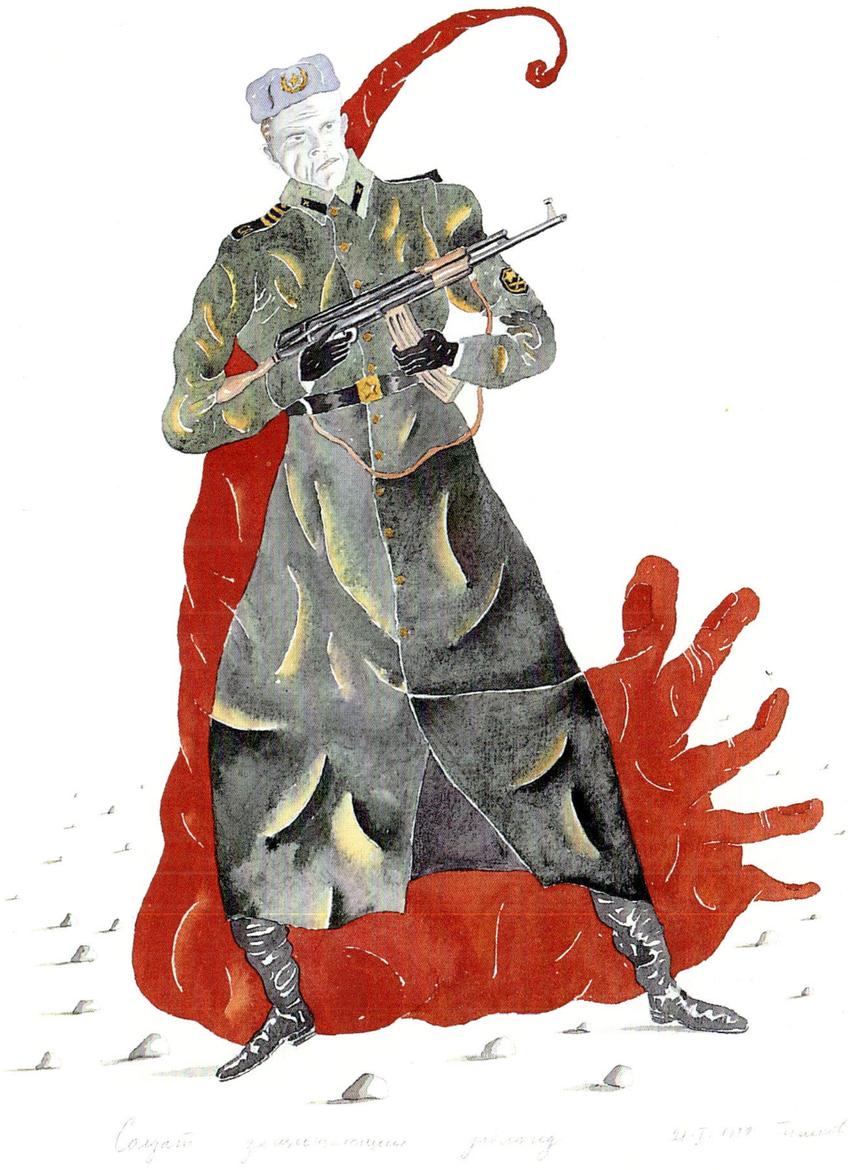

01.25.1990, pencil, watercolor on paper, 48x36 cm.

Soldier, defending a Dabloid

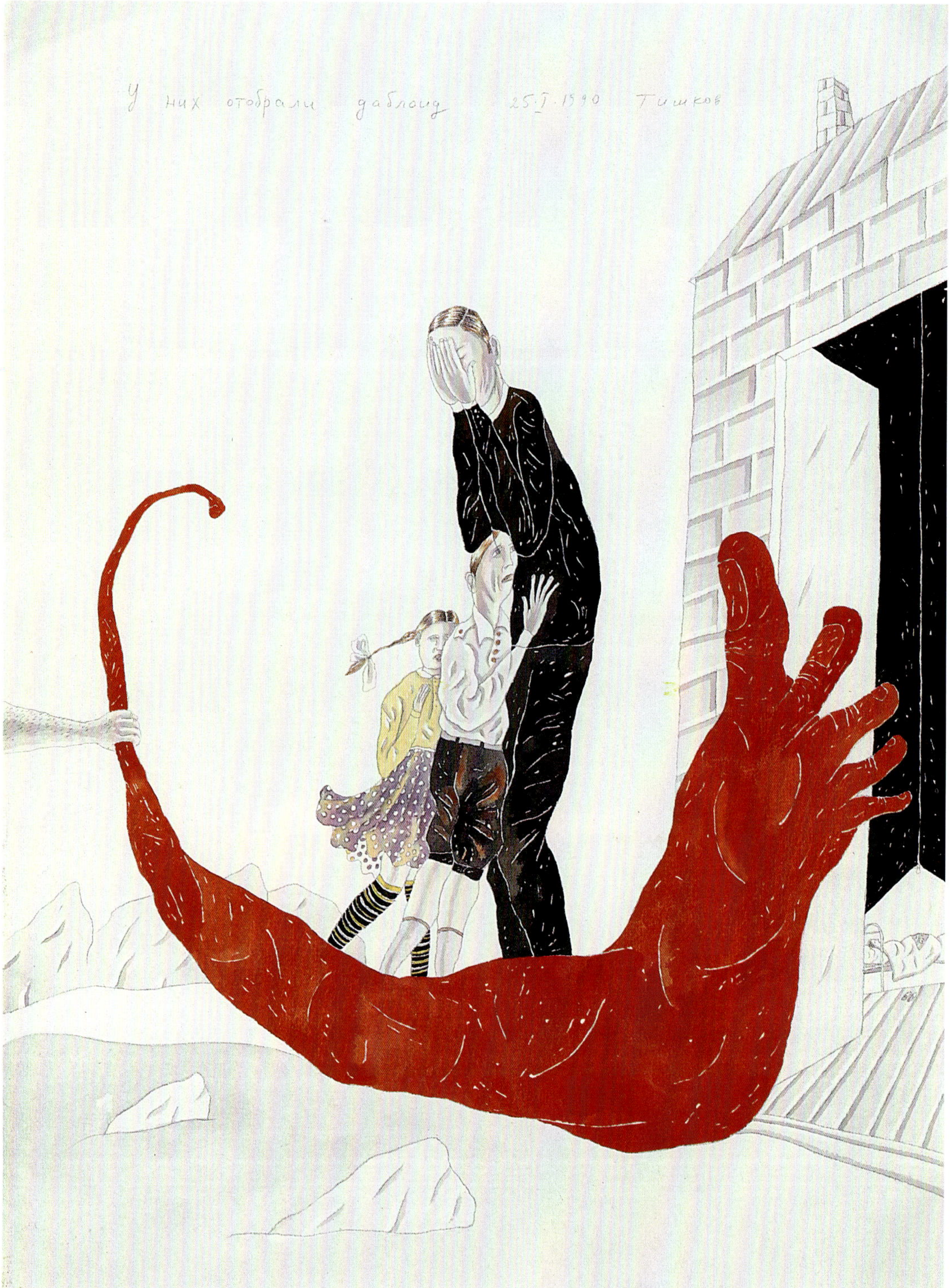

01.27.1990, pencil, watercolor on paper, 48x36 cm.

They took their Dabloid away

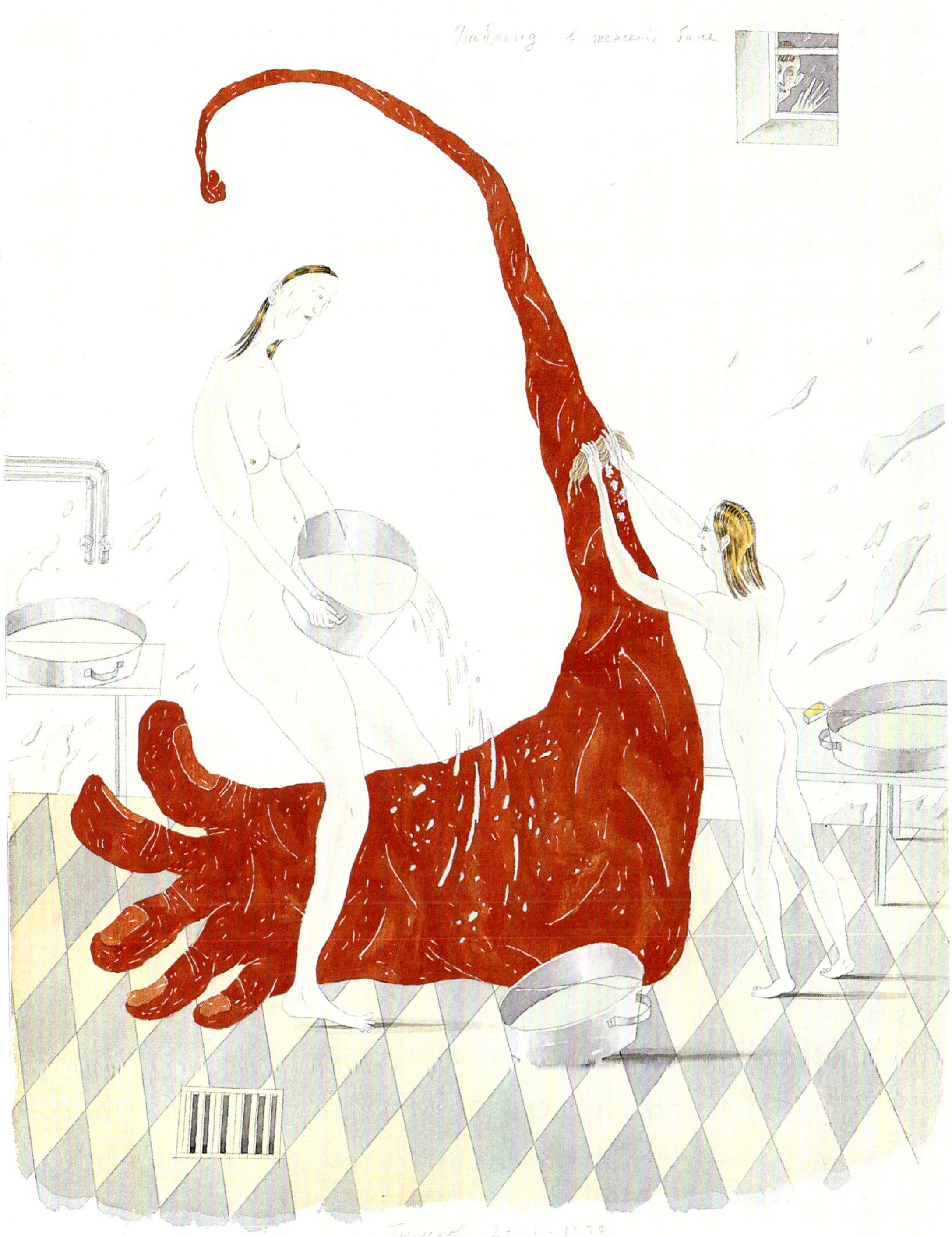

01.27.1990, pencil, watercolor on paper, 48x36 cm.

A Dabloid in the women's baths

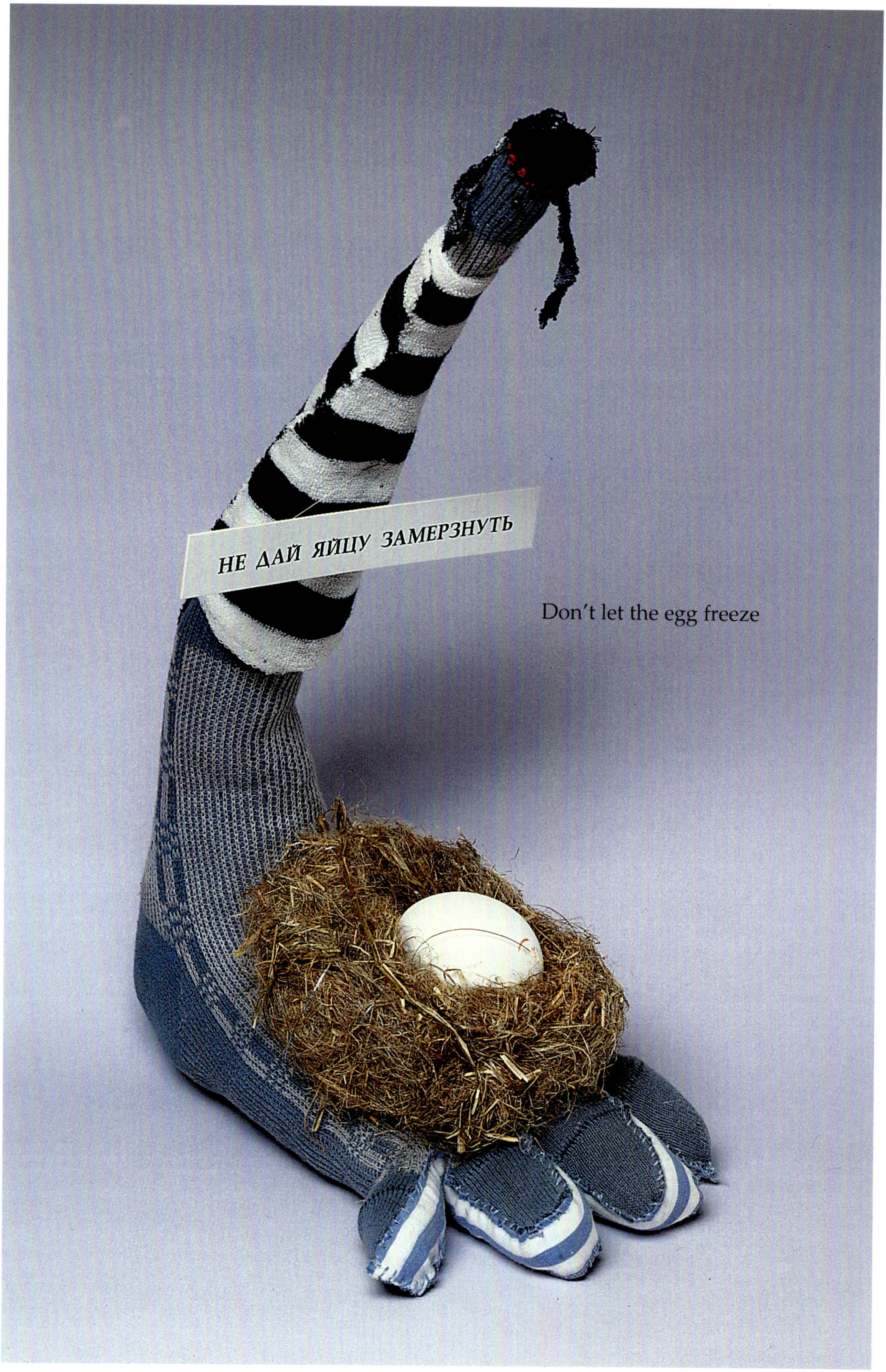

Don't let the egg freeze

MY VILLAGE FOLK

My mountains remained in the Urals. There among the mountains, by slow rivers, within the woods, my lonely village lives. On the outskirts, on the black earth, lies radiant Dablus. Amazing androgyne, the golden egg from folk tales, primogenitor of Dabloids, the female breast, phallic elongation, quiet confidence, the dignity of a god — this is all Dablus.

The village children recognized the god in him, decorated him, sang songs, but aggression, fear and the wicked fathers led to the birth of Dabloids who spread throughout our land. Forgotten is the religion of the ancestors, Victory Over the Sun is completed, the Bolsheviks and avant-garde created Dabloids and like dark, lame hunchbacks carry them on their backs and sing military marches.

Total dabloidization begins — the twentieth century ends. A black sea-gull flies over the lake, a frog falls in a pond, ripples spread along the water, along the land, where my lonely village stands, embracing a crippled birch tree. But I already see her only dimly, for my eyes are brimming with Dab-loids.

LEONID TISHKOV

MY VILLAGE FOLK

TERRE DES DABLOIDES

1 9 8 9

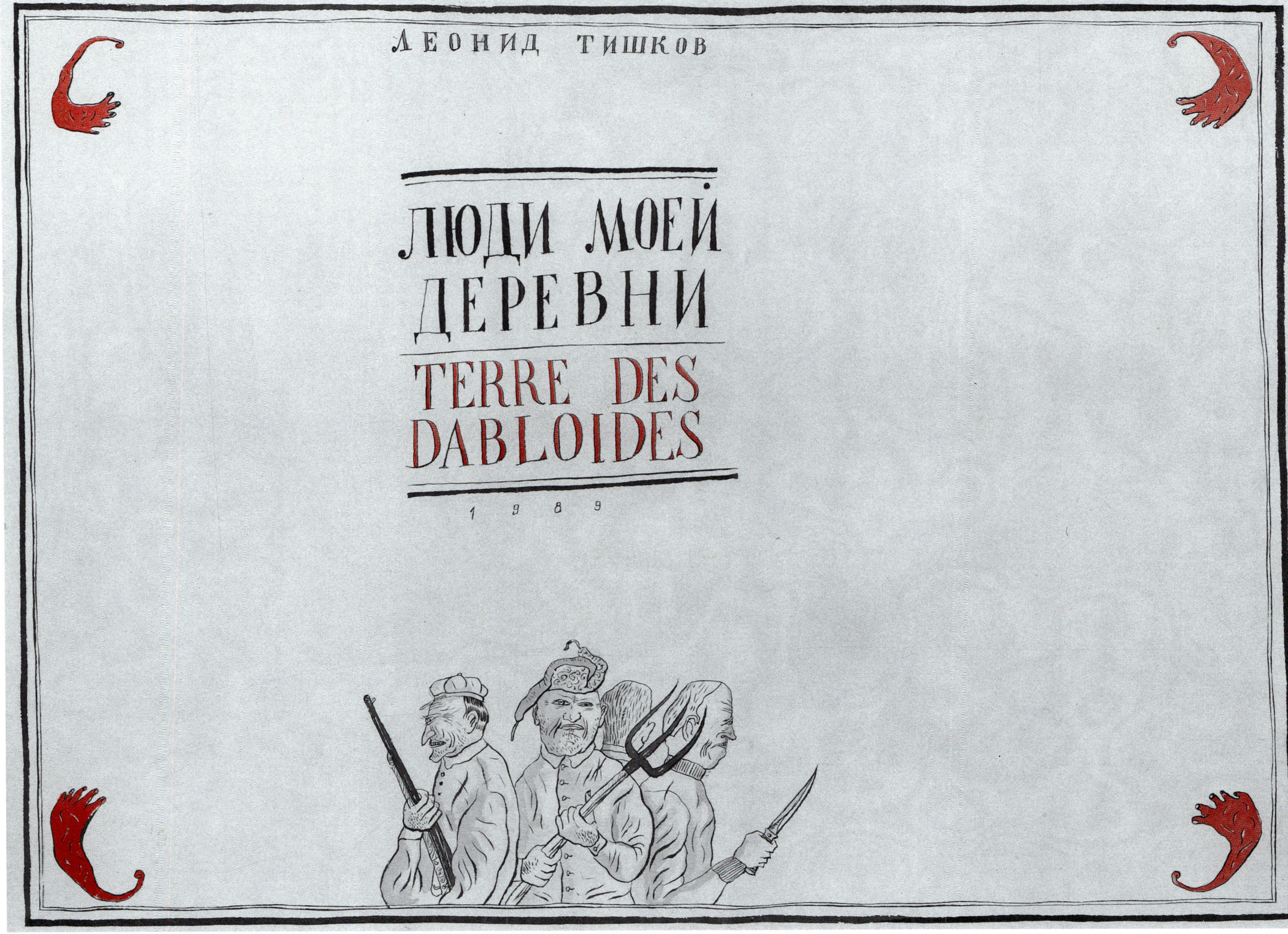

ЛЕОНИД ТИШКОВ
ЛЮДИ МОЕЙ ДЕРЕВНИ
TERRE DES DABLOIDES
1989

MY VILLAGE FOLK FIND A DABLUS

[1]

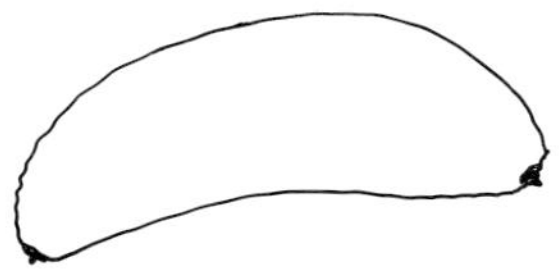

DABLUS VULGARIS

Was found outside our village in the wild growth of weeds near the woods. Mousy saw it first — that lad is always around. We call him Mousy, but no one knows his real name. Who are his parents? Where's his granny? — All a mystery.

Don't touch it, you'll be asking for trouble — thinks Comrade Lapin. He's the sheep-counter and Secretary of the Communist Party branch at th meat-packing factory.

Stoopy — our fisherman — grabbed an oar and ran to the woods... a desperate fellow, as we all know. Daredevil — said his mates in the army. He poked the find with his oar.

Shall we call a doctor? But we have no doctor, only a nurse. (When we fall ill, we use home cures or die) We'll call the militia. Also the Party Committee. Yes — specially invite them.

Clearly the village authorities will be called in to deside this question or the day will come when it will somehow sort itself out? Then we'll need no one else.

What's
inside there?
(Is it a bomb?)

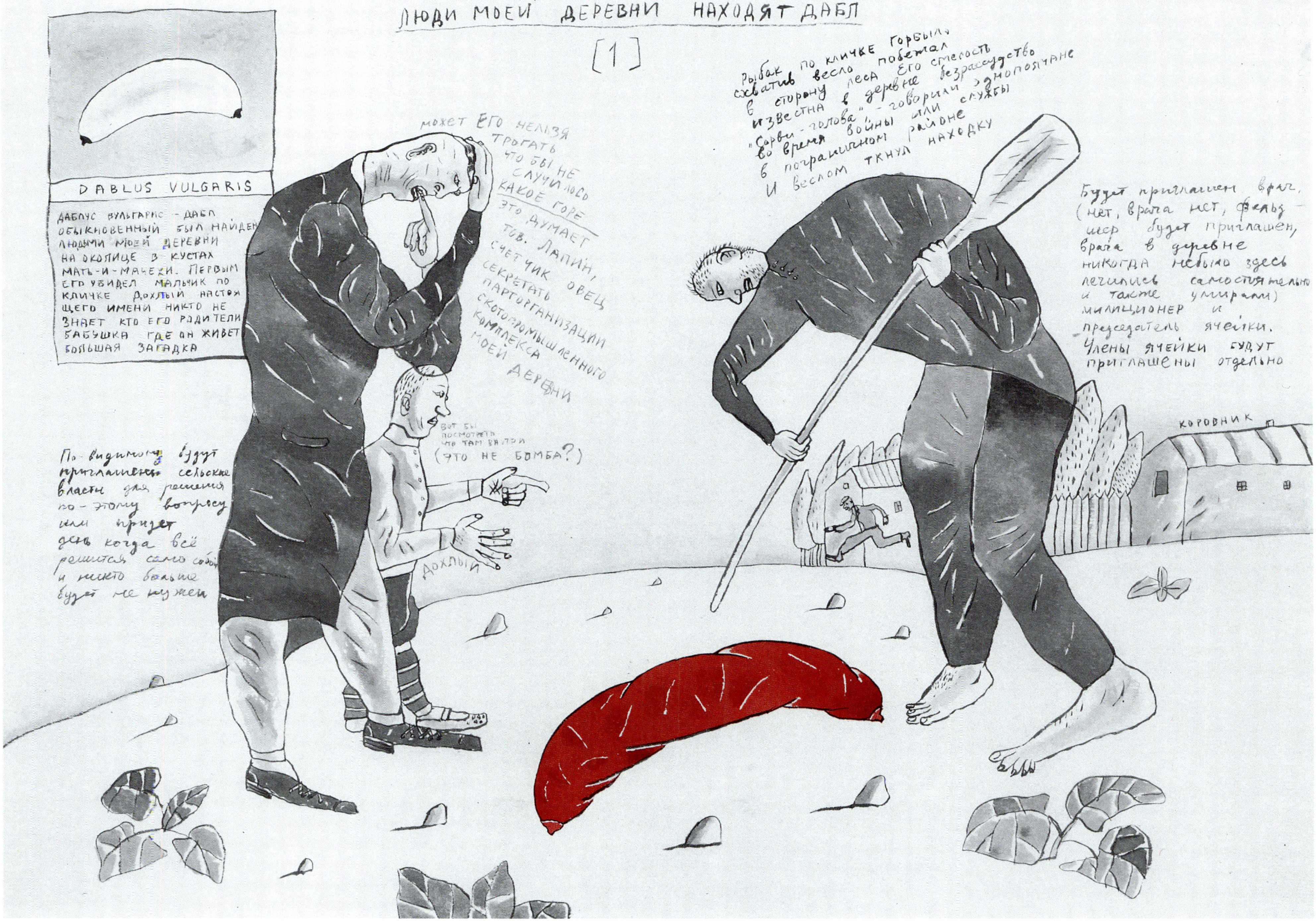

ЛЮДИ МОЕЙ ДЕРЕВНИ НАХОДЯТ ДАБЛ
[1]
DABLUS VULGARIS
ДАБЛУС ВУЛЬГАРИС – ДАБЛ ОБЫКНОВЕННЫЙ БЫЛ НАЙДЕН ЛЮДЬМИ МОЕЙ ДЕРЕВНИ НА ОКОЛИЦЕ В КУСТАХ МАТЬ-И-МАЧЕХИ. ПЕРВЫМ ЕГО УВИДЕЛ МАЛЬЧИК ПО КЛИЧКЕ ДОХЛЫЙ НАСТОЯЩЕГО ИМЕНИ НИКТО НЕ ЗНАЕТ КТО ЕГО РОДИТЕЛИ БАБУШКА ГДЕ ОН ЖИВЕТ БОЛЬШАЯ ЗАГАДКА
МОЖЕТ ЕГО НЕЛЬЗЯ ТРОГАТЬ ЧТО БЫ НЕ СЛУЧИЛОСЬ КАКОЕ ГОРЕ
ЭТО ДУМАЕТ ТОВ. ЛАПИН, СЧЕТЧИК ОВЕЦ СЕКРЕТАРЬ ПАРТОРГАНИЗАЦИИ СКОТОПРОМЫШЛЕННОГО КОМПЛЕКСА МОЕЙ ДЕРЕВНИ
ВОТ БЫ ПОСМОТРЕТЬ ЧТО ТАМ ВНУТРИ (ЭТО НЕ БОМБА?)
ДОХЛЫЙ
По-видимому будут приглашены сельские власти для решения по этому вопросу или придет день когда всё решится само собой и никто больше будет не нужен
Рыбак по кличке Горбыль схватив весло побежал в сторону леса Его смелость известна в деревне безрассудство "Сорви-голова" – говорили однополчане во время войны или службы в пограничном районе и веслом ткнул находку
Будут приглашен врач, (нет, врача нет, фельдшер будет приглашен, врача в деревне никогда не было здесь лечились самостоятельно и также умирали) милиционер и председатель ячейки. Члены ячейки будут приглашены отдельно
КОРОВНИК

DABLUS EXAMINED IN THE COLLECTIVE FARM'S OFFICE IN THE INSTRUCTOR'S PRESENCE

[2]

Our farmers' good honest faces

Instructor Markelov of the District Party

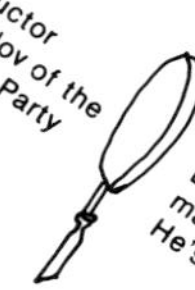

Committee examines DABLUS through a magnifying glass. He's thinking.

The wise old Commissar from the Army Enlistment Office-he marched from Moscow to Prague (1968) — applied his military mind to the puzzle. «Eyes left! Eyes right!» he barked. Not much else in his gray-haired head.

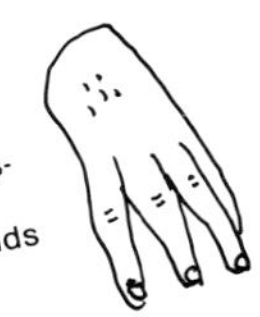

The Commis-sar's well-worked hands

Farm-hands wrapped DABLUS in sackcoth and with many an oath — carried it to the office — the Chairman's instructions.

birch-tree on the way. Sweet Russian birch-tree!

Our Chairman's pale-gray head and dark-gray suit. You can't see his face. He's looking up to the Instructor. He called up the Party Committee, «What shall we do?» Secretary Pryakhin heard it in his black phone and nervously eyed the red one. «Go out there, Boris,» he said to Instructor Markelov.

underground. What's under my village?

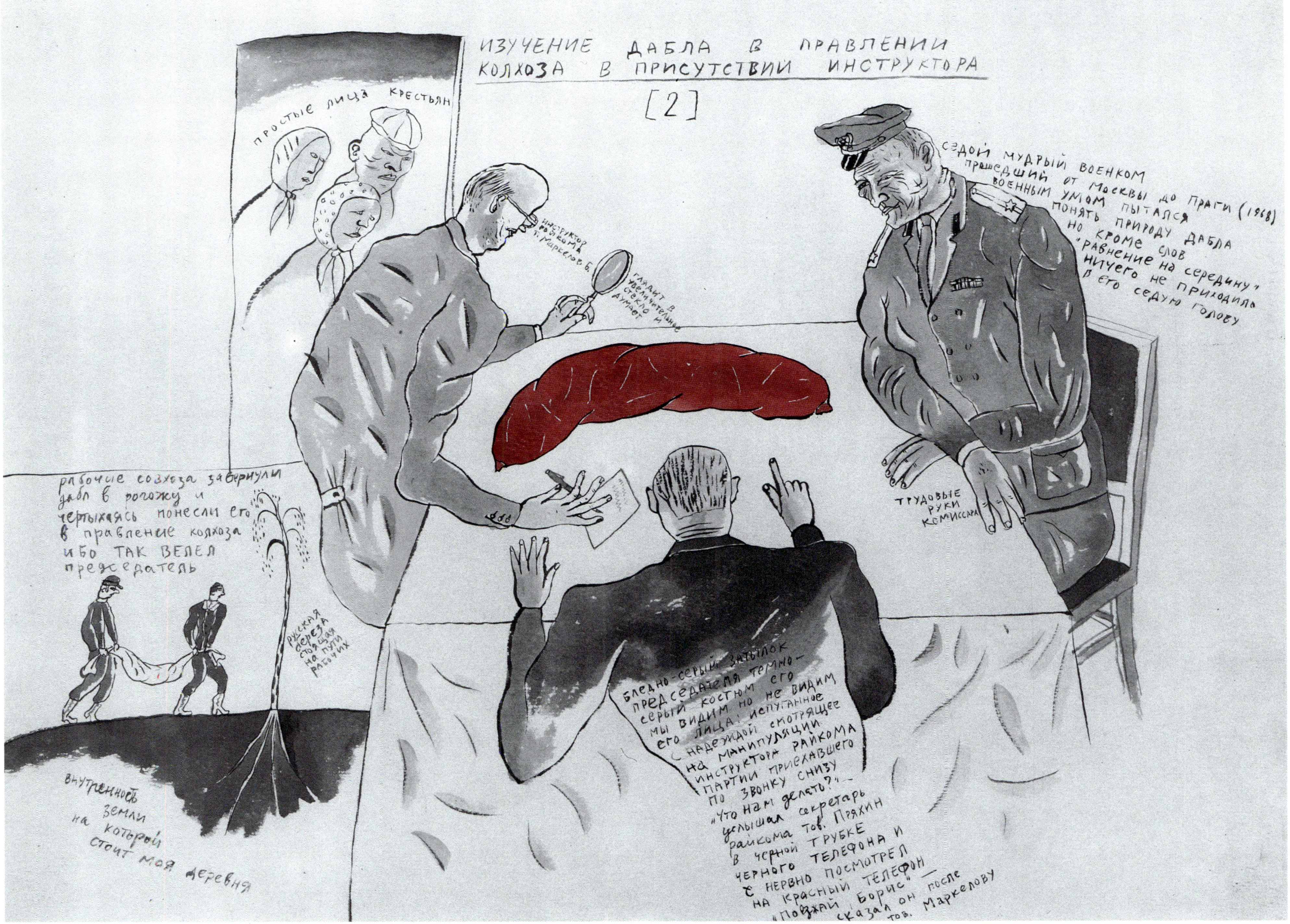

ИЗУЧЕНИЕ ДАБЛА В ПРАВЛЕНИИ КОЛХОЗА В ПРИСУТСТВИИ ИНСТРУКТОРА
[2]
простые лица крестьян
инструктор райкома т. Маркелов Б.
глядит в увеличительное стекло и думает
седой мудрый военком прошедший от Москвы до Праги (1968) военным умом пытался понять природу дабла но кроме слов „равнение на середину" ничего не приходило в его седую голову
трудовые руки комиссара
рабочие совхоза завернули дабл в рогожу и чертыхаясь понесли его в правление колхоза ибо так велел председатель
русская береза стоящая на пути рабочих
внутренность земли на которой стоит моя деревня
бледно-серый затылок председателя темно-серый костюм его мы видим но не видим его лица: испуганное с надеждой смотрящее на манипуляции инструктора райкома партии приехавшего по звонку снизу
„что нам делать?" — услышал секретарь райкома тов. Пряхин в черной трубке черного телефона и с нервно посмотрел на красный телефон
„Поезжай Борис" — сказал он после тов. Маркелову

OUR CHAIRMAN SLEEPS IN HIS OF FICE [3]

When everyone left and the black Volga carried off Markelov and his report for Comrade Pryakhin with his doubts about DABLUS, our Chairman Matvey Ivanovich was somehow drawn to DABLUS. He picked it up and pressed it to his sturdy broad chest as if it was the dearest thing he had. He lay with it on the sofa in his office and went to sleep, his cold pale cheek against its smooth and warm skin

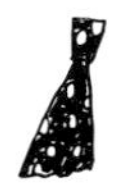

The leader's portrait in a prominent place on the wall — «his kind face with high cheekbones and laughing wrinkles round the eyes»

Who's there? Where am I? What do you want? What's this on the sofa with me?

The charwoman — Aunt Dunya — came to clean the office at 5 : 30, as usual. She opened the door — boss on the sofa, sleeping. «Must have worked all night through...»

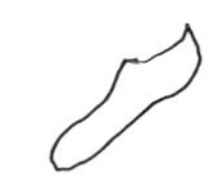

Best wear your rubbers to wash the floor

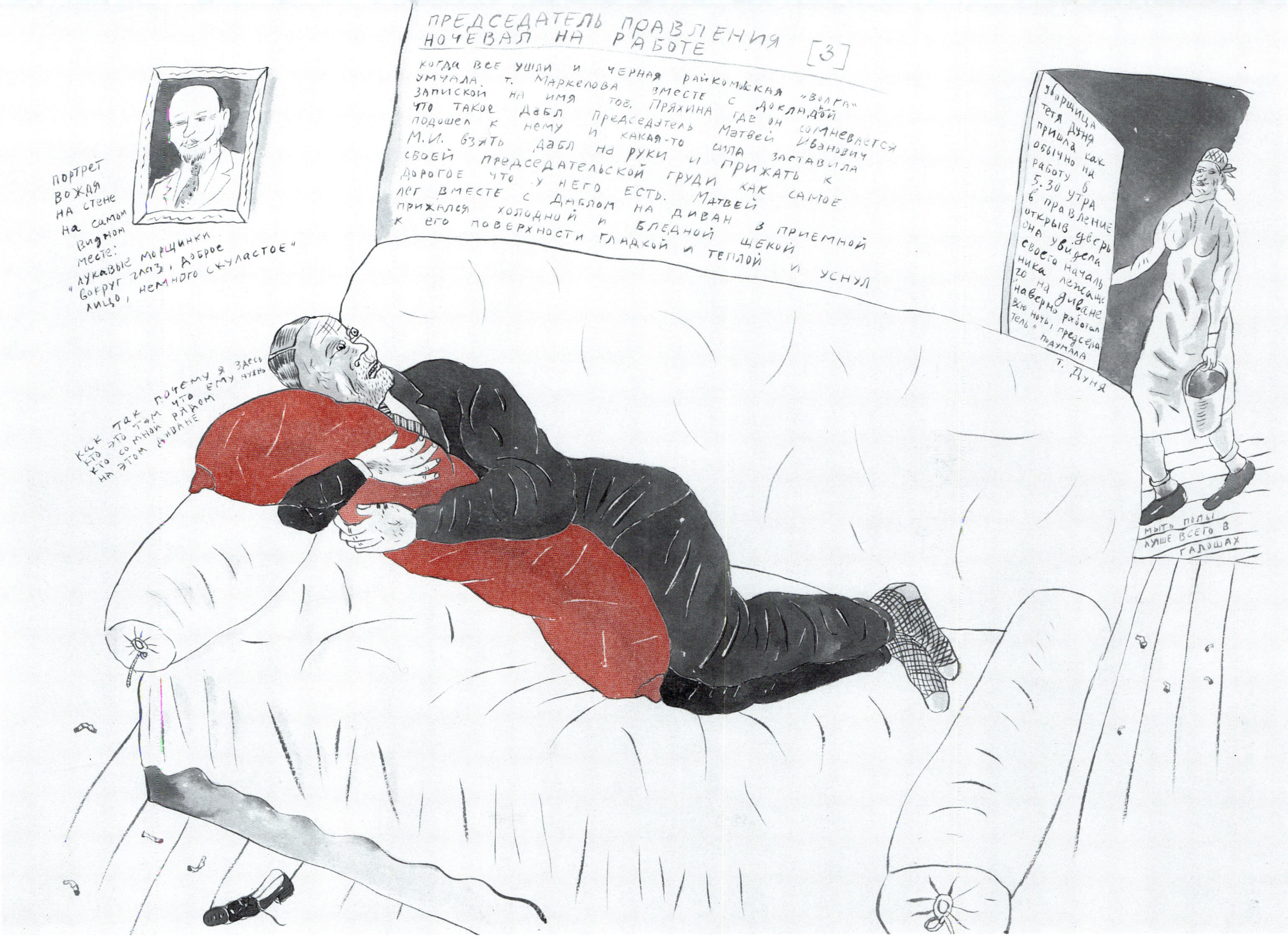

ПРЕДСЕДАТЕЛЬ ПРАВЛЕНИЯ НОЧЕВАЛ НА РАБОТЕ [3]
КОГДА ВСЕ УШЛИ И ЧЕРНАЯ РАЙКОМОВСКАЯ «ВОЛГА» УМЧАЛА Т. МАРКЕЛОВА ВМЕСТЕ С ДОКЛАДОЙ ЗАПИСКОЙ НА ИМЯ ТОВ. ПРЯХИНА ГДЕ ОН СОМНЕВАЕТСЯ ЧТО ТАКОЕ ДАБЛ ПРЕДСЕДАТЕЛЬ МАТВЕЙ ИВАНОВИЧ ПОДОШЕЛ К НЕМУ И КАКАЯ-ТО СИЛА ЗАСТАВИЛА М.И. ВЗЯТЬ ДАБЛ НА РУКИ И ПРИЖАТЬ К СВОЕЙ ПРЕДСЕДАТЕЛЬСКОЙ ГРУДИ КАК САМОЕ ДОРОГОЕ ЧТО У НЕГО ЕСТЬ. МАТВЕЙ ЛЕГ ВМЕСТЕ С ДАБЛОМ НА ДИВАН В ПРИЕМНОЙ ПРИЖАЛСЯ ХОЛОДНОЙ И БЛЕДНОЙ ЩЕКОЙ К ЕГО ПОВЕРХНОСТИ ГЛАДКОЙ И ТЕПЛОЙ И УСНУЛ
портрет вождя на стене на самом видном месте: «лукавые морщинки вокруг глаз, доброе лицо, немного скуластое»
как так почему я здесь кто это там что ему нужно кто со мной рядом на этом диване
уборщица тетя Дуня пришла как обычно на работу в 5.30 утра в правление открыв дверь она увидела своего начальника лежащего на диване «наверно всю ночь работал председатель» подумала т. Дуня
мыть полы лучше всего в галошах

DABLUS IS PUT IN THE BARN [4]

night teeming with stars

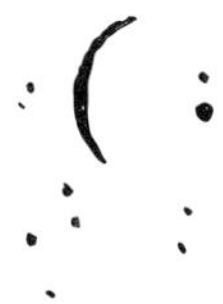

The Chairman ordered to keep DABLUS in the far-off empty barn, suspended to the ceiling with 2 (two) ropes. He felt embarrassed about last night — asked Aunt Dunya to tell no one what she'd seen in the office. He resolved to be firm.

drizzling rain

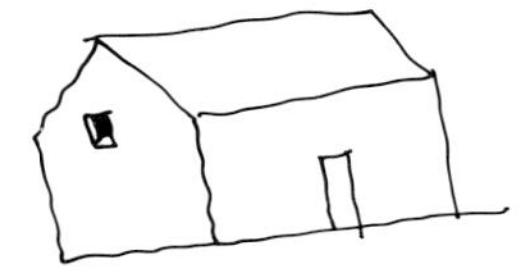

The barn door was left open. Two tramps — no, just two drunks drifted in from the rain. On the hay, in the quiet (how the hay smells and the rain taps quietly on the roof) they opened a botle of cheap port and talked about the rotten life in the village.

local alcoholic, sacked from the meat-packing plant for drinking bouts

MOONLIGHT

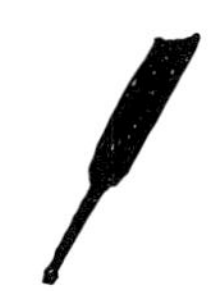

An Afghan veteran — he hasn't been working anywhere for quite a time

When Senya and the Afghan veteran saw DABLUS, they didn't take fright for they were high. They laughed and sang. They were drawn to the thing — they felt hungry. They sucked its Dabloic milk out of it. Secretly, in the night.

my friend's sweatshirt

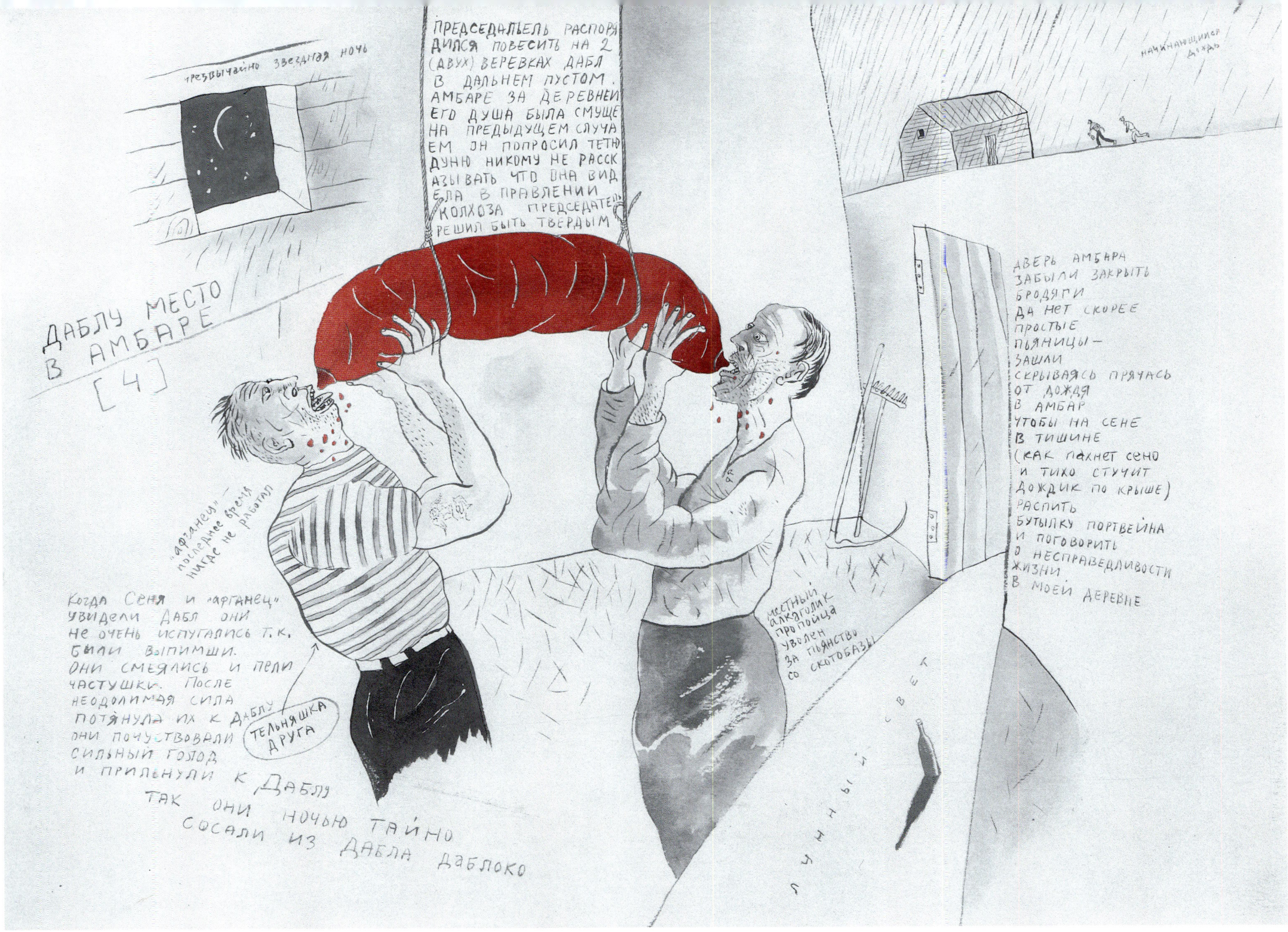

ДАБЛУ МЕСТО
В АМБАРЕ
[4]
чрезвычайно звездная ночь
ПРЕДСЕДАТЕЛЬ РАСПОРЯ
ДИЛСЯ ПОВЕСИТЬ НА 2
(ДВУХ) ВЕРЕВКАХ ДАБЛ
В ДАЛЬНЕМ ПУСТОМ
АМБАРЕ ЗА ДЕРЕВНЕЙ
ЕГО ДУША БЫЛА СМУЩЕ
НА ПРЕДЫДУЩЕМ СЛУЧА
ЕМ ОН ПОПРОСИЛ ТЕТЮ
ДУНЮ НИКОМУ НЕ РАССК
АЗЫВАТЬ ЧТО ОНА ВИД
ЕЛА В ПРАВЛЕНИИ
КОЛХОЗА ПРЕДСЕДАТЕЛЬ
РЕШИЛ БЫТЬ ТВЕРДЫМ
начинающийся дождь
ДВЕРЬ АМБАРА
ЗАБЫЛИ ЗАКРЫТЬ
БРОДЯГИ
ДА НЕТ СКОРЕЕ
ПРОСТЫЕ
ПЬЯНИЦЫ—
ЗАШЛИ
СКРЫВАЯСЬ ПРЯЧАСЬ
ОТ ДОЖДЯ
В АМБАР
ЧТОБЫ НА СЕНЕ
В ТИШИНЕ
(КАК ПАХНЕТ СЕНО
И ТИХО СТУЧИТ
ДОЖДИК ПО КРЫШЕ)
РАСПИТЬ
БУТЫЛКУ ПОРТВЕЙНА
И ПОГОВОРИТЬ
О НЕСПРАВЕДЛИВОСТИ
ЖИЗНИ
В МОЕЙ ДЕРЕВНЕ
«афганец» — последнее время нигде не работал
местный алкоголик пропойца уволен за пьянство со скотобазы
Когда Сеня и «афганец»
увидели Дабл они
не очень испугались т. к.
были выпимши.
Они смеялись и пели
частушки. После
неодолимая сила
потянула их к Даблу
они почуствовали
сильный голод
и прильнули к Даблу
ТЕЛЬНЯШКА ДРУГА
ТАК ОНИ НОЧЬЮ ТАЙНО
СОСАЛИ ИЗ ДАБЛА ДАБЛОКО
ЛУННЫЙ СВЕТ

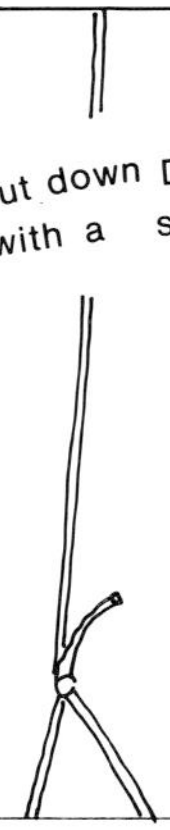

she cut down DABLUS
with a sharp sickle

DABLUS IS RESCUED

The history of [5] DABULUS continued

One night, as the village was sleeping, Granny Yefimovna walked to the barn and cut down DABLUS with a sharp sickle. She took it on her

shoulders and carried it off.

a bath-house in the kitchen garden

«I have a bath-house
in my kitchen garden —
it can live there.

The bath-house
goblin will be
glad to have
company».

THE DABLUS CONSTELLATION

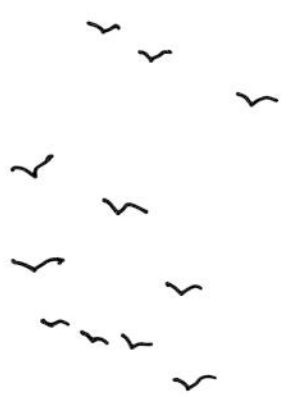

crows
flying
up like a

like black ashes

the near wood

THE FENCE

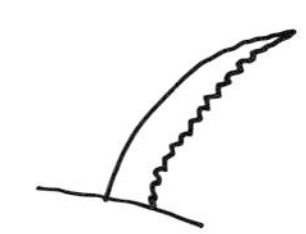

A CROP OF SICKLES

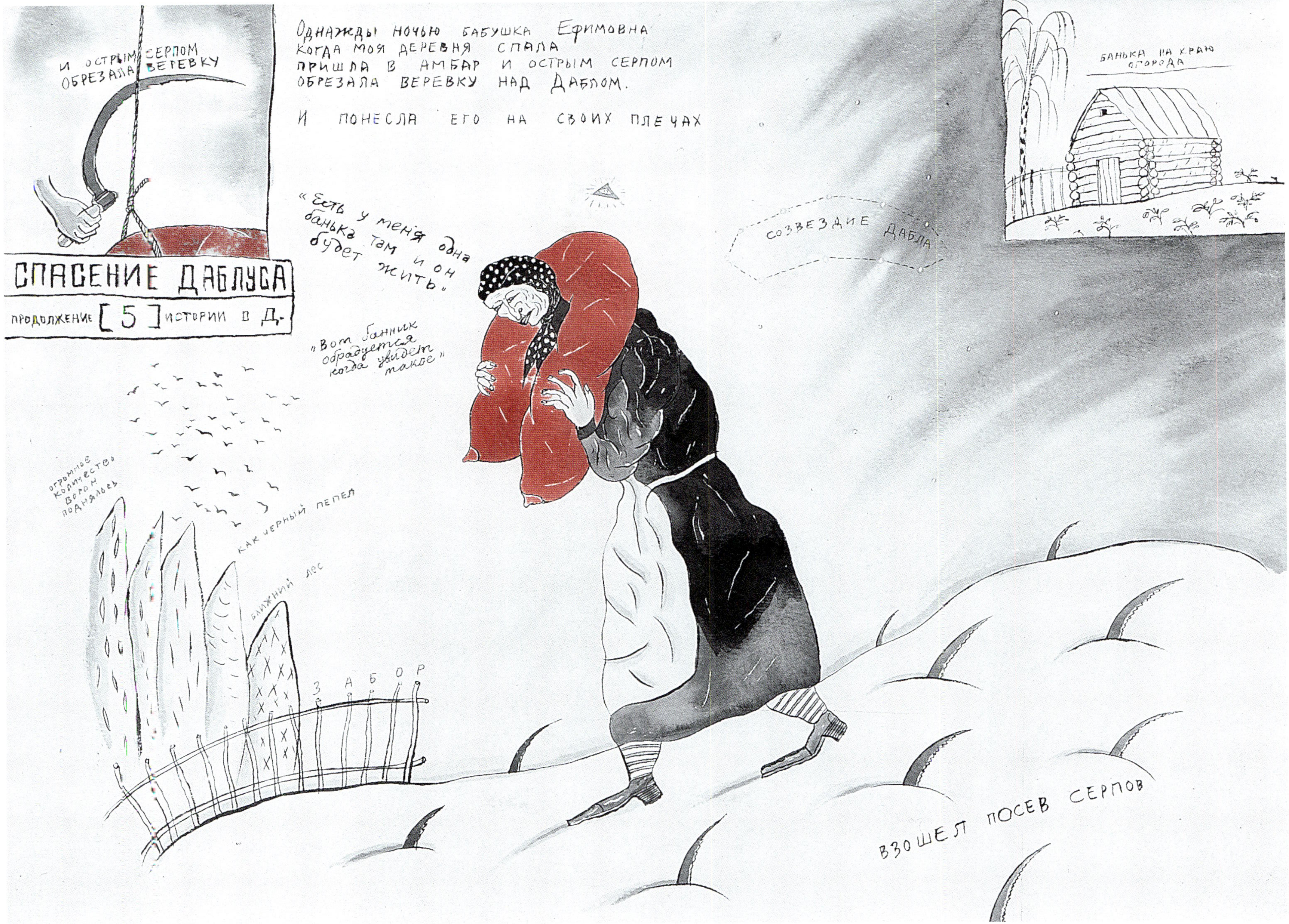
И острым серпом обрезала веревку
СПАСЕНИЕ ДАБЛУСА
продолжение [5] истории о Д.
Однажды ночью бабушка Ефимовна
когда моя деревня спала
пришла в амбар и острым серпом
обрезала веревку над Даблом.
И понесла его на своих плечах
«Есть у меня одна банька там и он будет жить»
«Вот банник обрадуется когда увидет такое»
созвездие Дабла
банька на краю огорода
огромное количество ворон поднялось
как черный пепел
ближний лес
забор
взошел посев серпов

GIRLS PLAY WITH DABLUS [6]

Getting on with the story I must tell you about the bath-house where Granny Yefimovna took DABLUS. She put a soft mattress under its side — «There, love, take a rest», and called some village lasses to take a look.

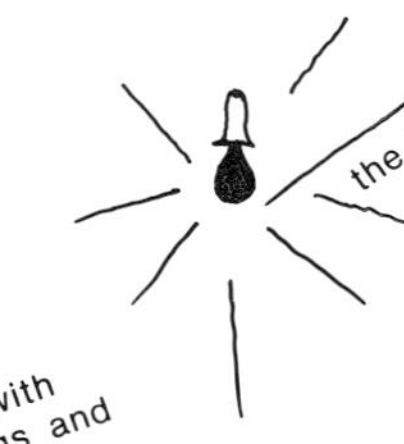

the lamp of Sergeyevich

Brother: has nothing to say. He's a half-wit. «retarded» says Mother.

Father asks: what shell we do about our girls?

Mother: what can we do? let them play around while they're young and still in good health.

girls racing to the bath-house

they decorate it with ribbons and sprigs and other pretty things

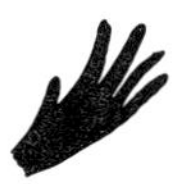

My village folk — families with young daughters — were outraged. «That Dablus, you know, in the bath-house at the far end... I looked in th-rough the window — the wenches were playing with it — that mute legless thing — that monster... Wh-at's the use of that DABLUS? Doing no work, just lying there — the fat swine.», that's what they said. And others said, «Do way with it — shoot it at dawn — let it die to the nightingale's song, to the toad's cr-oak». Still others, «Naked in the ba-thhouse — and that thing with them!»

(That's libel, a dirty slur on our innocent daughters)

she took a step

what fun for the little ones...

Of an evening the village lasses flock to the bath-house to play with DABLUS. With not a word to their parents, taking no leave, they play ...h DABLUS each night — all ...ight.

Who is hiding?

Who is it in the cellar?

Who?

carrots scattered around

RABBITS IN THE BOX

rabbits sitting in the box — biding the time — dull — creaking floor-boards — who's there? who goes?

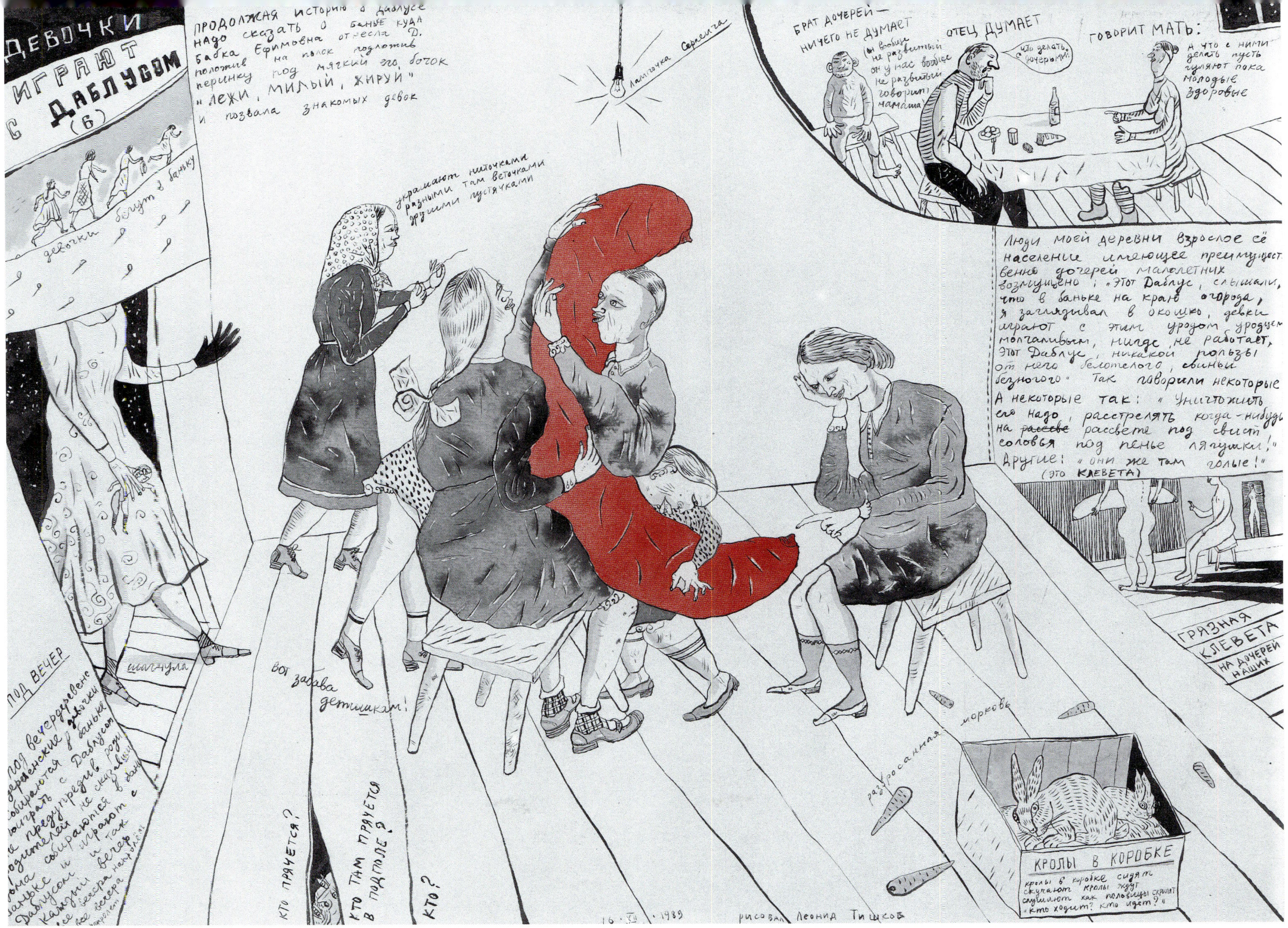

ДЕВОЧКИ ИГРАЮТ С ДАБЛУСОМ (6)
Продолжая историю о Даблусе надо сказать о баньке куда бабка Ефимовна отнесла Д. положив на полок подложив перинку под мягкий его бочок «лежи, милый, жируй» и позвала знакомых девок
лампочка Серёгина
девочки бегут в баньку
украшают ниточками разными там веточками другими пустячками
вот забава детишкам!
шагнула
ПОД ВЕЧЕР
кто прячется?
кто там прячется в подполе?
кто?
БРАТ ДОЧЕРЕЙ — НИЧЕГО НЕ ДУМАЕТ
(он вообще не развитый он у нас вообще не развитый говорит мамаша)
ОТЕЦ ДУМАЕТ
что делать, дочерями?
ГОВОРИТ МАТЬ:
а что с ними делать пусть гуляют пока молодые здоровые
Люди моей деревни взрослое её население имеющее преимущественно дочерей малолетних возмущено: «Этот Даблус, слышали, что в баньке на краю огорода, я заглядывал в окошко, девки играют с этим уродом уродцем молчаливым, нигде не работает, этот Даблус, никакой пользы от него белотелого, свиньи безногого». Так говорили некоторые
А некоторые так: «Уничтожить его надо, расстрелять когда-нибудь на рассвете под свист соловья под пение лягушки!»
Другие: «они же там голые!»
(это КЛЕВЕТА)
ГРЯЗНАЯ КЛЕВЕТА НА ДОЧЕРЕЙ НАШИХ
разбросанная морковь
КРОЛЫ В КОРОБКЕ
кролы в коробке сидят скучают кролы ждут слушают как половицы скрипят «кто ходит? кто идет?»
16 · … · 1989
рисовал Леонид Тишков

CONTINUED

UP IN ARMS — PITCHFORKS AND OARS [7]

Assault on the notorious bath-house: waving their hap-hazard weapons, shouting slogans to keep up the morale: death to Masons! (fasces unfastened in the hands of the man on the flang) No more wasting our national wealth! — and other newspaper stuff. Basta! How long can we suffer Dablus on our land! Out with the creature — out of our village!

dressed up in a shirt with a tie — what fun!

EARNEST AND ANGRY FACES OF OUR FATHERS.

faces

just wrathful

clear eyes

strong arms best

intentions of our fathers

Kill the vermin!

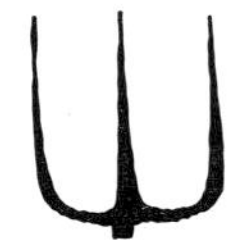

the ring-leader

Bath on the edge of the garden

in front

Ancient already— but still wrathful

pointing finger

blood will flow

We'll hack that DABLUS into mince-meat!

Theyre corrupting our daughters!

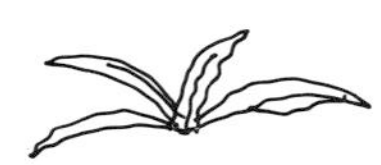

SEEKING JUSTICE

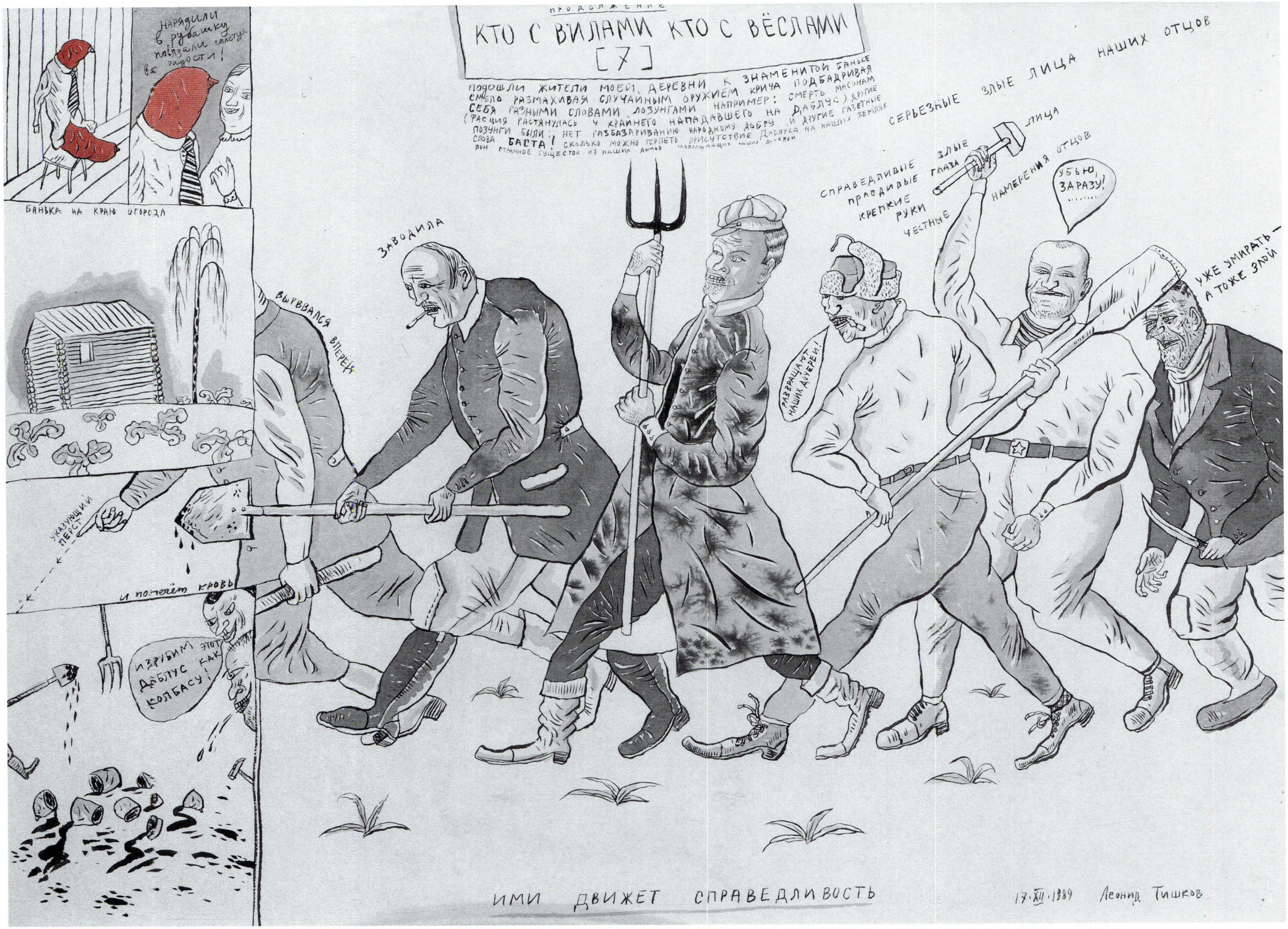
ПРОДОЛЖЕНИЕ
КТО С ВИЛАМИ КТО С ВЁСЛАМИ
[7]
ПОДОШЛИ ЖИТЕЛИ МОЕЙ ДЕРЕВНИ К ЗНАМЕНИТОЙ БАНЬКЕ
СМЕЛО РАЗМАХИВАЯ СЛУЧАЙНЫМ ОРУЖИЕМ КРИЧА ПОДБАДРИВАЯ
СЕБЯ РАЗНЫМИ СЛОВАМИ, ЛОЗУНГАМИ НАПРИМЕР: СМЕРТЬ МАСОНАМ
(ФАСЦИЯ РАСТЯНУЛАСЬ У КРАЙНЕГО НАПАДАВШЕГО НА ДАБЛУС) ДРУГИЕ
ЛОЗУНГИ БЫЛИ: НЕТ РАЗБАЗАРИВАНИЮ НАРОДНОМУ ДОБРУ И ДРУГИЕ ГАЗЕТНЫЕ
СЛОВА БАСТА! СКОЛЬКО МОЖНО ТЕРПЕТЬ ПРИСУТСТВИЕ ДАБЛУСА НА НАШИХ ЗЕМЛЯХ
ВОН СТРАННОЕ СУЩЕСТВО ИЗ НАШИХ ДОМОВ РАЗВРАЩАЮЩИХ НАШИХ ДОЧЕРЕЙ
НАРЯДИЛИ В РУБАШКУ ПОВЯЗАЛИ ГАЛСТУК ВЕ ГАДОСТИ!
БАНЬКА НА КРАЮ ОГОРОДА
УКАЗУЮЩИЙ ПЕРСТ
И ПОТЕЧЁТ КРОВЬ
ИЗРУБИМ ЭТОГО ДАБЛУС КАК КОЛБАСУ!
ВЫРВВАЛСЯ ВПЕРЕД
ЗАВОДИЛА
РАЗВРАЩАЮТ НАШИХ ДОЧЕРЕЙ!
СПРАВЕДЛИВЫЕ ЗЛЫЕ
ПРАВДИВЫЕ ГЛАЗА
КРЕПКИЕ РУКИ
ЧЕСТНЫЕ НАМЕРЕНИЯ ОТЦОВ
СЕРЬЕЗНЫЕ ЗЛЫЕ ЛИЦА НАШИХ ОТЦОВ
ЛИЦА
УБЬЮ, ЗАРАЗУ! ......
УЖЕ УМИРАТЬ — А ТОЖЕ ЗАДИ
ИМИ ДВИЖЕТ СПРАВЕДЛИВОСТЬ
17·XII·1989 Леонид Тишков

KILL THE VERMIN [8]

The book about my village folk continued — about my native place where DABLUS was once found.

HACK IT! PIERCE IT!

The men forced the lock, and burst in swearing viciously, pushing the lasses aside. They were waving their pitchforks and oars, hammers and knives — death to the fascist! Shouting they pressed on, disregarding the girls' tears. Nikodimov raised his sharp spade... his spade over the victim... his spade. He had used it to plant trees round the school.

But that's a diffe
rent story — quite
quite another story
— another story
about other
trees. About
no trees at all.

An old snapshot:
Nikodimov as a
young sailor,
— taken by the
boatswain.

Counting the
seagulls...

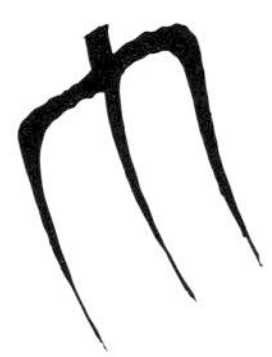

Stop, Daddy,
stop!

MOTHERS
CRYING
FOR THEIR
G
I
R
L
S

N. Nikodimova

M. Nikodimova,

The Box Trampled

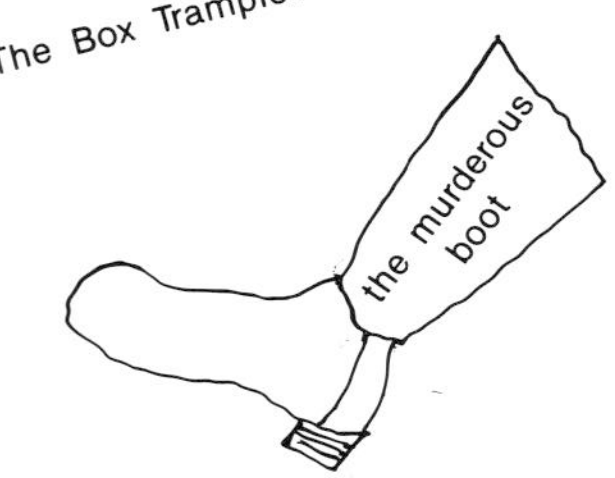

the rabbits scampering
away

Who's in
the cellar?
Who is it
hiding so
...ep?

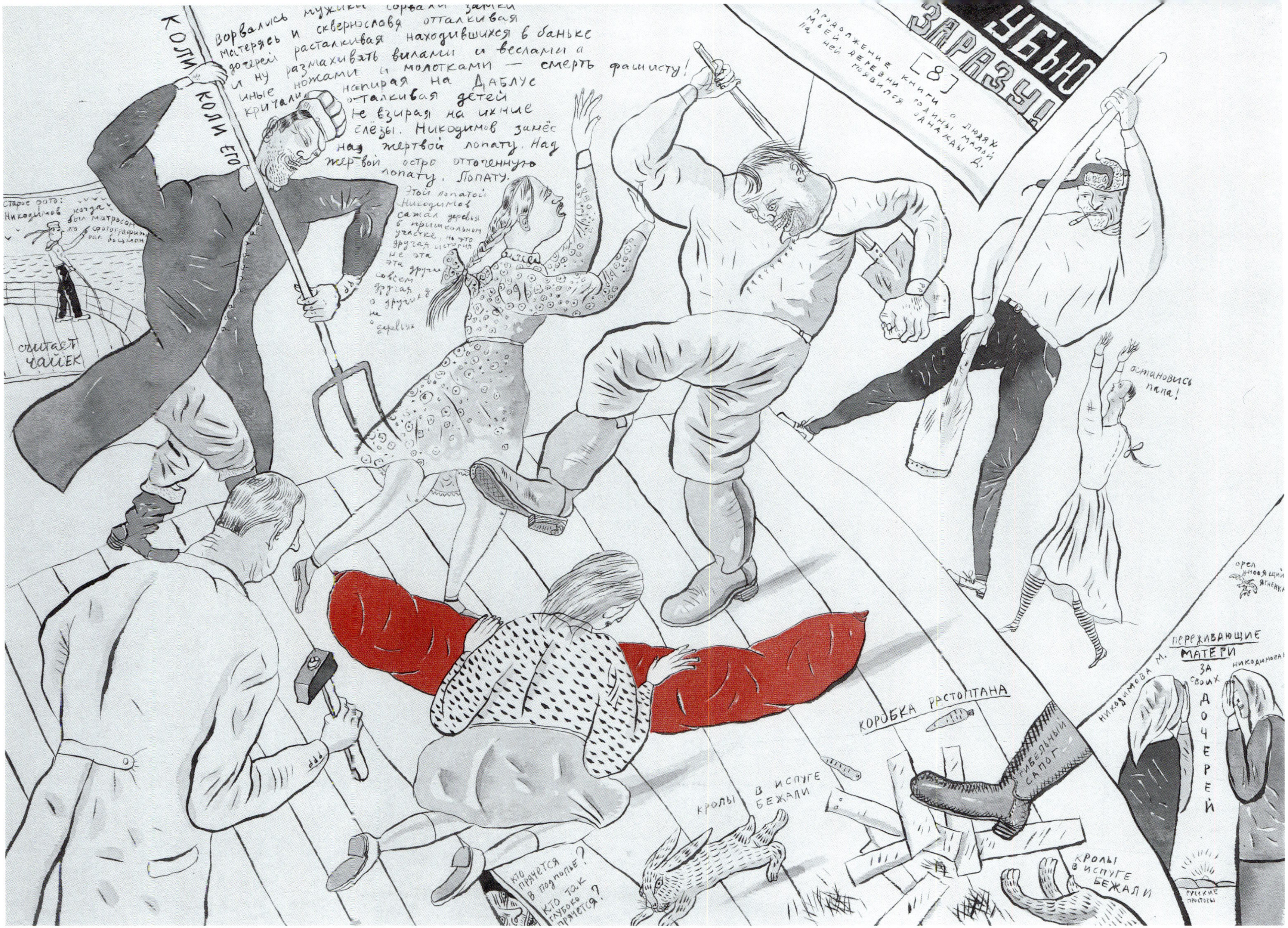

КОЛИ КОЛИ ЕГО
Ворвались мужики сорвали замки матерясь и сквернословя отталкивая дочерей расталкивая находившихся в баньке и ну размахивать вилами и веслами а иные ножами и молотками — смерть фашисту!
кричали напирая на Даблус отталкивая детей не взирая на ихние слёзы. Никодимов занёс над жертвой лопату. Над жертвой остро отточенную лопату. Лопату.
Этой лопатой Никодимов сажал деревья в пришкольном участке, но это другая история не эта
считает чаек
УБЬЮ ЗАРАЗУ!
[8]
продолжение книги о людях моей деревни родины малой на ней появился Даблус Д.
остановись папа!
коробка растоптана
гибельный сапог
кролы в испуге бежали
кто прячется в подполье? кто так глубоко прячется?
переживающие матери за своих дочерей
Никодимова М.
Никодимова

CONTINUED — NEXT PART

The desperate assault met a sudden rebuff — DABLUS strained and somewhat blew out, wriggled away from the beating weapons — spades, oars and knives — and burst open in several spots. The offensive halted.

DABLOIDES SPRING UP

[9]

The girls held on
to each other —

«Call Granny!
Yefimovna!
Yefimovna!»

No use — she is dead.
Dead and buried. In the
graveyard over
the hill.

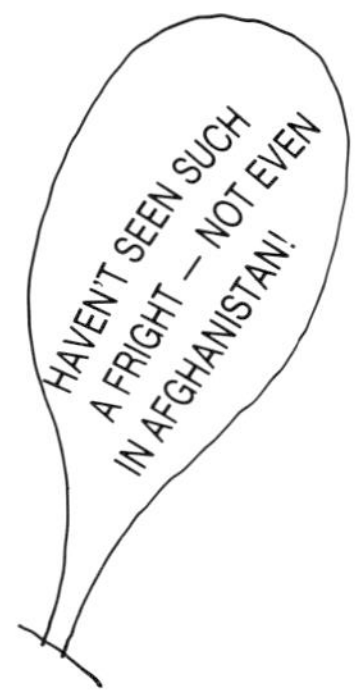

The constellation of DABLUS has flared up

KONDRATIEV IS FRIGHTENED

NIKODIMOV IS FRIGHTENED

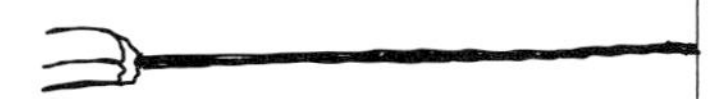

Horror,

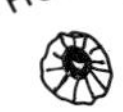

THE YOUNG AGRONOMIST
WRITES TO HIS MOTHER

Our young farming expert's
letter to his Mum in the city:
«Dear Mother, we have
found a DABLUS in our
village, no one knows what
it is or where it comes from
not even our Chairman.

I lodge with the Nikiforofs,
they' re nice people.

Can you send
...e 3 kgs of
...ugar?

My salary
is 110 roubles.

UNCLE IS FIGHTENED.

IN FRIGHT

ALSO FLEEING

PETROV IS FRIGHTENED

HABULAYEV IS FRIGHTENED.

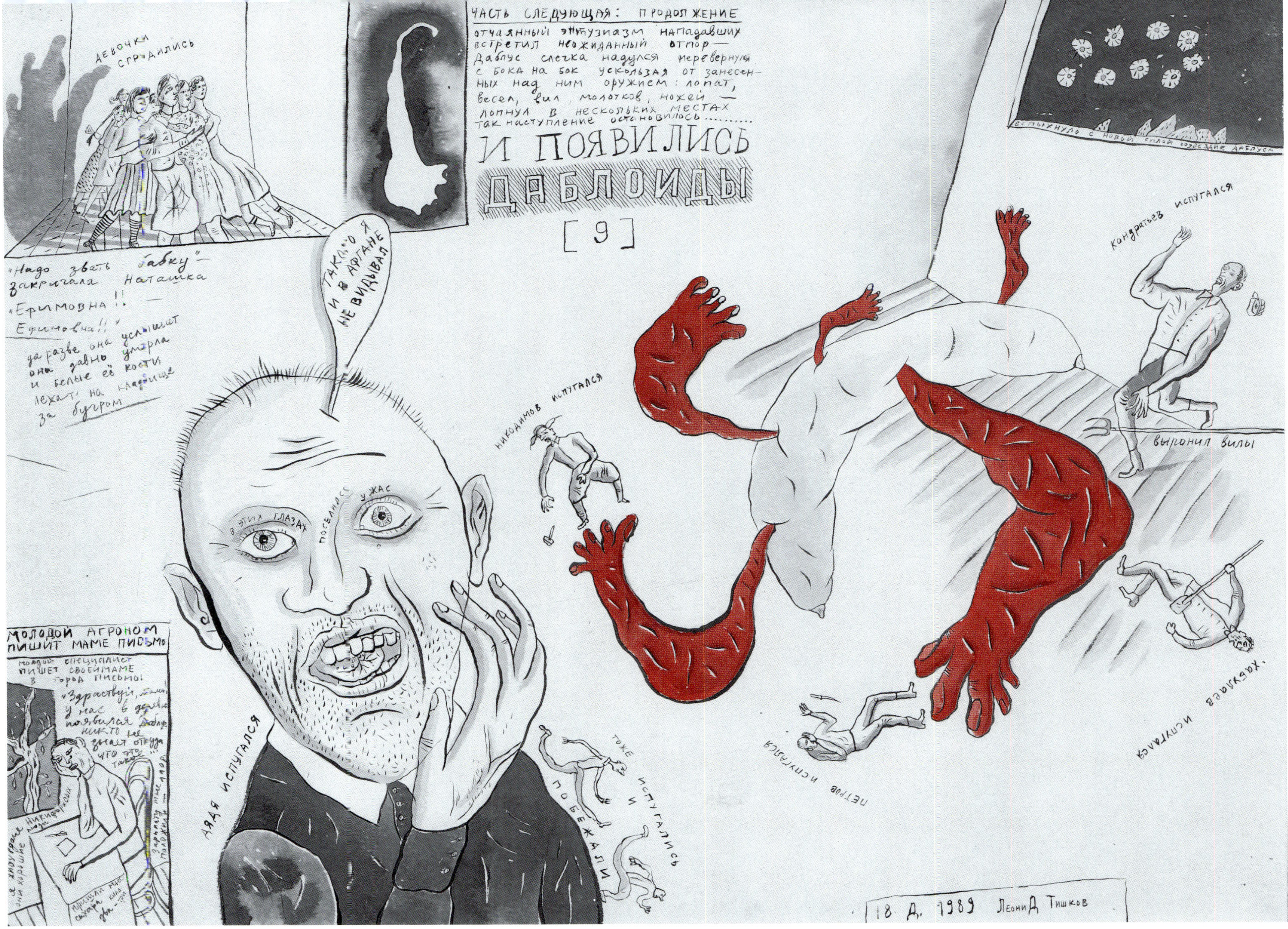
Девочки сгрудились
«Надо звать бабку» — закричала Наташка
«Ефимовна!! — Ефимовна!!»
да разве она услышит она давно умерла и белые её кости лежат на кладбище за бугром
Такого я и в Афгане не видывал
ЧАСТЬ СЛЕДУЮЩАЯ: ПРОДОЛЖЕНИЕ
отчаянный энтузиазм нападавших встретил неожиданный отпор — Даблус слегка надулся перевернулся с бока на бок ускользая от занесенных над ним оружием: лопат, весел, вил, молотков, ножей — лопнул в нескольких местах так наступление остановилось.........
И ПОЯВИЛИСЬ ДАБЛОИДЫ
[9]
в этих глазах поселился ужас
Никодимов испугался
Кондратьев испугался
выронил вилы
Хабулаев испугался
Петров испугался
тоже испугались и побежали
Дядя испугался
МОЛОДОЙ АГРОНОМ ПИШИТ МАМЕ ПИСЬМО
молодой специалист пишет своей маме в город письмо:
«Здраствуй, мама! у нас в деревне появился даблус никто не знает откуда что это такое»
18 Д. 1989 ЛеониД Тишков

CONFRONTATION

continued [10] the story

One two three — from the bath-house DABLOIDES spread over the village. There they are — in the field, swaying back and forth. Apparently harmless. The male population is out to meet them. The women are hiding their children. Hiding and tidying, spinning and combing, coming — who's coming? Dabloides are coming.

shaking his fist: asking for more? ...

Where are the bosses from the regional Party Committee?

fighting a *dabloid.*

Our village strong man Pyotr Silayev.

The girls are watching dabloids being born.

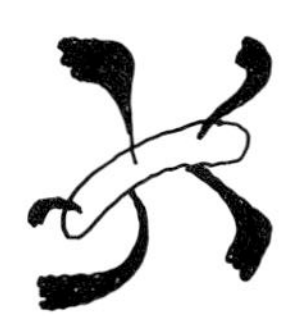

Dabloids spreading out from the bath-house.

the dear Russian birch-tree...

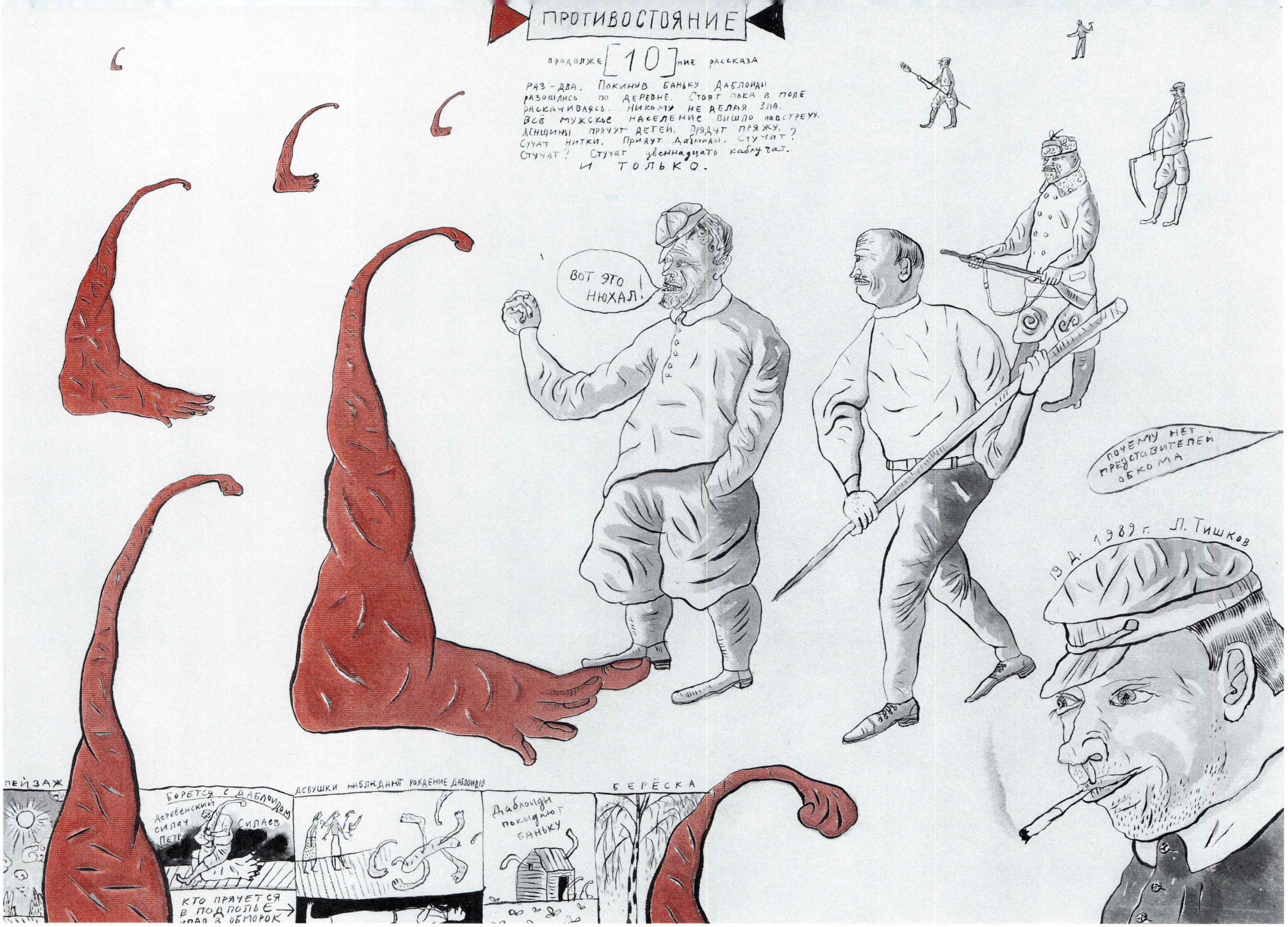
ПРОТИВОСТОЯНИЕ
продолже[10]ние рассказа
РАЗ-ДВА. Покинув баньку Даблоиды разошлись по деревне. Стоят пока в поле раскачиваясь. Никому не делая зла. Всё мужское население вышло навстречу. Женщины прячут детей. Прядут пряжу. Сучат нитки. Прядут Даблоиды. Стучат? Стучат? Стучат двенадцать каблучат.
И ТОЛЬКО.
ВОТ ЭТО НЮХАЛ!
ПОЧЕМУ НЕТ ПРЕДСТАВИТЕЛЕЙ ОБКОМА
19 Д. 1989 г. Л. Тишков
ПЕЙЗАЖ
БОРЕТСЯ С ДАБЛОИДОМ
Деревенский силач Петр Силаев
ДЕВУШКИ НАБЛЮДАЮТ РОЖДЕНИЕ ДАБЛОИДОВ
КТО ПРЯЧЕТСЯ В ПОДПОЛЬЕ →
Даблоиды покидают баньку
БЕРЁСКА

As Always In Extreme Situations The Army Came In To Help [11]

CONTINUED

BIRCH-TREES

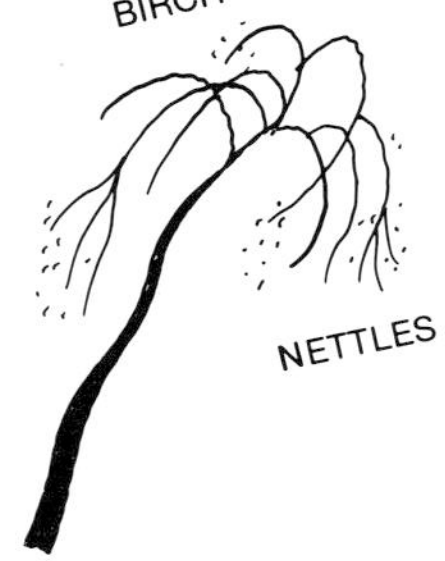

NETTLES

COW-SHEDS.

THIS ONE HIDES IN A DITCH.

SEN. SERG. BABENKO

CONCERTRATION AND PERSEVERENCE IN ARMY TRAINING.

GETTING DABLOIDES FROM THE REAR.

THE MARINE'S DARING MANEEUVRE.

MODEST PETROVICH MUSSORGSKY

IGOR PETROVICH STRAVINSKY

MARINE GUARD SERGEANT I. BABENKO

MIGHTY OAK

HE'S GUILTY — LOOKS LIKE A DABLOID.

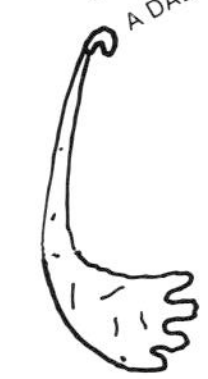

MISTAKES BREED DABLOIDS.

ZIGANSHIN

INVALID M.

BARRACKS.

BURDOCKS AND THISTLES.

THIS ONE WANTS TO HIDE IN A BOX.

JUNIOR SERGEANT M. Mukbelshoyev.

THIS IS MY OFFICERS OVERSIGHT: HE HAS MASTERED THE SKILLS, BUT HAS NO SUBORDINATION — SIGNED SGT M. Mukbelshoyev.

WELCOME

TAKE THIS, YOU BEAST!

A.T. TVARDOVSKY

MARSHAL SOKOLOVSKY

This one has covered himself with a sheet.

ROWAN-TREE

BLUEBELLS

VARIOUS STRAINS OF dabloides

THE CLUB

Polar EXPLORER KRENKEL

COSMONAUT ANDRIAN NIKOLAYEV

INTENTIONS

AND RESULTS

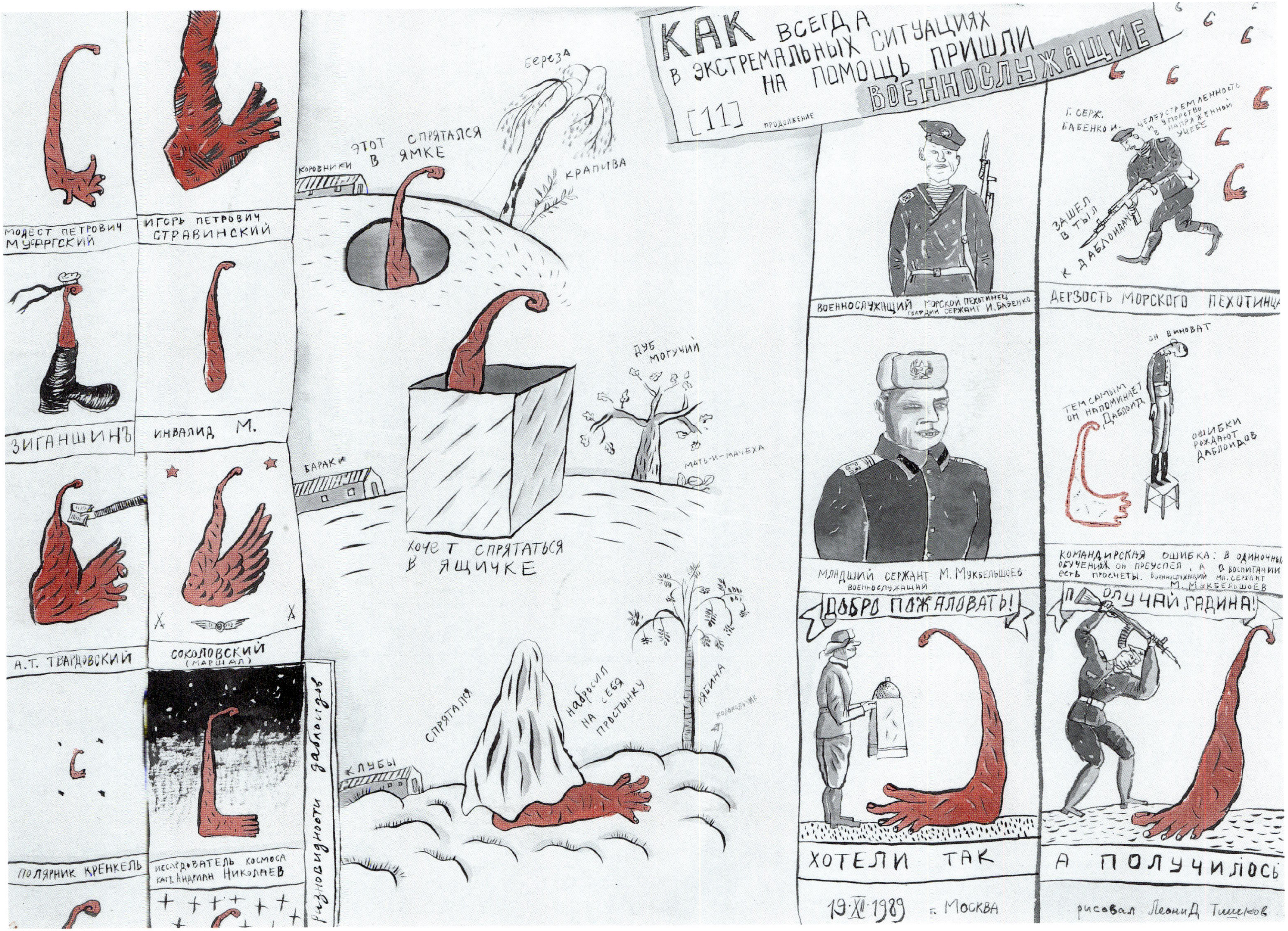

КАК ВСЕГДА В ЭКСТРЕМАЛЬНЫХ СИТУАЦИЯХ НА ПОМОЩЬ ПРИШЛИ ВОЕННОСЛУЖАЩИЕ
[11] продолжение
ВОЕННОСЛУЖАЩИЙ МОРСКОЙ ПЕХОТИНЕЦ ГВАРДИИ СЕРЖАНТ И. БАБЕНКО
Г. СЕРЖ. БАБЕНКО И. ЦЕЛЕУСТРЕМЛЕННОСТЬ И УПОРСТВО В НАПРЯЖЕННОЙ УЧЕБЕ
ЗАШЕЛ В ТЫЛ К ДАБЛОИДАМ
ДЕРЗОСТЬ МОРСКОГО ПЕХОТИНЦА
МЛАДШИЙ СЕРЖАНТ М. МУКБЕЛЬШОЕВ ВОЕННОСЛУЖАЩИЙ
ОН ВИНОВАТ
ТЕМ САМЫМ ОН НАПОМИНАЕТ ДАБЛОИД
ОШИБКИ РОЖДАЮТ ДАБЛОИДОВ
КОМАНДИРСКАЯ ОШИБКА: В ОДИНОЧНЫХ ОБУЧЕНИЯХ ОН ПРЕУСПЕЛ, А В ВОСПИТАНИИ ЕСТЬ ПРОСЧЕТЫ. ВОЕННОСЛУЖАЩИЙ МЛ. СЕРЖАНТ М. МУКБЕЛЬШОЕВ
ДОБРО ПОЖАЛОВАТЬ!
ПОЛУЧАЙ, ГАДИНА!
ХОТЕЛИ ТАК
А ПОЛУЧИЛОСЬ
19·XII·1989 г. МОСКВА
рисовал Леонид Тишков
МОДЕСТ ПЕТРОВИЧ МУСОРГСКИЙ
ИГОРЬ ПЕТРОВИЧ СТРАВИНСКИЙ
ЗИГАНШИНЪ
ИНВАЛИД М.
А.Т. ТВАРДОВСКИЙ
СОКОЛОВСКИЙ (МАРШАЛ)
ПОЛЯРНИК КРЕНКЕЛЬ
ИССЛЕДОВАТЕЛЬ КОСМОСА КАП. АНДРИАН НИКОЛАЕВ
РАЗНОВИДНОСТИ ДАБЛОИДОВ
ЭТОТ СПРЯТАЛСЯ В ЯМКЕ
КОРОВНИКИ
БЕРЕЗА
КРАПИВА
ХОЧЕТ СПРЯТАТЬСЯ В ЯЩИЧКЕ
БАРАКИ
ДУБ МОГУЧИЙ
МАТЬ-И-МАЧЕХА
СПРЯТАЛСЯ
НАБРОСИЛ НА СЕБЯ ПРОСТЫНКУ
РЯБИНА
КОЛОКОЛЬЧИК
КЛУБЫ

Guerilla tactics.

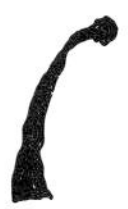

Air cover.

A BOY-SCOUT IS RESCUING HIS DABLOID FRIEND.

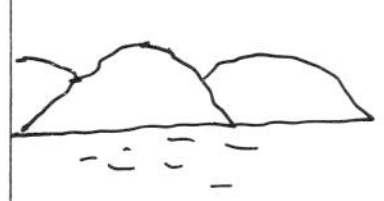

THIS WILL GO DOWN IN HISTORY

[12]

SERGEANT KRAVTSOV'S EXPLOIT.

He fired on from the cover of bushes to his last bullet. Dabloids were near, they surounded the Sergeant, and stood around him silently. Then Kravtsov got out a cluster of antitank grenades, shouted «Come on, you bastards!» and pulled the pin.

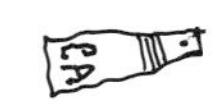

Submachine-gun has stalled.

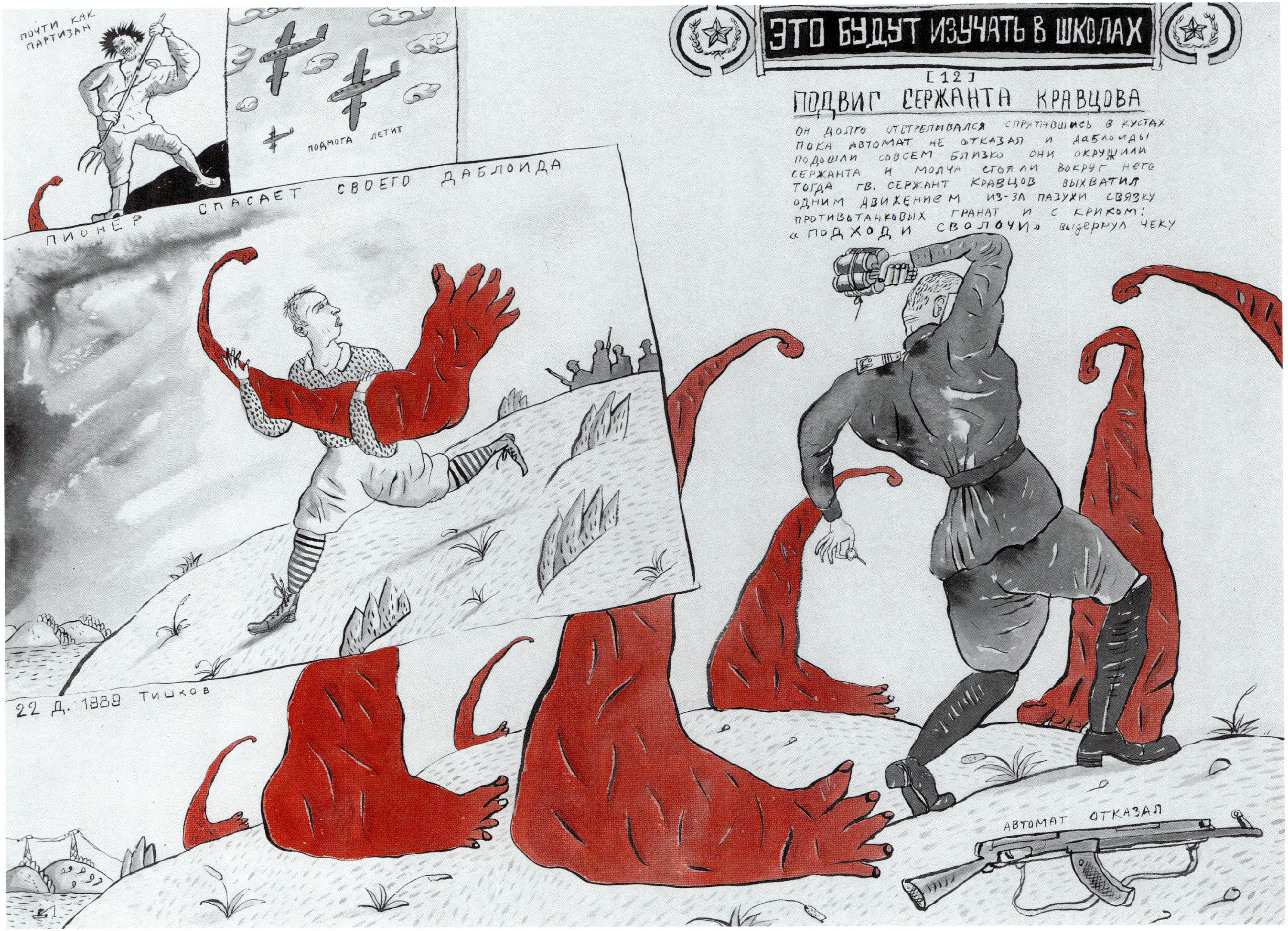
ЭТО БУДУТ ИЗУЧАТЬ В ШКОЛАХ
[12]
ПОДВИГ СЕРЖАНТА КРАВЦОВА
ОН ДОЛГО ОТСТРЕЛИВАЛСЯ СПРЯТАВШИСЬ В КУСТАХ ПОКА АВТОМАТ НЕ ОТКАЗАЛ И ДАБЛОИДЫ ПОДОШЛИ СОВСЕМ БЛИЗКО ОНИ ОКРУЖИЛИ СЕРЖАНТА И МОЛЧА СТОЯЛИ ВОКРУГ НЕГО ТОГДА ГВ. СЕРЖАНТ КРАВЦОВ ВЫХВАТИЛ ОДНИМ ДВИЖЕНИЕМ ИЗ-ЗА ПАЗУХИ СВЯЗКУ ПРОТИВОТАНКОВЫХ ГРАНАТ И С КРИКОМ: «ПОДХОДИ СВОЛОЧИ» ВЫДЕРНУЛ ЧЕКУ
ПОЧТИ КАК ПАРТИЗАН
ПОДМОГА ЛЕТИТ
ПИОНЕР СПАСАЕТ СВОЕГО ДАБЛОИДА
22 Д. 1989 ТИШКОВ
АВТОМАТ ОТКАЗАЛ

THE FORCE OF ARMS IS OF NO AVAIL

The more they battled, the more they fired, the more they attacked, the more DABLOIDES there were around.

The General Staff meeting.

THE MAP
OF THE FRONT
IS SPREAD
ON THE COLONEL'S TABLE

CONTINUED
13
SEE FIG. 12

MY VILLAGE FOLK
cont-d

Zia River

villa ge

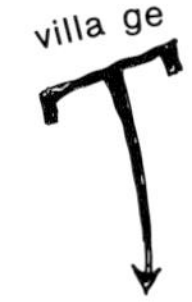

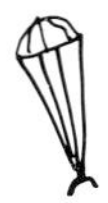

AN AIR-DROP ON
THE FOREST CLEARING

THEY FELL IN BATTLE DOING DUTY TO MOTHERLAND

COMMUNIST

Warrant officer N. Kapanin. Sergeant R. Ablatipov. Private K. Khoreshko.

They died with honour. Exemplary courage. Gallant soldiers.

WE OWE EVERYTHING TO OUR MOTHERLAND

The local women are saving their babies from stray shells and from dabloids.

Khoreshko's
chute
has failed.

Holding on
to his gun.

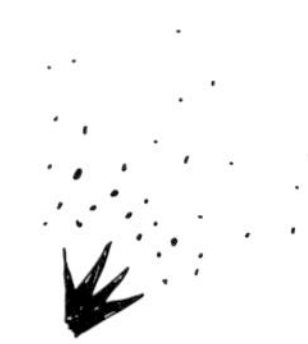

Safe landing
by Private
B. Mirkasimov.

OUR LONG-SUFFER-
ING RUSSIA

CREAKING ARTIFICIAL LIMBS

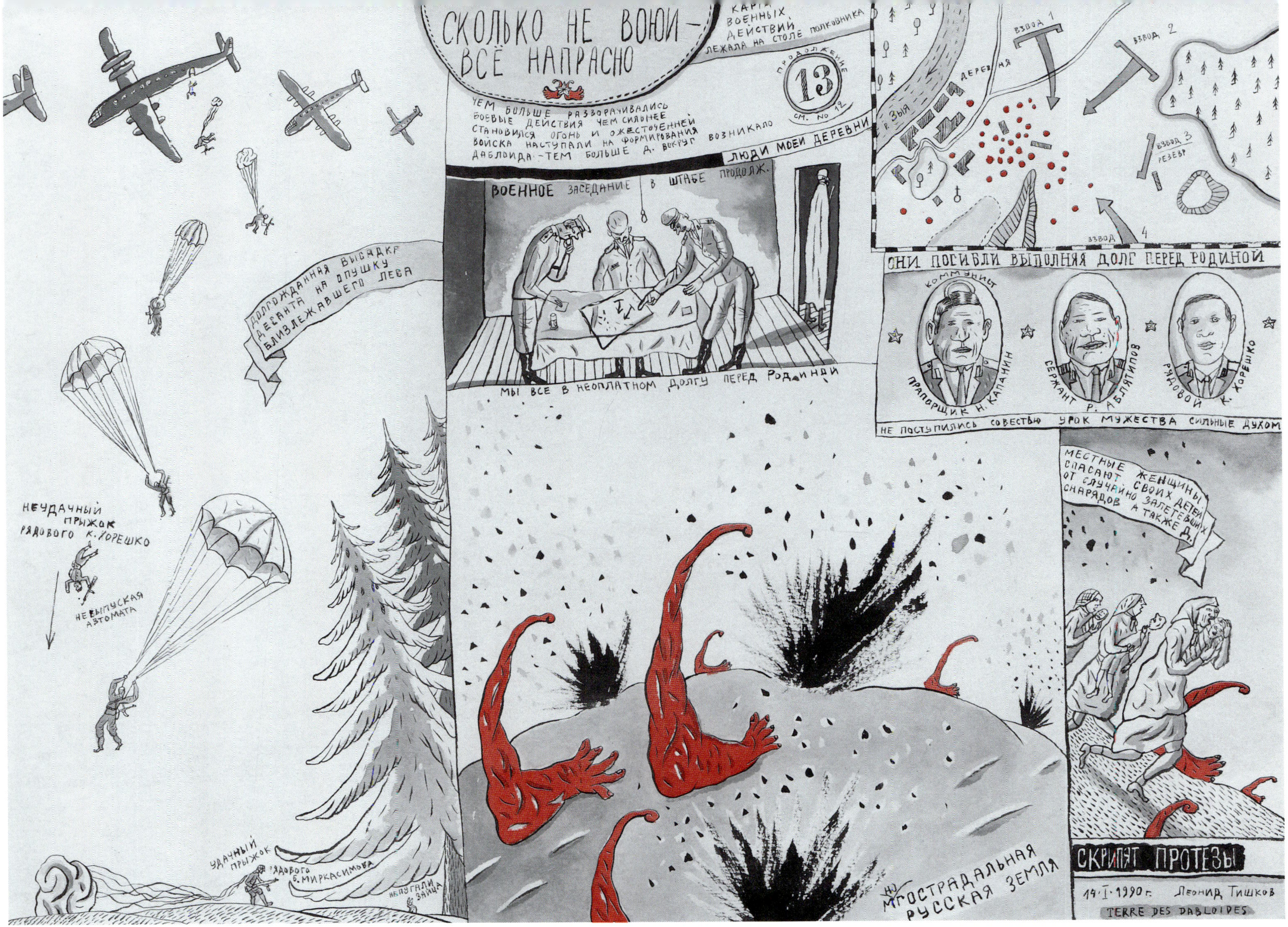
СКОЛЬКО НЕ ВОЮЙ — ВСЁ НАПРАСНО
ЧЕМ БОЛЬШЕ РАЗВОРАЧИВАЛИСЬ БОЕВЫЕ ДЕЙСТВИЯ ЧЕМ СИЛЬНЕЕ СТАНОВИЛСЯ ОГОНЬ И ОЖЕСТОЧЕННЕЙ ВОЙСКА НАСТУПАЛИ НА ФОРМИРОВАНИЯ ДАБЛОИДА — ТЕМ БОЛЬШЕ Д. ВОКРУГ ВОЗНИКАЛО
ПРОДОЛЖЕНИЕ 13 СМ. № 12
КАРТА ВОЕННЫХ ДЕЙСТВИЙ ЛЕЖАЛА НА СТОЛЕ ПОЛКОВНИКА
ЛЮДИ МОЕЙ ДЕРЕВНИ
ВОЕННОЕ ЗАСЕДАНИЕ В ШТАБЕ ПРОДОЛЖ.
МЫ ВСЕ В НЕОПЛАТНОМ ДОЛГУ ПЕРЕД РОДИНОЙ
ДЕРЕВНЯ
ВЗВОД 1
ВЗВОД 2
ВЗВОД 3 РЕЗЕРВ
ВЗВОД 4
ОНИ ПОГИБЛИ ВЫПОЛНЯЯ ДОЛГ ПЕРЕД РОДИНОЙ
КОММУНИСТ
ПРАПОРЩИК Н. КАПАНИН
СЕРЖАНТ Р. АБЛЯПИПОВ
РЯДОВОЙ К. ХОРЕШКО
НЕ ПОСТУПИЛИСЬ СОВЕСТЬЮ УРОК МУЖЕСТВА СИЛЬНЫЕ ДУХОМ
ДОЛГОЖДАННАЯ ВЫСАДКА ДЕСАНТА НА ОПУШКУ БЛИЗЛЕЖАВШЕГО ЛЕСА
НЕУДАЧНЫЙ ПРЫЖОК РЯДОВОГО К. ХОРЕШКО
НЕ ВЫПУСКАЯ АВТОМАТА
УДАЧНЫЙ ПРЫЖОК РЯДОВОГО Б. МИРКАСИМОВА
НЕ ВСПУГАЛИ ЗАЙЦА
МНОГОСТРАДАЛЬНАЯ РУССКАЯ ЗЕМЛЯ
МЕСТНЫЕ ЖЕНЩИНЫ СПАСАЮТ СВОИХ ДЕТЕЙ ОТ СЛУЧАЙНО ЗАЛЕТЕВШИХ СНАРЯДОВ А ТАКЖЕ Д.
СКРИПЯТ ПРОТЕЗЫ
14·I·1990 г. ЛЕОНИД ТИШКОВ
TERRE DES DABLOIDES

I've run out catridges ....

MY VILLAGE REFORMED — TIME OF DABLOIDES HAS COME

OUR SVETKA IS ROCKING ON A DABLOID

A time has arrived for DABLOIDES. The troops have returned to the barracks. All their fighting has only increased the number of DABLOIDES by 159 times

ELDER SON PAVLIK IS DOING HIS ARMY SERVICE IN THE FAR EAST

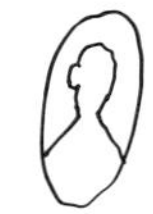

DA — BLO — BLO — BLO

ID — DA

DA — DA

— DAA — AAAA

14

CONTINUED

Terre des Dabloides

My Village Folk

Tiny tot Mishka (with spots all over from eating eggs)

The green shoot of new life

«Since these dabloids popped up, sugar has vanished from the shops.»

THIS FAMILY HAS A DABLOID OF THER OWN

«Can it be used to unload the sacks? Let's see...»

Boyscouts salute DABLOIDES.

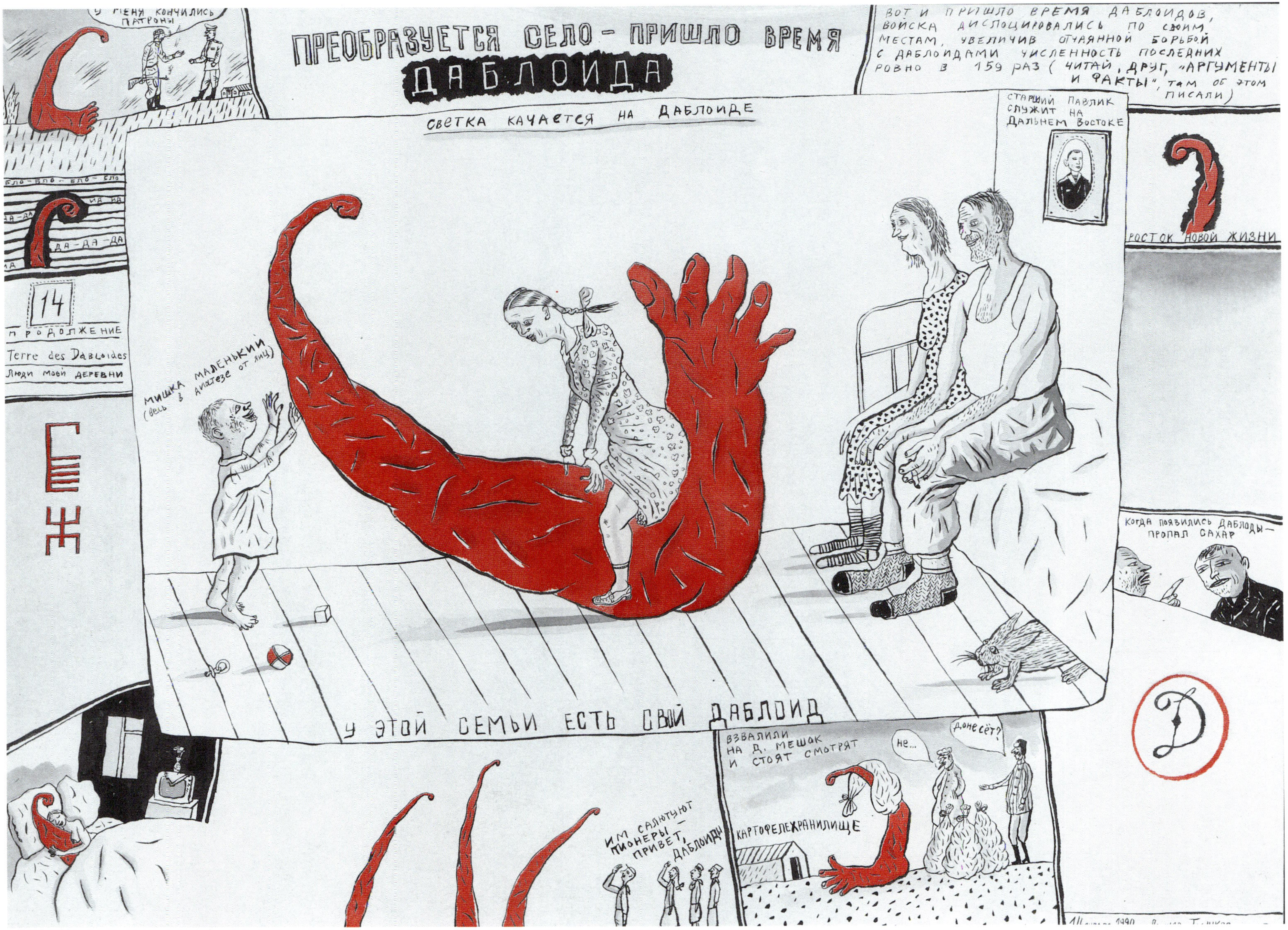

У меня кончились патроны
ПРЕОБРАЗУЕТСЯ СЕЛО - ПРИШЛО ВРЕМЯ ДАБЛОИДА
ВОТ И ПРИШЛО ВРЕМЯ ДАБЛОИДОВ, ВОЙСКА ДИСЛОЦИРОВАЛИСЬ ПО СВОИМ МЕСТАМ, УВЕЛИЧИВ ОТЧАЯННОЙ БОРЬБОЙ С ДАБЛОИДАМИ ЧИСЛЕННОСТЬ ПОСЛЕДНИХ РОВНО В 159 РАЗ (ЧИТАЙ, ДРУГ, "АРГУМЕНТЫ И ФАКТЫ", ТАМ ОБ ЭТОМ ПИСАЛИ)
СВЕТКА КАЧАЕТСЯ НА ДАБЛОИДЕ
СТАРШИЙ ПАВЛИК СЛУЖИТ НА ДАЛЬНЕМ ВОСТОКЕ
РОСТОК НОВОЙ ЖИЗНИ
14
ПРОДОЛЖЕНИЕ
Terre des Dabloides
Люди моей деревни
МИШКА МАЛЕНЬКИЙ (весь в аистезе от яиц)
ДА-ДА-ДА
КОГДА ПОЯВИЛИСЬ ДАБЛОДЫ — ПРОПАЛ САХАР
У ЭТОЙ СЕМЬИ ЕСТЬ СВОЙ ДАБЛОИД
ВЗВАЛИЛИ НА Д. МЕШОК И СТОЯТ СМОТРЯТ
Не...
Донесёт?
КАРТОФЕЛЕХРАНИЛИЩЕ
ИМ САЛЮТУЮТ ПИОНЕРЫ — ПРИВЕТ, ДАБЛОИДЫ

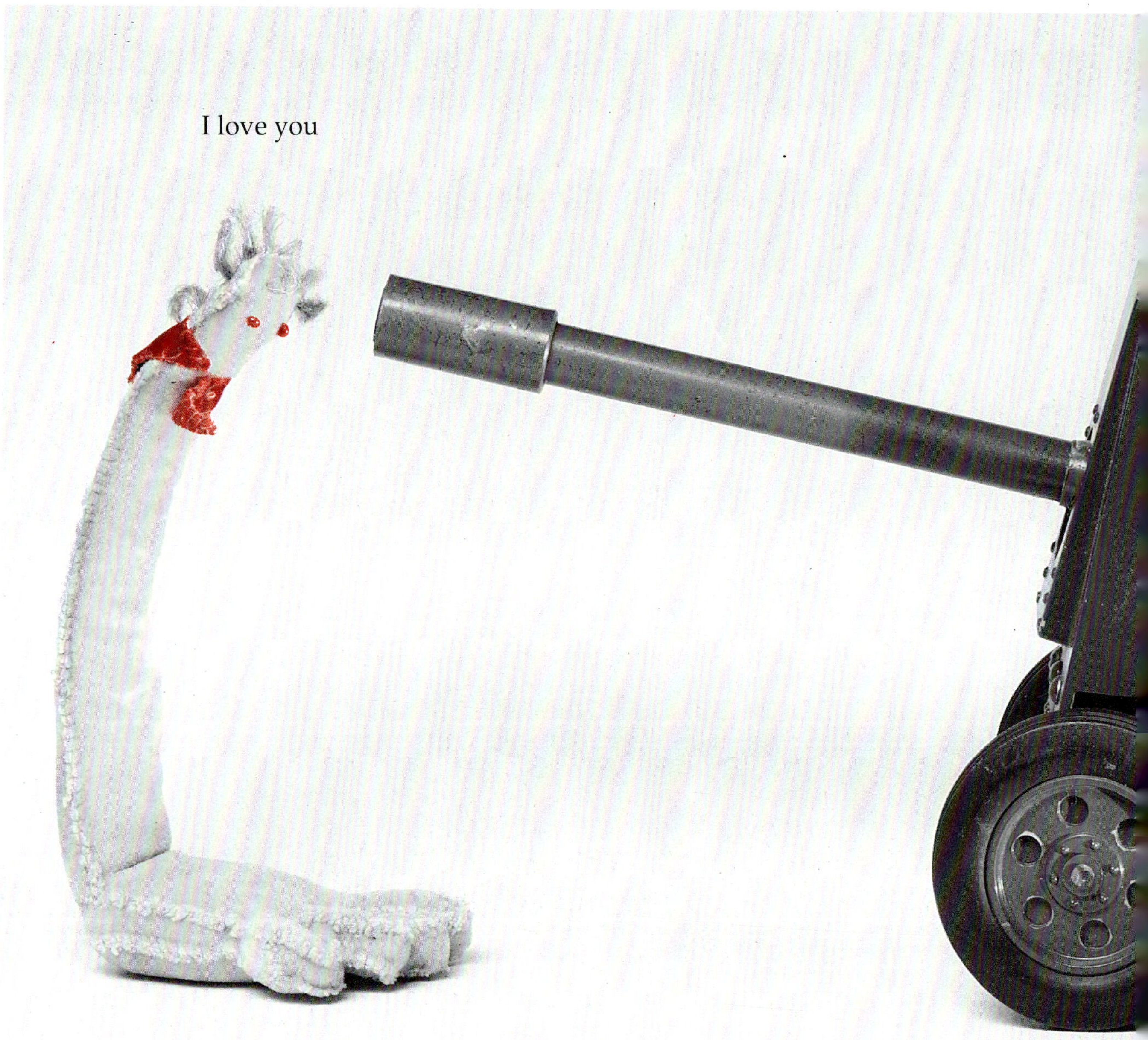
I love you

Make up a story, draw a picture, present everything as it is in life, and theatre will arise by itself, like magical Dablus, opening its secrets. Remembering the Russian Futurists, I compose my «Victory Over the Sun,» and as a true mythoholic want to make the myth reality. Dabloids come to life, they have young faces, Letishkov (remember Letatlin!) flies above the hall and grandmother returns. Again and again she brings us Dablus and bends over my sleeping face.

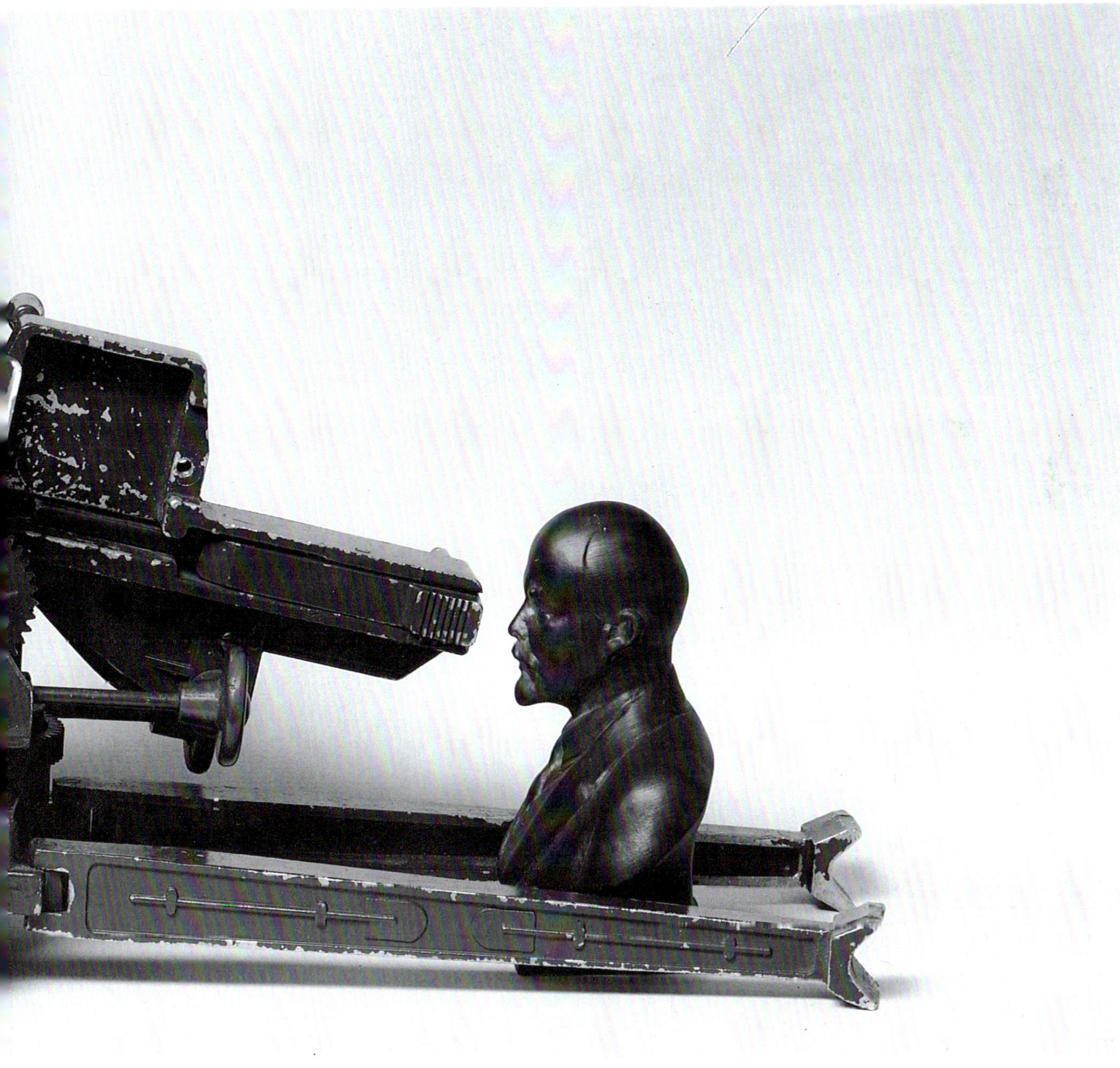

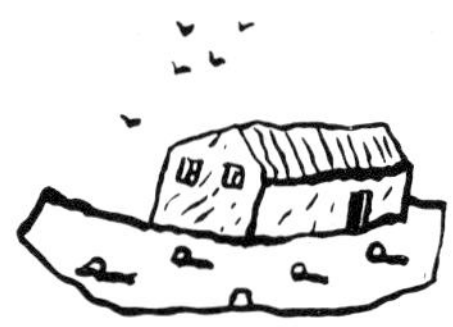

A Fantasy

A Play in Two Parts

CHARACTERS:

DABLUS*[1]
Dabloids
Matvei Ivanovich, director of a collective farm
Natalia, his wife
Svetka and a boy, their children
Arkady Zhilin*
Kostylin*[2]
Myasin*
Kozhina*[3]
Pyotr Yegorovich Diakov
Lapin, secretary of the party committee
Vasily Sergeevich, trade union committee chairman
Alyoshka, Afghanistan war veteran
Pavlik, drunkard
Dunya, custodian
Papilin, military commissar
Granny (Babushka)
Zlokazov*[4], militiaman
A blind madman
Brothers Kondratiev
The Alabushevs and other collective farmers
Girls
Boy Smorchkov
Colonel Sychev
Major Nekhoroshko*[5]
Corporal Zimin
Fomin, commander of civil defense HQ
Kryukov and other soldiers, medical personnel, commandos
A choir of collective farmers

1. *Dablus - In Tishkov's own words («Not Only Dabloids. Selected Conversations»), the name reflects the double (bisexual) nature of the creature. Therefore, its offspring should be «dabloids» («I am Leonid - the son of Leon, they are dabloids - the sons of Dablus»). The transliteration from Russian «Dablus» fails to reveal this interpretation.*

2. *Zhilin and Kostylin - main characters (officers) in Leo Tolstoy's novel* ***Captive in the Caucasus*** *(from* ***The Fourth Russian Reading Book****), which was studied in every Russian and Soviet school. Zhilin is short and brave, Kostylin is fat, sweaty and cowardly. In the minds of Russians these two always go together.*

3. *Kozhina - there was a woman-hero named Vasilisa Kozhina, who was a chief of a Russian partisan group during the war against Napoleon in 1812. The four characters (Zhilin, Kostylin, Myasin, and Kozhina) are to be viewed from the point of view of a Soviet citizen visiting the meat department of a local grocery store. Their last names are derived from the following roots: Zhilin - «veins,» Kostylin (could well be Kostin, but cf. note2) - «bones,» Myasin - «meat,» Kozhina - «skin.»*

4. *Zlokazov - means «Causing evil.»*
5. *Nekhoroshko - means «Not good.»*

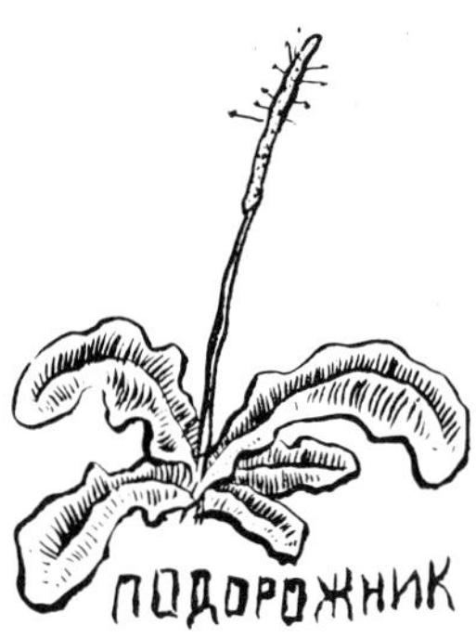

PLANTAIN

PART ONE

«DABLUS»

Action takes place in the «heartland» of Russia, on the collective farm «Garden Giant,»*[6] village Bazhukovo*[7], in 1989.

6. The real name of a collective farm located in southeast Moscow, not far from the house where Tishkov lives.

7. The name of a village near Tishkov's native town of Nizhnye Sergi, Sverdlovsk region, in the Urals.

INTRODUCTION

The landscape of a Russian wilderness. Birchtrees on the edge of a field. Morning birds are singing. The field is covered with morning fog. Dawn is breaking. A melodious and energetic song (music by Pakhmutova, words by Dolmatovski)*[8] is coming from far-away:

8. A very popular «official» Soviet composer and her poet husband, whose songs were on the radio and on TV almost every day.

OUR TRUTH IS IN THE LAND,
OUR ROOTS ARE IN THE LAND,
AND THE STRENGTH OF OUR SHOULDERS
COMES FROM MEADOWS AND FIELDS.
THE LAND WILL DRESS US, THE LAND WILL ALSO FEED US,
WE MUST SACRIFICE EVERYTHING FOR THE LAND.
THE LAND IS UNDER A CLEAR BLUE SKY —
LIKE A DREAM COME TRUE.
CALL ME YOUR DAUGHTER,
CALL ME YOUR SON,
BUT SINCE CHILDHOOD I HAVE BEEN
CALLING YOU MY MOTHER.
THE LAND BECOMES MORE BEAUTIFUL
WHILE GREETING A FRIEND,
BUT FOR AN ENEMY, THE LAND IS AS HOT AS FIRE...

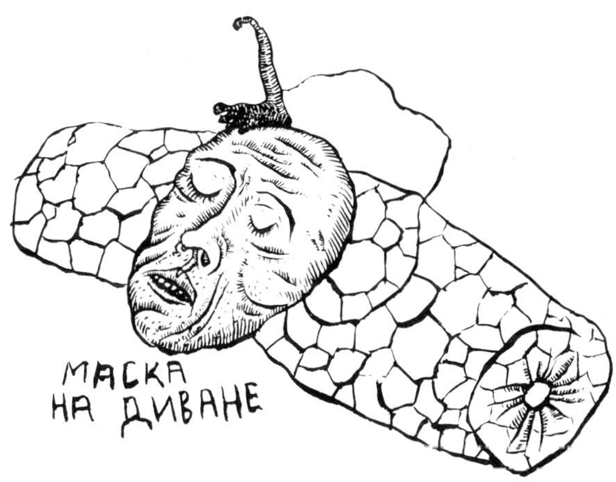

MASK ON THE SOFA

PROLOGUE

«THE PRAISE OF DABLUS»

Out of the soft black soil of a freshly ploughed field crawls DABLUS, with the light sound of a broken string.*[9] Frightened birds loudly take off.

9. «The light sound of a broken string» is from Chekhov's play «The Cherry Orchard.»

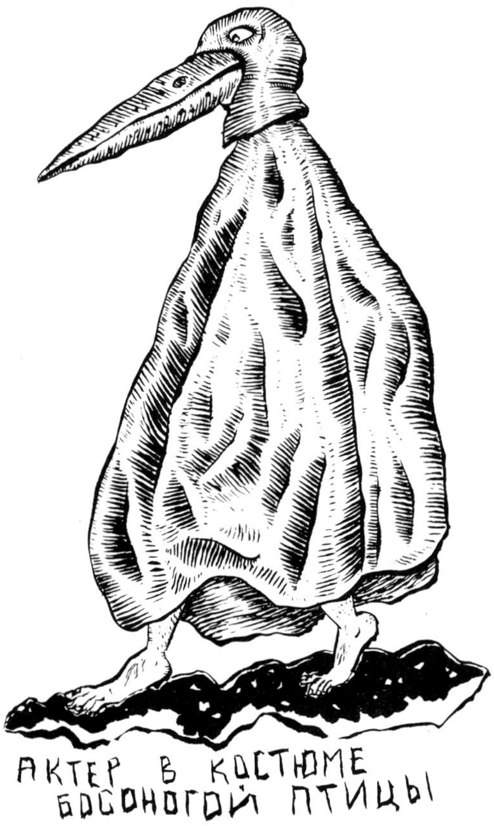

ACTOR IN COSTUME
OF BAREFOOT BIRD

CHOIR:
(merging with the opening song and finally overcoming it)

OH, DABLUS, THE BEAUTIFUL AND
JUST FATHER, YIELDING
THE AROMAS OF EDEN
THE FLESH AND FRUIT OF A CROWNBEARING TREE
THE IMMORTAL DUAL-TITTED OBJECT
THE SIMPLE LIGHT-CARRYING ORGANISM
THE VESSEL FULL OF BLISS
EVAPORATING THE DROPS OF THE INVIGORATING
SWEET-RUBY JUICE
THE PALE-MILKY MOTHER STUFFED WITH MEAT AND JUICE,
HE IS LYING IN MUD, THE GREAT AND ETERNAL
HANDSOME DABLUS.

EPISODE ONE

Scene one

(Kostylin enters)

On the fresh soil, where a barefooted bird with a beak-shaped face has just walked, Kostylin, a peasant wandering in the morning along a moist road, sees Dablus lying oval-shaped, pale as a rose, round-frosted and red, the sunbeams illuminating its length-wise horizon.

Kostylin:
FUCK IT - THAT SON OF A BITCH TRACTOR-DRIVER
DROPPED HIS UNISEXUAL LOVE OBJECT AGAIN.
Kostylin
(wandering in the morning along a moist road, sees Dablus. He comes up closer, and with his glasses on a rope, he bends over to have a better look):
WHAT IS IT? NO, THIS IS NOT PETRUKHA'S*[10] SHIT.
WHAT THE FUCK IS LYING HERE IN THE ROAD?
I SHOULD CALL FOR MY FELLOW-ELDERS AND FELLOW-VETERANS FROM THE KOLKHOZ.*[11]

10. *Petrukha - a «redneck» variant of Pyotr (Petr).*

11. *Kolkhozniks are the people who work on kolkhoz, a Soviet collective farm. Kolkhozs were imposed in Russian agriculture by Stalin in the late 1920s during collectivization. In the modern urban mentality kolkhozniks are considered rednecks and simpletons.*

(Kostylin is running, holding the flaps of his coat with his hands, his boots clattering, stepping on the lips of the land.*[12])

12. *A metaphor, very close to a one used in one of the songs by a popular Soviet singer Vladimir Vysotsky (died in 1980), «the naked nerves of the land.»*

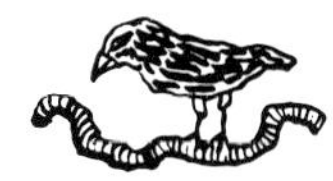

Scene two
(half an hour later)

A small crowd of collective farm people gather around Dablus, nudging one another, laughing and mombling something in Russian.

Kostylin:
HERE IT IS LYING IN FRONT OF YOU ON THE GROUND.
Zhilin:
(short, wearing a cap, rubbers on his feet but without socks. He is a blue-eyed white-haired carpenter with an oar*[13] in his right hand.)
I DON'T GET IT, IT DOESN'T LOOK
LIKE CRAP...
(touches Dablus with the oar)

13. *A girl with an oar or a man with an oar - typical sculptures of Soviet socialist realism in the 1930s, especially in parks and other recreational areas.*

Kozhin:
(a collective farmer of average height, former page-maker and landsurveyer,*[14] presently retired)
MAYBE PYOTR YEGOREVICH LOST IT?

14. *Tishkov makes fun of different professions, because they are real professions, but sound very funny and bureaucratic.*

Pyotr Yegorovich Diakov:
NO, I DIDN'T LOSE ANYTHING,
EVERYTHING HAS BEEN ALREADY LOST,
I OWN NOTHING, LOST AND LONELY
IS PETRUSHA*[15] IN THE UNIVERSE.

15. *Petrusha - diminutive of Pyotr (Petr).*

Myasin:
(a short collective farmer, bandy-legged, in a straw-hat, an honorary milkman, presently herdsman, the Minister of Cows, with a black bag around his neck)
SO, WHAT IS IT YOU SAY?

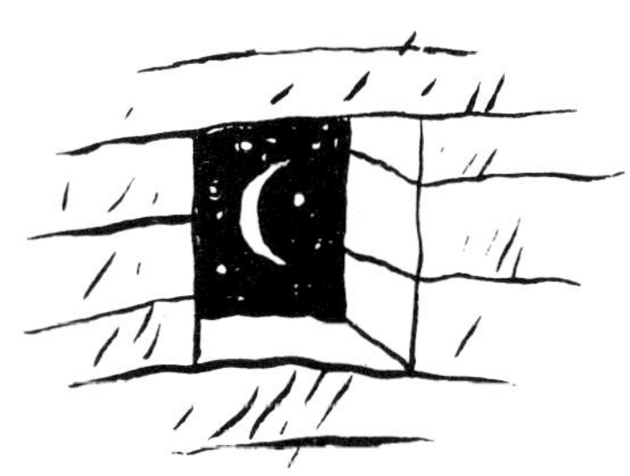

Kostylin:
YES, WHAT DO YOU SAY, VASILY SERGEEVICH?
Vasily Sergeevich
(chairman of the trade union committee of the collective farm «Garden Giant»)
WE SHOULD TAKE IT OFF THE FIELD, WE'LL GATHER THE EXECUTIVE BOARD, TALK IT OVER...

A boy:

OH, I AM SCARED, IT WILL BRING MISFORTUNE TO OUR KOLKHOZ.

Zhilina:

(in a shawl, boots, a heavy wadded jacket, with a pail, laughing into her small fist)

LOOKS A LOT LIKE MY TITS, HA-HA-HA,

LISTEN, ARKADY, TELL THEM, HOW MUCH LIKE.

(pushes Zhilin on his side)

Militiaman Zlokazov:

YES, COMRADE CHAIRMAN VASILY SERGEEVICH,

I'LL ATTEND TO IT IMMEDIATELY.

(pulls a burlap matting out of Myasin's bag, carefully wraps Dablus in it, orders Zhilin and Kostylin to pick up the matting and carry it into the collective farm executive office.)

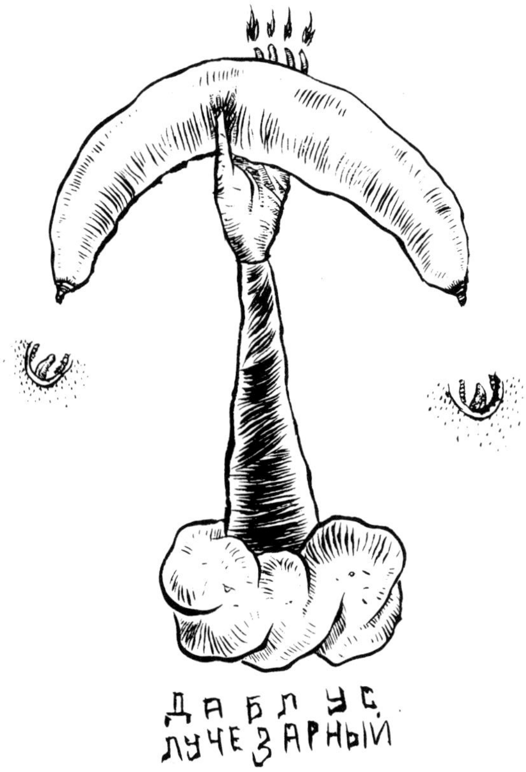

RADIANT DABLUS

Tchaikovsky's music is playing, birch-trees rustle in the wind as if whispering something to one another, the song is heard again from far-away:

CALL ME YOUR DAUGHTER, CALL ME YOUR SON,

BUT SINCE CHILDHOOD I HAVE BEEN

CALLING YOU MY MOTHER.

IN THE CORNFIELDS AND PLOUGHLANDS THERE ARE BEAUTIFUL PEOPLE,

THEY HAVE GOTTEN THE BEAUTY FROM THE LAND.

BUT IF YOU DON'T LOVE THE LAND

WITH ALL YOUR HEART,

YOU'RE NOT THE ONE WHO DESERVES REAL LOVE.

A blind madman:[*16]

(sitting on the porch of a church)

WHERE DID THEY TAKE DABLUS TO, I WONDER?

EPISODE TWO

Scene one

The executive office of the collective farm. A simple and spacious room with white walls and a TVset on the right.

Hanging near it on the wall are portraits of Lenin, Gorbachev

16. *From an ancient Greek tragedy. He is the first to call the thing Dablus.*

and Yeltsin in frames. Pinned to the wall is Sakharov's portrait from a magazine and the window shows a sad landscape of Russia. Through the open doors one can see simple, sun-tanned faces of peasants, they are the CHOIR.

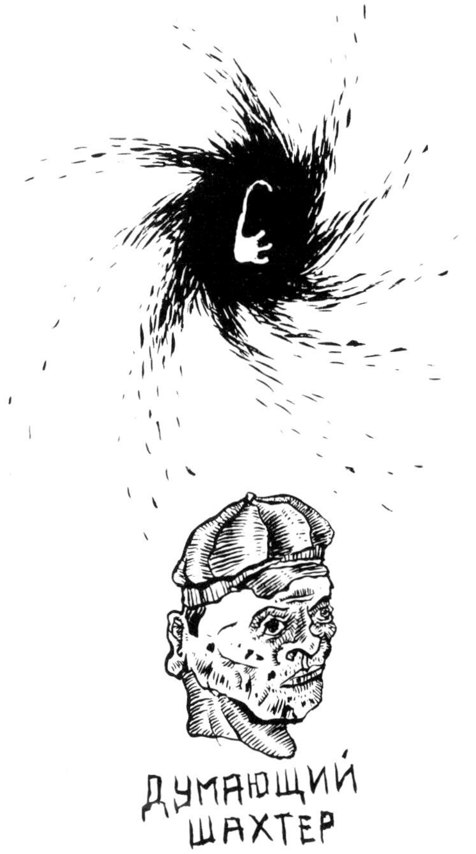

THINKING MINER

CHOIR:
O, HEAVENLY AND JUST
INVIGORATING DABLUS - FATHER AND MOTHER
SENT DOWN FROM ABOVE, TRANSFIGURED
GRANTING TRUTH, ETERNAL, VIVIPAROUS,
RADIANT, SENT DOWN TO US BY THE DAWN AND DEW
TO OUR JOY, BRINGING US DELIVERANCE
AND ETERNAL JOY, PEACE AND PROGRESS.

Matvei Ivanovich:
(director of the collective farm «Garden Giant»)
PROGRESS WILL NOT BE STOPPED BY
A GANG OF BASTARDS!
WE WILL SOW SEED GRAIN, WE WILL THROW OUR HOT
SEMEN INTO THE LAND AND THE LAND
WILL GIVE BIRTH BY THE TIME THAT THE PARTY
GIVES THE ORDER TO SOW.
(points his hardened finger above at the ceiling)

Vasily Sergeevich:
(lights a cigarette*[17])
MATVEI, LOOK HERE!
(He points at the table where Dablus is lying on green velvet, lighting the red faces of «the executive board» with a paleamber light!)

The director:
(throws the cigarette away)
GOD DAMN IT! WHAT THE FUCK IS THIS?

Vasily Sergeevich:
(lights a cigarette)
GOD KNOWS!
HOW THE HELL SHOULD I KNOW!
KOSTYLIN FOUND IT IN THE FIELD TODAY,
JUST THIS MORNING. THE DAMN THING
WAS JUST LYING THERE AND SHINING!

17. *In fact, it is a «papirosa,» a cigarette with a cardboard holder, very typical of Russia and prewar Europe.*

The director:

(lights a cigarette)

WHAT DO YOU SAY, LAPIN?

Lapin:

(secretary of the party committee.) (He throws the cigarette away.)

COMRADES, WE SHOULD CALL THE REGIONAL PARTY
COMMITTEE, THEY WILL TELL US
WHAT IS TO BE DONE.*[18]

18. *«What is to be done?» - the title of the famous novel by Chernyshevsky and one of Lenin's first books. One of the most popular questions in Russian culture.*

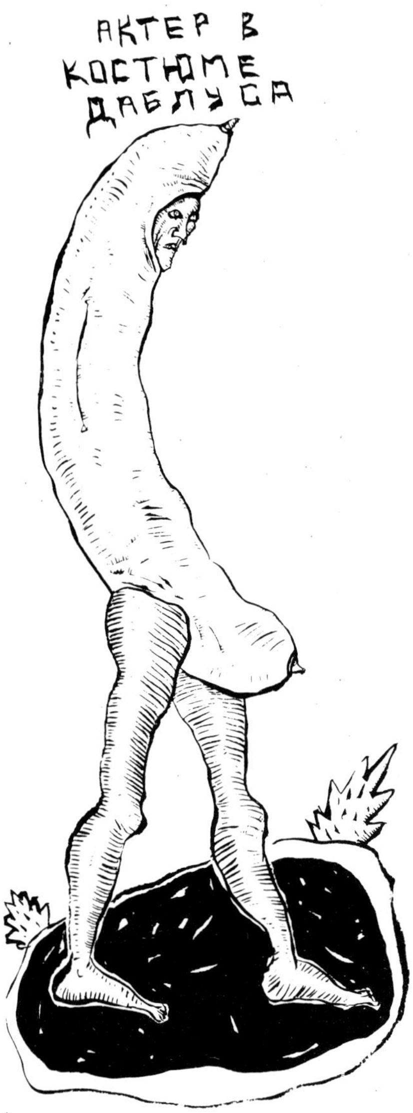

ACTOR IN
DABLUS COSTUME

Scene two

Early morning. It is quiet in the executive office of the collective farm. The sun is shining joyfully through the light curtains. There are cigarettebutts all over the floor. The director is sleeping on the couch, in clothes, in socks, embracing Dablus with both hands, leaning his unshaven cheek against the soft and warm surface of Dablus. The door creaks. Dunya, the custodian, enters with a pail and floor-cloth.

Dunya:

AND AGAIN MATVEI IVANOVICH PULLED AN ALL
NIGHTER FOR THE BENEFIT OF THE KOLKHOZ.
HE IS TOTALLY WIPED OUT FROM MAKING UP THE
SOWING REPORT,
AND NOW, MY SWEETIE, HE'S SLEEPING ON THE COUCH,
I WILL QUIETLY SWEEP UP THE CIGARETTE BUTTS,
WASH THE FLOOR
TWICE, FIRST WITH THE WET CLOTH, AND THEN
WITH THE DRY ONE... OH, WHAT IS THAT THING
MATVEI IVANOVICH IS HOLDING IN HIS ARMS?
WHAT CAN IT BE, IT'S SO WHITE?

The director:

(waking up)

AH, WHAT IS IT? WHO IS IT? DUNYA, IS THAT YOU?
YOU WON'T BELIEVE IT, BUT WHEN EVERYBODY LEFT,
I SUDDENLY FELT LIKE EMBRACING THIS...
THIS... THING. AND THEN I FELL ASLEEP
CUDDLING UP TO IT, FORGETTING MYSELF, FORGETTING
ABOUT EVERYTHING.

(pushes Dablus away from himself, jumps up)

LISTEN, DUNYASHA, DON'T TELL ANYBODY WHAT YOU HAVE JUST SEEN,

ESPECIALLY DON'T TELL NATASHKA AND THE CHILDREN. GO TAKE IT TO THE SHED,

OH IT'S CONFUSED MY SOUL. TAKE IT AWAY,

FAST, AND I, I WILL GO TO

THE STORE, MY THROAT FEELS DRY. LET'S SEE NOW, I HAD MY VODKA COUPONS

SOMEWHERE...*[19]

(walks away, fumbling in his pockets, leaving Dunya with-Dablus)

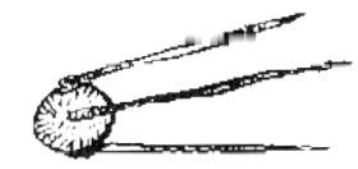

19. *Coupons for vodka or wine were introduced almost everywhere in the Soviet Union as a result of Gorbachev's anti-alcohol campaign.*

CHOIR:

O DABLUS, IMMORTAL AND SWEET

THE FATHER, WARM AND SOFT, STUFFED

WITH BLISS

SMELLING OF BREAD, FAIR-HAIRED

REJOICE YOU STRONG, VIRGINLY-PURE

SINLESS AND TENDER DABLUS.

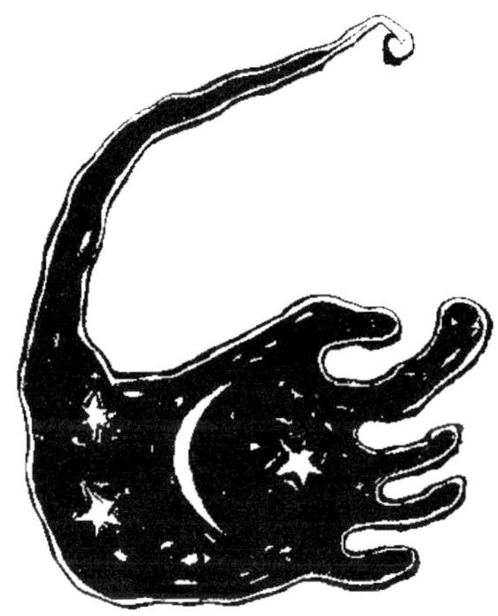

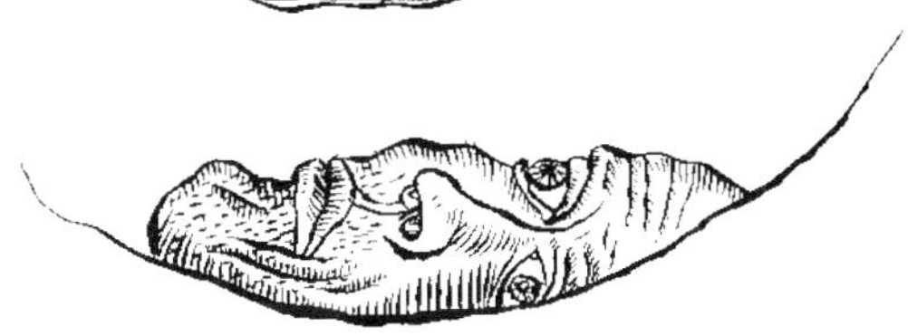

Д D

EPISODE THREE

Scene one

The shed. Scattered all over the place are boards and planks, various farming equipment, very rustic: rakes, shovels, hoes, chains, hammers, crow-bars, shafts, cart wheels, everything is old, half-broken. The moonlight is seen through the boards, a shaft of moonlight comes through the half-opened door.*[20] The same light illuminates Dablus hanging on ropes in the middle of the shed

20. *This scene should have an oriental (possibly Chinese) flavor.*

The rain is starting, occasional raindrops are falling on the roof. Amidst the noise of rain one can hear somebody running, now coming closer. Two men run in through the door.

One is thickset in a sleeveless Navy tunic, a tattoo on his shoulder. The other is thin, tall, in a gray coat and torn shoes. Both men are a bit tipsy.

First:

GOT FUCKING WET, DAMN IT, OOH,

THIS STINKING FUCKING RAIN.

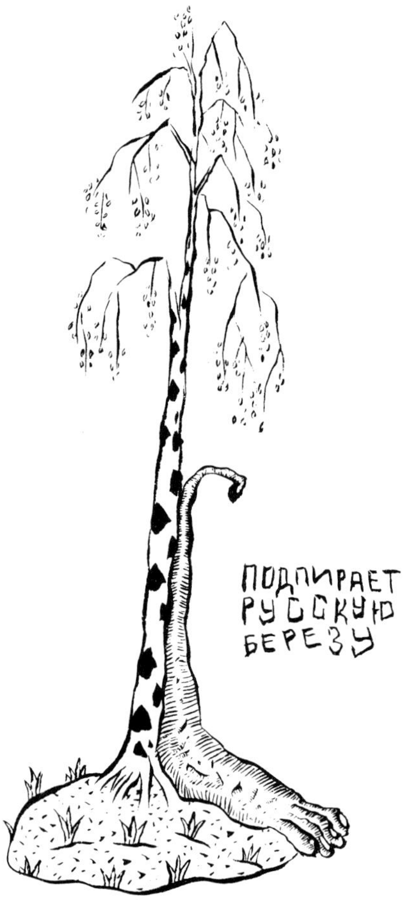

HE SUPPORTS THE RUSSIAN BIRCH

Second:

AND WE HAD JUST OPENED A BOTTLE, SLICED A CUCUMBER, HERE (offers), WHO ASKED THIS FUCKING RAIN TO START.

First:

I REMEMBER IN AFGHANISTAN, THE SAME THING...

(hits his head against the hanging Dablus, staggers back in fright)

PAVLIK, WHAT IS THIS THING HANGING HERE?

Second:

HOLY FUCKING SHIT, FUCKING HELL, HOW THE FUCK DO I KNOW WHAT IT IS.

First:

IT LOOKS LIKE A SAUSAGE!

Second: (laughing)

A TIDBIT TO EAT, ALYOSHKA! JUST IN TIME!

First:

(still with fear, but seeing that his comrade didn't get scared, takes out a bottle of Port and hands it to him)

DRINK THEN!

Second:

(drinks, then puts the bottle on the floor and tries to thrust his finger into Dablus)

SOFT AND WARM. IT SMELLS LIKE BREAD. TOUCH IT, ALYOSHKA, IT FEELS SO GOOD!

(grabs Dablus with both hands and starts to squeeze it from all sides)

The first:

OOH, PAVLIK, IT FEELS SO FUCKING GOOD!

(now they both squeeze Dablus, then catch the tits with their mouths and, smacking their lips, start sucking Dablus from both its ends) The noise of the rain and the music of Tchaikovsky are amplified, a heavy downpour hits the shed. But the moonlight is getting brighter, pouring through all the chinks and holes, illuminating the drunk and joyful Pavlik and Alyoshka. Like babies, they suck Dablus enthusiastically, and a warm pink juice runs down their cheeks, breaking into winding rills on their wrinkled skin, on their bristly chins, on their necks, dripping on their breasts and pants, flooding the plank floor of the shed, and blending with the pale and bright-amber light of the nightly moon.

Scene two.

The shed again. The morning has not yet started, but the night is drawing to its close. The rain has stopped, silence is all around, only the snoring of the sleeping Pavlik and Alyoshka breaks the silence. The door squeaks. A babushka enters. You can't see her face. She is bent double, with a stick in her right hand and a sickle in the left hand.

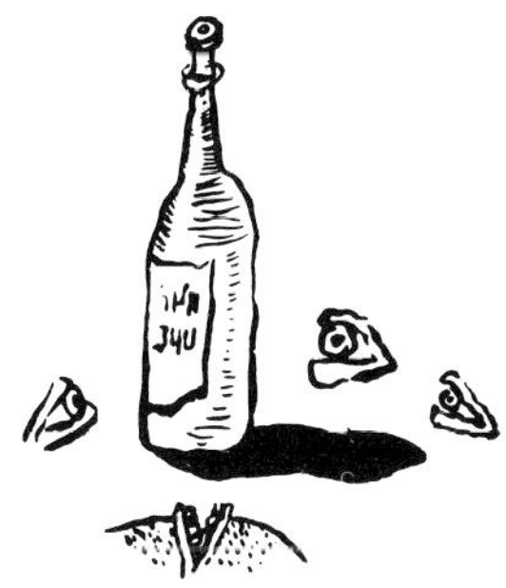

Babushka:

KHO-KHO, WELL DONE, NOW THE POOR THING IS TIED AND FASTENED WITH ROPES. GOOD. DUNYASHA, MY SWEETIE, TOLD ME EVERYTHING. HEY, LOOK AT THESE DRUNK BASTARDS.

(Steps over the sleeping guys, brandishes her sickle and cuts the ropes, carefully puts Dablus on her shoulders, as if it were a yoke, hangs the sickle on a nail in the wall next to the hammer.)*[21]

IT WILL BE SO BEAUTIFUL*[22]
WHEN A CROP OF SICKLES*[23] COMES UP
THE GRAIN WILL FILL THE EARS.
AND OOZING OUT THE MOTHER-OF-PEARL OF THE DAWN
WILL BE A HEADBAND IN THE ASHES
THE BOY WILL RETURN HOME
THE MILK WILL CURDLE
THE CALL-UP PAPERS WILL BE FORGOTTEN
THE HAMMER WILL MELT

(walks out through the door)

21. *To resemble the Soviet hammer and sickle.*

22. *This song is a reference to the war in Afghanistan.*

23. *May be an allusion to «A Crop of Pricks,» one of the erotic «Secret Tales of Russia» from A.Afanas'ev's collection.*

EPISODE FOUR

Scene one

The director's house. A modest room, in the middle of it is a table loaded with food,*[24]there are several chairs around the table. The director is sitting on one of these chairs, his wife Natalia, on another. To the right there is a chest of drawers. A sideboard is to the left. To the side is a TVset «Gorizont, model 206,» on legs. There is a portrait of a sailor above the chest of drawers. Further, there is a children's play-pen, a 10year old boy is sitting in it, wearing a shirt, without pants. He is building a pyramid out of many colored rings. There is a bed next to it, a rug is above the bed, and hanging above it is a reproduction of Van Gogh's **Red Vineyards in Arles**.*[25]

The radio is on.

24. *Food is emphasized like this, because of its importance and deep meaning to a Russian peasant. The foodom the table can be just about anything.*

25. *This painting is in the collection of The Pushkin State Museum of Fine Arts in Moscow.*

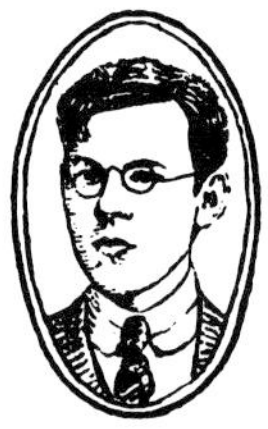

Announcer on the radio:

AND NOW AT THE REQUEST OF GALINA MIKHAILOVNA GUZ IN KISHINEV, WE HAVE

SYMPHONY NUMBER ONE BY PYOTR ILYICH TCHAIKO-VSKY, PERFORMED BY THE

SYMPHONY ORCHESTRA OF THE STATE COMMITTEE ON RADIO AND TELEVISION,

CONDUCTED BY SERGEI SKRIPKA.*[26]

26. *A real person, a popular Soviet orchestra conductor. «Skripka» in Russian means violin.*

Natalia:

I BOUGHT SEVEN BARS OF SOAP YESTERDAY, GOOD SOAP, «FOR ALL HOUSEHOLD

PURPOSES.» TRUE, WE ALREADY HAVE TWENTY FIVE BARS. BUT THAT IS FINE,

JUST LET IT BE.

The director:

THEY'RE PLAYING TCHAIKOVSKY AGAIN, NICE MUSIC. AND SKIS, DID THEY HAVE SKIS?

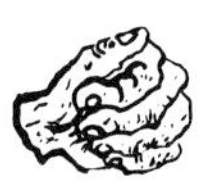

Natalia:

YES, SOAP MAKES GOOD LUBRICATION FOR SKIS.

The director:

WE SHOULD STOCK UP ON SKIS, JUST IN CASE —

WE ONLY HAVE ELEVEN PAIRS AND WINTER IS JUST ROUND THE CORNER. THEY MIGHT NOT BE ENOUGH,

AND THE STORE MAY RUN OUT OF THEM SOON.*[27]

27. *These comments reflect the subtle psychology of a Soviet consumer who stockpiles goods without even thinking what he will do with them afterwards. There is no exact English equivalent to the Russian phrase. The help of Michael Conrad in finding suitable English equivalents for such vague phrases is greatly appreciated.*

(The boy takes a trumpet and plays along with Tchaikovsky.)

Natalia:

STOP IT, YOU STUPID FOOL, OR I'LL HIT YOU WITH A BAR OF SOAP.

(takes a bar of soap from the table and throws it at the boy)

The director:

OH, WHAT, MISSED AGAIN, YOU SQUINTY OLD FOOL? LET'S GO TO BED.

Natalia:

WHAT TIME IS IT, MATVEI? WHERE THE HELL IS SVETKA? WHERE IS SHE WANDERING? MAYBE SHE IS IN THE BATH-HOUSE AT THE END OF THE GARDEN?*[28] WAITING IN LINE TO BUY SOAP TODAY ZHILINA TOLD ME THAT A BABUSHKA

28. *In Russian rural areas every household used to have a small bathhouse in the backyard or in the corner of a garden, usually close to a river or a pond.*

TOOK THAT THING THAT THEY FOUND IN THE FIELD TO HER BATHHOUSE. AND THE GIRLS HAVE STARTED GOING

THERE IN FLOCKS. AND THEY ARE ALWAYS CARRYING SOMETHING THERE. THEY ARE PARTYING AND YOU CAN HEAR SONGS COMING FROM THE WINDOW.

THEY ARE UP TO NO GOOD.

The director:

(lights a cigarette)

I THINK SO TOO.

Natalia:

GO AND PUFF ON THE PORCH!

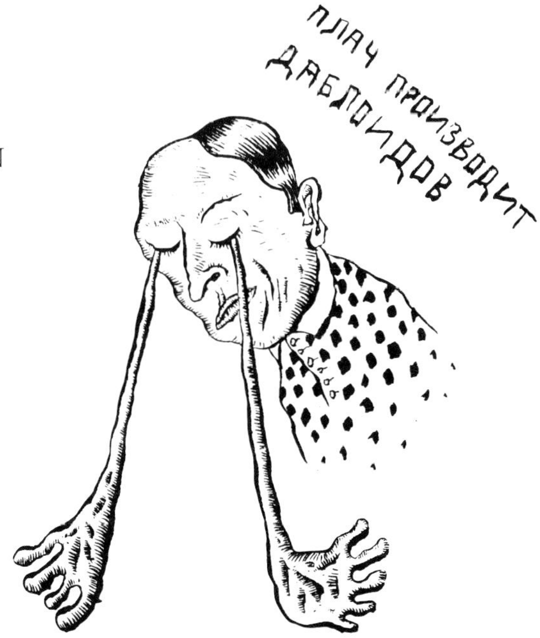

TEARS PRODUCE DABLOIDS

Scene two

The director comes out of the house, gets himself a cigarette, lights it, starts to smoke, sits down on a bench. Far away somebody plays an accordion and one can hear a song. Kostylin, Zhilin and brothers Kondratiev are passing by.

Kostylin:

GOOD EVENING, MATVEI IVANOVICH.

Zhilin:

DID YOU HEAR WHAT IS GOING ON IN THE VILLAGE, MATVEI IVANOVICH? SOMETHING BAD IS HAPPENING. AND ALL BECAUSE OF THAT OBJECT. IT'S FOOLING US ALL THE WAY. THE GIRLS ARE GOING NUTS, SPENDING DAY AND NIGHT IN THAT BATHHOUSE, AND NOBODY KNOWS WHAT THEY ARE UP TO.

Kostylin:

WHY DO YOU SAY NOBODY KNOWS? WHAT THEY ARE DOING THERE IS OBVIOUS: INDECENCY IS WHAT. SUCH ACTIVITIES CORRUPT OUR DAUGHTERS. WHAT IS TO BE DONE, MATVEI IVANOVICH?

The director:

I DON'T EVEN KNOW WHAT TO SAY, GUYS, BUT YOU ARE CERTAINLY RIGHT ABOUT IT.

Brothers Kondratiev:

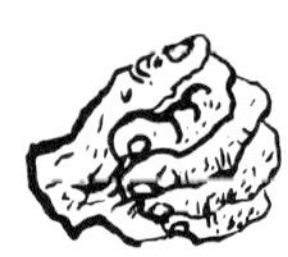

(there are many of them, all of them are tall, round-headed, with curly hair, in red dress-shirts, in shoes - gesticulating bluntly, almost shouting)

WE HAVE TO RUB IT OUT, WE ARE LOSING TIME. JUST SHOOT IT AS A FASCIST. WHO KNOWS WHAT IT REALLY IS, IT DOESN'T LOOK LIKE ANYTHING ELSE. IT PERVERTS OUR

DAUGHTERS. THERE IS NOTHING IN THE STORES, THEY DON'T GIVE YOU ANYTHING TO EAT IN THE CAFETERIA, APARTMENTS ARE NO LONGER BEING BUILT, WHAT THE HELL IS IT? IT IS SO FAT AND LAZY, WE'LL CUT IT INTO PIECES, WIPE OUT THE FREAK AS AN ENEMY OF THE WORKING PEOPLE, AS A PARASITE ON REGULAR HARD WORKERS, A BLOOD-SUCKER OF THE RUSSIAN PEASANTS!

(they run away)

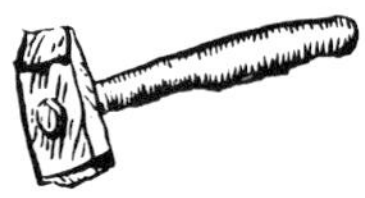

Scene three

Coming up are Myasin, elder Koroedov*[29], Terenty Maltsev*[30], an operator of brass hooks*[31] Lekandry Izotov, a weaver and barkthrasher Kolesnikov, half-smith and Lekandry's friend Kozhin, Silaev, Alabushev-junior and the boy Smorchkov. The evening shade has covered their gloomy faces. Their eyes start to twinkle in their eyesockets. There is no truth on earth and unhappy people live in the village. The brothers Kondratiev come back; in their hands they are holding pitchforks, shovels, crowbars, sickles, oars, knives, scythes, shafts, brooms, and hammers.

29. *Koroedov - «one who eats bark.»*

30. *A well-known real person, a tractordriver and a director of a collective farm, Hero of Socialist Labor, he was even elected Academician of the USSR Academy of Agriculture.*

31. *Here again Tishkov makes fun of professions which sound very funny and bureaucratic, almost absurd.*

Brothers Kondratiev:

WE HAVE BEEN IN THE SHED! THESE ARE OUR WEAPONS COMRADES, TAKE THEM, EVERYBODY GET READY FOR A FIGHT, WE MUST DESTROY THIS THING THAT BRINGS US TROUBLE.

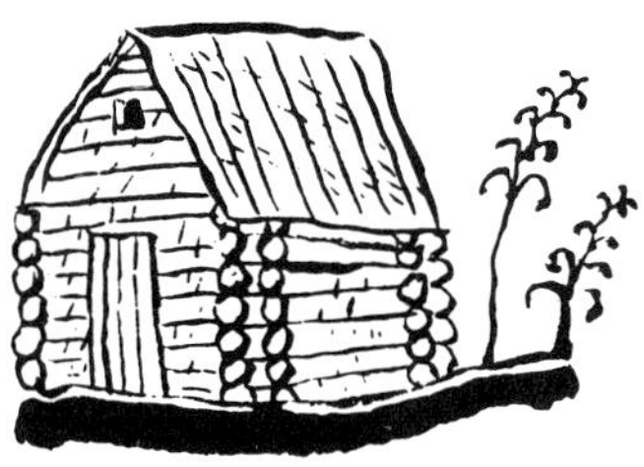

(They give out the tools to the peasants; the director refuses to take them and silently returns to his house, the rest of the crowd loudly walks away.)

The blind madman:

(sitting on the porch of the church)

ONE SHOULDN'T BOTHER DABLUS! STOP YOU MADMEN!

Tchaikovsky's music gets louder, transforms into the music of Shostakovich. Against the background of the music appears the CHOIR.

EPISODE FIVE

CHOIR:

OH DABLUS! OH DABLUS WHO IS LYING STRAIGHT,
DOUBLE-LAYERED AND RAIN-CARRYING,
DEATH-BRINGING, SPRING-BRINGING,
SOFT-FLESHED, VIVIPAROUS,
OH DABLUS! THE CARNIVOROUS GROOM,
THE FATHER OF THE GOLDEN GRAIN.
OH DABLUS - THE BIG-BREASTED BRIDE,
THE GRAVID MOTHER OF WHEAT!

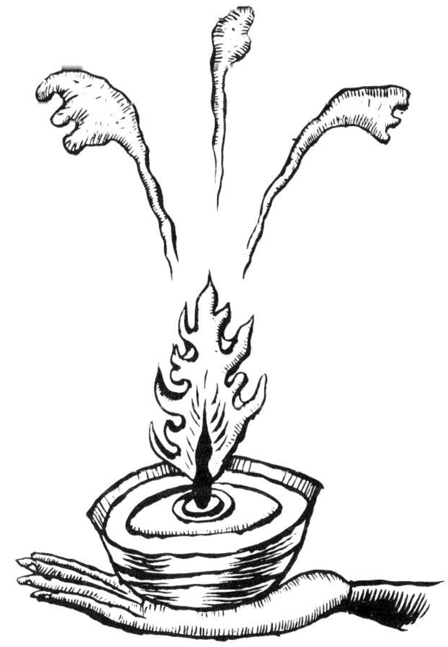

МАРМЕ И ДЫМ

MARME AND SMOKE

Scene one

The same evening. The bathhouse in the farcorner of the garden. A fence. Birds, like ashes, are scattered along the fence.

Far away is the black forest standing like a wall. Shining above the forest is the Dablus constellation. Beggars are sleeping everywhere, a fighter-jet is flying above the world. Even higher, cosmonaut Krikalev and Colonel Sergeev*[32] have left the MIR space-station and walked out into outer space, having tied themselves to the station with a clothesline.

It is warm in the bathhouse. Roomy and clean. On the wooden berth is Dablus, half-standing, half-lying. Children are around it of female sex, ages 10 to 15. They stand in a semicircle and are dressing Dablus in a shirt, knotting a necktie and a white scarf. Lyuba Zhilina has made a wreath of yellow wheat and is placing it on Dablus.

Lyuba:

NECK! NECK! NECK! NECK!*[33]

Vera Kondratieva has made a pile out of little stones, several glass fragments, two shreds of cloth, a chewinggum wrapper, a red bead, and her own milktooth.

Vera:

(singing)

CALL ME YOUR DAUGHTER,
CALL ME YOUR SON,
BUT SINCE CHILDHOOD
I HAVE BEEN CALLING
YOU MY MOTHER.

32. *Real cosmonauts*

33. *«Crying the neck»: This episode is taken from J.G.F. Frazier's, **The Golden Bough: A Study in Magic and Religion**. Part V. Spirits of the Corn and of the Wild. Chapter VII: Lityerses. It is connected with a custom of «crying the neck» in the harvest in Devonshire at the beginning of the 19th century. The neck is a small bundle of all the best ears of wheat that a harvester collects from the fields before reaping the last field of wheat.*

From the right, out of the parlor, comes Natasha Kostylina bringing in a box with rabbits.

Natasha:

HERE ARE RABBITS FOR YOU, FATHER,
THE FURRY RECEPTACLES OF THE SOUL,
THEY HAVE JUST EATEN SOME BREAD,
NOW THEY ARE READY TO CROAK.

All the girls rush to Dablus and start undressing it, shouting:

OUR MILKY GRANNY,
DEAR BABUSHKA DEMETER,
GIVE US BACK YOUR WEALTH,
THE JUICE OF A YOUNG FATHER!

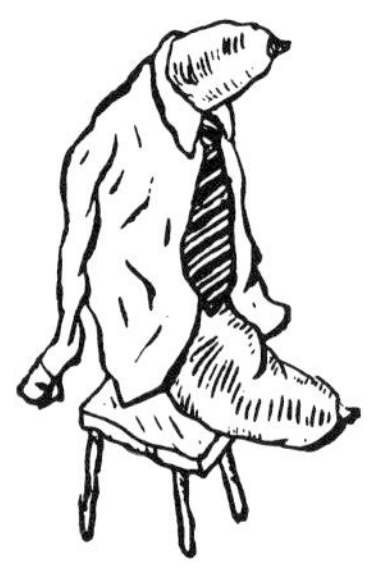

They are undressing Dablus, they start to pour water on it and to lubricate it with soap. Svetka takes off her dress, takes a rabbit into her hands and soaps it and rubs the rabbit against the soft body of Dablus.

Svetka:

LET THE WATER-OUR LORD, WASH AWAY,
THE EXHAUSTED FISHERMAN[*34] WILL AWAKE.
I AM WASHING WITH THE WATER THAT NOBODY DRANK,
THE SKIN DOUSED WITH THE VESSEL'S BLOOD.

34. *The fisherman - Christ.*

After the bath is over, the children wrap up ,Dablus into a fresh sheet and carry it to Elvira Myasina, who is sitting on a stool, and they put Dablus on her knees as if it were a baby.

Vera:

NECK! NECK! NECK!

Scene two

Suddenly the door opens with a wild noise, and frightful and furious peasants run into the bathhouse. Ahead of everybody are the brothers Kondratiev with scythes. Boris, the eldest brother, is blindfolded and has a sickle in his hand. Behind them are:

Zhilin with an oar, Kostylin with a hammer, Myasin with a screwdriver, cosmonaut Krikalev with a clothes-line, Terenty Maltsev with a crowbar, Izotov with a scoop, Kolesnikov with a shovel, Alabushev-junior with a shovel, Alabushev-senior with a hoe, Alabushev-middle with a rake, Silaev with a shaft, the boy Smorchkov with a brick, and the elder Koroedov with a knife (although he is old, he is still spiteful).

FAREWELL FOOT!
HELLO
DABLOID

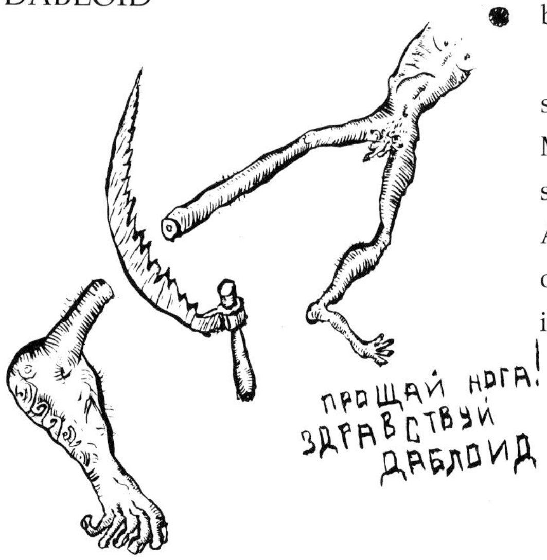

Kondratiev:

(makes as if to strike)

AEKH-HA!

The end of part one.

PART TWO

DABLOIDS

INTRODUCTION

CHOIR:

OH DABLUS BORN TWICE,
IMMORTAL RADIANT DOUBLE,
YOU DWELLED ABOVE, YOU DWELLED BENEATH,
GOVERNING THE CELESTIAL WILDERNESS.
WHAT WILL BECOME OF YOU NOW?

EPISODE ONE.

Scene one.

Both young and old, blinded with spite and holding their tools high, fill the bathhouse, overturn the rabbit-house, destroy the stone pyramid, scatter the colorful glass fragments, and frighten the girls. Now, screaming and yelling, they are ready to fight Dablus tooth and nail.

Men shouting:

SCUM, SWINE, SLIME, SCHMUCK, SLUT

Elvira Myasina:

(having thrown Dablus on the ground, runs away)

THE PEOPLE ARE READY! *[35]

Old Man Koroedov:

THE SCYTHES ARE BENT,THE SHARP-TOOTHED SICKLES,
THE SHOVELS, THE OARS,
THE SHAFTS AND THE SPINDLES.

The boy Smorchkov:

THIS MASTER MUST BE MOWED!

Boris Kondratiev:

(spinning and brandishing the sickle in all directions)

WE'LL CUT THIS BRUTE INTO LITTLE PIECES, LIKE A SAUSAGE!

BIRTH
OF DABLOIDS

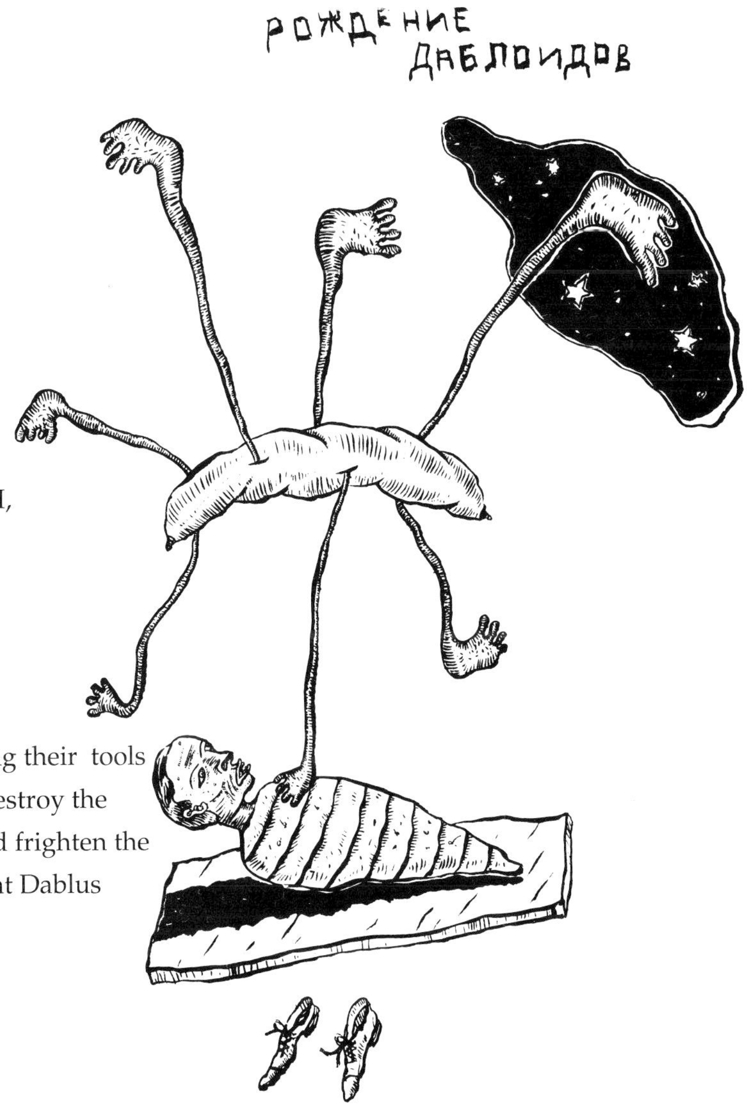

35. *This episode is also connected with the description of ceremonies performed in different parts of Europe at the end of the harvest season. All of these examples are taken again from Chapter VII of Frazer's book. Tishkov borrowed a few lines directly from the Russian translation of* ***The Golden Bough****.*
The kolkhozniks want to kill Dablus as an incarnation of the Corn Spirit. They perform the equivalent of a ritual wide-spread in Germany in which the reapers seized passing strangers and bound them with a corn stalk rope. The strangers were released only after they had paid a forfeit. This ritual is called, «The killing of the corn spirit.»

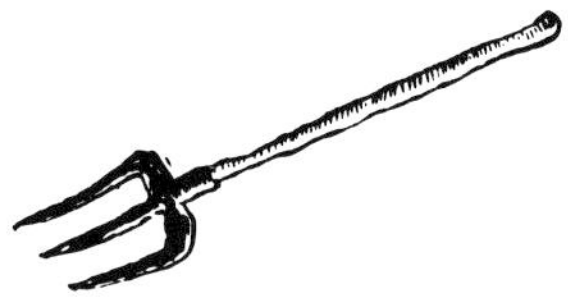

The girls are clinging to the wall in fright.
The rabbits are flinging themselves about the bathhouse.
The men with the tools
high above their heads have surrounded Dablus.
Suddenly Dablus starts to tremble, swells, glares red,
and out of it come dabloids, slowly at first,
then faster and faster. They hang above the crowd.
Everyone gets scared and their faces turn pale,
whiter than sheets. Shovels and pitchforks
in the hands of many start to tremble.
The girls come closer to one another, the rabbits
huddle under the bench, and somebody
shouts out in fear.
All of them are seen with their toothful
and toothless empty mouths open wide.
Zhilin falls to his knees.
Kostylin screws up his blue eyes.
Many, hastily throwing aside
all kinds of weaponry, rush out
of the bathhouse. Only Boris Kondratiev
keeps on spinning, holding high
his shining sickle, as if it
were the moon.

WARMING IN THE SUN

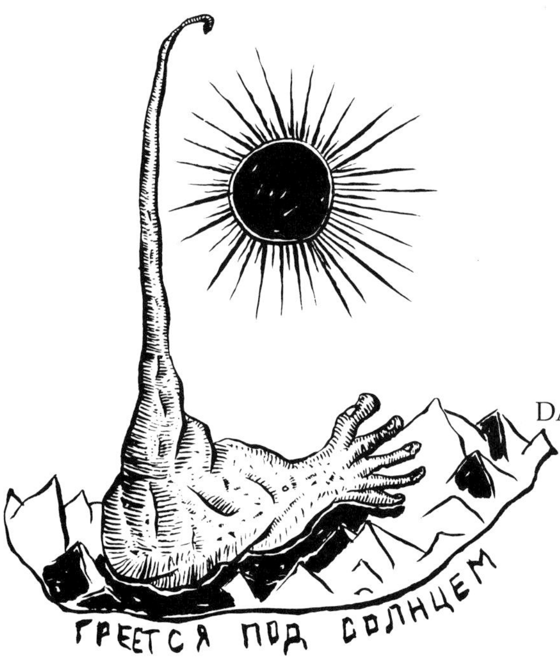

EPISODE TWO

CHOIR:
ALAS, OH DABLUS, THEY WERE BORN AND NOW
THERE IS NO PEACE FOR THEM, THE BLISSFUL, FATEFUL DAY
WILL NOT COME DOWN TO THE ILL-STARRED LAND,
ASHES, STONES AND BLOOD, GUNPOWDER,
TEARS AND SWEAT,
AND THE BITTER SMOKE OF BOOTS, OF BOOTS, OF BOOTS. . .

Scene one

A small room with a low ceiling. It looks like a dugout. There is a large table in the foreground with a scale model of a tank and a few books on it. Sitting around the table are Colonel Sychev, Major Nekhoroshko, the secretary of the party committee of the collective farm Lapin, and the military commissar Papilin. On the wall of the dugout is a big map of the theater of military operation. Near the map is the chief of civil defense of the compound, Fomin. Higher, above the roof of the dugout, one can see the edge of the village, a ravine, a field and a forest on the right. The brothers Kondratiev are running along the road in torn clothes, unshaven, some have scythes in their hands, one of them has a double-barrelled shotgun.

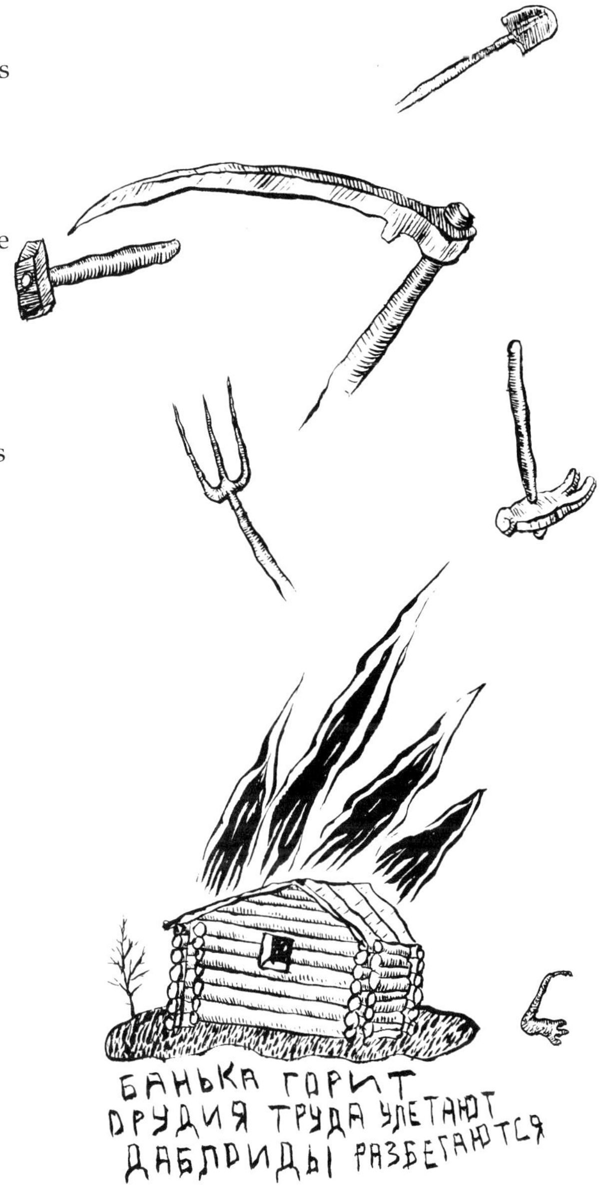

THE BATHS ARE BURNING
TOOLS OF LABOR FLY OUT
DABLOIDS SCATTER

A Kondratiev:

SHIT, ESCAPED BY THE SKIN OF OUR TEETH!

Another Kondratiev:

WE'VE BEATEN THE FUCK OUT OF THEM - LOOK, HOW GOOD THE BATHHOUSE BURNS

Yet another Kondratiev:

KOSTYLIN'S FUEL DIDN'T LET US DOWN

(turns around and shouts)

HEY YOU, WHERE THE FUCK ARE YOU?

From the left, out of the ravine, come two men. They are dragging the third, who has either drunk too much or is fatally wounded. Down in the dugout the conference continues.

Colonel Sychev:

GO ON, FOMIN.

Fomin:

WE'VE CREATED INTELLIGENCE UNITS FOR EVERY SHIFT. THEY ARE BEING TRAINED NOT ONLY ON THE TERRITORY OF THE COMPOUND, BUT ALSO IN THE SUBURBAN AREA, WHERE WORKERS, PEASANTS AND FAMILY MEMBERS WILL BE EVACUATED IN CASE OF EMERGENCY.

OUR INTELLIGENCE PERSONNEL ARE FULLY EQUIPPED WITH MEANS OF PERSONAL PROTECTION, WITH TOOLS AND

INSTRUMENTS, WITH MEANS OF COMMUNICATION AND

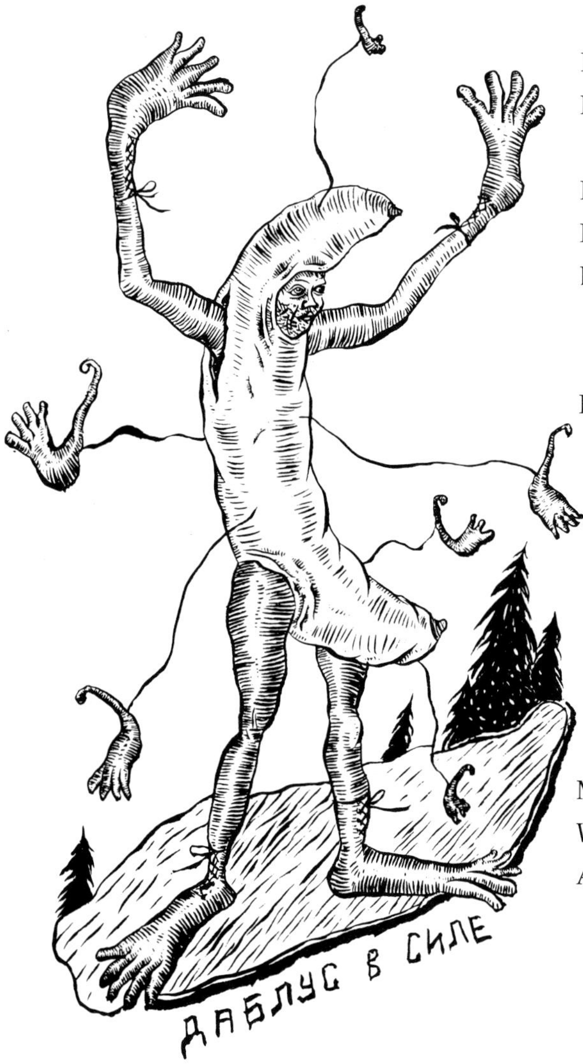

DABLUS IN FULL STRENGTH

TRANSPORTATION, AND WITH SETS OF ROAD SIGNS. THE FOLLOWING COMRADES HAVE PROVEN THEMSELVES AS HIGHLY SKILLED UNIT COMMANDERS: ENGINEERS BAYEV, KUZNETSOV, MALAKHAEV, KOSTYLIN, KOZHIN, ZHILIN, MYASIN, LEKANDRY IZOTOV, SILAEV, ALABUSHEV, THE BROTHERS KONDRATIEV, AND THE BOY SMORCHKOV. FROM YEAR TO YEAR OUR INTELLIGENCE UNIT TAKES PART IN THE REGIONAL CHAMPIONSHIPS AND NEVER COMES BACK WITHOUT A PRIZE.

Colonel Sychev:

GOOD, SIT DOWN, COMRADE. ARE THERE ANY QUESTIONS FOR THE COMRADE?

Major Nekhoroshko:

WHAT ABOUT OUR WOMEN IN THE AMBULANCE SQUAD? I MEAN THE STATE OF THEIR READINESS?

Fomin:

AT THE HEAD OF THE AMBULANCE SQUAD IS VERA BORISOVNA ZHILINA, THE EXPERIENCED FIGHTING COMMANDER OF OUR MEDICAL UNIT. THEIR NAMES ARE: KOZHINA, MYASINA, AVDOTYA SMORCHKOVA... GAS-MASKS ARE IN THE GAS-MASK BAGS, POCKETS ARE STUFFED WITH BANDAGES AND COTTON WOOL, STRETCHERS ARE ALSO READY.

Colonel Sychev:

STOP COMMANDER, THAT'S ENOUGH, BE SEATED.

Fomin sits down, the military commissar Papilin stands up.

Papilin:

THE SOLDIER STOOD WHERE STEEL BROKE DOWN,
THE SOLDIER STOOD WHERE ARMOR MELTED.*[36]

Colonel Sychev:

BE SEATED, COMRADE. ENOUGH!

NOW ABOUT VITAL ISSUES. THE MOTHERLAND IS IN DANGER. THE CREATIVE LABOR OF THE SOVIET PEOPLE IS IN DANGER AS WELL: DABLOIDS HAVE INVADED OUR LAND. COMRADE, PLEASE TELL US HOW YOU ALLOWED THIS TO HAPPEN?

Lapin:

THEY APPEARED OUT OF A BATHHOUSE THAT STANDS ON THE CORNER OF THE GARDEN OF THE COLLECTIVE FARM «GARDEN GIANT.» THERE WERE SEVEN OF THEM IN THE

36. *The lines from a song performed by The Red Army Choir.*

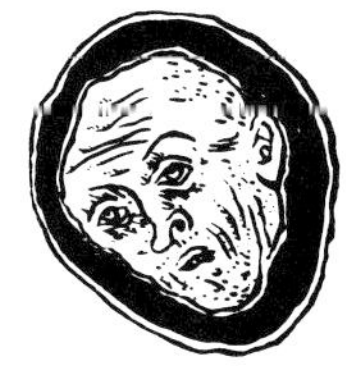

BEGINNING, BUT WHEN THE EIGHT BRAVE COLLECTIVE FARMERS DECIDED TO DESTROY THEM - THERE BECAME THIRTY FOUR OF THEM. AFTER THAT WE LOST COUNT. THERE ARE TONS OF THEM IN THE FIELD, AND IN THE FOREST AS WELL. THE VILLAGERS ARE IN PANIC, STAYING INSIDE. NO ONE DARES TO GO OUT. WORK IN THE FIELD HAS STOPPED AND THE SOWING SEASON IS JUST ROUND THE CORNER.

Colonel Sychev:

WHAT DO YOU SAY, MAJOR?

Major Nekhoroshko:

COMRADE COLONEL, WITHOUT LOSS OF TIME, WE SHOULD ENGAGE THE 90th UZBEK SPECIAL BRIGADE, SUPPORTED BY A LOCAL SPECIAL TASK FORCE UNIT , THE KGB, VOLUNTEERS OF CIVIL DEFENSE AND GUERRILLA UNITS. GIVE OUT MACHINE GUNS TO ALL KOMSOMOLS.*[37]

37. *Members of Young Communist League.*

Scene two

The dugout plunges into darkness. The field with standing dabloids is lit, one can hear mine explosions, gunfire and somebody shouting «Hurrah!». Tanks appear, they turn their turrets, alternatively firing blank and regular projectiles from time to time.

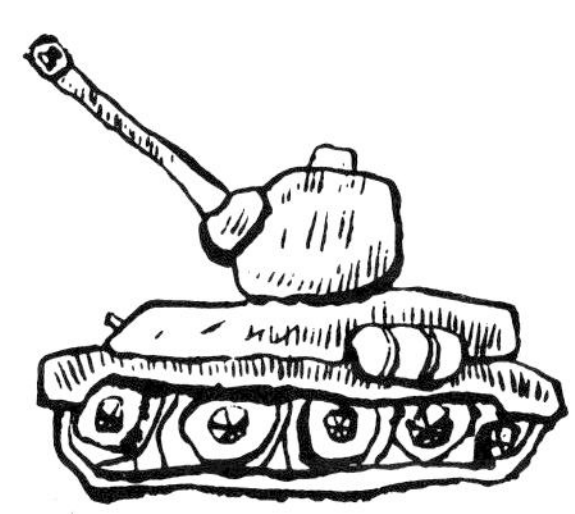

The tanks drive through the ranks of dabloids, pushing them away and crushing them with their tracks. The number of dabloids increases, now almost every space is full of dabloids. Marching behind the last tank are the infantry firing their guns. Running towards the infantry and a little to the left are women pressing their babies to their hearts. The infantry departs. The number of dabloids becomes even larger. Appearing in the center, surrounded by dabloids, is the figure of the hero Corporal Kryukov with a grenade in hand. His rifle is jammed*[38] and it is lying somewhere in the grass.

38. *It is very unusual for AK-47 automatic rifle to jam.*

Kryukov:

(pulls out the pin)

COME CLOSER, YOU BASTARDS, FUCK YOU ALL!

(a deafening explosion, little stones fly high together with glass fragments, shreds of cloth, grass, the hero's arm and his liver*[39])

39. *According to old beliefs, the soul is in the liver.*

CHOIR:

MOTHER, LOOK, THE WARRIOR'S SOUL

HAS FOUND PEACE AT LAST.

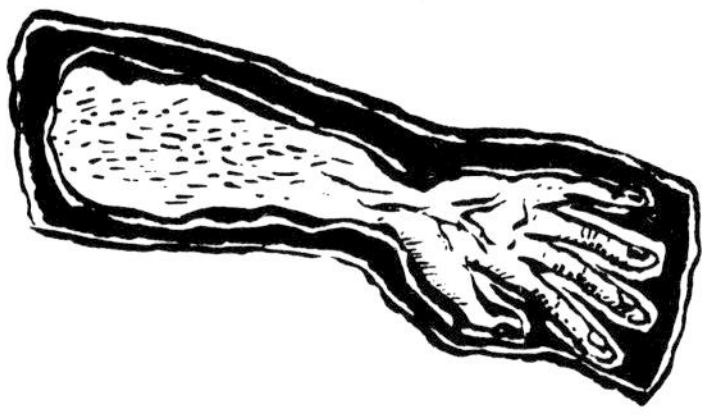

(The field plunges into darkness, the dugout is lit.)

Voices of those in the dugout:
...A HERO HAS DIED, BUT HE FULFILLED HIS DUTY
...THEY'LL STUDY THIS IN SCHOOLS
...HEAVY OFFENSIVE-DEFENSIVE FIGHTING
...«FALCON, FALCON»! - THIS IS «FORGET-ME-NOT»

Scene three

The same scene, only the war has distorted the landscape. There

are ruins on the left and on the right is a pile of scrap-metal in the forest. Birch-trees are broken. On a pole between the stumps there is a sign which reads «CONTAMINATED.» Falling suddenly from above, making noise and raising clouds of dust, is somebody in a military uniform, with a sack on his back and another on the front. Zhilin and Kostylin run in from both sides.

ACTOR
IN DABLOID
COSTUME

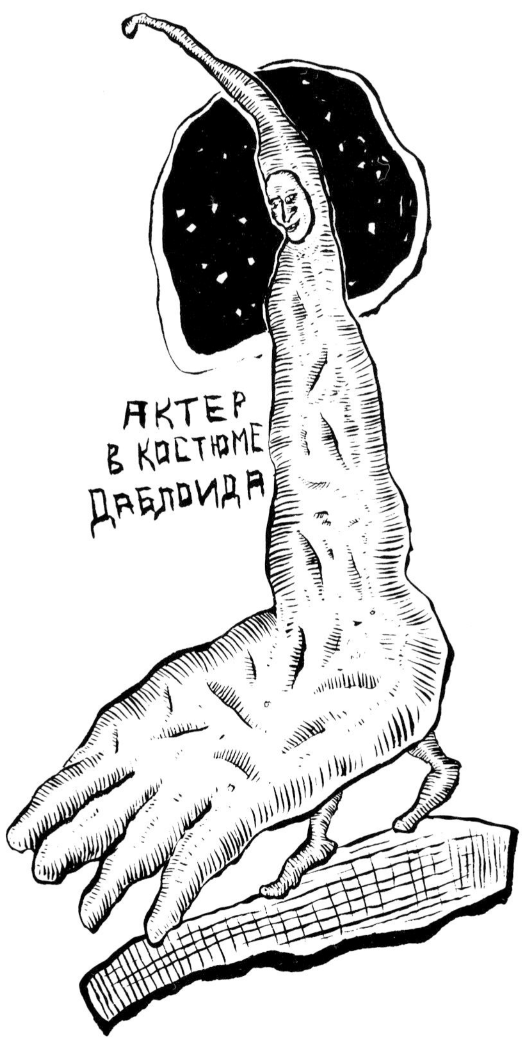

Kostylin:
ANOTHER PARATROOPER GOT HIS FINAL BLOW, THE SEVENTH SINCE THE BEGINNING OF THE GREAT BATTLE.
Zhilin:
(sadly)
AND HE KILLED A RABBIT.
Kostylin:
THE CENTER HOLDS FIRM, AND WE DON'T CARE ANY-MORE. THEY'VE BEEN LIVING IN MY GARDEN FOR AGES... DID YOU HEAR THAT, ZHILIN, THE BLIND MAN CALLS THEM A VERY STRANGE NAME...
DABLOIDS.
Zhilin:
ME? I DON'T CARE, I'M ALREADY USED TO THEM, I HAVE A DABLOID OF MY OWN, IN THE SHED. I KEEP'EM, INSTEAD OF PIGLETS, ON LAST YEAR'S HAY.
Kostylin:
WHAT IS IT, WHAT IS THAT NOISE ABOUT, FIRING AGAIN, HIDE YOURSELF, ZHILIN!
(both run away into the forest)

(from behind the leaning fence runs a young pioneer-boy,*[40] pressing a dabloid to his heart)

The young pioneer:

WHERE TO RUN, WHERE TO HIDE MYSELF,

HOW TO SAVE MY LIFE, HOW TO SURVIVE...*[41]

(runs away into the forest)

40. *Young Pioneers - members of the Pioneer organization, a type of boy-scout and girl-scout organization. All Soviet schoolchildren from 10 to 14 years of age were pioneers.*

41. *As if he is reading the titles of chapters in a survival manual for boy-scouts.*

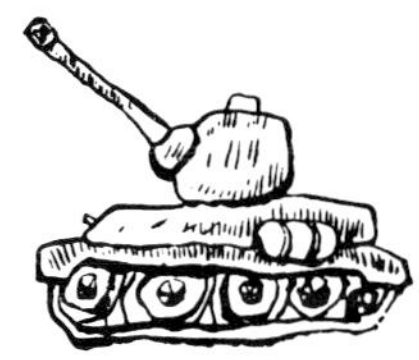

Three paratroopers appear, they have just landed in their parachutes, but they are already surveying the terrain carefully. Having detected no one, they disappear in the forest.

The dugout is lit, Colonel Sychev and Major Nekhoroshko are sitting there and drinking tea, militiaman Zlokazov is standing on the right.

Major Nekhoroshko:

AND YOU'RE TELLING ME THAT EVEN IN THE PEOPLE'S PALACE, IN THE MEMORIAL HALL, THERE IS A DABLOID, AND NOBODY...

Zlokazov:

NOT ONLY IN THE PEOPLE'S PALACE, BUT MANY HAVE THEM IN THEIR BACKYARDS, I'VE SEEN IT MYSELF. THEY ARE EVERYWHERE NOW.

Colonel Sychev:

WE HAVE LOST MANY SERVICEMEN SINCE THE BEGINNING OF THE BATTLE - THEY ARE: CAPTAIN LATYPOV, PARTY MEMBER , FELL DOWN FROM THE GUN-CARRIAGE; KRYUKOV, THE HERO; ABDULYATDINOV*[42] ALSO BLEW HIMSELF UP; LIFAR*[43] - DIED OF DYSENTERY; ALSO PARATROOPERS, TWO FROM THE SPECIAL TASK FORCE UNIT, AND TOO MANY OF THE RANK-AND-FILE TO COUNT...

42. *Abdulyatdinov - A Tatar by nationality. Representatives of all Soviet ethnic groups served in the Soviet Army in the same units with the Russians. For many non-Russians it was even more difficult because the official language of the Soviet Army was Russian.*

43. *Sergei Lifar - was a world-famous Russian ballet-dancer. (A very rare name).*

Zlokazov:

IN OUR VILLAGE, KONDRATIEV, THE MIDDLE BROTHER, STABBED HIMSELF TO DEATH WITH A SICKLE.

Major Nekhoroshko:

NOBODY WANTS TO FIGHT ANYMORE, THEY ARE DESERTING FROM THEIR UNITS AND FORGETTING ALL ABOUT THEIR DUTY, BUT THERE IS ONLY ONE FOOTHOLD LEFT -

THE CENTER WITH ITS PLATOON OF PARATROOPERS.

Colonel Sychev:

NO, MAJOR, THERE IS NO HOPE, WE WON'T BE ALIVE TO SEE VICTORY, TELEGRAM THE CENTER - WE ARE PULLING OUT TO THE BASE.*44

44. *«I went to the base» (base = depot, warehouse) - a typical sign in a window of a closed store, to the disappointment of the Soviet customer.*

Appearing from above, in the field, and in the forest are dabloids. They stand waving their heads. Women from the medical squad put the dead commando on the stretcher and leave singing a song:

IN THE OPEN BATTLE-FIELD AN UNFORGOTTEN SOLDIER
GAVE HIS LIFE FOR HIS DEAR MOTHERLAND.
ABOVE HIS DEAR GRAVE
LITTLE BELLS RING GENTLY.

Down in the dugout the door opens and Corporal Zimin runs in holding two dabloids in both hands.

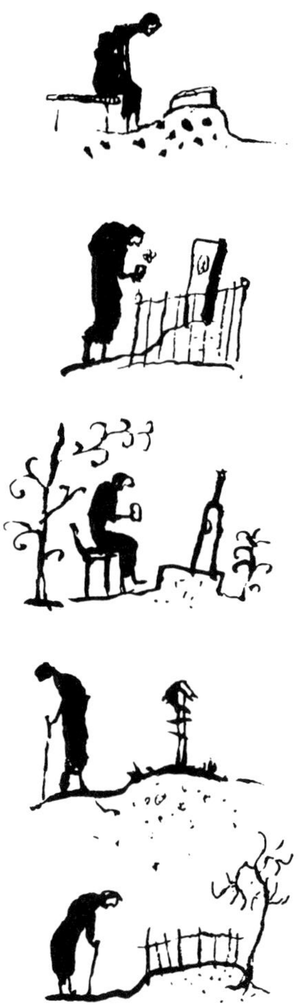

Zimin:

REQUEST PERMISSION TO REPORT, COMRADE COLONEL! TWO DABLOIDS ARE TAKEN PRISONERS. WHAT SHALL WE DO WITH THEM?

Major Nekhoroshko:

CORPORAL, I'M FED UP WITH YOUR DABLOIDS, LEAVE THEM OUT IN THE STREET.

Colonel Sychev:

ENOUGH, I CAN'T STAND IT ANY LONGER.

Zlokazov:

I ALREADY HAVE ONE, I DON'T NEED ANY MORE.
(puts his cap on and leaves)

EPISODE THREE

The innards of the director's house. The same setting. Next to the painting **Red Vineyards in Arles** there is a painting (cut out from the magazine OGONYOK*45), **A Soldier Defending His Dabloid**. Tchaikovsky's music is quietly played on the radio.

45. *The most popular Soviet weekly illustrated magazine, each issue carried not less than four full-page and full-color reproductions and an article about the featured artist. It became a very liberal political and literary magazine with the largest circulation in the Soviet Union during the Perestroika.*

It is evening. Matvei Ivanovich is sitting at the table and reading the newspaper **New Life**. The boy is sitting in the play-pen and playing with a dabloid. In the proscenium, Svetka is swinging on a dabloid.

CHOIR:
(on the radio):

THE HOUR OF RELIEF HAS COME, THE TIME OF PIETY HAS COME,
THE BLISSFUL DABLUS HAS BROUGHT TO US A REST FROM HEAVY LABOR
EVERYONE HAS RECEIVED HIS DABLOID,
WE HAVE NO OTHER CONCERN THAN FOR THEM.
WE WORSHIP DABLUS, THE DECEASED GOD,
AND AWAIT HIS RESURRECTION!

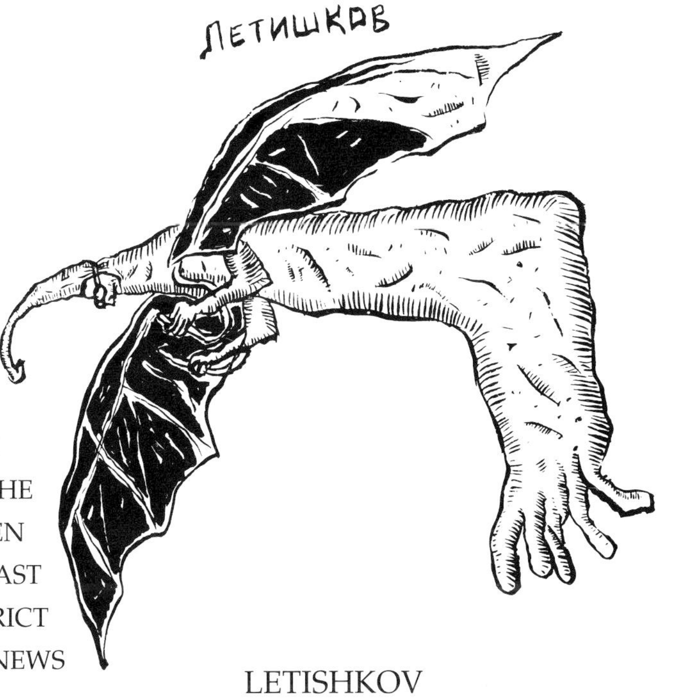

LETISHKOV

Matvei:
WHAT A NUISANCE - RAIN IS POURING FOR THE FIFTH CONSECUTIVE DAY, THE DAM IS WASHED AWAY, THE GRAIN HAS ROTTED, THE HAYFIELDS HAVE BEEN BEATEN DOWN BY HAIL, THERE IS AND WILL BE NO FUEL. THE LAST HORSE AND THE LAST TELEGRAPH POLE IN THE DISTRICT HAVE JUST COLLAPSED. AND THAT'S JUST THE LATEST NEWS IN OUR LOCAL PAPER.

Svetka:
(sings, sitting on a dabloid and swinging)
OUR TRUTH IS IN THE LAND, OUR ROOTS ARE IN THE LAND,
AND THE STRENGTH OF OUR SHOULDERS COMES FROM MEADOWS AND FIELDS.
THE LAND WILL DRESS US, THE LAND WILL ALSO FEED US,
WE MUST SACRIFICE EVERYTHING FOR THE LAND.

Natalia comes into the room out of the kitchen with a basin full of water.

Natalia:
(joining with the song)
THE LAND IS UNDER A CLEAR BLUE SKY
LIKE A DREAM COME TRUE.
CALL ME YOUR DAUGHTER, CALL ME YOUR SON,
BUT SINCE CHILDHOOD I HAVE BEEN
CALLING YOU MY MOTHER.

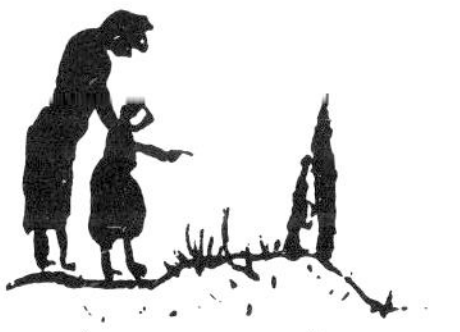

(puts the basin next to a dabloid)

I'VE WASHED MY DABLOID, NOW, SVETKA, IT IS TIME TO WASH YOURS, STOP SWINGING, GET OFF. MATVEI, HELP.

(They all stand around the dabloid and wash it, Matvei holds the basin and a towel. They all start singing.)

THE DIAMONDS OF MORNING DEW-DROPS ARE SHINING,
AND STARS ARE FALLING INTO THE GRASS.
CALL ME YOUR DAUGHTER, CALL ME YOUR SON, BUT SINCE
CHILDHOOD I HAVE BEEN CALLING YOU MY MOTHER.

(The boy also wants to join them. He takes his dabloid and blows it as if it were a trumpet.)

TAM, BA-RA-BA-RA,
PA-RA-PA-PA,
PAM, PAM, PAM,
PAM, BA-RA-BA-PA,
PA-RA-PA-PA-PAM!

A sudden knock on the door stops the celebration, Matvei walks out, returns in a second, all pale and excited. Natalia, Svetka and the boy glance at the director inquiringly.

Matvei Ivanovich:

GRANNY HAS COME!

(He puts on his heavy wadded jacket, takes the keys from the bathhouse and leaves.)*46

THE END

46.*Tishkov believes that «an artist should always be somewhere in proximity to his creations.» Therefore, he makes this mysterious ending so that his readers and the audience should look for another written text by the author or for the author himself in search of an explanation (Deus ex machina). This is what he could have told the audience. The people don't realize that the more they fight dabloids, the more destruction they are bringing on themselves, because dabloids are reflections of their souls. It is pretty simple: the angrier someone gets, the more furious and red his/her dabloid (alter ego) turns. This lasts until someone realizes that he or she has a dabloid. The awareness of your dabloid makes you control your behavior. When you forget about your dabloid it can leave you and start a fight with another abandoned dabloid. Thus, it is useless and foolish to fight dabloids. Only children and wise elders know the wisdom or perhaps subconsciously feel it: one should love Dablus and one's dabloid, and Dablus and your dabloid will bring you peace in return. That is why children liked to play with Dablus and Matvei felt so good when he fell asleep near Dablus in the collective farm office. The children, the blind madman who is the first to give the name to Dablus and who actually «sees» what is happening to it, Matvei who doesn't go to fight dabloids, and Granny (Babushka) who saves Dablus from the fire in her bathhouse, are the only «normal» people in the play. It takes a lot of destruction and sufferings for others to regain their «normality.» Now Babushka brings Dablus to Matvei and they go to his bath-house. There are people to take care of Dablus, and this means that there is still some hope left for the salvation of the world.*

Commentaries and translation from Russian by Mikhail Novikov (I would like to express my thanks to Michael Conrad and Dominique Gore for their assistance with this text). 12/9/92.

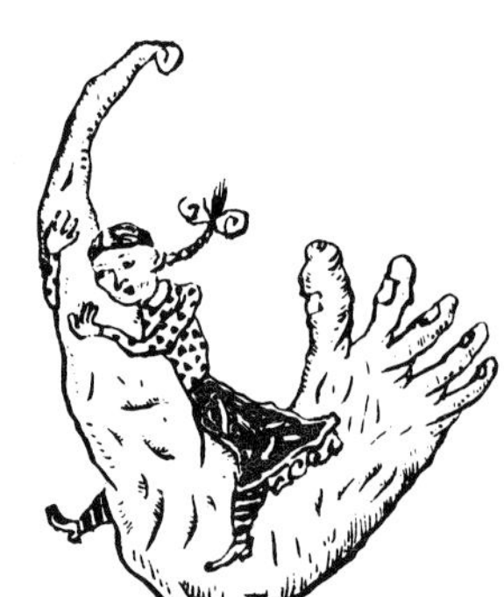

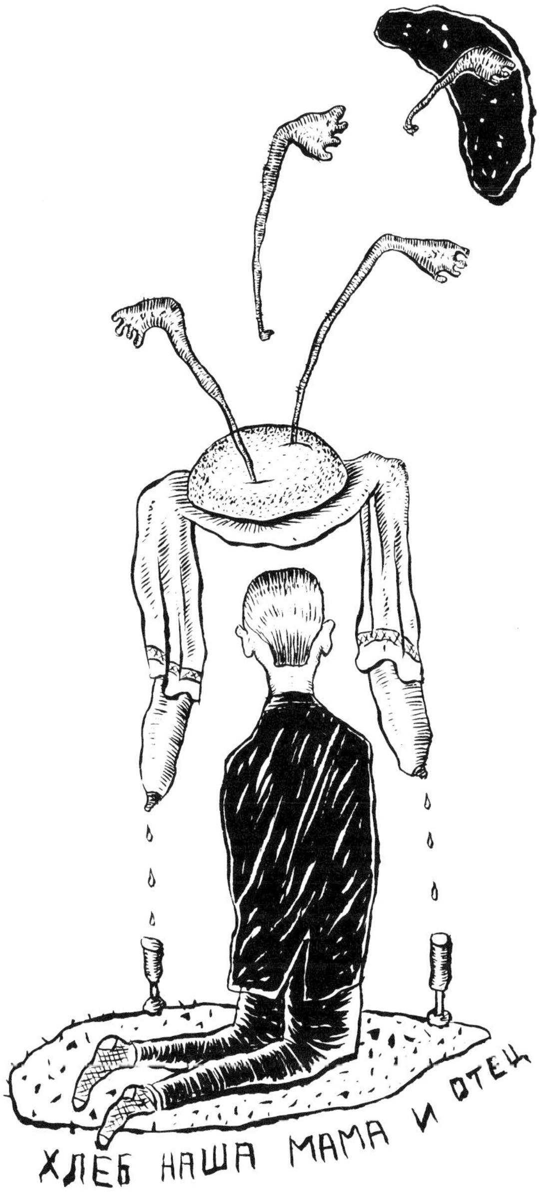

BREAD IS OUR MOTHER AND FATHER

Michael P. Mezzatesta

DABLOIDS AND MOTHER EARTH

NOTES ON RUSSIAN FOLK CULTURE AND THE ART OF LEONID TISHKOV

As the curtain rises for Act I of Tishkov's play, **Dabloids**, dawn is breaking over the soft black soil of a recently plowed field at the collective farm, Garden Giant. A cold morning fog hangs thick and low over the deep furrows. In the distance the Russian wilderness of endless birch forest looms above the black earth. Birds are singing. It is early spring.

From far away, music is heard and a song gradually grows in volume until its words ring clear:

Our truth is in the land, our roots are in the land,
And the strength of our shoulders
comes from meadows and fields.
The land will dress us, the land will also feed us,
We must sacrifice everything for the land.
The land is under a clear blue sky —
Like a dream come true.
Call me your daughter,
Call me your son,
But since childhood I have been calling you my mother.

As the song concludes, the light sound of a broken string pierces the air. Frightened birds loudly take flight. Suddenly, we see emerging from the moist, rich earth a large object. Incredibly, it is shaped like a gigantic sausage with a female breast at each end! It is Dablus. A Malevich-inspired choir appears and chants:

Oh, Dablus, the beautiful and
Just father, yielding
The aromas of Eden.
The flesh and fruit of a crown-bearing tree.
The immortal dual-titted object.
The vessel full of bliss
Evaporating the drops of the invigorating
Sweet-ruby juice.
The pale-milky mother stuffed with meat and juice.
He is lying in mud
The great and eternal
Handsome Dablus.

So, with a mystical and mysterious aura, Tishkov sets the scene for **Dabloids**. Although subsequent events recounting the astounding tale of the Dabloid's miraculous birth from Dablus are often hilarious, **Dabloids**, far from being a farce, is nothing less than a modern day morality play where burlesque and satire mask the action's messianic core. Even the setting, a farm in the heartland--the symbolic center of Russian life--conveys the immediacy of the play's message. **Dabloids** are creatures that occupy the center of Tishkov's universe, a universe which, as we shall see, is deeply rooted in a thousand years of Russian cultural tradition.

The song that opens **Dabloids**, with its reference to the land as «mother,» provides the key for understanding the play, for it recalls the age old worship among the Russian peasantry of «Mother Earth.» Russian historian George Fedotov saw this widespread and deeply held devotion as the heart of Russian faith. «In Mother Earth, who remains the core of Russian religion, converge the most secret and deep religious feelings of the folk. Beneath the beautiful veil of grass and flowers, the people venerate with awe the black, moist depths, the source of all fertilizing powers, the nourishing breast of nature, and their own last resting place. The very epithet of the earth in the folk songs, "Mother Earth, the Humid," alludes to the womb rather than to the face of the Earth. It means that not beauty but fertility is the supreme virtue of the earth. . .Earth is the Russian "Eternal Womanhood," not the celestial image of it: mother, not virgin; fertile, not pure; and black, for the best Russian soil is black.»[1] «Mother Earth» is everywhere. She is the very land upon which all things grow. She controls the patterns of life through the rituals of the agrarian calendar. She is the source of all life. We emerge from her when we are born and return to her when we die.[2] «"Mother Earth" was perceived, then, as a cosmic egg containing humanity between the breast of the sky and the womb of the soil.»[3]

This cosmic conception of the land and its protective relationship to the people traces its origin to the pre-Christian period of Russian history and the worship of Mokosh, the Mother Goddess. The rise at Kiev of the Slavic kingdom of the Varangians, the founders of the Russian state, in the 9th and 10th centuries witnessed the establishment of an official pantheon of divinities among whom was Mokosh, the only female goddess.[4] This «moist» goddess roamed the land to insure the fertility of the soil. She assured the generation and maintenance of life and was the goddess of women, childbirth, and animals. She had no mate, and needed none. She was the very image of fertility and abundance.[5]

The conversion of Russia to Christianity in 988 witnessed the gradual disappearance of Mokosh, but not the ideas that she embodied. The notion of a maternal protector was, of course, subsumed to the person of the Mother of God. Byzantine icons of the Blessed Virgin offered an official substitute for the pagan divinity. Yet, despite the efforts of the Russian Orthodox Church to eradicate pagan traditions, the cult of Mother Earth survived in the folk consciousness. A popular Russian proverb illustrates the persistence of the notion of Mother Earth: «Your first mother is Mary; your second mother is the earth, and your third mother is your own mother.»[6]

As Russia was a predominantly agrarian, peasant society well into the 20th century, this is not surprising, for the cycle of daily life was governed by people's relationship to the earth and the changing of the seasons. «In peasant tradition,. . ., all things are borne by the earth and derive from her fertility. . . The soil is sacred: The peasants implore "Mother Moist Earth" for aid in their lives. She seems to need no mate. She is self-moistened, self-inseminated.»[7] This deep, spiritual connection to the land remains one of the central forces in Russian life, for the notion of Mother Russia as a national identification, and Mother Earth as a socio-religious mythological legacy, were fused into a powerfully spiritual, common cultural bond. Tishkov's opening song invokes this centuries old folk tradition of «Mother Earth,» a life force providing strength and sustenance to her children.

The appearance of Dablus from the moist, black soil as the choir sings a paean in its honor, refers to what may be seen as the other side of the cultural coin--the role of the divine. From the conversion of Russia to Christianity in the 10th century, the Russian Orthodox Church has been the dominant influence in the spiritual life of the nation. The continuous construction of monasteries and churches throughout various periods of

Russian history attested to the deep spiritual faith of the Russian people.[8] This was amply demonstrated not only in the magnificent structures that covered the breadth of the land, but also on a more humble scale. In every peasant home hung, in the sacred «red corner,» a painted icon of Christ or the Virgin Mary. These images were the average person's link to the divine and so played a profoundly important role in the individual's and family's religious devotions.9 It is, therefore, particularly interesting that Tishkov has revealed the source for Dablus is the oval bolster which appears on the throne of the Blessed Virgin Mary in Russian icons!

Of course, Dablus could hardly be considered an orthodox image from the lexicon of Russian icons. Rather, it is a combination of folk and religious traditions, one which also reflects a fundamental aspect of Russian culture. Historians long have seen Russian history in terms of what has been called «dual faith» (*dvoeverie*) — a parallel system of folk-pagan beliefs versus the Russian Orthodox creed.[10] However, these two systems were not mutually exclusive. Over the centuries there occurred a syncretic fusion expressing the integral relationship between pagan and Christian beliefs, beliefs that «were tightly knit in a cultural-religious synthesis expressing the age-old traditions and interests of a rural community and class.» [11] These systems were not contradictory and incompatible--the parallel lines of «dual faith»--but complementary and natural parts of the daily life of the people.[12]

Dablus rises from the soil of «Moist Mother Earth.» Yet, like Christ, Dablus comes to us from on high:

O heavenly and just
Invigorating Dablus - Father and Mother
Sent down to us from above, transfigured
Granting truth, eternal, viviparous,
Radiant, sent down to us by the dawn
and dew
To our joy, bringing us deliverance
And eternal joy, peace and progress.
(Episode 2, Scene 1)

Despite Dablus' curious, hybrid nature, there is no doubt that we are in the presence of the divine. But what kind of god? Tishkov has fused the female--the life sustaining support of Mother Earth («The pale-milky mother stuffed with meat and juice») and the seminal role of the Mother of God («Vessel full of bliss»), with the male--God the Father («Yielding the aromas of Eden»), and Christ («The flesh and fruit of a crown-bearing tree»), to create a new divinity--one who emerges from the sacred soil of Mother Earth--DABLUS. Like Mother Earth, Dablus needs no consort for it is self-inseminating, containing the essence of both sexes in its very form--phallus and breast. It is, in sum, the divine androgyne.

The ideal of perfect androgyny--the fusion of male and female characteristics--was a basic element in the philosophical system of Jacob Boehme, the 19th century philosopher who was the dominant figure in the development of a Russian philosophical tradition. In Boehme's system, the whole universe was an expression of the wisdom of God and all of man's actions were part of his effort to regain the lost unity between God and man. Before the Fall, Adam knew perfect union with God, a spiritual perfection attained without sex. Part of man's return to God would be the achievement of the principle of «eternal femininity» through the attainment of perfect androgyny.[13] In Dablus, we have the paradigm of spiritual perfection.

Dablus is not really a new divinity but, as we have seen, a combination of Russian folk and Orthodox traditions, a synthesis expressing Tishkov's family background and his own deep interest in folk culture.[14] Pagan folk beliefs and rituals survived for centuries as an integral part of Russian life; a fact mirrored by the wealth of allusions to Russian folk ritual and art that appear throughout the play. Perhaps the most significant of these allusions is related to the time of year. It is no accident that Tishkov sets the action in early spring, the moment when the birds have returned and the fields have been plowed and are ready to be seeded. This is a critical period in the agrarian calendar, one that for centuries has been marked by a number of elaborate folk rituals celebrating the return of life to the land.

The earliest of these, *Semik*, took place on the seventh Thursday after Easter. During this period the young women of the village went into the woods, selected a young birch tree, decorated it with flowers and ribbons, and sang and danced around it. Later, the tree was felled, dressed in women's clothes, and brought to the village where it was placed in a house and treated as an honored guest. On Pentecost Sunday, it was stripped of its finery, carried to the river and thrown in, ceremonially drowned, so as to release the spirit of spring.[15] Similar rituals were enacted at other times during the spring or summer. Closest to *Semik* was *Kostroma*. Here again the women of the village were the leaders, making a flax doll, either male or female, which was dressed in clothes and flowers, carried in procession, honored in the village, then ritually burned, buried, and resurrected--a rite to insure fertility and renewal.[16]

These folk ceremonies recall the events in the collective farm bathhouse in Episode 5, Scene 1. The location of the action is especially significant for the bathhouse occupied a position of special importance in Russian folk culture. It was a «*bozhena* (from *bog*, "god") or "temple" in Russian folklore, the traditional focus of all prophecy, sorcery, and magical cures».[17] In the scene, young girls ages 10-15 stand around Dablus dressing him/her with a shirt, tie, scarf, and wreath of yellow wheat. Like the maidens who dressed the birch tree in the Semik rituals, they too chant and sing as they now dance around Dablus; undress him/her; pour water on him/her; and prepare to wash Dablus with a rabbit, «the furry receptacle of the soul.»[18]

The concern of the collective farm's men that something lewd is taking place in the bathhouse is misplaced. Clearly they have forgotten the rituals of their grandparents. Although the scene is certainly charged sexually, the energy is ritualistic and focused on Dablus as the symbolic giver of life. In this regard, the «bacchic» celebrations are reminiscent of the major *Semik* ceremony called *kumstvo* that occurred after the dressing of the birch tree. Young girls, wearing birch garlands with wheat entwined, circled the tree, kissed one another and embraced, pledging eternal blood ties, *kumstvo*, on behalf of their families.[19] The ceremony was meant to signify the unification of nature and humanity as the garlands of birch and wheat symbolically trapped the girls' fertility until they were ready to marry, thereby assuring the continuity of the village.[20] This notion of fertility is conveyed in the girls' chants as they begin to undress Dablus:

Our milky Granny,
Dear Babushka Demeter,
Give us back your wealth,
The juice of a young father!

Demeter, of course, is the goddess of the earth whose daughter Kore (Persephone) was abducted by Pluto to live in the underworld as his wife. Kore's annual return to visit her mother marked the beginning of spring. The young girls of the collective farm--granddaughters of the Russified Greek goddess «*Babushka* Demeter»--mark the beginning of spring by invoking the fertilizing powers of Dablus/Demeter/Mother Earth.

This bath scene also recalls the folk ritual of the cleansing of the newborn child in the bathhouse, the temple of the pagan *rozhanitsy* (goddesses of fate), and the child's reception into the pagan cult of Mother Earth.[21] Indeed, after Dablus has been undressed and washed/baptized, he/she is carried to Elvira Myasina and placed on her knees, «as if it were a baby».[22] Subsequent events confirm the generative symbolism of the ritual when Dablus--attacked by the men of the farm--swells, grows, glows red and gives birth to dozens and then hundreds of **dabloids** (Part II, Episode 1, Scene 1).

The **Dabloids** represent another important connection to Russian folk tradition. Their arrival, though charged with apocalyptic overtones in the midst of battle, is actually a sign of hope. These **Dabloids**, far from being frightening, threatening, or dangerous, harm no one. Indeed, all the human casualties in the ensuing battle are caused by accidents or self-inflicted wounds. Gradually, the fighting subsides as the soldiers and farmers adopt a Dabloid for themselves. **Dabloids** become the patrons and protectors of their human friends, providing their owners a sense of security and peace. In this, **Dabloids** recall the fantastic creatures of Russian folklore, creatures who mirrored aspects of nature and dwelled in the trees, rivers, and springs of the forest land: *Bereginy* and *Rusalki*, mermaid-like women with long hair who lived in the rivers and protected travelers; *Sirens*, bird-woman, originally connected with water, rain, and fertility; *Senmurvy*, dogs with wings who, by flapping their wings, made spring come; and the *Simarql*, «a singing creature, part bird and part dog, who lived in an oak tree at the edge of the world and would spread his wings to make the wind come and distribute seeds.»[23]

In addition to these fabulous creatures, almost every aspect of village life had a special «spirit» associated with it. The *leshi* lived in the forest; the *domovoi* lived in the house; the *bannik* in the bathhouse; and the *vodianoi* in the rivers. These spirits, and others, were both feared and loved, blamed for bad luck or invoked for protection.[24]

Guardians of houses, farmland, animals, and people, they formed an integral part of the mystical-religious world of the Russian peasant. They appeared on carvings, embroidery, distaffs, prints--all manner of folk art--as invocations for protection and support. These powerful beings were essential elements in the complex cycle of human life, «and were foci for ritual activities in which entire communities participated.»[25] **Dabloids** too fill this mytho-religious role, serving as modern day folk spirits/guardian angels, spirits whose ancestors dwell in the endless reaches of the Russian forests and in village barns, bathhouses, or homes.

Ritual activities often were accompanied by music and song. In this regard, Tishkov's use of a choir is also of special interest in its evocation of classical Greek theater, although here with an amusingly incongruous tone of high drama. However, the comic allusion to a convention of ancient theater masks a serious intention. Tishkov's chorus, far from being dressed in Attic robes, appears as the peasantry--life-sized cutouts borrowed directly from Malevich's late paintings. Thus, like all the play's protagonists, the chorus too is directly linked to the earth. Their songs, or chants, evoke the folk spells, or *zagovor*, used to communicate with the folk spirits. Such chants and ritual songs were performed at the special occasions of village life or even in response to daily mishaps or problems.[26] These magical incantations charged the proceeding with the power to summon the beneficent influences of the spirits. Throughout **Dabloids**, the peasant-choir affords the magical link between heaven and Mother Earth.

As we have seen, the action of **Dabloids** unfolds during the early spring, the beginning of the season of renewal and growth. Equally significant is the fact that it is 1989, the twilight of *perestroika*. Framed portraits of Lenin, Gorbachev, and Yeltsin hang in the office of the Garden Giant's director, Matvei Ivanovich. The moment affords Tishkov a final opportunity to skewer familiar characters and social situations of the Soviet system.

Our first encounter with Matvei Ivanovich sees him railing against Communist Party bureaucracy, «a gang of bastards» whose inefficiency is delaying the sowing of the fields (Episode 1, Scene 1). Yet, government stupidity is only part of the problem at Garden Giant, where shopping means buying whatever happens to appear in the stores, regardless of whether you need it. Natalia, Matvei's wife, announces that she bought seven bars of soap even though she already has twenty-five. Matvei himself suggests that they stock up on skis. They only have eleven pairs and, even though it is spring, winter is just around the corner (Episode 4, Scene 1)! This is not fantasy or theater of the absurd but, as any Russian will testify, the harsh reality of consumer shortages in the centrally planned Soviet economic system. However, Tishkov's burlesque masks a situation more serious than the shortage of consumer goods. Far more troubling than economic hardship is a spiritual poverty that affects the members of the collective farm. A sense of alienation and isolation pervades the farm, a fact we are made aware of by startlingly frank and unexpected statements from characters and author. In response to the suggestion that the object discovered in the field may have been lost by Pyotr Yegorovich, we hear him respond: «No, I didn't lose anything. Everything has already been lost. I own nothing. Lost and lonely is Petrusha in the universe.» (Episode 2, Scene 1). In Episode 4, Scene 3, tucked within the mundane description of the scene and its characters is the statement, «There is no truth on earth and unhappy people live in the village.» Outside the bathhouse in Episode 5, Scene 1, «beggars are sleeping everywhere.»

It is to this «sad landscape» of spiritual desolation and existential isolation that Dablus arrives as a redeemer.[27] Dablus' appearance is, in effect, a kind of second coming. Like the first, Dablus is not immediately recognized or accepted. Only the blind madman, symbolically located on the church porch, «sees» Dablus for what it is. Yet, the attraction, though at first inexplicable, is undeniable. Matvei Ivanovich awakes embarrassed finding that he has fallen asleep embracing Dablus:

You won't believe it, but when everybody left I suddenly felt like embracing this... this... thing. And then, I fell asleep cuddling up to it, forgetting myself. Forgetting about everything. . .Oh, it has confused my soul. Take it away, fast, (Episode 2, Scene 2).

Dablus also provides comfort for the two drunks, Pavlik and Alyoshka, who discover Dablus hanging in the shed (Episode 3, Scene 1). At first frightened by the strange object, they discover that it is soft and warm and smells like bread. Then like babies, they suckle, one from each end, and warm pink juice runs down their cheeks and floods the floor. Bread and wine, the ingredients of salvation, are Dablus.[28]

By the end of the play, almost everyone has acquired a Dabloid and, consequently, is happy. The final scene takes place in Matvei Ivanovich's house where his two children play contentedly with their **Dabloids** to the sound of Tchaikovsky's music. Natalia appears from the kitchen with a basin of water. She has washed her Dabloid and now urges Matvei to join her and Svetka as they clean Svetka's Dabloid too. As they do, all sing a song reminiscent of that which opened the play:

The diamonds of morning dew drops are shining,
And stars are falling onto the grass.
Call me your daughter,
Call me your son,
But since childhood I have been calling you my mother.

A sudden knock on the door stops the celebration. Matvei leaves to answer it, returns momentarily «all pale and excited» and announces «Granny has come.» Taking the keys to the bathhouse, he leaves with her. The curtain falls.

And so the play ends, as mysteriously as it began, presumably with Granny, the keeper of Dablus and the font of folk tradition, taking Matvei to the family bathhouse--the temple of Dablus--to be initiated into the cult of Dablus (Mother Earth) and to receive his own Dabloid. Matvei's exit symbolizes the beginning of a «new life» for him, as it does for anyone who embraces Dablus and the **Dabloids**.[29]

Like the ancient rituals of Russian folk culture that celebrate birth and the return of spring after the long, dark winter, **Dabloids** celebrates the end of a Bolshevik winter that lasted for seventy-two years. Prophetically, the month and year in which **Dabloids** takes place, May 1989, is one thousand years after the conversion of Russia to Christianity in May of 988. **Dabloids** marks the end of the Soviet era and, most importantly, the beginning of the second millenium of Russian history. The rebirth of Mother Russia and the Age of **Dabloids** have arrived.

NOTES

1. G. P. Fedotov, *The Russian Religious Mind: Kievan Christianity - The Tenth to the Thirteenth Century*, I, Cambridge, Massachusetts (1966), 12-13.

2. Joanna Hubbs, *Mother Russia: The Feminine Myth in Russian Culture*, Bloomington and Indianapolis (1988), 56.

3. Hubbs, *Mother Russia*, 56

4. Hubbs, *Mother Russia*, 16.

5. Hubbs, *Mother Russia*, 20.

6. Hubbs, *Mother Russia*, 21. See also James H. Billington, *The Icon and the Axe: An Interpretive History of Russian Culture*, New York (1966), 20, on the notion of motherhood and the Russian national consciousness.

7. Hubbs, *Mother Russia*, xiii-xiv.

8. A particularly interesting example was the construction by the Istar River outside Moscow in the 17th century of the Monastery of the New Jerusalem. The complex of buildings included a church modelled on the church over the Holy Sepulchre in Jerusalem. See Billington, *The Icon and the Axe*, 142.

9. Billington, *The Icon and the Axe*, 35.

10. Billington, *The Icon and the Axe*, 18f. See also, Moshe Lewin, *The Making of the Soviet System: Essays in the Social History of Interwar Russia*, New York (1985), 69-71; Alison Hilton, «Piety and Pragmatism: Orthodox Saints and Slavic Nature Gods in Russian Folk Art,» 55ff, and Margarita Mazo, «We Don't Summon Spring in the Summer: Traditional Music and Beliefs of the Contemporary Russian Village,» 76, both in *Christianity and the Arts in Russia*, William C. Brumfield and Milos M. Velimirovic (eds.), Cambridge, 1991.

11. Lewin, *Soviet System*, 70.

12. Mazo, «Traditional Music,» 78.

13. Billington, *The Icon and the Axe*, 310-311.

14. For Tishkov's family background, see the essay by Ludmila Lunina in this catalogue.

15. Hilton, «Piety and Pragmatism,» 63; Hubbs, Mother Russia, 73; and Elizabeth A.Warner, *The Russian Folk Theatre*, The Hague - Paris (1927), 22-23.

16. Hubbs, *Mother Russia*, 74-78, and Warner, *Russian Folk Theatre*, 24-27. For the related Jarilo celebrations, see Warner, 27-29.

17. Hubbs, Mother Russia, 15.

18. From Episode 5, Scene 1.

19. Hubbs, *Mother Russia*, 72.

20. Hubbs, *Mother Russia*, 73.

21. Hubbs, *Mother Russia*, 59. Hubbs also noted that, «marriage rituals in the bathhouse were as important as church ceremonies. The bathhouse and the *rozhanitsy* were the center of the cult of the Family, and in Kievan and Muscovite Russia, old women were censured by the priesthood, most particularly for the special feasts which they prepared in honor of the goddess of fate who presided over childbirth.» Hubbs, *Mother Russia*, 15.

22. A Christological allusion is conveyed in Svetka's call for water to wash «the exhausted fisherman» whose «skin [is] doused with the vessel's blood.» Episode 5, Scene 1.

23. Hilton, «Piety and Pragmatism,» 61.

24. Mazo, «Traditional Music,» 79.

25. Hilton, «Piety and Pragmatism,» 62.

26. Mazo, «Traditional Music,» 79.

27. The view from the office of the Garden Giant's director is called «a sad landscape of Russia,» Episode 2, Scene 1. For Dablus the redeemer, see the choir's chant, Part II, Episode 1, «Oh Dablus born twice ...,» and Part II, Episode 3, «We worship Dablus, the deceased God, and are awaiting his resurrection.»

28. See Episode 5, Scene 1, where the choirs chant: «Oh Dablus!. . . The Father of Golden Grain. . .The Gravid Mother of Wheat» and the choir's chant, «Sweet-ruby Juice,» at the opening of the play.

29. The final scene sees Matvei sitting on a chair reading the newspaper, *New Life*. The idea of redemption also is signaled by the presence in Matvei Ivonovich's home of a copy of Van Gogh's, *Red Vineyards in Arles*, with its obvious dabloidian (red) and eucharistic symbolism.

CATALOGUE

1. While they haven't their own elephants they must sit in anthills, 09.18.1989, India ink on paper, 75x100 cm.

2. Each of us has his own elephant, 06.04. 1989, India ink on paper, 75x100 cm.

3. Living In a Trunk enjoys the sun, 09.27. 1989, India ink on paper, 75x100 cm.

4. One must look after Living In a Trunk and with food nourish living in a trunk, 06.17.1989, India ink on paper, 75x100 cm.

5. Living In a Trunk also wants a little love, 06.17.1989, Indian ink on paper, 75x100 cm.

6. L.I.T. goes to the North Pole to leave a rag on a stick there, 07.04. 1989, India ink on paper, 75x100 cm.

7. A very heavy suitcase but in it are Living In a Trunk's things, 09.27.1989, India ink on paper, 75x100 cm.

8. What has this freedom given him L.I.T. crawls along the ground like a worm, 06.27.1989, India ink on paper, 75x100 cm.

9. L.I.T. looks in a microscope and sees: even the smallest microbe lives in a trunk, 07.04. 1989, India ink on paper, 75x100 cm.

10. Thus sleep Living In Trunks roll up in balls close their eyes and silently lie crying in the dark, 09.27.1989, India ink on paper, 75x100 cm.

11. Entertainment for L.I.T.: bird-shooting, 09.27.1989,India ink on paper, 75x100 cm.

12. Living In Trunks' play on the violin pleases their elephants, 09.05.1989, India ink on paper, 75x100 cm, Collection of Mr. and Mrs. Gosnell.

13. Living In Trunks are armed to the teeth both these and those, 09.03.1989, India ink on paper, 75x100 cm.

14. At night they awakened Living In Trunks in alarm and they ran with gasmasks on, 09.05.1989, India ink on paper, 75x100 cm.

15. L.I.T's elephant grows to the size of the universe, 09.27.1987, India ink on paper, 75x100 cm.

16. What a fool, thinks he's L.I.T. — until the first rain, 07.04.1989, India ink on paper, 75x100 cm.

17. This one that's left his trunk will still be lying on the ground when the others move ahead, 06.18.1989, India ink on paper, 75x100 cm.

18. His elephant died of radiation and L.I.T. is still trying to put out the fire, 07.04.1989, India ink on paper, 75x100 cm.

19. Living In a Trunk's elephant went out of his mind, 06.26.1989, India ink on paper, 75x100 cm.

20. L.I.T. takes care of his elephant licking his hide, 09.02.1989, India ink on paper, 75x100 cm.

21. Happy L.I.T.s: in one trunk for life!, 09.27.1989, India ink on paper, 75x100 cm.

22. Living In a Trunk's elephant drowns in a swamp, 06.26.1989, India ink on paper, 75x100 cm.

23. It's very easy to kill L.I.T. with a shot to the back of the head just feed his elephant hay, 07.04.1989, India ink on paper, 75x100 cm.

24. Fatal mistake of a lunatic: Living In a Trunk commits the suicide of his elephant, 12.02.1989, India ink on paper, 75x100 cm.

25. There is always hope to save yourself just firmly clench your teeth and let the wind rock us all it can — Living In a Trunk, 12.01. 1989, India ink on paper, 75x100 cm.

26. In the desert will remain only the pale bones of an elephant and Living In a Trunk, 12.02.1989, India ink on paper, 75x100 cm.

27. Large Dabloid, 1990-93, acrylic on canvas, 200x200 cm.

28. Dabloid track, 1990, oil on canvas, 32x25 cm.

29. Simplified Dabloid, 1990, oil on canvas, 32x25 cm.

30. Dabloid Rune, 1990, oil on canvas, 32x25 cm.

31. A sunken ship — danger for a sailing Dabloid, 1990, oil on canvas, 25x32 cm.

32. From what depths do Dabloids arise?, 1990, oil on canvas, 32x25 cm.

33. Their eyes are directed to this sky, 1990, oil on canvas, 32x25 cm.

34. The rocky shore is a danger to Dabloid, 1990, oil on canvas, 32x25 cm.

35. Ancient symbols of Dabloid and Man, 1990, oil on canvas, 32x25 cm.

36. Simple Dablus, 1990, oil on canvas, 32x25 cm.

37. His skin is like human skin, 1990, oil on canvas, 25x32cm.

38. When the Dabloid disappears, 1990, oil on canvas, 32x25 cm.

39. It's nothing to do with the team «Dynamo» — it's the sign of the Dabloid, 1990, oil on canvas, 32x25 cm.

40. Dablus, twelve Dabloids and television, installation, 1993, cloth, threads, applique, video.

41. Red Dabloid: my mountains remained in the Urals — my favorite stones live there, 1992, cloth, 120x70x30 cm.

42. Black Dabloid: stroke me, a poor thing, oh big-headed person, 1992, cloth, 120x80x25 cm.

43. New About Dabloid, folio cover, 1992, pencil, watercolor, collage on paper, 52x39 cm.

44. Descent From the Mountain Kukan, page of folio, 1992, pencil, watercolor, India ink on paper, 52x39 cm.
45. Flat-footedness gives us the joy to feel life more fully, page of folio, 1992, pencil, watercolor, India ink, collage on paper, 52x39 cm.
46. Where did Dabloids come from, page from folio, 1992, pencil, watercolor, India ink on paper, 52x39 cm.
47. Brahman, page from folio, 1992, pencil, watercolor, India ink, collage on paper, 52x39 cm.
48. Four Dabloids, folio page, 1992, pencil, watercolor, India ink, collage on paper, 52x39 cm.
49. Chinese money, folio page, 1992, pencil, watercolor, India ink, collage on paper, 52x39 cm.
50. Dabloid music, folio page, 1992, pencil, watercolor, India ink, collage on paper, 52x39 cm.
51. How to Make Your Own Dabloid, folio page, 1992, pencil, watercolor, India ink, collage on paper, 52x39 cm.
52. Tilling of the Fields, page from folio «Dabloid Pedagogy», 1991, pencil, watercolor on paper, 54x38 cm.
53. I studied with them, list from folio «Dabloid Pedagogy», 1991, pencil, watercolor on paper, 48x36 cm.
54. Offense is punished, page from folio «Dabloid Pedagogy», 1991, pencil, watercolor on paper, 54x38 cm.
55. Little girl with Dabloid, 01.23.1990, pencil, watercolor on paper, 48x36 cm.
56. Taking a Dabloid home, 01.20.1990, pencil, watercolor on paper, 48x36 cm.
57. Soldier, defending a Dabloid, 01.21.1990, pencil, watercolor on paper, 48x36 cm.
58. They took their Dabloid away, 01.25. 1990, pencil, watercolor on paper, 48x36 cm.
59. A Dabloid in the women's baths, 01.27.1990, pencil, watercolor on paper, 48x36 cm.
60. Afraid of stumbling, 01.24.1990, pencil, watercolor on paper, 48x36 cm.
61. Dabloid no. 4; St. Sebastian firmly tied to a tree, 1989, oil on canvas, 200x150 cm.
62. Dabloid no. 5; St. Barbara extinquishes the burning tree with her own blood flowing from her body, 1989, oil on canvas, 200x150 cm.
63. Yellow Nile I, scroll from the Diver's Library, paper, tracing paper, acrylic, India ink, ink, collage, glue, wood, twine, 104x650 cm.
64. Yellow Nile II, scroll from the Diver's Library, paper, tracing paper, acrylic, India ink, ink, collage, glue, wood, twine, 200x700 cm.
65. Yellow Nile III, scroll from the Diver's Library, paper, tracing paper, acrylic, India ink, ink, collage, glue, wood, twine, 150x650 cm.
66. Windows facing within I, 1989, paper, tracing paper, India ink, ink, glue, collage, 105x77 cm.
67. Windows facing within II, 1989, paper, tracing paper, India ink, ink, glue, collage, 105x77 cm.
68. Windows facing within III, 1989, paper, tracing paper, India ink, ink, glue, collage, 105x77 cm.
69. Windows facing within IV, 1989, paper, tracing paper, India ink, ink, glue, collage, 105x77 cm.
70. Reed hut, book from the Diver's Library, 8 pages, 1992, watercolor, India ink, tracing paper, collage on paper, cardboard, 44x31 cm.
71. One hundred and thirty five descriptions of the unrealized, book from the Diver's Library, 1992, watercolor, India ink, tracing paper, collage on paper, cardboard, 47x200 cm.
72. The Accountant, book from the Diver's Library, 1993, watercolor, India ink, tracing paper, collage on paper, cardboard, 27x140 cm.
73. New songs, book, 1992, 12 pages, lithograph on paper, 27x19 cm.
74. Book of Blockheads, 25 pages, 1990-93, India ink on paper, 55x42 cm. Courtesy of The J. Paul Getty Center, Santa Monica, California.
75. Poems, book, 95 pages, 1989, India ink, ink, gouache on paper, cardboard, 14.5x11 cm. Courtesy of The J. Paul Getty Center, Santa Monica, California.
76. Fish Track, book, 10 pages, 1990, India ink on tracing paper, paper, 38x28. Courtesy of The J. Paul Getty Center, Santa Monica, California.
77. The Simple Actions of D.,1992, Six page folder, cover, 21 copies, two color lithographs on paper, 68x46 cm.
78. Still lifes, 1992, Folder of 16 pages, cover, 50 copies, two color lithographs on paper, 61x44 cm.
79. Dabloids, dinner service, 5 copies, 1993. 80. Dabloids, 1992 -1993, toys.

BIOGRAPHY

1953, May 4 - born in the town Nizhnye Sergi in the Urals.

1974 - began drawing. First published caricatures.

1975 - began participating in exhibitions.

1976 - awarded certificates at humor festivals in Akshexire, Turkey, and Marostik, Italy.

1977 - Grand Prize and gold medal at the International Caricature Competition in Skope, Yugoslavia.

1978 - graduated from the Sechenov Institute of Medicine.

1975-1982 - participated in international caricature exhibitions in Belgium, Canada, Italy, Poland, Russia and elsewhere

1985 - joined the Artists Union

1989 - Grand Prize with N. Kozlovy at the International Book Design Exhibition in Leipzig for illustration of E. Zamiatin's «We».

1990 - founded «Dablus-Press».

Leonid Tishkov's works are in the collections of: The Tretyakov Gallery, The Pushkin Museum of Fine Arts, Moscow; The British Library (British Museum), London; The International Museum of Caricature, Basel, Switzerland; The J. Paul Getty Center, Santa Monica, USA; Artoteka Documenta, Kassel, Germany; The Klingspor Museum, Frankfurt, Germany; Lyric-cabinette, Munich, Germany; Duke University Museum of Art.

BOOKS

Leonid Tishkov's Books:
«Dablus» publishers,
1990 - Dabloids.
Gazelles.
The Simple Actions of D.
1991 - Life of a Little Person.
The Fisherman's Dream.
«Dablus» publishers in collaboration with IMA-Press:
1991 - Dabloids.
1992 - «Not only Dabloids». Conversations.
1993 - Stomachs.

EXHIBITIONS

Primary Exhibitions:

1985 - XVI Exhibition of Young Moscow Artists, Kuznetsky Bridge, Moscow.

1986 - XVII Exhibition of Young Moscow Artists, Kuznetsky Bridge, Moscow.

1988 - Biennale Book Illustration, Brno, Czechoslovakia.

1989 - International Book Design Exhibition, Leipzig, Germany.

1989 - «Furmanny Lane», Warsaw, Poland.

1990 - «Contemporary Soviet Art», The Moscow Palette Association, Melbourne, Australia.

1990 - «Six Contemporary Soviet Artists», Mona Bismarck Fund, Paris.

1990 - «Concrete». International Exhibition of Visual Poetry. City Museum of Gotha, Germany.

1990 - «Transfuture». International Exhibition of Visual Poetry, Kassel, Hauptman-schule, Germany.

1990 - «Trio». Central House of Artists, Moscow.

1990 - «Graphomania,» drawings and texts. Exhibition in the cycle «Graphic Seasons,» 25 Tverskaya St., Moscow.

1991 - «Furmanny Artists,» Martigni, Switzerland.

1991 - «Agasphere». Moscow Youth Palace, Moscow.

1991 - «Dablus» Publishers, XI International Book Salon, Paris.

1991 - International Moscow Art Fair «ART-MIF-2,» Manege, Moscow.

1992 - Exhibition in «Lyric-Cabinette» in Munich, Germany.

1992 - «Paper Theatre». Anna Akhmatova Museum, St. Petersburg.

1992 - «Communication». Ex Libris Museum, Moscow.

1992 - «International Exhibition of Visual Poetry». Pankow Gallery, Berlin, Germany. 1992 - «Dablus» in Scotland. Art College, Edinburgh, Great Britain.

1992-93 - «A Time of Transition,» City Museum and Art Gallery, Bristol, Great Britain; Ferens Art Gallery, Hull, Great Britain.

1992 - One Man Show, «Soft and Hard». Paintings, drawings, lithographs, installations, music. «Velta» Gallery, Moscow.

1992 - One Man Show, «Not only Dabloids». Large and small format books, drawings, scrolls. «Al'yans» Gallery, Moscow.

1993 - One Man Show, **Leonid Tishkov Creatures**, Duke University Museum of Art, Durham, North Carolina.

1. Nenarokomov, M. «The Paradoxality of Thinking.» *Tvorchestvo*, 1987, No 9
2. Lakin, Ya. «Leonid Tishkov's "Hot Solo",» *Literaturnaya ucheba*, 1989, No 2.
3. Nikich, G. «Introductory article to the exhibition catalogue «Six Contemporary Soviet Artists.» Mona Bismarck Fund, Paris, 1990.
4. Tsentsiper, I. «Dabloids.» IMA-Press - Dablus, 1991.
5. Gavrilov, A. «In the Little Garden of the Empire», «Dabloids» and others. *Stolitsa*, 1991, Nos 11-12.
6. Vasil'eva, Zh. «Bestseller in One Copy.» *Literaturnaya Gazeta*, 1991, No 31.
7. Pisarev, I. «In the Artist's Studio. Leonid Tishkov.» *Druzhba Narodov*, 1991, No 3.
8. Pesok, L. «Leonid Tishkov's Gift.» *Chas pik*, 1991, No 15.
9. Tsentsiper, I. «Interview with a Publisher.» *Dekorativnoe Iskusstvo*, 1991, No 9-10.
10. «Man from the Provinces. Leonid Tishkov, Poems and Drawings.» *Dirizhable*, 1992, No 1.
11. Tuchkov, V. The Stomach's Homeland — A Person. *Vechernii Klub*, 1992, Nos 97-98. 12. Tsentsiper, I. «In Praise of Common Sense.» *Ogonek*, 1991, No 6.
13. «Where Are You Going, Oh Heart of Mine?» Yuri Nechiporenko interview with Leonid Tishkov. *Moskovskie Novosti*, 1992, no. 49.
14. «Dabloids. A Play.» *Mesto Pechati*, Moscow, 1992, no 1.
15. Lunina, L. «Tishkov.» *Tvorchestvo*, 1992, no 2.
16. Uvarova, I. *Dekorativnoe Iskusstvo*, 1993, no 1.
17. El'shevskaya, G. *Detskaya Literatura*, 1992, nos 8-9.
18.Gerchuk, Yu. «The Disappearance of Things. Where is Still Life of the End of the 20th?» *Nezavisimaya Gazeta*, 1992, no 124.
19. L. Tishkov, Poems and Drawings. *Voum*, 1992, no 1.
20. «Life of a Little Person.»Poems and Drawings. *Dirizhable*, 1993, no 2.
21. «The Doctor from Ward 6.»Interview Irina Lyubarskaya with Leonid Tishkov. *Stolitsa*, 1993, no 5.
22. «The World at Stool Level.» Catalogue for «Still Life at the End of the 20th...», Moscow Palette Association, 1993
23.Glotser, V. «IMA-Press. Non-traditional Literature.» Kur'er Unesco, 1993, September.
24. Pesok, L., Lunina, L. «Interview with Leonid Tishkov. Selected Conversations.» Book published with the Exhibition «Not Only Dabloids». IMA-Press, Dablus, 1992.
25. Lunina, L., Ford, P. Article in catalogue for «Time of Transition.»
26. Courtney, C. «Artists Books Out of the USSR/ Liver and Lights.» *Art Monthly*, 1993, November.

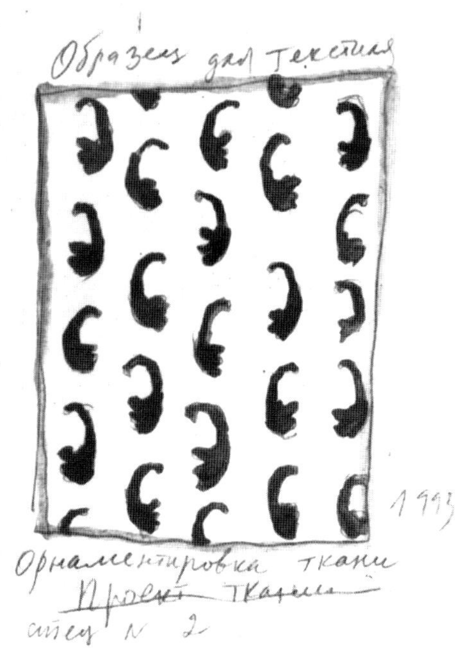

Design of a textile